CW00519433

STRINGS ATTACHED
The Life & Music of
JOHN WILLIAMS

William Starling

The Robson Press

First published in Great Britain in 2012 by
The Robson Press (an imprint of Biteback Publishing Ltd)
Westminster Tower
3 Albert Embankment
London SE1 7SP
Copyright © William Starling 2012

ISBN 978-1-84954-404-7

10 9 8 7 6 5 4 3 2 1

A CIP catalogue record for this book is available from the British Library.

Set in Sabon

Printed and bound in Great Britain by
CPI Group (UK) Ltd, Croydon CR0 4YY

For Charles Edward Fox

*Without whose art this adventure
would never have happened.*

CONTENTS

ACKNOWLEDGEMENTS

I owe an enormous debt of gratitude to all those who were so kind as to grant me interviews to help with the research for this book. Their regard, admiration and affection for John Williams made my task of persuading them to do so far easier that I could have imagined. In England, Australia and elsewhere they gave time, offered hospitality and shared their memories with generosity and patience. It was a pleasure and a privilege to meet each and every one of them and I thank them all sincerely. That many of them have become friends is a blessing and a bonus beyond the dreams of the most avaricious banker.

Sadly, some very special people who helped me with their contributions shall not read this book and I pay my humble respects to the memories of Sir John Dankworth, Matcham Skipper, Eric Sykes and Gareth Walters.

The process of actually writing a book and getting it into its final form is very different than researching it and I benefited from great generosity in this phase, too. The professionals at The Robson Press have been just that: generous, indispensable and supportive throughout.

My admiration of the redoubtable Richard Sliwa is

matched by my gratitude for his generous provision of the discography included here and Tony Long, friend of many years, is due thanks, too, for accepting being put upon without complaint; he provided assistance and support when it was most needed. My daughter Anna-Marika was always available with encouragement when concentration and inspiration were in short supply and I shall never forget the help I received from Val Doonican, surely one of the nicest human beings ever to draw breath.

Most of all I thank John Williams for his generosity with time and his recollections. Without interference or demands, he has supported and encouraged me along the journey leading to this book and I value his trust, confidence and friendship enormously.

Finally, to my dear patient wife, Eila, who has developed the special discipline needed to live with a writer and stoically tolerated the disruption to our life together for the past few years, *kiitoksia paljon!*

PREFACE

To do justice, in a single volume, to the life of a decidedly still-active musician with a stellar fifty-year plus career behind him is a tall order. The task becomes even more daunting, however, when the subject has not been content with a linear musical life, achieving and settling for mastery of the path on which he was set as a boy. Not so for John Williams, and consequently there is not 'just' a story to relate but some curious questions to consider. Why, as he reached and exceeded the heights expected of him, did John Williams choose to challenge norms and expectations in repertoire and presentation? Why did he form groundbreaking, perhaps risky collaborations, commission and promote unexpected works and confound orthodoxy in the design of his chosen instrument?

Then there is what lies beyond the music. While this particular life may appear to be neatly bound around with guitar strings, there are other, metaphorical strings extending from the musical core to other, less obvious factors in John's make-up: his lifelong humanitarian involvement, his pride in being determinedly Australian, and a bloodline that includes a Cockney cabinet-maker and a Chinese barrister.

How do these and other such factors contribute to defining John Williams?

Woven through much of the above and perhaps shedding some light is the profoundly influential role of John's charismatic father and teacher, Len, whose own eventful story sets the scene. This book reflects John's life against Len's and invites its reader to consider the effects of that influence, for good and ill, as it contributed to making John Williams the supremely accomplished, complex and compassionate person he was to become. Can any of John's great achievements be attributed to his reaction to the ambition his father had for him from early childhood?

Concerned primarily as it is with the man and his making, this work has no intention of providing an exhaustive concert-by-concert, recording-by-recording account of John Williams's musical career, a worthy aim but one that can wait for now. Rather, it tells of the life and development of a fascinating man who happens to be one of the most important musicians of his time.

William Starling
Suffolk
September 2012

INTRODUCTION

In the course of research for this book I have had the pleasure and privilege of meeting and interviewing members of John Williams's family and a great number of his friends and musical associates. Almost without exception, they expressed their amazement that John had finally sanctioned the writing of his biography; they had believed it would simply never come to pass. The idea of the book was conceived over a post-concert dinner on the terrace of a restaurant on the Rhine in Cologne. It was a balmy September evening and John Williams and John Etheridge were relaxing after their enthusiastically received performance at the city's superb Philharmonie concert hall. I lived with my family in Cologne for most of the nineties and, with my wife, Eila, I went to celebrate her birthday and to watch our friends in action at the venue where we had enjoyed so many great concerts. Eila's day was made when the Johns dedicated their encore number to her and the icing on the cake came when John Williams gallantly presented his platform bouquet to her after the show.

The two Johns are always great company and were in that special afterglow that makes musicians such great company after a successful gig. We enjoyed badly pronounced but beautifully cooked German food, taking our time over the small glasses of Kölsch, the excellent local beer. The conversation meandered pleasantly alighting on a variety of random topics but always gently veering away from anything in danger of becoming too serious. As the sun dipped and the cabbages and kings began to wane, John Etheridge posed a regular question of me, 'When are you going to write my life story?' He was not expecting a sensible answer since this was a standing joke between us born of my having written odd biographical pieces for him combined with his desire for even more immortality than his formidable musical legacy will provide. The question was laughed off, as ever, but it prompted me to ask John Williams why he had never been the subject of a biography. I received the answer that I think I was expecting. Paradoxically, one of the most widely known things about John Williams is that he is a very private person. Despite his fame, worldwide following and incredible career, he eschews celebrity and is utterly devoid of any sense of 'showbiz' or self-promotion. Certainly, he is aware of his standing as a musician and of his role in modern music but his answer was that it would never happen.

I respected his position of course but, as we returned to England, I became more and more fixated on the idea, so just before we left the country again for a long-planned holiday, I wrote to John making a case for the biography and for me as its author. Beyond swearing that blackmail or threats of violence never came into it and there was very little in the way of coercion or duress, I shall not reveal exactly how I persuaded him. Suffice to say that the letter did the trick. John called me when I returned from my holiday, inviting me to lunch to discuss the matter further and, to my amazement, agreed not just to the notion of the book but also to co-operating with me as its author. Having done so, he embraced the idea with his characteristic, wholehearted enthusiasm. He made clear that, while he would co-operate fully, giving me interview time, access to his papers and introductions to his friends, it was totally my project. This was welcome news since I feared there was a chance that perhaps his agreement would come with the cloying condition of editorial control. As I have grown to know John better I realise what an absurd concern that was.

It is necessary to travel back some time before that Rhine encounter to record my introduction to John Williams and, for that, I am indebted both to our mutual friend John Etheridge and to an American guitar maker I have never met. I had known Etheridge for some time through encounters at various jazz clubs. He played a guitar of mine that he really took a shine to and said it was 'Just what I need for my tour with John Williams', a tour of which I knew nothing. The two Johns were soon to start rehearsing and he asked if I might consider selling the guitar. I declined but offered it on loan for the duration. John was not keen on the idea so that was that – at least until I thought about how I might be able to help.

I got in touch with Charles Fox, now based in Portland, Oregon, the man who had made my guitar. Although we knew nothing of each other's existence I thought he might be interested to learn that his guitar had narrowly missed touring in the hands of a great jazz player alongside probably the best-known classical guitarist of his time and that he might choose to do something with that knowledge. When I emailed Fox I was not sure what to expect but I could never have dreamt that he would send a beautiful example of his latest revolutionary work for John to use. Anyone who knows Etheridge will be aware that he is not the person best suited to the kind of bureaucracy that goes with the importation of an expensive guitar so I was enlisted as his go-between with Charles and Denise, his wife and business partner. Between us we helped the guitar, an Ergo Noir model, make it across the world in one piece and it did not fail to delight. Etheridge loved it; it was a superb substitute for my own Fox as he toured and recorded with it. Somewhere along the way I was introduced to John Williams.

‡

This book is a broadly chronological record of the life of the man and the musician, with rather more emphasis on the former. I knew John first as the musician but as I grew to know the man, I felt more and more strongly that a treatise on his musical career would not really tell his story. There are many other dimensions and influences that fascinate and inform alongside his life as a virtuoso musician and I set out to explore them. Even as I began, I had some sense of the importance of the influence of John's father, Len, in the way in which John's life unfolded and, as my research progressed, I realised that my original instinct to assess John's life in the light of his father's had served me well.

ONE

ROOTS

Len Williams, guitar designer and jazz guitarist.

THE MAN WHO STARTED IT ALL

Leonard Arthur Williams was a highly motivated, extremely gifted and rather idiosyncratic man. He was also an enormous influence in his son John's life, far more so than is the case in most father–son relationships, and this was not just in terms of John's career as a musician but also in the creation of his complex identity.

Len was an excellent musician, teacher and business-man who had scant regard for convention in any of these fields. An autodidact polymath, possessed of a formidable and inquiring intellect, enormous energy and unshakeable focus, in post-war London he championed the classic guitar and pioneered methods of tuition and technique to become one of the most influential forces in the development of the instrument. In later life, he became an authority on certain aspects of animal behaviour, publishing several books on the subject in typically uncompromising style. Commenting on Len Williams's 1971 book, the loftily titled '*Challenge to Survival: A Philosophy of Evolution*', his friend Gavin Maxwell (of *Ring of Bright Water* fame) said of him, 'Williams writes as he talks, with acid humour and disturb-ing frankness. He personifies the uncompromising force of a revolutionary who combines a devastating logic with the intuitions of an artist.'

Maxwell's choice of the word 'revolutionary' is highly apposite. Williams challenged or ignored received wisdom in most activities in which he was involved and had the determination and strength of character, leavened with a streak of ruthlessness, that powered him not just to follow his own path but to succeed. Len lived an adult personal life as complex and unpredictable as his career. It was undeniably a pretty bohemian existence and, in an era when divorce was far from common, he was divorced twice and married three times. He held strongly left-wing political views throughout his life that were to determine and shape many of the decisions and choices he made.

John Williams credits his father as being his best and most important teacher. Not only does he acknowledge the importance of Len's role in his own development as a musician, valuing his contribution far above that of Andrés Segovia, the 'father of the guitar', but he also holds a strong conviction that Len was, by any standard, a highly influential teacher of the guitar, 'The best of his generation'. Len was an evangelist of the classic guitar, and his mission – vocation even – to teach reached its zenith when he established the London Spanish Guitar Centre in 1952.

A proud Londoner, he was born at the home of his paternal grandparents at 250 Dalston Lane, Hackney on 11 August 1910, the first child to Art (Arthur) and Flo (Florence), née Madlin. His father, Art Williams, was the son of a very accomplished cabinetmaker, some of whose creations are still in use in the home of Len's younger sister Marjorie, his junior by thirteen years. The family was well regarded and fairly typical of the area where they lived. One of the few things that may have set them apart was that most other couples of their class and generation would probably have had more than the two children that completed the Williams family. Following to some extent in his father's footsteps, Art became a draftsman, designing furniture for Frank Windsor, a substantial and respected company with its premises on Cambridge Heath Road in the heart of the East End. His designs ranged from Arts and Crafts to Art Deco and Marjorie still treasures some of the beautiful drawings he produced as working references and as illustrations for the company's sales catalogues.

Although it was far less usual for married women to go out to work in the years before the First World War than today, Flo made a modest contribution to the family exchequer by doing some dressmaking. When war broke out in 1914, she played her part for the nation by working in the royal telephone exchange where she handled calls between government officials, ministers and, she claimed, royalty. After the war the family moved the short distance to 76 Mildenhall Road in Clapton, a larger house with the additional benefit of a sizeable basement. The three-generation family home was warm and welcoming. Friends, relatives who lived close by and clients for both cabinetry and musical tuition came and went, and the place was abustle with family life. Visitors were announced by the barking of whichever dog was at the heart of the family at the time, greeting them boisterously and then being indulgently fussed over in the narrow hall. The family was always very fond of animals, something that was to result in Marjorie's future profession as a breeder of Irish Wolfhounds and to play an important part in Len's life, too. Their grandmother bred Chow Chows, which Len loved and enjoyed playing with, and Pomeranians, which he was disinclined to acknowledge as real dogs. Like those generations of his family before him, John grew up with animals around and remains very much a dog person; an indulged and languid lurcher is an important part of the Williams' household today. Len and Marjorie both attended Millfields Road School, which is still in existence.

The household was not notably more musical than many of the time, but many homes had a piano as the font of entertainment and the Williams's was no exception. Art and Flo both played, she to a much higher standard, and Flo would sometimes perform duets for the family and their friends with her sister, Belinda (Belle), who was a piano teacher. It was Belle who introduced Len to the joys and disciplines of music and she taught both Len and Marjorie to play the piano although the young girl was far less enthusiastic about it than her naturally gifted brother. Len began lessons at the age of four and evidently enjoyed them as he recalls the pain of changing teachers when he was ten from 'dear old Aunt Belinda to a local tyrant who rapped my fingers with a ruler whenever I made a mistake'.

Len's grandfather was more indulgent of the boy than his father, and when Art was able to find time to spend with his son, he was strict and disciplinarian – never, for example, giving the boy the benefit of letting him win a soft game of draughts or chess and berating him when he lost. One thing he did get from his father was a smoking habit that would remain with him throughout his life and contribute to his death. From his early teens Len seemed to be either smoking a cigarette or rolling the next one up; apart from those he was given or cadged, he never smoked ready-made cigarettes. Like his attachment to his grandpa, Len also felt that he received 'more mothering' from Aunt Belle, who gave her piano tuition at the house, than from his mother, who worked away from home as a telephonist during his formative years. The thirteen-year age gap between Len and his only sibling, Marjorie, meant that, although they were mutually supportive throughout their lives, their childhood activities did not overlap very much outside of family time and events. They were as close as their ages allowed and the teenage Len was sometimes pressed into service to push his little sister around the neighbourhood in a pram. Although he was only called upon to do this from time to time and often escaped the chore, it was a non-negotiable duty on a Sunday afternoon when the adults demanded some quiet time at home for themselves. This was a typical East End routine: Mum stayed at home and cooked the Sunday roast while the men-folk went off to enjoy a pint or two at the local. Often a child was sent to let them know when it was time to come home and they returned, hungry for the biggest meal of the week. Then everyone settled down for a lazy afternoon in preparation for the week's work ahead.

Young Len was a good student of music who gained an excellent grounding from his lessons; he played well and had a strong grasp of musical theory but he was also a capable improviser. He was confident player whose natural gift soon soared beyond what he had been taught and, when he was just fourteen, he began earning a living by playing piano around the numerous working men's clubs in the area. This was well-paid work and the youngster would typically receive around three shillings and six pence per gig. As one of the most influential guitarists of the twentieth century, it is interesting to note that, in interviews in later life, Len recalled with some pride: 'I started my musical life as a jazz pianist'. He must have been pretty good because there was a lot of competition for piano jobs in those days; most families had someone who was competent on the instrument, playing for family parties and neighbourhood singsongs, and many of these pianists would welcome the chance to earn an extra few bob playing in a pub or club. This kind of work got Len noticed and a London-based Irish band recruited the sixteen-year-old to join them on piano for a tour in Belgium. This was a very big step forward for the lad, a real achievement that reinforced his determination to make a career as a musician. However, his triumphant return home from the European adventure was soured somewhat by his father's glowering resentment that Len was now earning more than he himself was. The young man was precocious in many ways and his achievement added to the tension that always lay just below the surface of their relationship.

Never a great one for sports, music and everything that went with it more or less filled his life. On the rare occasions when he was not seeking out or playing gigs, he enjoyed a hand of cards and there were regular games in the basement of his grandparents' house at Mildenhall Road. Pontoon and rummy were the preferred games and Len sometimes lost money he could not afford at the table.

On the musical front, Len being Len and revelling in his playing, he decided to look for an alternative to the piano that would give him an edge with finding work. He found it first in the form of a tenor banjo that came his way through fortuitous circumstances. To help the family budget, the Madlin household took the occasional lodger and one of their paying guests 'did a moonlight flit'. In his hurry to leave he forgot to take his banjo, which Len promptly adopted. The banjo had a degree of novelty and there were far fewer players to compete with than was the case for piano so he took to studying it in earnest. Len landed a regular job with J. G. Abbott, which gave him access to the various instruments that were on sale and that he had to demonstrate. He took every opportunity to listen to recordings of American banjo players and, after a while, stumbled across a disc by the US guitarist Eddie Lang, a seminal discovery that was to turn him seriously towards the guitar. Len's musical hero, Django Reinhardt, also graduated from the banjo to the guitar, although he started his journey into music on the violin, not the piano. Django was the gypsy guitarist often described as the greatest European jazz musician ever and he has been a source of inspiration for thousands of players. Despite throwing himself into acquiring some skill with the instrument, Len dallied with the banjo for less than a year before hearing Eddie Lang and transferring his affection to the instrument that would shape his future and become the destiny of his son, John. Williams worked hard in his efforts to master his new instrument, playing out whenever possible, grabbing every chance to show off the guitar to potential buyers for his employer and practising in every moment that circumstances allowed. In this, he had a head start because his piano playing provided him with a good grounding in musical theory. He played a steel string arch-top guitar with a plectrum and sought to emulate the Eddie Lang style that had been his inspiration to take up the instrument. Lang was the model for many players of that generation and was cited as *'the first'* by no less than Les Paul and dubbed *'the father of jazz guitar'* by George Van Eps – few would argue.

Luck soon smiled on Len again. One truly fateful day in 1931, the great Italian luthier and guitarist Mario Maccaferri wandered into the shop and saw the young beginner practis-ing guitar. Although Len had only been playing for around six months, the Italian was very impressed with what he saw and took the nineteen-year-old under his wing, inviting him to dinner and then offering to help. Regular lessons with Mario followed, but they were always strictly in the classical technique. Maccaferri's solidly classical repertoire included works by Sor, Coste, Bach, Granados, Tarréga and his own teacher and mentor, Luigi Mozzani. It was from Mozzani that he had acquired his one deviation from the classical 'Segovia style' in that he always used a metal thumbpick, a peccadillo he happily did not impose too determinedly on his new young pupil. Maccaferri also spared Len the trials of playing a 'harp guitar', an unusual instrument which the Italian particularly enjoyed playing and for which he was famous. It was an ungainly device that was like a conven-tional guitar but with extra 'drone strings' added in parallel to the conventional six.

Len Williams could hardly believe his luck with the

opportunity that had presented itself. He was already an accomplished and hard-working jazz guitarist and Maccaferri's appearance in his life was precisely at a time when he was open to the new challenge of taking up the classical style of playing. He and other 'plectrists', including Ron Moore, Terry Usher and Louis Gallo, who plied their trade in London dance-bands and jazz clubs, had been mightily impressed by the HMV recordings of Segovia imported to the UK, and they made determined efforts to try and lay their hands on the sheet music. The teenager was in no doubt about just how incredibly fortunate he was to be learning from one of the great European masters of the instrument; Maccaferri also gave lessons to the Prince of Wales. His Royal Highness might even have used his guitar to serenade Wallis Simpson a few years later.

The highly accomplished Maccaferri was still only twenty-nine himself, but by François Charle's account in his definitive book on Selmer Maccaferri guitars, he had studied at the Siena Academy and emerged with every possible honour before being appointed in 1926 as the first guitar teacher there. Williams was extremely impressed with Maccaferri's playing and said, in later life, that he thought that it was as good as the recordings he had heard of Segovia. This view was no doubt coloured by a number of factors, not least that he was able to observe as well as hear the Italian playing. However, many contemporary critics compared Maccaferri extremely favourably to the Spanish maestro; Charle writes: 'For several years, Maccaferri and Segovia were the two leading guitarists of European renown who regularly performed in concerts and recitals.' Another Maccaferri biographer, Michael Wright, records that the Italian became friends with Segovia after they met in 1926. Len had all the 'bad habits' that a classical player would identify in his jazz counterpart. As well as weaning the jazzer off playing with a plectrum, Maccaferri schooled him in the 'apoyando' technique in which the 'plucking finger', after plucking a string, comes to rest on the adjacent string. This is a fundamental skill for classical and, indeed, many other fingerstyle players and contrasts with 'tirando', a more intuitive technique in which the plucking finger avoids contact with other strings. Apoyando is quite demanding of the player and requires serious practice and discipline. In loose translation from Spanish, apoyando means 'resting' and tirando means 'free stroke'.

Segovia gave a recital in London a few months after Maccaferri's departure from the city and Len Williams made sure of his place in the front row at his concert, from where he intently observed and absorbed everything he could about his hero's technique and approach to his repertoire. Williams immediately confirmed that, unlike Maccaferri, the maestro did not use a thumbpick. He also picked up on hand positions both left and right, sitting poise and position and many other important points of style and performance. He made copious notes and sketches, and tried out everything he had learned as soon as he could get home to his own guitar. Len became an important teacher to his son and later to thousands of others, and it is remarkable that the fundamentals of his teaching were drawn from what he had learned of Segovia's playing style and technique through extremely limited opportunities for observation. He acquired his knowledge only from the few occasions when he was able to watch the Spaniard in person and from listening to recordings. There were no tuition or concert DVDs or YouTube clips that could be played repeatedly and analysed frame-by-frame. Quite apart from all his other talents and achievements, Len Williams merits recognition as a highly astute and analytical observer with an exceptional memory.

Williams only ever had two musical heroes, the guitarists Andrés Segovia and Django Reinhardt, giants in the classical and jazz worlds respectively. Their music could be heard wherever the Williams family lived and it provided a soundtrack to John's growing years. For Len, it was a matter of pride in later life to reflect that, in some modest sense, he had been a living link between the two. It is remarkable enough that Maccaferri taught Len and Segovia taught John, but the link of which Len was so proud hinges upon the Italian's connection with Reinhardt. Mario Maccaferri's place in the history of the guitar comes not for his playing, great as it was, but as the designer of the guitar most associated with Django, which remains the definitive instrument for 'gypsy jazz' guitarists. Many guitarists will be totally unaware its creator was also a feted classical player. His revolutionary design was manufactured by the Paris-based Selmer company and surviving examples of the thousand or so guitars made to his specification are highly prized and command astronomical prices.

Now playing what he called 'jazz and straight' guitar, Len's capability with both improved; it was becoming his instrument of choice and he played piano less frequently. The guitar allowed him to explore new musical forms as he attempted to emulate his two heroes and, when seeking gigs, he had a great edge as one of the few guitarists around. His performances were in the jazz or dance-band style but his study was increasingly dedicated to the classical style and repertoire. He still played piano to some extent, of course, since it remained a source of income and an important part of his social life but his future clearly lay with the guitar. Music was what Len was all about at that time and he applied himself to it with his usual single-mindedness and dedication. Williams also made quite a mark on the commercial side of the UK music scene. By the tender age of twenty-four, he was firmly established as the sales manager and designer (Terry Usher was his co-designer) for Aristone, a manufacturer of high-quality guitars, mandolins and banjos. The company was headed up by managing director J. G. Abbott Sr., a luthier with a long and distinguished track record, particularly with banjos and there was support and investment from Besson, a major French musical instrument maker.

A 1934 catalogue for Aristone instruments features photographs of the three principals, the elder statesman Abbott flanked by the youthful Williams and Usher. Many musicians had to avail themselves of the easy payment facility detailed within in order to pay over time for the Aristone of their choice as these were very high-class and handmade instruments that equalled if not surpassed the big name American brands such as Gibson and Epiphone and, of course, the prices reflected this. Pre-war Aristones are now highly sought after and command large figures when they do occasionally surface for sale. The catalogue featured a range of archtop guitars that Williams had designed and which were named after him – models included the LW, the LWo, the LW1 and so on. A hand-carved spruce and maple LW3 retailed for twenty-seven pounds and six shillings, a truly princely sum. The final page of the sales brochure was devoted to the promotion of *'Fretted Harmony – The World's Leading Publication Dedicated to Fretted Instruments'*. This periodical magazine, edited by Len Williams, promised *'Twelve pages of instructive matter, solos, arrangements and technical articles by professional players'* and more. *'In short ... Everything of Vital Interest to the Modern Player'*.

Len's achievement in attaining this role was remarkable. Having left school at the age of thirteen, he had no further formal education to help him make his way into this impressive corporate position. On the design front, he had enjoyed the benefit of exposure to the cabinet-making skills of his grandfather working in the basement of the family home and insights into his father's profession as a furniture draftsman. No doubt both men were available to provide advice and guidance, should the younger man have needed or been prepared to accept it. As a gig-hardened player, he knew what was required of a good guitar and he was able to analyse and marshal his experience to very good effect. John was to do something similar many years later by sharing his knowledge and suggestions with the Australian guitar-maker Greg Smallman (see Appendix B). Added to these resources were an innate entrepreneurial streak and his supreme self-confidence: he simply wanted to make his mark. Len was never driven by a desire for wealth and he was famously very generous with what money he did acquire over time.

It was not quite all music for the young Cockney, though. He was quite a ladies' man and found plenty of time for the girls, drawn to the confident and charismatic musician who lived a pretty glamorous life by the standards of the East End. Len liked the company of women, especially those inclined to devotion to him and there were plenty of them around. But there were also other, intellectually weightier interests that increasingly intrigued and seduced the young Leonard. As was the case with many young working-class men with precocious intelligence, he was curious about many matters that tested the mind and the conscience. There was, for example, a phase when he took an interest in the occult and the paranormal. This was in the era when the so-called 'Great Beast', Aleister Crowley, was at the height of his notoriety and many people including Ian Fleming, intelligence agent and creator of James Bond, were dabbling in the occult. Len's spiritual activities ranged from séances at his home (which sister Marjorie found very disturbing) to friendship and involvement with the notorious Colin Evans, famed for his apparent skills at levitation. The guitarist was present at the infamous demonstration in 1938 at Regent's Park when Evans was photographed in mid-air.

Another diversion for the young musician was in London's Denmark Street, known since the twenties as 'Tin Pan Alley'. This short road, less than 150 yards long, has always been the hub of popular music in the capital. Over decades publishers, songwriters, the odd agent, instrument shops and then recordings studios kept the heritage of the street firmly based in music and it is now the home of some of the best guitar shops in Europe. It has always been somewhere for musicians to hang out and exchange gossip, news and gig prospects. In Len's day, deals were done, the men were sorted from the boys for music jobs and it was where you went to keep in touch, a kind of musical stock exchange. Apart from these temptations, however, the place held even more attractions for Len. He used to meet up there with friends to play chess, becoming a very combative and accomplished player, and it is also where he received his introduction and grounding in philosophy. His guru was known only as 'Old J' and he helped Len to acquire a substantial knowledge of the works of Hegel, Kant and Croce. The thoughts of all three were to underpin his worldview for the rest of his life and he would quote them frequently, particularly Hegel, to students, friends and the world at large from then on.

Len's music continued to occupy his evenings with both his playing and his employment as he moved on to a job with one of the world's largest music publishers, Francis, Day and Hunter of Charing Cross Road, where he worked as a salesman and demonstrator by day. The company also sold instruments and, at that time, were the British importers of Gibson guitars made in the original factory in Kalamazoo, Michigan. Len sometimes borrowed one of the Francis, Day and Hunter-branded 'FDH Special' or 'Style FDH' guitars to road test at gigs.

Django Reinhardt was always an idol to Williams and he missed no opportunity to see Django and his band play during their pre-war tours of the UK. The Quintet of the

Hotclub of France also featured Stéphane Grappelli, a superb violinist and Reinhardt's greatest musical partner. Reinhardt, who was then, like Len, just twenty-eight years old, recorded and performed in a curious variety of venues, particularly during his tour of 1938. The most memorable of these might have been the London Palladium, the leading variety theatre, where the band shared top billing with the film star Tom Mix, 'King of the Cowboys', and his horse! Reinhardt was said to be less than impressed. He had also been irate about the audience at his earlier gig at the Empire Theatre in Wood Green and that fit of pique cost Len his only chance to meet and interview the great player. Len was there as a devoted fan but also to take advantage of his status as editor of *Modern Guitar*. After the performance, he and Louis Gallo went backstage to meet and talk with their hero. Unfortunately, the gypsy genius had come off-stage incensed that a sizeable number of audience members had filed out while he was still in full flow. He did not know that they had probably left reluctantly but simply had to catch the last trains and buses home. All he could think was that they had shown him great disrespect. Len and Louis went round to the back of the theatre and managed to negotiate their way past the stage doorkeeper. They got as far as the dressing room but were met with a musician who was temperamental at the best of times and now, smarting from the perceived affront, would have no truck with journalists and he flatly refused to see them.

Len was becoming quite a capable classical player with a growing repertoire of Bach transcriptions and pieces by Sor under his belt, but his employment was due to his jazz and dance playing and he was kept busy on the London club and dancehall circuit. He took another 'day job' in the music business to work for John Alvey Turner, a renowned and highly respected musical instrument dealer. At that time the firm boasted of being an importer of 'Italian strings', a fairly prosaic description for goods that included violins and cellos from famous Cremona makers such as Stradivari and Guarneri.

Len had found time, alongside his music, for quite a number of girlfriends over the years and he finally settled to marry a local girl, Phyllis Pace, in a civil ceremony at St Pancras Register Office on a wet and windy 28 February 1935. He had met his new bride while he was playing, he the charismatic musician, she the adoring fan. She was a good-looking and intelligent woman, some three years younger than him, living at the time with her parents in Grange Street, Hoxton, not far from Len's home in Mildenhall Road. His parents took to the girl and thought their son had done rather well for himself. The marriage certificate records his 'rank or profession' as a 'Music Teacher'. Phyllis, the daughter of a motor engineer, has no employment status recorded. Len's future seemed set: he had a substantial repu-tation not just as a musician but as a respected if rather demanding music teacher, with a pretty new wife and the energy and commitment to make a great life for them both. Fate intervened, however; just two weeks after the wedding, Adolf Hitler violated the Versailles Treaty by ordering German rearmament, an action that began a chain of events that would spread war across Europe and eventually drive the young couple to seek a more secure future Down Under. Australia beckoned.

John Williams and Sebastian Jörgensen compare notes.

TWO

WHERE GALLANT COOK FROM ALBION SAILED

Len and Phyllis left England for Australia in August 1939. It was just a couple of weeks after his twenty-ninth birthday and there was quite a party at the dockside to see the young émigrés off on their adventure. The Madlin, Williams and Pace families all turned out in number to wish the couple bon voyage, having barely recovered from a boisterous East End knees-up at a pub just round the corner from Mildenhall Road the previous evening. In the face of some competition, the couple had secured a berth on one of the last ships to carry emigrants from the UK to Australia just days before the declaration of war on Germany. It was Len who had been in the driving seat in making what would have been a difficult, somewhat uninformed and generally unpopular decision to get out of Britain before the country became embroiled in trying to stem Hitler's territorial ambitions. Phyllis had some misgivings about the move but finally went along with her husband's plan, although in truth she had little idea of what to expect. She was not a soft touch by any means but Len was so determined that she feared he might even go it alone, leaving her in London. This was typical manipulation by Len who, once he had set his mind to something, would use whatever tactics he thought necessary to make it happen. Neither of the couple's families had any previous association with Australia and they had no contacts there who could have provided any assistance or advice but Len managed to persuade his employers that having some kind of connection in Australia could only be a good thing and he talked them into chipping in towards the cost of the move.

Even though Len received a contribution for the promised promotion of John Alvey Turner's interests, he still needed to find quite a sum from his own resources. Contrary to the belief held by many, including some members of the Williams family, Len and Phyllis were not so-called 'Ten Pound Poms', since the heavily subsidised passage through a generous Australian government scheme did not come into being until after the war. Marjorie, Len's younger sister, was in her mid-teens when the bombshell of her only sibling's plan to emigrate was dropped on the family. The world was a much bigger place back then and the backdrop of the impending war added to the uncertainty of whether she would ever see her brother again. Their parents' generation had lived through the 1914–18 war and Flo and Art were probably quite sympathetic to Len's desire to avoid a similar experience, even though they would have been the ones back home facing any criticism of their son's decision. After war was declared a few days later, anyone who failed to support the war effort was strongly criticised and might receive a white feather, the World War I symbol of cowardice. But there was no opposition at all to the move from his parents, rather, generous support combined with confidence that Len and his young wife would make a go of life in a different and safer setting in their new homeland. For Art's part, he might have been happy for some respite from his go-getter son. The Pace family were not so keen but they too knew that war was looming and that their only daughter Phyllis, at least, would be well off out of it.

When the couple left, war was spreading like a contagion across Europe and Britain's involvement seemed inevitable; conflict was now at the country's doorstep and there is no doubt that the probability of his country declaring war on Germany was the primary reason for Len's decision to get out and head to Australia.

Mr and Mrs Williams were not the only people driven to up sticks and leave. By coincidence, Django Reinhardt was in Britain at the time and he, too, was to change his mind about staying. He and the Quintet started their tour playing in Len's backyard: on 1 August 1939, the band began a week-long stint at the Hackney Empire Music Hall in Mare Street, less than a mile from the Williams family home. Len went to the show, of course, but again failed to meet the great man, despite his best and fairly desperate efforts and he bitterly resigned himself to never seeing the gypsy genius again. After Hackney the musicians moved on to other dates in London and Glasgow and to make a recording at the BBC TV Studios in White City. This particular visit to London marks a milestone in the history of the band as the final audio recordings by the pre-war Quintet were laid down at the Decca studios, now long gone. The Quintet was still in England when, on 3 September 1939, Britain and

France declared war on Germany. Reinhardt immediately cancelled his remaining concert obligations and rushed back across the channel with the rhythm section in tow. Stéphane Grappelli took a more pessimistic view of the prospects of the conflict for France and decided to remain in London. When asked later why he had returned to France, Django is reported as saying 'It is better to be frightened in your own country than in another one' which is a slightly puzzling answer as he was, in fact, Belgian by birth and, in any event, normally identified himself more through his gypsy culture than any nationality. Len Williams left England to avoid the war just a matter of days before Django Reinhardt returned to France supposedly to confront it.

Whether or not there was a genuine intention for business to be done for the London company, Len Williams's first employment in the Antipodes was not related to his musical experience and interests at all. Somewhat surprisingly, he went to work for the Australian Air Ministry, where he secured a job as a general clerk. This role was very out of character but was driven by the urgent and basic need to put food on the table and, at least, the job with its regular and secure income gave him a base from which to seek out a more fitting employment, whatever that might prove to be. Not long after arriving, and given that no formal qualifications were required in those days, Len set himself up as a psychotherapist under the adopted name of 'Ormerod', an affectation which he felt bestowed more gravitas than his own. This little enterprise required no more than a lot of front, a small ad in a newspaper and the renting of an office by the hour and Williams gave 'consultations' in the evenings and at weekends – it seems his busking skills were not limited to music! Whatever free time he had left was devoted to getting himself known in musical circles, and the combination of his convincing manner and excellent musicianship meant he had few problems in securing guitar jobs at clubs and dancehalls.

To begin with, Leonard Williams was perfectly at home in Melbourne and he loved the Aussie character. Phyllis, however, had major reservations right from the outset and they were soon to take their toll on the couple's relationship. She was very disappointed with what she found in Australia and the informal and casual lifestyle did not sit well with her knowing, as she did, what her family and friends were enduring back in Blighty. They heard of the harsh realities of war in Europe through news reports in the Australian media and the letters they received somewhat infrequently from family in Britain. It seems that Phyllis was far more affected by the trials of her homeland than Len. Her conscience was clearly troubled about running out and leaving Britain to its fate, and the difference in attitudes soon spelt the end for the couple's relationship.

In reality, the Williams's marriage was doomed from the day they left England. Phyllis's heart had never really been in the move and she had fallen victim to the charm and guile of her husband. In the event, she was to leave Len and quit Australia before they had been there for a year. On her return to England, she immediately signed up to serve in the Women's Royal Navy Service (WRNS), a confirmation that her motive was her regret of abandoning the UK to its fate. She had a kind and generous nature so it was no surprise that she stayed friends with Len thereafter, keeping in touch by mail from England. Phyllis soon remarried after her return home, this time choosing someone very different to Len in character and standing; her second husband was a captain in the Royal Navy. Both served throughout the war and when they were demobbed they, too, emigrated and settled in New Zealand, where they had one son. Whenever she visited England many years later, after Len's own return there, Phyllis always made a point of looking up the family. Although she had never been part of his childhood, John had some affection for his father's first wife and when his tours took him to New Zealand, he always enjoyed catching up with Phyllis.

Len was never shy when it came to self-promotion and his fortunes and, indeed, fame increased. Phyllis's departure provided him with more freedom to explore and exploit the many opportunities that came his way and he took most of them. He had previously been pretty successful in making his mark in a highly competitive London that was beginning to tighten its belt in anticipation of war. How much more he flourished in a Melbourne ripe with opportunity and possessed of a more positive way of life. He carried on with his pattern of daytime employment and playing in the evenings and at weekends. By mid-1940 he was already well established in the city as a musician, his recent arrival from Europe giving him something of a cachet. He made sure that people knew he was a man who had seen Segovia and Reinhardt perform and who had played in London jazz clubs that were known and revered around the world. He secured the plum job as guitar guru and teacher with Sutton

Brothers Music Store, one of the largest such companies in Australia, which satisfied the need for a steady income and gave him access to the city's network of musicians.

Len became a popular and in-demand jazz guitarist in the clubs and dancehalls around the city and soon held the guitar chair in the much-feted ABC Dance Band, which broadcast regularly. After a time, he became 'resident guitarist' for the national broadcaster and, although the job was not especially lucrative, it raised his profile for the ever-increasing amount of work that was to be had as a session musician in the burgeoning recording industry. As a salesman and demonstrator in Melbourne's biggest music shop, he met and impressed many other musicians and he was right at the heart of the city's music scene.

Williams thrived in his new surroundings and his life began another exciting chapter when he met Melaan Ah Ket, the woman who was to become his second wife and mother of John, in a jazz club in that city. Melaan was a keen and knowledgeable jazz fan and had watched Len play many times before they got together. Like him, she was a devotee of Django Reinhardt and the music of the Quintet of the Hotclub of France was often to be heard in the Ah Ket home. But the couple had much more than a love of jazz in common: both were restless and raring to do something new. They shared radical left-wing views and actively supported various causes such as foreign aid for China and workers rights. Melaan's younger sister, Toylaan, recalls that Len and Melaan could regularly be found at political gatherings, the Melbourne 'Speakers' Corner' at Yarra Bank being a frequent and lively haunt. The couple mixed with like-minded people and were to be found in the company of some who would go on to have substantial political careers, One of them was John McClelland, a sometime friend of Toylaan, who became a star of the Labor Party and a minister in the national government. Surprisingly, given the strength of his convictions, Len was never a confident public speaker and he would not take to the soapbox, no matter how passionately he felt about the topics under discussion. It was a different matter entirely with small groups of people, particularly friends and followers, to whom he would happily hold forth at length. Len and Melaan held similar social and political views and they were both especially enamoured of the authoritarian aspects of left-wing politics that characterised China and the Soviet Union. They had absolutely no problem with the paradox of notional equality but with firm, if not stern leadership and Len would himself apply this philosophy when his chance came.

With a highly respectable job as secretary to the Chinese Consul, Melaan reflected, at least superficially, the values that her parents espoused. The Ah Kets had a social standing that was very different from Len and his family back in Hackney. She had a younger sister, Toylaan, and two brothers, William Marc (Bill) and Stanley (Stan). Her father, who died some years before she met Len, was William Ah Ket, a second generation Chinese who was very prominent in Melbourne society circles. Her mother, Gertrude, was first generation Australian of British extraction. Melaan was, like all her siblings, very intelligent and accomplished. She was also strong-willed and extremely confident. Judging her elder and more striking sister to be someone with whom she could not compete, Toylaan settled for the role that she herself describes as 'family show-off' and she was quite a girl about town. Toylaan remembers that, too often for her comfort, someone meeting the two girls together for the first time would remark on Melaan's stunning looks and then throw a condescending afterthought to the younger girl, 'And you're pretty, too'.

Although William Ah Ket had passed on, his stamp remained firmly on the family. He was a man who throughout his life always knew what he wanted and found a way to get it, although his methods would have borne greater scrutiny than Len's. His courtship of Melaan's mother, Gertrude Bullock, had been conducted clandestinely due to opposition from her father who, like her mother, was of English stock and reluctant to countenance the introduction of Chinese blood into the family. Gertrude was very highly thought of in her work at a bank and when her boss learned of the romance he interceded successfully with her parents on her behalf, pointing out that Ah Ket was a man of standing and growing reputation. Gertrude herself was bold and confident enough to withstand any social buffeting that was likely to result from her love of the ambitious and successful young Chinese. It is a testament to both William's charm and his substance that he was soon genuinely to be embraced by the family at a time when this type of inter-racial relationship was very rare and invariably viewed with disapproval. But the couple were evidently much in love and were married at Kew Methodist Church in 1911 with the blessing of both families. They made a handsome and striking couple.

The Ah Ket family were soon well established in the upper middle-class circles of the select Melbourne suburb where they were welcomed and totally at ease in both the Chinese and non-Chinese circles of society. Toylaan has continued some of her father's work to promote the cause of Chinese Australians and particularly to document their history; they are both celebrated in the Immigration Museum in Melbourne. The Ah Ket boys worked hard and did well in their chosen professions – Bill, the elder of the two, became a physician while Stan, a solicitor, had the incredible misfortune to be killed in action in 1945 on the very last day of the war while serving in Military Intelligence in the Borneo Campaign.

William Ah Ket's life was extraordinary. He was born to Chinese parents, a solitary son with six sisters, all seven of them arriving in a ten-year period. William attended Wangaratta High School and went up to the University of Melbourne to read Law. He was called to the Bar in 1904, the first Chinese Australian to achieve this status in Melbourne; no other Chinese barrister or solicitor was to serve in Melbourne for almost three decades. Ah Ket was popular with colleagues, clients and with the press, particularly the cartoonists of the day, who drew him as a Chinese 'Rumpole' character.

William Ah Ket made enormous progress in pursuing his personal philosophy of 'building bridges between the East and the West' but, although so much of what he did was specifically for the benefit of the Chinese community, Willie also left a memorable mark on Victorians at large as he was famously responsible for helping to bring about the legalisation of 'poker machines', which had been outlawed as they were deemed to be 'games of chance'. William died, aged sixty-one, at Malvern, where he was cremated following an Anglican and Masonic funeral service.

Although Len could not be compared in any way to Willie Ah Ket, it is somewhat ironic that Gertrude was to be as disapproving and unforgiving of Melaan's choice of partner as her parents initially had been of her own, even though her misgivings were based upon differences of class rather than of race. She was unimpressed and somewhat affronted by the confident and, by the standards of her society, upstart Londoner. The degree of maternal resistance was substantial and long-lived, and Len was made to understand that the woman who was, after some time, to become his mother-in-law was someone to be reckoned with. Gertrude had been widowed in 1936 and took her responsibilities as head of the family and protector of Willie Ah Ket's legacy very seriously. The combination of her middle-class English conditioning as a child and her knowing how hard her husband had worked to make his way in life meant that she wanted the best for their children and she did not take to Len at all. She had issues with his attitude to life and his profession, and she held a strong conviction that her daughter could do better. The history of his flight from England and the recent divorce from Phyllis just served to compound her misgivings. There were rows about the relationship and also about Len's attitude to some family friends. He phoned Toylaan at home, advising against her seeing her current boyfriend, and her brother Bill grabbed the phone, telling Len to keep his opinions to himself. Gertrude and Toylaan soon formed a shared view of Len as a bit of a bully and 'someone who wasn't in this world to take on the strong'. Toylaan concluded that Len would 'catch your weak point and get you on it and have you under his thumb for the rest of your life'. This observation is endorsed by many others who knew Len, including his third wife, June, and it perfectly captures one of the devices the man used to dominate people around him.

Quite apart from the nature of the man she fell for, Melaan was also criticised for the manner in which the relationship was conducted. Going to live with Len rather than to marry him was something that was rare in any event and downright scandalous to the circles of society in which Gertrude Ah Ket lived and to which William had fought to introduce and establish his family. Melbourne was relaxed but there were limits. Melaan, though, clearly had her father's genes, which manifested themselves in her self-confident and determined way of proceeding with her life in the way she wanted to live it. William may have been quite a man but Melaan was quite a woman, too. As well as Gertrude's disapproval, she and Len risked and, indeed, suffered some wider opprobrium by living together and were finally wed in 1951 at the Kew Registry Office with the ten-year-old John in attendance and standing as a witness. Despite their love and genuine commitment to each other, the formality of the eventual marriage ceremony was for less than romantic motives. It was not to appease the scandalised Gertrude or to finally embrace convention; rather it was to ease the formalities that their move to England would entail.

The couple first set up home at 6 Alston Grove in Melbourne's St. Kilda East district, south of the city centre.

They had made many friends through musical and political connections and they regularly hosted social evenings at which music was played and discussions conducted which roamed across philosophy, politics and matters of social conscience. When John was born it was probably an unplanned event in the couple's life but it was one that brought them great joy without seriously changing their lifestyle. John has fond memories of his time at the house; Len was a very hands-on father who let his son be part of everything that was going on in the family's life, even though this was almost entirely with adults (John had very few friends of his own). The boy loved the fact that there were orange trees and a fishpond in the back garden, where his father kept and nurtured some very exotic fish, one particularly fine example of which was stolen, to Len's fury. And John will never forget that it was at Alston Grove where their dog went mad. This came about because the dog was sniffing around a barbecue and somehow managed to inhale some hot coals. Unsurprisingly, the hound went crazy and became so frantic and violent that everyone was obliged to retreat into the house to await the arrival of a veterinarian who had been called. Sadly the vet had no choice but to put the dog down.

They shared the house with another couple, George and Nancy Millain, who had a daughter named Susie, who was about the same age as John. They also let a room to their close friend and guitarist Lockhart Aitken, who would later travel with them to England and remain an important presence in their lives for a long time to come. John has great memories of raiding Lock's room on a Sunday morning with Susie and the pair of them bouncing up and down on the poor man as he lay in bed.

Although many of their friends came from the artistic community, the couple's interest in political and philosophical matters meant that a crowded house at the weekend could include characters from vastly differing backgrounds. One of Len's pals was Ron Kenny, a truck driver. Invasion fever struck when the Japanese Navy managed to sneak a submarine into Sydney Harbour, which they also bombed from the air. Len prepared for a possible Japanese occupation by buying up a huge stock of canned food – John was amazed to see the garage completely packed with tins. Len and Ron's plan was that, when the invasion was imminent, the two would load the food onto the truck and head off into the mountains with their families to ride out the storm. As part of their preparation, they decided they needed to ensure that the contents of the truck would be securely out of sight, so, one dark evening, Len and Ron sneaked into a railway yard and stole a tarpaulin large enough to conceal the substantial cargo of canned comestibles. History records that the invasion never came to pass and John Williams records that the family lived exclusively on tinned food for a very long time!

At this time John was a pupil at Grimwade House, today the 600-strong junior school of Melbourne Grammar School. Unlikely as it sounds, his fellow pupils had no idea that he was receiving guitar tuition from his father and that they had a future giant of the instrument in their midst. The school now includes the Netley Music School, which was opened in 1991, and it is tempting to muse on what might have come to pass had that facility been around in John's day. Had his musical potential been spotted by teachers, Len's role in its development might have been reduced or supplanted with who knows what outcome. Grimwade House was only a kilometre or so from home and the young John would walk there, sometimes with Melaan for company, north along Orong Road to the campus on Balaclava Road. He did not have any particular friends from school or even any social life based around Grimwade House and, even though the house was usually buzzing with visitors, none of them had children so, apart from playing with Susie, John spent much of his time – too much – just listening to and observing the adults. As an adult, he holds a strong view that life as an only child might be unhealthy in some ways; John also believes that he might have benefited from having a bigger circle of young friends.

There is no blue plaque or its Australian equivalent in place recording the fact, but Alston Grove goes down in history as the place where John Williams first played a guitar. Len gave him his first instrument when he was four years old and the boy's future was cast. To begin with, it was just to become familiar with the feel of an instrument and tuition in earnest did not begin for another year or so. John enjoyed watching his father and his friends play and there was always music to be heard at home. Recordings of Django Reinhardt and Andrés Segovia were among the favourites but some of the great jazz pianists also got a hearing. Guitars were still quite hard to come by and it was particularly difficult to find one to suit the hands of a young boy, even for someone with Len's connections. Len got hold of a small Martin and built up the neck with a plastic wood filler so its profile would be more like that of a classical guitar than a steel string. French artist and teacher Robert Felix was among the many regulars at the house, and apart from his other achievements and whatever particular contribution he paid to the house, Felix must be recorded as having taught the five-year-old John Williams to play the first few bars of 'La Marseillaise' on his mandolin. In the key of 'C' apparently! John, having already been introduced to the guitar at the age of four by Len, was soon told by his father in no uncertain terms to stop messing around with the mandolin. Although John has no memory of a mandolin or, indeed, the French national anthem in that context, Len recalls this as his first major act of musical discipline in his tuition of the son who was to become one of the world's greatest and most controlled players. John was endowed by nature with the intelligence and character that enabled him to receive tuition from his father, a great teacher, and to question and adapt when he thought fit. Nature also blessed him with a memory to match his father's and strong and durable fingernails. There is delightful clip of John aged six playing two pieces that his father recorded on a wire recorder to send to the family in England. Between them can be heard the voice of the young Aussie with a message, 'Hallo over there in England. Hallo Grandma, hallo Grandpa, hallo Marjorie. I hope you're all well and happy over there in England.' The message is quite sweet and the playing incredible for one so young.

Len discovered other talents. He had tried all kinds of tricks in his psychotherapy days and found along the way that he had a gift for graphology or so he was able to persuade the gullible. There were plenty of them around so, for a suitable fee, he did handwriting analyses using the takings for the unlikely purpose of funding the purchase of sheepskins, which he sent to charities in Russia. Len knew that his son was also creative – he had great imagination and was very resourceful. One day Len went looking for the sprinkler attachment he used for watering the lawn. Despite searching the garden he could not find it so, never one to give up, he turned the house upside down, still with no success. A few days later, a neighbour came round clutching the sprinkler and it was clear that it had been thrown over the fence and that only five-year-old John could have done the deed. Len took him to task and John said simply that the wind must have blown it over the fence. His father was so impressed by the inventiveness of this fantastical notion that he left it at that. It seemed that whenever John had to come up with an excuse for his behaviour, he would do so in a way that did not implicate anyone else and find a way of blaming whatever he was accused of on the elements. He also had a talent for negotiating his punishments. If Len caught him at something and, by way of punishment, offered his son a choice between, say, three hard smacks or not going to the pictures at the weekend, John's rejoinder would be 'How about two not-so-hard smacks?' And that was the deal that was reached.

In 1948, when John was aged seven, the family moved a short distance west to a house at 82 Brighton Road, St Kilda. It was a pleasant but unremarkable house fronted by a small garden and boasting a shady porch in which hung the cage of a sulphur-crested cockatoo called Jerry, of which

John was especially fond. There were other pets there, too, including a variety of lizards and an ill-tempered ferret. The house had a fairly small back garden with a shed at the end and there was a path behind the property that led to a block of flats where John's grandmother, Gert Ah Ket, lived with Toylaan and her husband Tom. By this time Gert and Len had reached a kind of accord in which they agreed to keep their differences and criticism to themselves. Gert was more likely to breach the boundaries of the agreement than Len, but generally they managed to rub along and it was good for John that he had his grandma close by. She was greatly amused when he recounted how Jerry the cockatoo had escaped. John spotted the bird in a nearby tree a few days later and it sat there, as if waiting for dog that was passing to move away. When the dog had gone Jerry flew down to the ground, tilted his head to one side and said 'Hello' before happily returning to his cage. As had been the case at Alston Grove, the Williamses did not have the whole house to themselves; this was a matter of economics but also one of their chosen lifestyle. Len and Melaan were highly sociable people who really enjoyed having others of similar mind around them and their new co-residents were a perfect foil. Living upstairs from the Williams family were Sadie Bishop, who was to become one of Len's most accomplished Australian students, and her husband, Joe Washington. He was an arranger and jazz guitarist later noted for his arrangements of Beatles tunes for the classical guitar although his earlier achievements as head arranger for the ABC orchestras were far more laudable. Sadie was a larger-than-life character with an earthy sense of humour and she played a strong role in the way in which the house-hold defined and conducted itself. She worked as a copyist for her husband, writing out the parts of his arrangements and she took the opportunity to study guitar with Len. Sadie, who kept the name Bishop throughout her life, once said, 'For three weeks I was a better guitar player than John Williams, but then I was thirty-two and he was nine.' Number 82 was a magnet that attracted a particular kind of person who was determined to have fun with like-minded folk. The musical, the hedonistic, the argumentative ... all would find something there to suit them. Many people stayed over at the house, making the most of the great time that was to be had and it seemed like there was always a party going on. The crowd that came together at the house on Brighton Road were drawn by their interests in politics, culture and art. Some were already well established and celebrated and others went on to become so, but it was almost manda-tory to be 'a character'. It was certainly not a place for the shy or the timid puritan. Anyone unsuspecting who came along with doubts or reservations faced the simple choice of whether to stay and subscribe or simply go away; most seemed to bend and few to leave.

One of the few things that Len would not allow in his home, though, was drug use of any kind, and this was a position he adhered to throughout his life. Alcohol was tolerated and helped things along but Len was not a drinker; he described himself as 'a cheap drunk' because even half a pint of beer would be enough to affect him and he liked to remain in control. The house was noisy in a boisterous rather than rowdy way and who knows what the neighbours made of this suburban outpost for artistic types, where frequent jam sessions were punctuated by recordings of Django Reinhardt and dancing, singing and laughter.

Weekends were when things really hotted up. It was 'open house' and visitors would stay over, sleeping wherever they could find a space and with whoever took their fancy. This was the norm for John's childhood. The goings-on could not be accurately described as orgiastic but it was very laissez-faire and all concerned seemed completely content and relaxed about what went on. Sexual relationships were very casual. Sadie Bishop recalled in later life that, 'It was so different there. It was like all the stupid rules that normally restrict everyone were considered ridiculous and just ignored', and when she was teaching in Canberra in the early seventies, there were shades of Brighton Road in the way she ran her own home. It was Len who set the pace and controlled everything that went on in the house and he ordained and blessed these arrangements – and they would be the model for the way he conducted the rest of his life.

John had a very bohemian upbringing in many ways and was, to quite a large extent, denied many of the experiences and norms of a conventional childhood. His status as an only child who spent much of his time alone practising the guitar already set him apart and the environment that his parents created, combined with their very particular social mores, forced him to grow up quickly. Len never expressed any regret for this and believed John benefited from living in this kind of unconventional environment, learning to be direct and forthright, qualities that the eight-year-old displayed in his resignation letter to the Chief of the Ovaltineys, announcing his switch of allegiance to the club associated with a children's radio programme.

> Dear Chief, I am sending back my golden book of rules and broken weak [sic] badge. I am not going to be an ovaltiney any more. I think it is an awful business all about kidding little children into buying your ovaltine. Some girls and boys like being ovaltinies, but yet know you are only trying to sell ovaltine. I am now an Argonaut and I think it is much better, because it is much more fun and educates you. Another thing is that you can't buy Argonaut in shops, but you can buy ovaltine in shops.
>
> Yours faithfully, John Williams

This was all well and good but directness and forthrightness without knowledge of or recourse to alternative behaviour can backfire badly on children, exposing them to ridicule, bullying or stigmatisation but the Williamses seem not to have considered that. Len later claimed that the environment in which John was raised explained his son's lack of stage fright or pre-concert nerves. Other views are that John withdrew into himself, lacking the peer interaction and stimulation of a conventional childhood, and that it was his own intelligence and strength of character that enabled him to overcome his upbringing and make the necessary adjustments. There is certainly a strong possibility that he may have felt resentful and ignored, having a sense that attention to his needs was of low priority to his parents and the other adults whose lives dominated and displaced his own. When circumstances demanded he had to interact with children to whom his lifestyle would have been totally alien he could have found it extremely difficult to relate to them and this might easily have resulted in the boy becoming self-conscious, introverted and shy. Fortunately for his parents and even more for him, this did not happen and John's ultimate response was to become self-reliant and to trust his own judgement above that of others. Paradoxically, it may have been fortunate that John's teenage years were also characterised by isolation and self-reliance and he had no need to confront and accommodate 'normality' until later. By the time he had to relate regularly to others, he was old enough to deal with it intellectually rather than through nurture and conditioning.

The Williams's circle included musician and journalist Sam Dunn and his wife, Faye, and Gerry and Barbara Newman. Both couples, along with the young John, were witnesses when Len and Melaan finally tied the knot towards the end of 1951. Stan Kupercyn, Marion and Lilian Krynski, and Bob Wilson, another guitarist who later travelled to London in the company of the Williams family, were among those who stayed occasionally or joined the open house at weekends. Another composer-resident was Miles Maxwell and possibly the most famous of the visitors was the noted Russian cellist, David Sisserman (Zisserman), who had toured Australia with Anna Pavlova in 1929 before moving to live there permanently in 1933. Then there was the actor Frank Thring, whose career was to range from Shakespeare with Olivier to playing Pontius Pilate in the blockbuster movie *Ben-Hur*. Thring came from a movie family and his film producer father was said to have invented the clapperboard. Felix Werder, a German who had come to the country around the same time as Len and promptly been interned (because of his nationality), went on to become one of Australia's most performed composers. Sadie and Joe brought Clifford Hocking into the circle and he was later, in partnership with David Vigo, to become Australia's most important and original impresario. Hocking was something of a Diaghilev figure in the Australian arts world, successfully enticing a vast array of artists to the country, including guitarists Leo Kottke, Paco Peña and Alirio Díaz, sitar master Ravi Shankar, Victor Borge, Oscar Peterson, Woody Herman, the Alvin Ailey Dance Company and many more, including touring versions of plays and musicals.

Frank Thring became notorious as a great Australian eccentric and, along with Barry Humphries and Germaine Greer, was famously celebrated in Keith Dunstan's wonderfully entitled book *Ratbags*. Many years later, John Williams happened across Frank in the Sebel Townhouse hotel in Sydney. Thring had the self-regarding presence typical of a particular kind of thespian and was standing in the lobby holding forth to the world at large. When Williams approached him and introduced himself as Len's son, the actor's response was just two words: 'Poor bastard!' Regardless of Thring's dismissive views, Len Williams had many loyal and devoted friends. He was not a social climber and his friends came from many different walks of life. Len was a fully paid-up member of the larger arts community including writers, actors and visual artists as well as musicians, where his interest in and knowledge of classical music and jazz proved to be highly acceptable credentials. But there was more that made him and his beautiful wife such sought-after company: their radical politics, bohemian approach to life and desire to enter into debate or discussion on any topic helped make sure that they were always in demand and welcomed. Len and Melaan both read the works of moral and political philosophers and used them to help form their own prospectus for life. The arts groups, of which there were many, were riven with petty differences and very factionalised. There were jealousies, rivalries, diverse philosophies and competition for popularity, commissions, funds and patronage. Strong personalities who may or may not have been among the most gifted artists courted followers to enhance and secure their own standing and security. The painter Justus Jörgensen was one of the most successful, having founded the Montsalvat artists' colony. Len got to know Jörgensen after accepting his son Sebastian as a guitar student and became a frequent visitor at Montsalvat, an habitué even, and a great, if grudging admirer of the artist. He was heavily influenced by Jörgensen and his rustic realm, which epitomised Len's own unconventional way of living, reinforcing and validating the freedoms and mores he chose for himself and encouraged in others.

Montsalvat, in Eltham, an outer suburb of Melbourne, declares itself to be the oldest artists' colony in Australia and to this day thrives as a home to painters, sculptors and instrument makers, but in a far less bohemian form than in the heady days when Justus was at the helm. Justus Jörgensen was an Australian-born artist whose father was a distinguished Norwegian seaman. He studied painting, first at the National Gallery School and then with the noted Max Meldrum. In 1924 he married Lillian Smith and, together with artist friends, they embarked upon a four-year long sojourn in Europe. Lily, who was a medical student when she met Jörgensen, took the opportunity to complete her degree in London and became interested in the work of pioneer psychoanalysts Freud and Jung.

Montsalvat was created in 1934 when Justus Jörgensen purchased land at Eltham and, with help and hard work from his friends, students and followers, began to construct the first buildings on the site in a wide variety of romantic styles. Financial support came from disciples such as Mervyn Skipper, the art and culture critic for the *Sydney Bulletin*, who was entranced by Justus and became the chronicler of Jörgensen's life despite being reviled and frequently abused by him. Years later Justus said of Skipper, 'If Mervyn had not had two pretty daughters I doubt I would have given him a second thought. Associationally he violated every fibre of my being. I had to make a conscious effort even to talk to him.' Jörgensen knew the extent of Skipper's devotion and exploited it quite shamelessly. In an interview with his niece Jenny Teichman in 1965 he boasted that the critic had become 'completely enamoured of me'.

Jörgensen's design was not just of the buildings and layout of Montsalvat but, fundamentally, also of the ethos that would ensure his dominion over everything that mattered there. His moral philosophy was typical of those so frequently attributed to artists and others said to be in 'pursuit of higher things', particularly in respect of sexual licence in that it gave him more freedom and choice than would convention. Although 'Lil' remained with her husband until his death in 1975, she was obliged throughout their life together to be witness to his sexual adventures, which included the routine seduction of his female students and his enduring affair with Helen Skipper, one of Mervyn's 'two pretty daughters', who became the mother of Jörgensen's two younger sons, Sebastian and Sigmund. Lily had just one child by Justus, a son called Max.

Matcham Skipper, Helen's brother and a Montsalvat 'original', was accomplished in many artistic disciplines, excelling particularly as a silversmith and jeweller. He dabbled with guitar and first taught the young Sebastian, who went on to study with Len Williams as a contemporary of Len's son, John. All the Skippers, including Matcham, got on well with Len and Melaan. The confident and outspoken Englishman was prepared to stand up to Justus and this was admired and envied. Melaan was also known to be no pushover and commanded respect in her own right.

The colony expanded as more and more artists took up residence. It offered painters, sculptors, silversmiths, writers and others, in the words of a biography of Justus Jörgensen by his son Sigmund, 'the chance of a freer, more meaningful life – a measure of heightened self-knowledge and the possibility of happiness, including artistic and sexual fulfilment'. Even more so than was the case at Len and Melaan's home, there were numerous 'part-time' or weekend visitors to what was now a fully-fledged artists' colony. The one constant was that Montsalvat was Justus's fiefdom and to survive there, it was necessary to accept subjugation to his

will. This was essential when he held court at the communal mealtimes. The subject matter could include philosophy,
aesthetics, sexual mores and other relationships, but regardless of the topic, Justus would always have the last word.

Some accounts, notably that of Betty Roland, a writer
who spent substantial time at Montsalvat, document
Jörgensen's harsh treatment of his two 'illegitimate' sons
and Helen Skipper, their mother. She notes the favouritism
shown to Max and that his mother, Lil, fared perhaps even
worse than Helen. In Jenny Teichman's record of her six
interviews with Justus in 1966, although he speaks fondly
of Matcham, he makes scant reference to Max and never
once mentions Sebastian or Sigmund. Regarding the social
arrangements that brought notoriety to the place, she
writes, 'While there are no scenes of wild debauchery on
Montsalvat, there are unmarried mothers and children born
out of wedlock ... He has flouted middle-class morality.'
She then quotes Jörgensen – 'I don't observe the social laws,
I make my own.'

Montsalvat, as an integrated community, was an artistic
dream, an experiment in communal living and a utopian
vision, but ultimately its flawed founder was as responsible for its decline as for its establishment. Today it retains
some sense of its former self but with clear evidence of the
necessary compromise and reconciliation with the world
outside. On Justus's death, Montsalvat became a charitable
trust, with Sigmund serving as chairman and administrator.
Sebastian lives nearby in the delightfully named Christmas
Hills and remains very much involved, particularly with the
musical side of things. Seb and Sig could be forgiven for

reproaching their father for the lifestyle he imposed on their early years but instead they have chosen to honour what he tried to achieve at Montsalvat.

Melaan and Len took John along to Eltham for weekends, where Len relished the opportunity to participate in the debates around the long communal meal table. Betty Roland places him at the lower end of the board, writing that, although Len sought to engage in argument with Justus, the master would not countenance it, probably fearing he would be out-shone. Not surprisingly, Williams did not take this slight well. Justus explained his decision with typical arrogance: 'I could not fail to humiliate him and that may make him react unfavourably towards my son.' This explanation says far more about Justus than about Len and demonstrates how little the artist knew of the man because Len, for all his faults, was never one to bear a grudge.

The young John's recollection of the tone and events at the dinners is at odds with Roland's as he recalls his father having sat close to Jörgensen. What can be said with confidence, however, is that Len was influenced and impressed by Justus and keen to spar with the older man. And Justus, for his part, valued Len because his mere presence had the effect of elevating the status of Montsalvat. He came, after all, from 'overseas', from the hub of the empire, and that in itself bestowed some exoticism. However, even with this head start, Len did not undersell himself when seeking to impress and enhance his standing. He himself was a demonstrably accomplished musician, who was teaching the Master's son alongside his own to play the guitar and he had some real credibility through his circle of writers, musicians and other artistic folk, but he could not resist enthusiastically embellishing this reality by laying claim to achievements and connections that, though pure fantasy, proved utterly irresistible to Justus.

Seb Jörgensen was John's only real friend at that time and he often came to the Williams's home in Brighton Road at weekends or during school holidays for lessons; the two boys encouraged each other and were often instructed together by Len. After dinner at Montsalvat, when the fledgling guitarists were called upon to perform, the marked differences in their characters became obvious. John was the better player but he was a comparatively shy and serious lad whereas Sebastian was far more light-hearted about performing. He had made great strides under Len's guidance and was happy to seize any chance to enjoy the limelight and demonstrate his skill. When Len revealed that he was thinking about taking his family back to London to allow Segovia to hear John play, Helen implored him to take her son, too – not least to get him away from the dominating clutches of Justus. Williams was willing to do so, but the patriarch would not hear of it and so Sebastian remained in Montsalvat. Quite a number of years were to pass before he would finally catch up with his fellow student in Britain. In 1964 he was to stay with John and his wife in London and in 1968 he performed at the Royal Festival Hall in a duo with Tim Walker at a bizarre 'Guitar-In' with Jimi Hendrix, Paco Peña and Bert Jansch.

Although never a permanent resident or listed among the twenty-six 'founders', Len Williams is considered and recorded in the history of Montsalvat as an alumnus, as indeed is John. Most people who knew Len at any stage in his life would say, with absolute conviction, that he was his own man, a self-confident and single-minded person having no need of role models. It is, however, impossible not to see much of Justus Jörgensen in Len in the way he chose to live his later life. Neither was keen on travelling, preferring to stay where they headed the pecking order. Both had high opinions of themselves and could be spiteful and bullying at the drop of a hat. Even if Len did not consciously adopt Justus, seventeen years his senior, as a role model, there can be little doubt that he was greatly influenced by the man and his methods and his later life resonates with echoes of the Master of Montsalvat. The two men each set up exclusive communities over which they had total control and within which they could explore and enjoy their interests, pursuits and predilections on their own terms. The monkey sanctuary that Len was to establish in Cornwall years later had a very different purpose than that which underpinned Montsalvat, but both places were the absolute domains of their originators, where the founder made the rules and held sway over all important matters.

Although Len put up the intellectual defence of espousing the concept of a 'group family', the two communities shared very liberal attitudes to sex. Both men were self-taught to a large extent, controversial in their approaches and each sought to be recognised as philosophers. Little would stop them holding forth on their thoughts and they would quash any gainsayers without mercy. Justus's influence was probably the final piece in the complex puzzle of Len's identity to be put in place in Australia.

Len Williams became restless; doubts and unfulfilled ambitions began to occupy his thoughts and he started to wonder what he wanted or perhaps needed to do next. John's remarkable progress and ability were beginning to make him realise that his limitations as a teacher were close to being reached and this really unsettled him. He was keenly aware of his son's talent and potential, and anxious that it was realised for John's sake. Another goal was emerging in his mind, that of teaching others to play the classical guitar; as he had developed John's playing so he developed his own awareness and capability as a teacher. These two strands coalesced into a conclusion that Australia was no longer the right place for him to be. He had become a little bored with Melbourne, a small city in comparison to his birthplace, and having achieved so much with the ABC job and his high standing in the arts community, he was beginning to feel like a big fish in a smallish pond. He felt he had somehow outgrown Australia. Thoughts of returning to England became more attractive and compelling, and in addition to his absolute conviction that his two greatest ambitions could only be realised there, he started to think about lesser considerations that also came down on the London side of the scales. The most siren of these was that he was missing out on chances to see Django play and maybe even, finally, to meet him. The gypsy guitarist only ever left Europe once.

When Len put the idea of quitting Melbourne for London to Melaan, she was very enthusiastic. He was by now sufficiently advanced in his thinking to be able to include in his pitch to her the notion of Segovia as the right man to take John's development further. His ideas for some kind of guitar academy were also becoming fleshed out and satisfied her concerns about how they might make a living. Gert and the rest of the family were broadly supportive of the move, not that Len would have been bothered or swayed had they been otherwise. She would miss John – she doted on her grandson – but was excited by the prospect of him studying with European masters of the guitar, added to which was the bonus that she would get to see the back of Len. Melaan was quite capable of taking care of herself as far as Gert was concerned, so why not? At the end of 1950, the couple were able to take advantage of a generous offer on their house, so they sold up. For their remaining time in Australia, they stayed with a variety of friends including Gerald and Barbara Newman and, for a short period, the family lived at Montsalvat. It was while staying with the Newman's at Kew, a few miles north of their old home, that the couple married as part of their travel preparation.

The course of action was clearly defined and plans were coming together. Len's charisma and confidence in the future he had mapped out may have been a factor in a number of friends of the couple deciding that London, now well on the way to recovering from the war, was quite a good prospect and began putting their own plans in place to accompany or follow the Williamses across the world. They were all swimming against the tide, since migration in the other direction was growing, not least due to the promises of a better life and financial inducements offered by the Australian government.

It is tempting to think that Len had done so many unlikely, not to say strange, things during his relatively short stay in

Australia that there could be no surprises left to come. But he was never predictable; he reduced his hours at Suttons Music Store to evenings only in order to allow him to take up a new career at Melbourne Zoo, a real piece of establishment Melbourne founded in 1862. He also gave up his chair at the ABC, passing it over to the same younger player who he had recommended as his successor at Suttons. It is not recorded exactly what credentials Len was able to present in order to secure the post of animal keeper, but secure it he did, and very soon after gaining employment at Melbourne Zoo he found himself taking care of the entire colony of hippopotamuses.

Len has good reason to remember his time as hippo-keeper; in his early days, he found himself trapped inside the hippo den, the refuge for the animals from the crowds outside. There was only one way into the den and, to use his words, 'the daylight went out as two tons of hippopotamus appeared in the entrance'. He stood still, petrified, as the beast came in, looked at him quizzically, then turned and made its exit. Although he enjoyed his experiences there, they helped confirm his belief that most animals cannot be kept or cared for adequately in a typical zoo regime. The job gave him a chance to indulge his interest and love of animals and crucially it paid better than his previous employment, helping fund the passage to London. He was certain that within his old home town there were enough potential students to support his dream of establishing a school with the sole purpose of spreading the gospel of the classical guitar. And his son would play for Andrés Segovia.

DESMOND DUPRE, *recitalist, recording artist*
B.B.C. television and radio

LEN WILLIAMS
Principal — Spanish Guitar Centre — London

JUNE WILLIAMS

JOHN DUARTE — *composer*

LORNA GRAY

STELLA McKENZIE

Spanish Guitar Centre Principal, staff and students.

THREE

LONDON, FLOWER OF CITIES

The voyage to England was far from plain sailing. The family set out from Australia in December 1951, along with two friends, Bob Wilson and Lock Aitken, and a new acquaintance, Brice Wilson (no relation) aboard the RMS *Orontes*, a proud ship of the Orient Line. The vessel had a primary function of transporting mail but also carried a sizeable passenger complement. It all started well as they steamed out of Melbourne harbour, the beginning of a great adventure for young John, sailing across the world heading for London, his father's birthplace and the crucible of his career. The 20,000-ton *Orontes* was big enough to have over a thousand berths, but John had plenty of time to find his way around every inch of it during the journey to the place that he would call home for the rest of his life. En route there were the usual shipboard distractions: games, entertainments and, a highlight that John enjoyed immensely, the traditional hi-jinks that go with crossing the equator.

The young guitarist practised diligently as usual, knowing that his future with the instrument was one of the reasons for the journey. He had a chance to perform, too, and there must have been a collective sigh of abject resignation from his competitors when he finished playing in the talent competition. He won, of course.

It was during the layover at Colombo in what was then still Ceylon that things went seriously awry. While Melaan stayed with John on the ship, Len Williams and Bob Wilson took the bumboat from the liner for an excursion into town. Unfortunately, they either indulged in too much of the local brew or were so deeply engaged in conversation that, on the return journey, they got off the small craft at the wrong liner and missed the sailing. By the time they realised their mistake and could even begin to think what they might do about it, the *Orontes* was steaming out to sea, heading for the horizon and, beyond, Blighty. The two hapless travellers were obliged to follow the rest of the Williams party some three weeks later by hitching a lift on the RMS *Oronsay*, another ship of the line, when it made a refuelling call at Colombo on its way to the UK. They were lucky as, only three months earlier, the *Oronsay* had been called upon to help in the evacuation of almost two hundred family members of British servicemen from Egypt after the Egyptian government had reneged on the century-old Anglo-Egyptian Treaty. Now, just back in regular service, it had two unexpected and chastened passengers on board.

Back on the *Orontes* Melaan was considerably less than pleased with the prospect of arriving in an unfamiliar country without her husband at her side. It fell to her and Lock to keep young John occupied and out of mischief for the rest of the trip and then to deal with all the bureaucracy and immigration formalities on arrival in England. Len and Bob had, of course, left their luggage on the ship. Melaan and

Lock were able to deal with that without too much trouble but complications arose because the two men had also left their passports in their cabins. This meant that arrangements had to be made with a shipping agent in England to board the *Oronsay* on its arrival and hand the passports over so the two could disembark, pass through Immigration and gain entry to the country. One quirky consequence of Len needing two ships to get him back to London was that he won the chess competitions on both of them so he arrived back home as a 'double champion'.

The *Orontes* docked in wintry weather at Tilbury, a busy port in the Thames estuary about twenty-five miles downstream from London. Waiting with a warm welcome was Len's energetic sister, Marjorie, who had come to drive them into town. She was the family 'fixer' who helped by preparing living arrangements for them, having found a home for the new arrivals in north London's Bounds Green area. The house was not immediately available on their arrival so the family moved into temporary accommodation in a flat in Talgarth Road, a road on the west side of London in an arrangement set up for them by Stan Kupercyn, their old friend who had moved from Melbourne to London some time earlier and was keen to help his friends in any way he could. Talgarth Road is now almost unrecognisable as part of the Cromwell Road extension but it still includes some of the most remarkable facades in London, the row of nineteenth-century artists' houses once known as St Paul's Studios although the Williams's flat was in a rather more modest building.

Even though the war had finished over five years earlier,

the journey along the A13 road into the city through the heavily-bombed post-war East End must have included some pretty sobering sights, but John says he does not remember seeing anything that lessened the excitement of the promised new life, 'It all looked so different to Melbourne.' Even the cold grey weather that greeted the ten-year-old failed to take the edge off his anticipation of what the city would offer. The route taken by Marjorie and the family ran parallel to the River Thames, taking them past the giant Ford works in Dagenham and through the dock area in the east of the city.

London's Docklands had been an important strategic target for the Luftwaffe and the seventy-six consecutive nights of remorseless bombing of the capital as the 'Blitz' of British cities began there at the end of 1940. This unparalleled assault left over 20,000 Londoners dead, many more wounded and countless thousands homeless as innumerable buildings, including a million houses, were destroyed or badly damaged. The urban landscape was still pockmarked with bombsites, where there were deep craters and the stark remains of fallen buildings. When the Williamses arrived, the Conservatives had just taken back control of the UK government and the UK was recovering from what had been a controversial General Election. The Labour Party had won an election eighteen months previously but with a precarious majority of only five seats. With some encouragement from the King, the party decided to go to the country again seeking a fresh mandate from the electorate and confident of securing an increased majority. In spite of polling more votes nationally than their main opposition, they lost to the Conservatives and Winston Churchill, as Prime Minister, crept into power with the support of the National Liberals, who helped consolidate their sixteen-seat majority over all other parties. There were still party posters in the windows of houses they passed and Melaan was quite shocked to see so much support for the Conservatives in districts that were obviously working-class.

Len caught up with Melaan and John, made his peace with them and busied himself settling in. He put lots of effort into looking how best to foster John's study in parallel with getting started on his dream project for a guitar centre, where he could teach and promote modern classical guitar playing. His ambitions were clear but the methods of achieving them somewhat less so: he needed an income and his most pressing priority was to find some paying work, which he did by re-establishing his old contacts in the music world. He still had a network of sorts and was very soon able to pick up jobs playing for dance bands and recording sessions but not all of his old friends were easy to find. Some had been casualties of the conflict and others had moved away from London; one or two may have even passed him on the high seas as they made their way to Australia or New Zealand.

Britain was still slowly recovering from the war; although its impact was easing, rationing of many basic foodstuffs was still in place and would remain so until 1954. After the relaxed lifestyle in Australia, times must have been very difficult for the family adapting to a crowded, still austere London. Len sometimes found himself subject to criticism for having avoided the conflict, particularly from those who had lost family members in the armed services or in bombing raids. He shrugged that off and kept his focus on his master plan although he always tried to remain attentive to the needs of his family. One thing he did to make life a little happier for them, perhaps not the most practical given they were living in the centre of London, was to acquire a beautiful and very lively German Shepherd dog, who became known as 'Max'. Marjorie helped fix this, too.

While Len and Melaan were busy settling in, getting the basics of a household together and then managing the move from the flat to the new home at 78 Maidstone Road, John was sent to live for a while with his grandparents at their new home in Shoeburyness, Essex. He went to the junior school there for the summer term of 1952 along with his cousin, Margaret, Marjorie's daughter, also taking temporary refuge from London. Shoeburyness is located on the coast at the mouth of the Thames estuary. A quiet, undistinguished town situated just beyond Southend-on-Sea, it was then the slightly tacky playground for Londoners needing a break from city life. It was a place of fish and chips and 'kiss-me-quick' hats, the destination of 'beano' charabanc outings. Such fame as it had came from having the longest pleasure pier in the world.

John found his time at the seaside to be a very different experience from living in the heavily scarred post-war London. The city had been the primary site of the morale-boosting 'Festival of Britain' in the previous year. The Festival was an effort by the government to raise the spirits of the nation and, although a national event, it is remembered best for the spectacular South Bank complex and the iconic Skylon. One of the most durable legacies of the festival is the Royal Festival Hall, the first post-war building to receive Grade 1 listing status, which sits in a commanding position on the South Bank of the River Thames. This is a venue at which John was to perform many notable concerts as a mature musician.

When John returned to the capital from his seaside break, his guitar studies became much more intense, not least because he was back under Len's direct tuition after the disruption to his playing through their enforced separation. The family were now ensconced, if not completely settled, at 78 Maidstone Road, Bounds Green. Money was very tight for the Williamses and the property had been carefully chosen for the ease and economy of travel to Leicester Square Station, just around the corner from the Guitar Centre, which was now starting to take serious shape. For the first time, Melaan was herself taking tentative guitar lessons from Len but it was a brief endeavour that sadly revealed her complete lack of aptitude for the instrument. John was pleased to be re-united with his parents and, especially, Max and he was soon enrolled in the local school, Bowes Park Primary.

Len pushed John hard in his guitar studies, knowing that he had to be at his best when any chance to move forward presented itself. Together they listened to a French radio programme made by Robert Vidal called 'Notes sur le Guitare'. It introduced them to new repertoire and to performers from across the European guitar scene, such as it was, and it was where they first heard Ida Presti, the great French guitarist. Later in life, John became great friends with Vidal, who was very important in advancing the guitar in Europe. Williams worked many times with the Frenchman, collaborating on concerts and radio and TV broadcasts and the guitar festivals that the Vidal set up in exotic places such as Martinique and the Côte d'Azur. Robert Vidal was not the easiest man to get along with but John became very close to him. He was always concerned, however, about being collected from the airport by the Frenchman because even by the standards of Paris the producer was a wild driver.

It was soon after returning from Essex that John made his first television appearance when he played on a BBC children's programme called 'All Your Own'. This was a showcase for children to show off their skills or achievements ranging from musical performance to training unusual pets. No tapes of the programme exist and it is most memorable for the future legends of the BBC who were its presenters: Huw Wheldon (later managing director of BBC Television), Cliff Morgan and Brian 'Johnners' Johnston (the celebrated cricket commentator). The producer was Cliff Michelmore. Another notable guitarist made his TV debut on the show in 1957: thirteen-year-old Jimmy Page playing in a skiffle group.

Wheldon seemed to be cursed; among other disasters he created one of the great moments of pathos. A young lad was proudly standing beside the full-size harpsichord that he had constructed from matchsticks. Wheldon asked what he planned to make next, leaning heavily on the model as he spoke. To sounds of disintegration coming from within the instrument, the boy plaintively replied, 'Another harpsichord.'

It was around this time that John's eyesight was beginning to give him problems that could no longer be ignored and his parents stepped in to take action. After complaining that he could not see the blackboard at school, John was sent for an eye examination just down the road at Arnos Grove, and was prescribed glasses for the first time. His father wore spectacles from childhood to the end of his life to compensate for his short-sightedness, so it was no surprise that John inherited the condition.

At Bowes Park School, along with most other children of his generation, John sat the 11-plus examination. This was a curious and surprisingly durable national test of academic ability combined with an IQ intelligence assessment that could determine and have a profound effect upon a child's future through streaming into 'appropriate' secondary schools. In those days, all children nearing the end of their time at primary school and their eleventh birthdays were required to sit the examination. The young Williams joined the school too late to be part of the first sitting of the exam but finally had the opportunity to take it. He passed, but only just and since there were more passes than there were places available at the local grammar school, he had to settle for spending the next two years at Arnos Grove Secondary Modern School. John says that he learned very little there and this must have been evident to Melaan and Len as they chose to exert their influence to get him moved to a grammar school elsewhere; he had the 11-plus pass in his back pocket and it just needed some determined parents and a little research and manoeuvring to ensure that their son had the chance his success warranted.

So it was off to Friern Barnet Grammar, an independent school with impressive credentials and a strong educational tradition dating back to 1884. Throughout its history it remained quite a small school, never exceeding 200 pupils, which meant that the relationship between masters and their charges was quite personal. At the time John attended, the school was run by a cultured and visionary headmaster, the Reverend Philip Thomas. Among his other accomplishments, the good priest was an amateur violinist of some repute and a close friend of the noted Sydney Humphreys of the Aeolian Quartet. Under the guidance, tutelage and watchful eye of the Reverend Thomas, John's schoolwork improved and he was permitted to be absent from school for the two afternoons each week that would be devoted to sports so he would have time to study music and practise the guitar. This allowed for what John calls 'A reasonable amount of prac- tice', but in recalling the generous accommodation provided by the school, he also remarks, slightly ruefully, 'Maybe I might have been better at sports', a comment that suggests regret at a loss of more ordinary schooldays.

It is always difficult for gifted children to balance their talents and the special treatment they generate against a temptation to envy 'the normal'. Someone who suffered a grotesquely distorted childhood as a consequence of his musical gifts was the violin virtuoso Sir Yehudi Menuhin. To help others avoid this fate, in 1963 he founded the eponymous school in Surrey. He wanted precocious musical talents to be nurtured, but in the context of a good general education and a feeling of normality. Menuhin always planned to include the classical guitar at the school and this was realised in 2004 due, to a large extent, to a generous and perhaps unlikely bursary from The Rolling Stones. The guitar teacher is the thoughtful and inspirational Richard

Wright, one of John's students at the Royal Northern College of Music, and the school has produced some outstanding players, including Laura Snowden and Tom Ellis.

Philip Thomas's concessions to John were well intentioned and the youngster was particularly fortunate to be at Friern Grammar during Thomas's time since the school never had a particularly marked leaning towards musical education and there is no record of similar indulgences being extended to any other pupil. The only other noted musical alumni appear to be Simon Nicol, a founder member of the folk-rock band 'Fairport Convention', and Chris Carter, who made his name and notoriety when he helped create the extraordinary avant-garde music and visual arts group 'Throbbing Gristle'. Neither was a contemporary of John's. Williams left Friern Grammar early, at the Easter break in 1956 – one of a number of far-reaching events that flowed from a proposal by Andrés Segovia that the teenager should be entered for a major guitar competition to take place in Geneva that summer (see Chapter 4).

A significant consequence of this premature departure, at least in the eyes of the school, was that John was unable to take the 'O' or 'Ordinary' level exams that would have followed in the summer term. The Reverend Thomas was especially disappointed at the decision to take the lad out of school at that critical time because the headmaster had high hopes of some good examination results from him. He also knew, however, that there was little doubt about the promising future that John would likely enjoy by exercising his talents and he soon came to terms with the prodigy moving on to the next phase in his musical development, albeit at the expense of conventional academic attainment. Thomas also knew how hard the young guitarist was working on his music and guitar technique, clearly having a very high degree of self-motivation. Or was it paternal pressure? He was wary and distrustful of Williams senior and became something of a confidant for Melaan, who had few others outside the family circle to whom she could refer for advice. When she turned to him at one point of particular stress, Philip Thomas advised her to take John and run, advice she chose not to heed. One can only wonder how different history might have been had she done so!

Through 1955 and 1956, John attended the Royal College of Music 'Saturday Junior College' for tuition in musical theory. His main tutor there was Stephen Dodgson, an extraordinarily gifted teacher and composer who was to have a profound and continuing effect on Williams's musical life. Dodgson has often been described as the best non-guitarist ever to compose for the instrument and he is certainly one of the most important and influential English composers of his generation. He also has the distinction of being the nearest living relative to bear the family name of Charles Dodgson, who, under his nom de plume Lewis Carroll, was the author of *Alice in Wonderland*.

Thomas also knew that, in addition to the demands of schoolwork, junior college and his father's lessons in technique, John was also taking musical theory lessons from Jack (John William) Duarte. He would later become a significant figure in advancing the classical guitar in Britain through his pedagogy, composition and, most notably, criticism. Duarte was someone who would remain in John's life for many years. He acquired his first guitar in 1934 then met Segovia thirteen years later, making an impression upon him that helped soften the Spaniard's profound disdain for all things guitar in the UK. John recalls that he used to walk up from Bounds Green every Sunday morning past Arnos Grove School to Duarte's home, where he would get a basic musical theory education. Other friends of the Williams family used their connections to good effect to advance John's musical knowledge and education. Basil Hogarth, a musician friend of Len's, had a link with Angus Wilson, now celebrated as one of Britain's greatest novelists and a knight of the realm. At that time Wilson held the important post of 'Librarian of the British Museum' and Hogarth managed to enlist him to the cause by granting a pass to the Reading Room for the young musician even though he was well below the official age limit for such a privilege. John used the facility well and spent much time poring over and copying works by Silvius Leopold Weiss (1687–1750).

Len and Melaan's relationship was under serious stress for a number of reasons. He was comfortable, back on his old stomping ground with great plans for John and for himself, with connections and friends, old and new, who would support him in his ventures. By contrast, Melaan suffered from what might be described as a 'colonial' worldview and had very high expectations of life in London, the past centre of an empire in the late throes of transition and one of the world's greatest capital cities. Printers of world atlases may have been able to reduce their orders for pink ink but old associations and old attitudes lingered. She was not expecting streets paved with gold but had been looking forward to a bit more historical legacy and pomp and circumstance than she had known hitherto.

It may be a sweeping generalisation but it is certainly true that among natives of countries such as Australia, there was a tendency to think of grand culture residing 'overseas' and more specifically in Europe with somewhere as iconic as London being an epicentre. This condition was known in Australia as the 'cultural cringe'. Melaan had English blood flowing through her veins and would have heard stories of the old country from her maternal grandparents. It is very common for expats to have a sentimental, nostalgic and frankly distorted view of the place they have left behind, and whether or not this was the case with Melaan's family, she definitely embraced a vision of a place with old world values and a romanticism that she had not experienced in her homeland. Regardless of the significant accomplishment and status achieved by her father, her upbringing was unremittingly western. There was never any effort to teach the Ah Ket children Chinese and the family would have regarded the UK, with all its faults and pomposity, as the motherland. Now she was at the very centre of the empire, Melaan was confronted with a pervasive class system, economic barriers and something of a sense of being the outsider. This, at least in the short term, resulted in some disillusionment, ironically echoing that of Phyllis, Len's first wife, when she tried to settle in the very different society that was 1940s Melbourne.

Although she was extremely personable, immensely charming and resourceful, Melaan had left her support network of her family and, far more importantly, most of her friends, back in Australia. Some of the closest friends of the Williams couple were to follow them to London but that would come later. For now, she was having to manage a home of a very different kind in a harsh post-war climate with unfamiliar bureaucracy. She never expected to arrive in an environment full of butlers and grand houses with porticoed entrances, something her socialist principles would have abhorred, but despite her commitment to the move as being absolutely necessary for John's advancement, she felt quite disappointed and disillusioned with her new life.

Len was also pre-occupied with his business plans, with which Melaan was hardly involved at all. He realised a major personal ambition when he founded the Spanish Guitar Centre in 1952, and this venture demanded lots of his energy, time and resourcefulness right from when he began work on it immediately after arriving in London. He spent all the time he could there and Melaan began to feel neglected. The first premises to be occupied by the centre were on the top floor of a building at 12 Little Newport Street, an undistinguished and then rather seedy little thoroughfare off Charing Cross Road, indeed, seedy enough for its founder to refer to his new workplace as 'the abortionist's office'. Although his pal, Lock Aitken, put up a great deal of the money for the centre, it was very much Len's project and, he made very plain, his vision that was being pursued. He had a clear view of what he intended to achieve with the centre: the spreading of the gospel of the guitar according to Andrés Segovia and Francisco Tarréga. No other kind of guitar would be allowed across the portal but the classical or, to use Len's preferred term at the time, the 'Spanish' guitar. He would teach only classical students and only in the style of the Spanish maestri. This was a novel approach and a great departure from current practice; the few other major guitar schools in London, such as that run by the noted jazz guitarist Ivor Mairants, offered a whole range of styles, including jazz, folk, fingerstyle and a little classical instruction. Len's creation was to be the first classical guitar centre anywhere in the world, an enormous ambition even for the determined East-Ender.

At the start Len did most of the teaching but he was aided by Lock, who taught in a very small space behind a curtain from Williams's own teaching area. Lock was a good enough player to teach initiates and, between lessons, made himself useful in other ways. As the centre was being slowly pulled together, he – along with Bob Wilson, who was also roped in to help – was charged with getting hold of enough guitars and, more prosaically, enough chairs for the students. The chairs that they rounded up were adapted by having footstools fitted to them. This relieved students of having to bring their own footstools, which are a fundamental requirement for achieving the correct playing position and something upon which Len insisted. The centre had a precarious existence for a while, dependent upon Lock's continuing generosity and it was quite a crude set-up to begin with but Len's single-mindedness and energy soon set the business on its way.

He did whatever was necessary to achieve his ends, whether by applying his charm and undoubted charisma to recruit students or using some of the less pleasant tools in his armoury to get the best business deals. Len was also quite shameless about taking advantage of the goodwill of friends and admirers, of which there were many. His personality was a powerful device, magnetic even: he had an extremely pleasant voice, great sense of humour and a very beguiling manner that he employed to good effect. The centre was exactly the right thing for its time and Len exploited this and every opportunity that came his way. It is important though to set these completely valid observations against his motives, which were undoubtedly honourable. He had a mission, not a profit motive and he was supremely good at delivering what he was selling. He was also a very intelligent man, with good instincts and ideas. For example, he recognised that many students would be working full-time so he made sure that the centre stayed open until 8 p.m. to accommodate them after work. He made lessons affordable and in those early days the fee was one pound for four lessons. Courses were promoted as 'Tuition in the Tarréga Method' and students were recruited mainly through advertisements on cards in the windows and on the noticeboards of the numerous bookshops along Charing Cross Road. Len felt that this approach would help ensure that he was attracting 'serious' students and although it is impossible to reflect on the level of commitment of his tutees, his recruitment strategy was clearly successful as they began to flock in and, more importantly, stick around.

Williams broke with the prevailing convention of the few classical guitar teachers around who taught on a one-to-one basis by working with groups of between five and eight students. A single guitar was used for each lesson, being passed around from student to student for each to demonstrate their progress. All the students worked on the same piece and they would usually be asked to play only a part of it. They played in turn and were subject to the scrutiny and comment of their fellows and to the advice and criticism of their teacher, sometimes quite bluntly expressed. The philosophy behind this method was that students would benefit by learning not just from their own efforts and mistakes but also by observing those of their colleagues. Instruments could be hired for use on the premises by those students who elected not to bring their own guitars along, perhaps through the difficulty of travelling with them. Another Len innovation and the most usual method by which guitars were provided to students was an imaginative lease/lend scheme. A beginner's guitar was priced at £19 10s. The student paid a deposit of £12 when starting lessons and the £7 10s balance at the end of their first four lessons. Should there be no desire to continue with study, the guitar would be returned and £10 refunded, meaning the student had effectively hired the guitar for just £2. This worked well and further new students were recruited by word of mouth as those who found the Williams' teaching regime effective and the teacher irresistible passed on news of the centre's existence. Len extended the business scope and student appeal of the centre further by hiring Dick Sadleir, who was skilled and experienced in repairing and setting up guitars.

Some three years or so after it was founded, the centre relocated to larger and more prestigious quarters at 36 Cranbourn Street, just a few paces from Charing Cross Road and Leicester Square tube station in the heart of London's West End, and where it now nestles between a pub called The Brewmaster and an Italian restaurant. Again, the space it occupied was on the upper floors and it is intriguing to think of all the great players who made their way up the steep staircase over the years. Fees were now double the original level at £2 for four lessons. Lock Aitken stayed behind in the Little Newport Street premises where he ran his own modest school, later transferred to 84 Newman Street.

There is a fascinating covenant in the lease for the Cranbourn Street premises. The lease-owner was and remains London Transport, an organisation more noted for its iconic red buses and Tube trains than for its property portfolio. For some unknown reason, the origins of which are lost in the mists of time, the lease stipulates that the property can only be used 'for guitar purposes'. In 2012, some sixty years on from its establishment, the business has combined with other guitar-based enterprises to become 'The London Guitar Centre'.

After the move to Cranbourn Street, Len remained firmly at the helm, teaching and advising, providing a range of quality instruments never before available in England and writing and arranging guitar music. A particular innovation was his arrangements of Vivaldi and other classical composers as guitar duets and ensemble pieces, some of which are still in print. A few of Len's pieces were published by Schotts and one was recorded by the Cuban guitarist Leo Brouwer with Ichiro Suzuki long before he began his association with John Williams. Len commanded some considerable respect in the music fraternity and among other requests he was approached at the centre by John Davis, a noted orchestral viola player, who asked him to write some arrangements for two guitars and viola.

Len imported cheap Spanish guitars from Italy and these were the mainstay for beginners to use. As time went on and the need for higher quality guitars became greater, Williams established a relationship with Harald Petersen, a Danish luthier who was based at the time in Barrow-in-Furness. Petersen made the top range of guitars that were offered through the centre.

Dick Sadleir's contribution was also an invaluable part of the success of the centre. He was an old friend of Len Williams and a well-respected guitar repairer. In addition to his work on setting up, fixing or even making the odd guitar, he later published many tutor books for a range of instruments and composed pieces for jazz guitar. Perhaps his greatest claim to fame, however, was unrelated to his work with Len Williams. It is as the designer of the very first solid body electric guitar to be produced in England. This was the Dallas Tuxedo, introduced in 1957, a small-bodied instrument with a single pickup in the neck position. Although understandably lacking in such refinements as a truss rod, it did have a 'through neck' – a feature now much prized, particularly in bass guitars. It was marketed by the Dallas Arbiter company and narrowly preceded other early guitars such as the Watkins Rapier and the designs of Jim Burns, the first of which were sold under the Supersound brand.

In 1996, builders working in John Lennon's childhood home at 251 Menlove Avenue in Liverpool stumbled across a two pickup Dallas Tuxedo gathering dust in the loft. As tempting as it is for all concerned to wish so, it is yet to be confirmed that the guitar actually belonged to Lennon. Investigations continue to this day...

Christopher Nupen, later the distinguished producer of many fine and award-garnering musical documentary films, was one of the early students at the centre, who eventually went on to give private lessons of his own. Nupen employed the Williams' group teaching technique and summed up its benefits well: he told his students that he did not teach them very much at all, they learned from each other and through their own practice and mistakes at home; his role at lessons was to give them a status report on their progress. He believes that you can tell someone most of what is required to play the guitar in the space of a couple of hours but little would be learned because the learning is only in the doing.

Nupen had impressed Len mightily when he responded to the postcard advertisements. He was a South African who came to London for four years to study law. Before his arrival, he had had great ambitions for his leisure time in the city, planning to visit galleries and museums at weekends and learn all the Beethoven Piano Sonatas during the week. He was the son of the great and fabled Test cricketer Buster Nupen who, despite his blindness in one eye, was a national sporting hero in South Africa. Unable to afford a flat large enough to accommodate a piano, Christopher ditched the Beethoven idea and decided to go for the guitar instead. On spying the advertising card outside a bookshop he went straight to the centre, where he encountered Williams at the top of the stairs. Nupen asked about lessons, enquiring whether he might expect to be able to master the classical guitar in four years – a question that delighted Len, who responded: 'Most people who come up those stairs expect to do that in one or two months.' The South African became close to the Williams family and also very important to the centre, for it was he who set up the regular supply of nylon guitar strings from a Turkish contact called Rifat Esenbel. He seems to have particularly good recollection of the females among his fellow students, who included Stella McKenzie, Sadie Bishop (both of whom went on to teach at the centre) and the model Juanita Forbes, the first wife of film star Anthony Steel. Forbes was immortalised in significant works by Jacob Epstein and Pietro Annigoni and was to be succeeded in 1956 in her role as Mrs Steel by Anita Ekberg.

The teaching philosophy never changed. There were no one-to-one lessons except for a few advanced players whose performance and, more importantly, commitment and application, merited this treatment. Such lessons would focus upon very specific matters of technique and interpretation. All tuition, without exception, took place at the centre. Approaches were made on behalf of Princess Margaret for Len to provide personal lessons at Buckingham Palace but he would not compromise his approach and, perhaps, his socialist principles, even for the remote prospect of a Royal Warrant. He made it clear, however, in an echo of the stance taken by Lionel Logue, the speech therapist in *The King's Speech* who refused to treat his royal patient anywhere but in his consulting rooms, that Her Royal Highness would be warmly welcomed at a beginners' class at Cranbourn Street.

Len remained a political being who loved an argument and it was not unknown for that side of his character to get the better of him. He occasionally got into arguments on the subject of politics or philosophy with his students, many of whom were well educated, articulate and possessed of youthful fervour on such matters. Several times this activity so dominated proceedings that he was obliged to abandon the class, sending his students home with their fees refunded. Some of those who had travelled in from the suburbs were not pleased to have endured the time and expense of making the journey into central London only to sit through a discourse or debate on something in which they had no interest. On one memorable occasion when debate displaced instruction, Len was vigorously challenged by a Canadian student who objected to what was happening. It was an affront to which the teacher took great exception. He reached into his pocket, took out his wallet as if to offer a cash refund and invited his interlocutor to consider returning to his homeland forthwith.

The Williams's old Aussie housemate Sadie Bishop arrived at the centre in 1955 to resume her studies with Len. She stayed with the family for a short time and was a frequent visitor thereafter. Among the many other students who went on to have great careers as guitarists and teachers were Gordon Crosskey, John Mills and Michael Watson, who replicated the Williams' teaching philosophy and methods at his own centre in Bristol. Another important figure was the Londoner Peter Calvo who, like Bishop, was first a student but soon graduated to teaching.

Calvo was referred to Len for audition by his previous guitar teacher. He had originally been a violinist but had been advised against continuing with the instrument for health reasons and had transferred his musical interest to the classical guitar. Arriving at the centre was quite nerve-wracking and Len was not one to make it easy for a potential student showing signs of nerves. He wanted students to come to him, of course, but in situations such as this he could be quite brutal and very intimidating. Calvo had not taken his own guitar for fear it would be considered inadequate and he knew in any case that he could use one of the centre's instruments. Instead, he took his violin with the intention of using it to demonstrate his strong left hand technique. He performed a Caprice by Paganini on the violin and played three pieces on the borrowed guitar. Len accepted him and Calvo was assigned to the Monday evening master class. Williams unceremoniously dumped a pile of music on his violin case and told him to get to work.

Like most students, Peter would often feel the rough edge of Len's tongue. The teacher would ask questions in class and any student failing to answer quickly and appropriately would be dismissed from the room. It was all too easy to invoke the wrath of the master and his arrogance could be breathtaking. It is difficult to understand why so many students tolerated the rudeness and arrogance of the man but Peter Calvo provides some clues as to why this was the case: 'In summer, Len would take students, some with guitars, to the local pub in Cambridge Circus. He was very relaxed and a completely different person away from the centre. Someone would play and Len would wallow in the attention he received as he related tales of characters and adventures. The students hung on every word.' Len had some quality, some strange charisma that made people tolerate his boorishness and, in a masochistic way, draw even closer to him, grateful should he speak to them even if in the most arrogant or insulting manner.

Peter Calvo later managed the centre after Len moved from London to Chislehurst and eventually went with his wife Athalie to live in Australia. He founded the Sydney Spanish Guitar Centre (later the Australian Institute of Music) and became perhaps the most important bearer of the pedagogical torch that Len had ignited, fittingly using similar teaching techniques to train hundreds of students in the land where the philosophy had been conceived. His work and achievements are a very important part of Len Williams's legacy to the world of the guitar.

Len had a major falling-out with Sadie Bishop over an invitation for someone to perform that had been dropped off at the centre. Sadie saw it first and successfully put herself forward for the job, but when Len heard about this he raged at her that he would have wanted that opportunity for John. Despite the occasional upset, the centre continued to thrive and the sustained growth in student numbers meant that another dimension of Len's tuition philosophy could be introduced. Students were graded and streamed into the class most suitable for their abilities and level of progress. Len worked hard to bring out the best in all of his students, bullying and cajoling, but there were rare and precious times when discretion was the better part of valour. Christopher Nupen recalls one instance when a fellow student played a scale that he describes as 'gloriously unmusical'. Len was so fascinated and bewitched by this display of crass incompetence that he couched his criticism in an unusual and lyrical way: 'Observe nature and learn,' he told the young man. 'Watch a bird as it lands on a slender branch. See how it gently adjusts its weight to the nature of its perch. This is how you should approach the guitar.' Despite having been the recipient of such poetic and useful advice, the unfortunate student was not given a chance to show Len that he had absorbed and followed it but was transferred forthwith to a less demanding class.

From Spain to Streatham, a 1959 BBC TV documentary film for the 'Monitor' series which recorded and celebrated the emergence and rise in popularity of the guitar, briefly showed John in performance and featured Len in teaching mode with a number of students. Compared to how much more relaxed a similar scene might look today, it appeared more like a finishing school for Sunday school teachers than instrumental tuition; students being addressed as 'Mister this' and 'Miss that'. The use of multiple guitars in the class that was filmed was probably a grudging concession on Len's part to satisfy the demands of the director and producer of the piece, Ken Russell and Humphrey Burton respectively, both of whom went on to make highly successful careers in the arts. Students came from all walks of life and social backgrounds but as the guitar gained in popularity, in some part due to the visibility and status it was being given (mainly by Julian Bream and, to a lesser extent, the emerging John Williams), so the student mix changed slightly. There were perhaps fewer of the earnest intellectual type who had predominated in the early days and an increase in the number coming from more privileged circles, people who now perceived the guitar as interesting, fun and, critically, respectable.

Someone especially notable to be brought into the fold by responding to the Charing Cross Road postcards was a young woman named June Peirce. She lived some forty miles out of the city on the border of Essex and Hertfordshire and had given up any chance of a career or going to university so that she could devote herself to looking after her mother, who was suffering from cancer. June used to allow herself one day a week to escape from her carer's role and immerse herself in the excitement of London's theatre district. She browsed bookshops, wandered round museums, attended the odd lecture and generally revelled in the life and energy that was so lacking in her everyday existence. Her interest in guitar had been initally sparked by hearing Julian Bream on the radio, and when she saw what she describes as a 'well designed advertisement' on the noticeboard of one of her favourite bookshops, she decided that this might be just the thing for her. She could take lessons in London and spend her spare time during the rest of the week at home practising.

So much for the theory and the plan, but when June first ventured up the stairs at Little Newport Street she lost her nerve and turned back. Eventually she returned and was duly signed up by the charming and persuasive Mr Williams. She didn't study with him for the first six months, though. As a rank beginner she was a pupil of the far less able and less-in-demand Lock Aitken, tucked away behind the curtain. June took to the instrument, applied herself diligently to her playing and in time progressed from Lock's beginner's class to studying with Len. She continued her pattern of attending the centre one day a week while putting in hours of study and practise back home.

June Peirce was in many ways a fairly typical student at the centre but she would, in time, dramatically distinguish herself from the others by becoming the third Mrs Leonard Williams.

TWO

A LIFE IN MUSIC

John's technique under scrutiny from fellow students and Maestro Segovia.

FOUR

A PRINCE OF THE GUITAR

Len Williams's ambition for John to realise his artistic potential was probably the most compelling motive for the family's move to England in 1952. Although, as a Briton and a highly self-confident one at that, he was immune to any sense of cultural cringe, Williams knew that there were no realistic prospects for John to develop musically in Australia at that time. There was really only one man who Len believed was better equipped than he to develop the boy technically and to provide the platform he craved for his son, and that was Andrés Segovia. There would be no chance to enlist the Spaniard to the cause while they were in Australia. Living in London, however, could make this a genuine prospect so Williams set about making this encounter possible with the steely determination, focus and zeal with which he made so many other unlikely things happen in his life. While he was working at the zoo and slowly getting together the funds needed for the move, he got in contact with friends in England who he thought might be able to help him achieve his objective of getting his son to play for Segovia. He had sufficient confidence in John's facility and potential to know that they would not come up short in an audition on that front, and in his own abilities as a salesman to be able to handle anything further that might be required to convince the maestro. All that was needed was the opportunity.

A number of Williams's old jazz-playing pals from pre-war days had got into the classical style, mainly as a result of having been inspired by recordings of Segovia. No matter how much they studied, practised and threw themselves into it, none of them had any prospect of making a living from playing classical guitar so in the cause of earning their daily bread they were still to be found in jazz combos, dance bands or recording studios. Len tracked some of them down and sounded them out as best he could across the globe. Terry Usher, to whom Len had passed his editorship of *Modern Guitar* before he left England, looked to be a potential entrée. He and fellow-Mancunian Jack Duarte both had previous contact with Segovia so they were the best prospects and when the Williamses arrived in London, it proved to be Usher who was able to arrange the meeting with the Spanish maestro on his very next visit to the city in November that year.

Long before that auspicious meeting with the great Segovia, Len had wasted no time in getting himself and his son known to the London guitar establishment. He had arranged and played quartet and trio pieces for guitar in Melbourne and both John and Bob Wilson had played them with him. Some of these works involved the use of soprano and bass guitars, unusual instruments and impossible to obtain in Australia, so Len had designed his own and had them made there to his specifications. He thought that writing for novel instruments might prove intriguing enough to help raise his profile so, immediately upon his arrival in London, Len contacted Dr Boris Perott of the Philharmonic Society of Guitarists, seeking the earliest opportunity for John to perform for its members. Len Williams, although known by reputation and through rumours of his plans for the first Spanish Guitar Centre in London, was something of an unknown quantity and may have proved too rough a diamond to embrace quickly. Perott decided he needed to know more about this whirlwind that had just blown in from Melbourne so invited him to a meeting at which Len spoke of his son, his plans for the centre and his ensemble arrangements. Perott was either reassured or intrigued and an invitation was forthcoming for John to be presented to the Society and for the hurriedly-assembled Len Williams Guitar Trio to perform at the meeting on Saturday 19 April 1952. This date was five days before John was to turn eleven and barely three months after Len's delayed arrival at Tilbury, quick work indeed!

With Len in the trio were London-based Desmond Dupré and Bob Wilson, on his familiar soprano guitar. Dupré was best regarded as a lutenist at the time and he had contacted Len soon after his arrival to learn about the planned Spanish Guitar Centre, of which he would become an associate. He was enlisted to play the bass guitar part for this first performance by Len's trio which, although politely received, perhaps with some concern that it was bit of a novelty, was comprehensively overshadowed by his son's solo performance. Many Society members were astounded, firstly that the ten-year-old played a full-size guitar and the more so by his mastery of the instrument and his mature technique. Julian Bream, who was the darling of the Society, also played that evening and he was moved to comment afterwards that he could not have played as well as John Williams at the same age. This was the first meeting of these two giants of the guitar, a genuinely historic occasion. A month later, Bream and both John and Len were back at the Society to play again, this time with the elder Williams playing solo. The Williamses each played pieces by J. S. Bach and Carcassi; John fittingly, given his father's discipleship of the man, also offered 'Adelita' by Tárrega. Although there were several other very accomplished performers including Peter Sensier and Deric Kennard, the impressively large attendance at such a gathering, over 100 in number, was drawn by the youthful Julian Bream and John Williams, aged eighteen and eleven respectively – the two men who would, alongside Segovia, dominate the classical guitar in the twentieth century.

So it was a pre-teen John still in short trousers who, in November 1952, was set before the man acknowledged as the world's foremost guitarist to demonstrate his aptitude and accomplishment. As was his custom during that period, Segovia was staying at the Piccadilly Hotel and he had agreed to audition the hopeful young player there. The Spanish maestro was more likely to be satisfying his curiosity regarding the young guitarist than expecting to find his successor as, over the years, he had been presented with numerous young players, all of whom had fallen short of his demands and expectations. True, he had heard many good reports of John's abilities, but most had come from Englishmen and he harboured a doubt that this was just another instance when they were desperately trying to promote one of their own.

Len and John were shown to Segovia's room and the great man generously put John at ease by chatting to him before inviting him to play. John, devoid of performance nerves as always, played some technically demanding pieces very well; his proud father bore a faint smile and an 'I told you as much' expression on his face as the maestro beamed and murmured his approval. After some brief discussion about John's musical history and the options that lay open, Segovia invited the lad to study with him at the following year's summer school at the Accademia Musicale Chigiani di Siena in Italy. He undertook to give John the highest recommendation. This was a huge breakthrough for the entire Williams family; Len had realised his immediate ambition for his son, John had his foot on the first rung of the ladder and when Melaan heard the news she felt like she had been welcomed into the higher echelons of European culture.

Len had no misgivings whatsoever about ceding his son's further guitar education to Segovia. When he was asked later if he was concerned about his surrender of influence, Len's reply was that he was happy that his son had the benefit of two afternoons free from school per week for practice; that he had done all he could for him; that Segovia was the boss and that the boy was fine practising on his own. All in all, Len was delighted to entrust his son's development to the greatest exponent of the classical guitar; he felt he had done his duty by John and, although he would probably not have couched it in such terms, honoured his talent.

After recommending that the Sor and Guiliani pieces

they had discussed should be acquired for John's study, Segovia accepted an invitation to visit the Williams's home in Maidstone Road before he left London and Len and John left the hotel cock-a-hoop. Ever the opportunist, after John's audition was over, Len had arranged to go back to the hotel the following day to see Segovia on his own and, indeed, on his own account in his role as a teacher of guitar. He asked about the scale system that the maestro used and copied the whole scheme out by hand with his hero, the great Segovia, demonstrating and dictating them to him. When he returned home and was showing John the fruits of his work, Len related his amusement at the maestro having referred to open or unstopped strings as 'empty strings' whenever he played or indicated one.

Regardless of this act of great generosity by Segovia, things were to change as Len got to know the man better. Although the two had the bond of a profound love for the guitar and now a shared interest in developing further its perhaps most promising talent, they took an instinctive dislike to each other and grew ever more mutually suspicious. It may have been through some sense of competition as teachers. Segovia gained his status primarily as a performer, something on which Len could not hold the dimmest of candles to him, but the Spaniard must have recognised that, regardless of the boy's innate talent, John could not have reached the standard and quality of technique he had demonstrated without the guidance of a very gifted teacher. Perhaps the most important factor, however, was that they had markedly different ways of dealing with their humble origins. Arguably Len's were the slightly more illustrious but they each dealt with the historical reality in their own way. Segovia sought to conceal his background and had for decades spun an image that he was from a cultured class, whereas Len had no compunction about acknowledging his working-class Cockney roots. The Englishman despised the hypocrisy of the man he admired so much as a musician. Segovia's desire for status was finally sated when he was ennobled in 1981 by King Juan Carlos I, who bestowed on him the newly created hereditary title of Marqués di Salobreña.

In the school summer holiday in 1953, just three months after his twelfth birthday, John and Melaan were full of excited expectations as Len saw them off from Paddington Station, where they boarded the boat train to begin the journey to Italy. They were bound for Siena, home of the famous Palio and a place of such historic beauty that it has since been designated a UNESCO World Heritage site. After the long and exhausting journey across the continent they received the customary warm welcome at the Accademia but were both, for different reasons, deeply disappointed that Segovia was not to be in attendance as he was undergoing a surgical procedure on his eyes. Absent he may have been but Andrés Segovia had honoured his pledge to John; he had secured a bursary providing him with free lodging and covering all tuition fees, something that would remain in place throughout the decade. The tuition would be good, too, as it had been arranged that another great Spanish guitarist, Emilio Pujol, would deputise and take the guitar classes.

Pujol was better known as a teacher, musicologist and composer than as a performer. He had studied with Tárrega himself and developed his own 'school' of guitar tuition. In some ways Segovia's absence might have been a boon for John – it gave him the opportunity to become close to a man who became a great influence and a life-long friend. The Venezuelan player Alirio Díaz, some eighteen years senior to the young Australian, was also there to study and he took John under his wing. Díaz had come to the guitar by a circuitous route, having first studied the saxophone and clarinet. After taking courses in English and typewriting he moved to Caracas and began his association with the guitar, learning from the great Raul Borges. His progress with the instrument was such that the Venezuelan government awarded him a scholarship to continue his studies in Spain and he first attended Siena as a pupil of Segovia in 1951. Díaz had been in danger of missing the course as he had suffered earlier in the year with appendicitis but he was by now fully recovered. Another guitar student, Gerasimos Miliaresis, from Greece, also adopted 'the younger brother' and the two helped look after John's interests and musical development during the four weeks of that first visit to Siena. Pujol's lessons were inspiring but John also learned immediately from Díaz, taking note of his posture and being particularly impressed by his right hand position, which was significantly different from the Segovia mode in which Len had schooled him. John had clearly inherited the powers of observation and critical analysis that his father employed to such great effect.

It is easy to rush through the events that John experienced in that torrid time without pausing to consider the impact on him, probably because it is so difficult to imagine what must have been going through the mind of the young lad whose life had changed so dramatically over the past eighteen months or so. Leaving behind his childhood home in Melbourne; the excitement and sometime boredom of a sea voyage across the globe; arrival in the great and battered metropolis of London; getting acquainted with previously unknown family; adapting to new schools, music teachers and now finding himself in the heady and romantic setting of summertime Siena made it a time of momentous challenge. It is said that children are very adaptable but John was now on the cusp of puberty and carrying enormous expectations; the upheaval through which he went at that time was immense by any measure. It speaks to the core of his character that nobody who was around him then can recall anything other than a polite, modest, slightly serious and very composed young man.

John learned a lot in that first summer in Siena about music, the guitar and life itself. His personal environment in both Australia and London had been one filled almost exclusively with adults, observing far more than interacting with them but here, with music as the leveller, he was for the first time truly among peers. He also had company and companionship, something he had been denied as a child and that was to be absent again throughout his teenage years. Although it was yet again the company of people mostly older than himself, they shared the bond of music and some of them had, in their time, experienced childhoods as extraordinary as John's.

The Accademia Musicale di Chigiana was not just for guitarists; John met an incredible array of musicians there over the years. There were all kinds of instrumentalists, string quartets, opera singers and orchestras all peppered with future stars and John was a contemporary of Zubin Mehta, Salvatore Accardo and cellist Rohan de Saram. The Welsh composer Gareth Walters, someone with whom John often worked at the BBC in later years, was enormously impressed by the musical accomplishment of the young Williams. There were not too many folk there from Britain and it greatly amused Gareth, then in his mid-twenties, that one of his few compatriots at the Accademia was still in short trousers.

It was while at Siena that John first met and became close friends with Daniel Barenboim. He was not only a prodigy as a pianist but also already making his very distinctive mark as a twelve-year-old conductor, having previously taken courses at the St Cecilia Academy in Rome. Unlike John, who had only his mother with him, Daniel was accompanied by both his parents and Melaan soon became great friends with them. Utterly seduced by her surroundings, she was revelling in the experience of being accepted within an international mix of refined and cultured people. Back in London, meanwhile, Len's existence was less colourful. He was still working tirelessly to grow both his business and his reputation at the Spanish Guitar Centre and the cost of the Siena trips, although recognised and accepted as an essential investment, was a huge draw on family resources, both financial and emotional.

The month in Siena passed all too quickly for mother and son. Back home in London, John's life resumed some semblance of what passed in the Williams clan for normality. On Friday evenings, he and his mother would head off to the

Guitar Centre to meet up with Len and they would all go to the cinema together, rounding off the evening with a meal at the brasserie in Lyons Corner House. Cinema trips were also quite frequent on Sunday afternoons, with a choice of either the lovely art deco theatre in Bowes Road or another in Turnpike Lane. When school and guitar practice allowed, John looked forward to playing table tennis in the back garden but he could rarely get the better of his father. Len was a very good player and would enjoy smashing the ball back across the net at great speed or putting a wicked spin on his return. John's only real school-friend, John Sanchez, would sometimes be presented at the table as a sacrifice for Len but the two boys usually played together and both became much-improved players. Sanchez was also a promising footballer who played for the youth team run by the Tottenham Hotspurs club, where John occasionally went to watch him play. Quite what made John Sanchez special in the friendship stakes is not clear; he had no interest in music and John Williams had little in sport. The two lost touch and John was surprised and delighted when Sanchez turned up to see him after a concert in Adelaide in the 1980s, having emigrated some years earlier. The young Aussie had hardly any other friends of his own age; guitar practice was the priority on getting home from school and the time off he had been granted for practice, beneficial as it was, meant his missing the rough and tumble of sports sessions in which many friendships in the all-boys school were forged.

As in Australia, the semi-detached house in Maidstone Road was always open to friends of the Williamses so John again endured a domestic life dominated by adults living by the same unconventional rules that had operated in Melbourne. The visitors were all confident, outgoing people and their presence helped ensure the house was always alive with jokes, games, music and sex. Family photos show friends who had also come over from Australia mixing with those who had joined the Williams circle through the Guitar Centre. Gerry and Barbara Newman, Michael Watson, Lock Aitken, Sadie Bishop (who came at Len's invitation, leaving her husband Joe Washington back in Melbourne), the Wilsons, Stella Mackenzie and guitar maker Harald Petersen can all be found in the family album along with the teenage John, bearing more than a passing resemblance to a youthful Woody Allen.

June identified an inner clique centred on Len, Lock and Sadie, who she described as 'a very brash and physical person'. Len was also close to Bob Wilson's wife. Many of Len's jazz guitarist friends also showed up at the house. The Williams gang were often pictured around the table tennis table and, as was common in those days, mostly with cigarette in hand. Both John's parents were still heavy smokers – Len continuing to roll his own cigarettes, Melaan happy to smoke them too. When John asked his dad about the subject in his early teens, Len dealt with the issue of smoking in a very matter-of-fact way. He said: 'It's entirely up to you. You can smoke if you want but you'd be bloody stupid if you did. It's an addiction that will cost you a fortune and end up killing you.' This from an eighty-a-day man who was to die from emphysema.

It was most definitely Len who set the rules for the household and paternal attitudes to money and sex were similarly liberal and liberating. John was told that if he needed cash for anything then he should just help himself from his father's wallet. The qualifying condition was that the lad should, however, be responsible about what he took. Apropos girls and sex, since the same loose attitude to casual partner-swapping among residents and visitors chez Williams prevailed in London as it had in Melbourne, Len could hardly take a tough stance, even had he been so inclined. Most thirteen-year-old boys would have been extremely envious of being told by their fathers to 'Bring any girls you meet back home to stay, if you want, it is not an issue. You know what we are like in this house.' It was an offer that John never took up. He describes the house as being, 'Very sociable, almost communal, with quite a few people virtually sharing it.'

When John had the time, he would take the Tube into town to visit the Guitar Centre, where Len encouraged him to spend time with other guitarists, and he made a number of durable friendships. Christopher Nupen and Luc Markies were both students at the centre and would later become flatmates of John's. Although the business of the centre was patently that of guitar tuition, numerous people who knew Len through his other interests used to turn up there to talk about philosophy and politics, entice him into a game of chess or, to use a modern term, just hang out. If Len turfed them out, a not infrequent occurrence, they would retire to the coffee bar downstairs and try again later.

John remembers Len urging him to spend time with one of this crowd, a larger-than-life character named Lou de Schwartz, who came into the West End from his home within the large Jewish community then centred on Whitechapel. Lou was articulate, funny, wise and well-read but you had to get close to him to fully appreciate those qualities. To most he was best known and instantly recognisable for his routinely filthy clothing, of which his tie was usually the pièce de resistance. He seemed to have an incurable habit of spilling food on the tie and he used to joke, 'I can boil it up once a week and make a lovely soup.' Lou became a bit of an 'uncle' to John and took him to watch cricket. They had a great time watching 'fearsome' Freddie Trueman, the Yorkshire fast bowler, in action. As two curious intellectuals with similar political inclinations, there was mutual respect between the unkempt philosopher and the centre's proprietor. They sparred verbally on a wide range of subjects, sharing and exchanging views and books. Lou got to know Len well enough to make a pithy observation of the man: 'The trouble with Len is that he can't reconcile himself to being above the animals but below the Gods.'

Melaan had immensely enjoyed the first trip to the sun and the old buildings and culture of Siena and was as keen as her son to return there the following year, having completely succumbed to the allure of the place and the people. Including the time needed for travelling, they were away for around five weeks and she positively wallowed in the exposure to the celebrated and sometimes aristocratic companions with whom she had time to relax and enjoy the Italian summer. John had made an immediate impression there and the respect that his talent and personality engendered served to bolster Melaan's sense of rightfully belonging within the Chigiana community. She was slightly unsettled by the presence of Sadie Bishop, who was a somewhat unwelcome reminder of the old days back in Australia, but regardless of this minor irritation, things were far more like what she had expected and hoped for in coming to Europe than the grey skies and daily struggle in London.

While his mother sunbathed and socialised, John was in musical heaven – learning, questioning and absorbing. That year he took classes with Segovia and he could not help noticing that all the other guitar students sat around looking absolutely terrified; they knew that the maestro would take them to task for the slightest mistake or deviation from his instruction. This prospect did not bother him at all – he had survived the academy of Len so what was left to fear? He renewed his acquaintance with his great friends Alirio and Gerasimos and continued to enjoy their support and influence. John has now realised, with the benefit of hindsight, that even though he had guidance and instruction from the undisputed father of the guitar, he actually learned much more from Díaz than from Segovia. Alirio was more accessible, less prescriptive and, crucially, he was part of the student milieu and hence devoid of the grandeur that Segovia never failed to affect. He was also one of a number of Latin American guitarists in attendance over the years and he helped introduce and guide Williams to the music of that region, something that would later help shape the Australian's career and for which he remains profoundly grateful.

The repertoire that John had taken to his first summer schools was understandably quite conservative and entirely euro-centric – Bach, Tárrega and Carcassi – as was the programme that Segovia followed in his classes. John enjoyed Alirio's playing of pieces based on Latin American folk music though this had to be done surreptitiously, well away from the ears of the maestro. There were some extremely accomplished musicians from that region who made their mark on John during his time at Siena, such as Raul Sanchez from Uruguay, the Mexican Gustavo Lopez and Alirio's colourful compatriot, Rodrigo Riera. John prizes a recording called 'El Uno y El Otro' that was made of Díaz and Riera by the French radio producer Robert Vidal, which has Riera improvising over various traditional South American pieces played by Díaz. For John, it conjures up treasured memories of the two playing for a few friends while seated around the ancient fountain below Siena cathedral in the wee small hours.

Alirio shared some very special pieces of music with John: a book of Venezuelan compositions published by the government of that country that included Lauro's 'Natalia', together with his own arrangement of Ponce's 'Scherzino Mexicano' and, most importantly, two pieces by the Paraguayan guitarist and composer, Agustín Barrios Mangoré. Segovia's snobbishness about much of South American music, especially that with popular roots, was evident to John from very early on and was something the young man struggled to understand and that damaged the great man's credibility in his eyes. The Spaniard was dismissive of Lauro's work and positively banned that of Barrios from his classes, although years later Alirio Díaz confided to John how excited he was that Segovia had finally shown an interest in 'Natalia'. Perhaps because of the way in which he had been taught by his father, John also found Segovia's teaching methods unsympathetic and unhelpful to the student. He and others have commented that the demand by the maestro that the student copy his every inflection stifled creativity and undermined any sense of personal ownership of a piece. It was as if Segovia had decided and ordained that there was but one valid transcription, one interpretation and one fingering of anything in the repertoire and they were his own. John feels that, perhaps because of this, he never played his best for Segovia and that many of the maestro's students would have been better if they were not so constrained.

John, with Melaan in eager support, went to Siena each summer and, while there in 1955, he made history at the Accademia Chigiana by becoming the first student of any instrument to be asked to perform a solo concert. What made this an even greater honour was that it was at the request of his fellow students. He chose a demanding programme and played brilliantly, confirming his place among the very best as someone truly special.

At Easter 1956 John left Friern Barnet Grammar School amid some intense and heated debate between his parents as to what the boy's immediate future should be. Len was happy that John was progressing superbly as a guitarist but they both felt the boy had a lot to learn to become a complete musician; he should go to music college to complete his education. There was an important guitar competition in Geneva towards the end of that year and Segovia was insistent that John should be entered. He was confident that the youth would win hands-down and consequently gain recognition on the world stage, where he would be identified as the Spaniard's protégé. This whole notion was very appealing to John's mother, who was in thrall to Segovia, a musical giant who was, to her, the very pinnacle of the world into which she wanted to see her son established, and she was not really looking any further than that. John's early exit from school had been in part to help prepare him for the competition and Len had let it happen, having, unusually for him, taken his eye off the ball. The Williamses were increasingly at odds over many things and they rowed constantly. Although Len dominated the family, dictating terms and manipulating events, Melaan had grown bolder and more self-confident, having rubbed shoulders with the great and good in Siena, and she made her voice heard and her opinions very clear. She won the battle about the boy leaving school to prepare for Geneva but this was because Len was, to her continuing annoyance and frustration, totally absorbed in promoting business at the Guitar Centre. She wanted her son to win the prize in Switzerland now and get a career underway; she reasoned that Segovia had to be right, he was the greatest guitarist in the world so what did Len know that the great Segovia did not? John's analysis of his mother's internal debate is that Melaan, for all her left-wing principles, was at heart conservative and inclined to excessive adulation of authority and the establishment. She had always struggled with a dichotomy between her craving for the embrace of the establishment and her socialist convictions and the relationship with Segovia brought that conflict to a head.

Len was concerned that John should not be diverted from acquiring a sound musical education simply, as he saw it, to serve the ego and selfish ambition of Andrés Segovia; he even went so far as to telephone Julian Bream to seek his opinion. Julian was in a difficult position because he was invited to be on the jury in Geneva so was not able to offer much to aid the debate. Ultimately Len was convinced that the Geneva competition would have been the start of a very long and very slippery slope into what he considered to be the uncaring exploitation of a prodigy and this was not what he thought was right for his son. Melaan probably failed to anticipate this consequence. Although Len retained his profound admiration for Segovia the musician, he felt his duty to his gifted son was paramount and he would stand his ground. Len despised what he termed 'the cult of the prodigy' and he knew that was what awaited John in Geneva. But he was no fool and he fully understood the importance of the 1956 competition to Segovia. This was the first year since its establishment in 1939 that the prestigious Geneva International Music Competition had accepted the guitar for inclusion as a concert instrument. It was almost a foregone conclusion that John would win and, in doing so, elevate Segovia's reputation to even greater heights, providing him with the legacy he sought. With some justification, Williams senior resented the kudos that would attach to the Spaniard at the expense of his own lengthy and fundamental contribution to John's success.

Melaan and Len each remained committed to their preferred course of action for their son and poor John was in the middle as the fights became more heated and the schism widened. He discussed the issues at length with both his parents. Even at that age John realised that Melaan's reasoning was based upon her excessively high opinion of Segovia and her yearning for acceptance, the evidence of which he had witnessed over the past few years in Siena. The fifteen-year-old made a point of laying out and considering all the pros and cons, an approach that, in his discussion with his father, was met with a rejoinder that Len used to him many times and in many circumstances throughout his life: 'The trouble with you, young Williams, is that you are excessively fair-minded.' At that tender age there was no way that John was adequately versed in the ways of the music profession to know what was the best course of action. Finally, in what Len would call 'taking charge of your own life', but what was really an appalling abdication of responsibility by both parents, it fell to the teenager to make the decision. His only frame of reference was Julian Bream's experience – he had gone to college and it did not seem to have slowed his progress; he was doing well and gaining greater acceptance all the time. After much soul-searching and lobbying from his parents, John opted to subscribe to Len's analysis, combined with his own observations and conclusions about Segovia, and he declined to participate in the competition, a decision he has never regretted. It was settled. John had been attending the RCM junior department on Saturday mornings and in June 1956, his application to the Royal College of Music proper was accepted.

When Segovia heard of John's decision, he telephoned the boy to remonstrate with him, soon resorting to venting his rage in Spanish, which, of course, John did not understand. The anger subsided and it was agreed that Melaan and John should travel to Siena that August as usual. Perhaps Segovia felt then that he could have one last try at persuasion there – in the event, he did not, having resigned himself to losing the fight.

John and Melaan went to Siena in August 1956 on what was an uncomfortable visit although John's extraordinary self-possession, combined with his excitement about enrolling at the RCM, meant that it did not upset him too much. They returned to London and it would soon be time for the next phase in John's development. He arrived at the portals of the Royal College of Music at the start of the autumn term to begin studying the piano and music theory. As a guitarist, this combination was hardly an ideal basis but the college simply had no guitar department, tutors or curriculum, a situation replicated at all conservatoires and colleges at that time. Like Bream, who had suffered similar limitations, he was right at the forefront of the pioneers who would establish the guitar as worthy of academic study as a concert instrument.

Segovia came to London some months later with Olga Coelho, the Brazilian singer and guitarist who had been his partner since 1944. Len went to their room at the Piccadilly Hotel to discuss John's future. He did not hold back in his criticism of the maestro who was, to his mind, blatantly out to exploit his son. There was very little chance of an accord being reached: the two were used to getting their own way and they were fighting about their influence over John. Emotions soon got the better of both men and after some verbal skirmishing the discussion became very heated. It culminated in Williams physically confronting Segovia after being subjected to his opinion that he was 'a very, very little man'. Olga called the hotel's porters and the irate Londoner was unceremoniously bustled off the premises.

The following day Segovia summoned John to the hotel. Knowing what had transpired between his two teachers, the fifteen-year-old was understandably trepidatious about what might be in store for him but he made his way to the hotel room where Segovia, in all his pomp, was waiting for him. The interview was brief. The older man did not attempt to go through the debate or argue the merits of his view that John should enter the competition. Instead, he said simply, 'I must tell you that I can no longer be your teacher and one day, I shall tell you why I detest your father,' then dismissed the youth. Poor John left the hotel totally perplexed, hardly knowing what to make of the harsh words. He headed off to relate the proceedings to his father, who was waiting for him in Peter Mario's Coffee Bar in Gerrard Street. Len was furious and ready to go right back to the Piccadilly to resume his own encounter with Segovia but, fortunately for John, some friends were also there to calm him down and try to help him make sense of Segovia's position.

The outcome of these seismic exchanges was that not only did John not compete in Geneva that year but he also did not go to Siena to take classes with Segovia the following year. However, on her own account and in her own as well as John's interests, Melaan, more and more her own woman, kept the lines of communication open with Segovia. She brokered a slightly uneasy rapprochement with him that allowed John to return to Siena in 1958; the determined barrister's daughter was not prepared to let such an important relationship wither. Len was completely sidelined.

In 1957 Len and Melaan finally ceased to be a couple. Even though she lost the battle of Geneva, his wife's determined assaults on his authority were something new to Len. He was going through a disturbing personality crisis; there were mood swings and signs that he was assailed by paranoia. He always had a bit of a chip on his shoulder about being an 'outsider' to the establishment, referring to anything he did not control as 'out there'. Now, even though he had a successful business and students, lured by his success and irresistible charisma, were queuing to register at the centre there were new and worrying signs. Len had confided in his friend Stan Kupercyn long ago that he had had lurid nightmares during which a chair in his room was intent on attacking him. Stan later told John that he thought this was the sign of a growing paranoia.

Len's behaviour became erratic and his temper more volatile. Salvation was to be found in his growing relationship with June Peirce and he moved the family to a flat at 40 Gordon Square in Bloomsbury so she could live with him. The two-floor apartment, which they rented from the University of London, had to accommodate all their needs and, in any event, Len and Melaan could not have afforded the upkeep of two separate dwellings. They explained to John why they had split, something that was a real burden for the teenage musician, knowing that his musical welfare had probably been yet another factor in them reaching the point of no return. The couple formalised their divorce soon afterwards.

The living arrangements at Gordon Square were unconventional, if not downright bizarre. Len lived with June in the downstairs rooms while John and Melaan were billeted upstairs. They all shared a kitchen and the single bathroom. Someone close enough to events to be considered a reliable observer commented of Williams around that time that 'Positive women were always a red flag to Len, half of him wanted a Melaan, half a June.' Melaan was very much her own person by then and he would not brook the challenges to his authority. June was much younger than Melaan and possessed of a sweeter, far more compliant nature and she was devoted to Len. Her enrolment at the centre had been a transforming experience that put something exciting, challenging and fulfilling into her dutiful but understandably reluctant role as dedicated carer to her mother. She was susceptible to the glamour and undoubted charisma that the worldly and confident Len possessed and regarded him as some kind of saviour. June had probably been smitten and carrying a torch for him since she had finally made it all the way up the stairs of the centre at her second attempt. Melaan had always liked June and continued to get on well with her, not quite like sisters but very chummy and there is no suggestion from anyone concerned that she was responsible for, or even contributed to the breakdown of the marriage. In fact, Len's now ex-wife probably felt sorry for the woman who was about to step into her shoes.

The other resident at Gordon Square almost from the start was the South African guitar student Christopher Nupen, who had become something of a favourite of Len's among his disciples. Nupen hung on every word that Len uttered and considered him to be a genius – a flawed one perhaps, but a genius of sorts. He was now working for a bank but

Nupen wanted to abandon the bowler-and-umbrella life of his job in the City to take a more creative path so left to become a trainee sound engineer at the BBC. He asked Len if he could lodge with him. Although the rooms in the flat were spacious, their number was limited and they were all spoken for; there was simply nowhere for Nupen to lay his head.

Determined to stay close to the man he revered and never less than supremely resourceful, however, Nupen suggested that he might move into the coal cellar of the building. Len scoffed at the idea, pointing out that the place was filthy and, even worse, permanently damp. Nupen pushed the point and extracted an agreement from his potential landlord that, if he could get the accommodation to a state where he was happy to move in and would not sue should pneumonia set in, then he would be permitted to do so.

Somewhere along the way, Christopher had come across an industrial additive that would make concrete waterproof. The product, 'Lillington's No. 2 Liquid', was intended to be used in the construction of large bore water pipes but Nupen's logic was that if concrete so treated would retain water in a pipe then it could be equally effective in keeping water out of a cellar. He set to work, first thoroughly cleaning the place and then rendering the inside of the walls and the ceiling with his modified cement mix, all with just a six-inch trowel. While he was working on the ceiling, John went down to check on his friend's progress and it was exactly at that point that the entire ceiling came down on the poor Nupen, John managing to scramble back through the door before he, too, became engulfed by the messy debris. The dogged springbok cleared up, overcame the problem, spruced the place up with a coat of paint and duly joined the household, paying thirty shillings a week for the privilege.

Christopher Nupen was the only objective close-up observer of the Williams clan during the important years of John's progression from child prodigy newly arrived in London to emerging star of the guitar on a world platform. And even his objectivity may be a little compromised by his profound admiration for Len, who he called 'the most interesting person I have ever met'. That is an enormous compliment to Williams given that Nupen went on to become the most important producer of documentary films on many truly great classical musicians with whom he had close relationships. He describes Len as 'dynamite' and observed both at the centre and in social life that 'people who came near Williams were either heavily influenced by him or turned tail and ran. You listen to him on his terms or go. When you are as intelligent and urgent as Len you don't compromise – you have no time for that.'

Nupen thinks that Melaan was perhaps too resilient for Len to cope with. She became far more resistant to his routine bullying than most people and learned not to be afraid to trade verbal blows with him. She had witnessed and tolerated the way that Len cheated, lied and exaggerated to achieve his ends and mostly lived with it. She had appreciated him as a gifted teacher of guitar to their son but had not always agreed with his methods and, although sexual fidelity was not of great concern to her or Len, she was not prepared to live with what Nupen calls the 'prominentengeil' or groupie culture that her husband encouraged and exploited among his students and other disciples. Nupen casts Melaan as a robust and critical character who had the mantra 'Criticism is the rallying point of intelligence'. Combine all these characteristics with her longing to become part of a respected elite and it is not difficult to see why her relationship with Len was destined to fail. Living in these new circumstances in the same flat was not easy for anyone concerned and John's loyalties must have been severely tested at times. Len now defined himself primarily through his role as founder and head teacher at the centre and became more autocratic and self-absorbed as time went on. June indulged him and was far less demanding and distracting than Melaan had been of late. He kept an eye on John's progress but that was taking care of itself to a great extent and Len spent a large proportion of his energy in making sure that his status as a highly successful teacher and entrepreneur was not only preserved but also made abundantly evident to the world at large.

John did not waste the 'gap year' that he had from attending the Accademia Chigiana. In June of that year, Clifford Williams, the director of the Arts Theatre in Great Newport Street, just a stone's throw from the centre, approached Len about his taking guitar lessons. During their conversation he mentioned that he was about to stage a production of 'Yerma' by Federico García Lorca and asked if there was someone from the centre who could help with assembling and arranging suitable guitar music. John was immediately conscripted and worked on the task with the help of actress Madelena Nicol. She had a volume of Iberian folk music compiled by Kurt Schindler that contained hundreds of tunes and themes. They plundered and adapted and what they finally put forward to the producer was adopted with delight. After completing this unusual and rewarding assignment, John took up an invitation from a Swedish friend, Dan Grenholm, a contact from Siena. Grenholm, a guitar aficionado, noted photographer and travel guide, had asked John to join him at his second home in southern Spain, high up in the Sierra Nevada. The two became life-long friends.

Although John did not go to Siena in 1957, Sadie Bishop made the trip to continue her studies there under Segovia. She had previously met and become close to Rodrigo Riera, the Venezuelan guitarist, and enthusiastically renewed her relationship with him, returning to England pregnant with his child. Their son Stephen was born in London in May 1958. He is now a successful artist, actor, singer and multi-instrumentalist who goes by the delightful adopted name of George Washingmachine. He is particularly celebrated as a jazz violinist and has recently re-established contact with Rodrigo's family in Venezuela.

At the end of July 1958, John Williams, now seventeen and fully familiar with the drill, travelled to Siena alone. On 8 August, he performed another solo concert at the Accademia and one month later to the day, June and Len took their marriage vows at St Pancras, the same register office where he had wed Phyllis Pace twenty-three years earlier.

‡

By kind permission of the Principal of the
Royal Manchester College of Music.

IN THE HALL OF THE ROYAL
MANCHESTER COLLEGE OF MUSIC

Ducie Street, Oxford Road, Manchester, 13.
Friday, December 9th, 1955, at 7-0 p.m.

A

GUITAR RECITAL
by
JOHN WILLIAMS

ADMISSION FREE BY PROGRAMME.

(This Recital is sponsored by the Manchester Guitar Circle and
programmes may be obtained from the President, Terence Usher,
5, Woodheys Drive, Sale, Cheshire).

(Programme inside)

Manchester recital programme.

On 6 November 1958, two months after his father had
married for the third time, John played the recital at the
Wigmore Hall that numerous references cite, incorrectly, as
his public debut. This is one of three great myths of Williams's
career. He had, in fact, already performed professionally in
1955 at the Conway Hall and at a recital arranged by his
father's friend and sometime student Michael Watson at the

Museum Lecture Theatre in Bristol. In 1955 he played at the Royal Manchester College of Music in a recital sponsored by the Manchester Guitar Circle, the President of which was one Terence Usher. He remembers the Manchester date not for the programme he played nor the warm reception he received from the audience but because when he stood up to take his bow, having just played the twenty-minute 'Variations and Fugue on Folies de Espagna' by Manuel Ponce, he found his foot had 'gone to sleep' and he toppled off the stage down the steps into the green room, where Terry Usher caught his guitar. Iconic though it might be, the Wigmore performance may not be entered in the annals with any validity as John Williams's debut but it undoubtedly deserves to be celebrated for the memorable and oft-quoted words of Andrés Segovia in the programme:

> A prince of the guitar has arrived in the musical world. God has laid a finger on his brow and it will not be long before his name becomes a byword in England and abroad thus contributing to the spiritual domain of his race. I hail this young artist on the occasion of his first public performance and make the heartfelt wish that success, like his shadow, may accompany him everywhere.

Given the generosity and fulsomeness of these words it would be churlish not to forgive the two inaccuracies they include. The concert played to a full house, generating reviews from music critics in the national press as well as in guitar magazines and musical journals. By and large, they endorsed Segovia's sentiments with just a few suggesting that his technique was perhaps a little too controlled. Len's reaction to the programme note was perhaps provoked to some degree by its authorship and was certainly far earthier than any review: 'Touch his brow? You'd get far more response by kicking his fucking arse!'

Melaan had arranged that she and her group would take John for a celebratory meal after he had performed but, before making his way to the restaurant, John called into the pub where he knew his father would be, along with his new wife June, Basil Hogarth and several other pals. Len was absolutely thrilled that John had 'cracked the Wigmore' and, when his son walked in to thank his father and accept his congratulations, Len turned to his friends and said, 'You never know what John is thinking – he'd never give his old Dad a kiss on the cheek.' John says, 'I was astonished at him saying that because I may be quiet but I am not emotionally detached. So I stepped right forward and gave him a kiss on the cheek.' Len, shocked, exclaimed: 'Well, I'll be buggered.'

The only real competition between John and Julian!

FIVE

JOHN AND JULIAN

To many listeners, the duet recordings of John Williams and Julian Bream represent a form of guitar perfection. Quite apart from their technical and artistic accomplishment the award-winning discs are an irrefutable testimony to the remarkable development of the modern classical guitar and a revelation of the richness of the diversity within that development. It is well known that the two musicians espouse very different playing styles and interpretative methods, seek very different things of their chosen instruments and approach their music in very different ways but they came together for their tours and recordings in what can be characterised and appreciated as a celebration of their differences. Their fans make up two loose camps but it is fair to say that very few from either have failed to appreciate and applaud what the two men achieved together.

These masters of the guitar have much in common, perhaps even more than in what distinguishes them. John and Julian were both important pioneers, breaking new ground, although Julian, being some eight years older and in career as well as age chronologically ahead of John, trod the more difficult path. The two each had fathers who worked tirelessly to promote the playing careers of their sons, who went on to become pillars of the modern classical guitar, not only in their backyard of Britain but across the world. Both fathers played jazz guitar, albeit at different levels of competence, but demanded something else of their sons, arguably projecting their own ambitions upon them. Both came from modest circumstances, fought fierce battles for their causes, made sacrifices and ultimately realised their goals, which were different even though they overlapped.

Bream senior was primarily driven by the aim of setting his son on the way to a career as a musician, firstly as a pianist or cellist then, hopefully and less certainly, as a guitarist. Len Williams was similarly committed in his ambition for his son John to become a concert guitarist but this objective was undoubtedly set alongside his proselytising of the guitar and the promotion of his own teaching. Although not much better funded for the task, John's father was undoubtedly the more organised and better equipped of the two. By the time that John's talent was becoming evident, Len Williams already had a substantial career as a working musician under his belt. He had played jazz, designed and marketed instruments, studied classical playing under Maccaferri, one of the masters of his time, and knew his way around the music business. In the context of developing and launching John, he also enjoyed the enormous benefit of at least a part of his vision being actively shared by his wife, Melaan, who played her own significant role in the odyssey, not least in her determination that the family would travel across the globe in its cause.

John Williams speaks with enormous regard and sincerity of Julian Bream's role in advancing the guitar as a serious concert instrument. He believes that the timing of his own father's bringing him to England was both fortuitous and beneficial, coming, as it did, after Julian and his father had already fought some of the inevitable and debilitating battles and had overcome enormous obstacles to help put the guitar on the map. John credits Julian as being an even more important influence on the development of the modern classical guitar than Segovia, especially in his contribution to the development of the repertoire. He feels that few, if any, of Segovia's commissions and collaborations could rival those of Bream with luminaries such as William Walton, Benjamin Britten, Michael Tippett, Malcolm Arnold and Hans Werner Henze.

Julian Bream's career nearly didn't get off the ground. His redoubtable father, Henry, had to fight long and hard to establish Julian as the first and, arguably, greatest British guitarist. This endeavour took place during the latter half of the 1940s and may be considered to have culminated when Bream junior made his Wigmore Hall debut on 26 November 1951, just two and a half weeks after Henry died.

Alexander Julian Bream was the first of four children for Henry and his wife, Violet, who Julian has described as 'very beautiful' and 'warm but crazy'. He was born in Battersea, south of the Thames in London, on St Swithin's day, 15 July 1933. Julian pithily describes his first home as lying 'between the Power Station and the Dogs' Home'. His father worked as a sign painter, specialising in advertising and promotional material for cinemas. Two years after Julian was born, Henry realised his ambition for slightly more artistic freedom by setting himself up in business as a freelance commercial artist. The family relocated to a bungalow at 25 Cleveland Avenue in the London suburb of Hampton, close to the home of Twickenham Rugby Club and Kempton Park racecourse. It was still a fairly modest home but was in a more desirable neighbourhood than Battersea.

Julian was given his first classical guitar as a birthday present when he was eleven, an age by which John Williams already had five or six years of expert tuition under his belt. The gift was prompted by the recent interest the boy had shown in the plectrum guitar, an instrument that Henry played in a local dance band. Although he derived some small income to supplement his earnings, Henry's playing was principally a source of pleasure and satisfaction so he was keen for his son to learn and share his enjoyment of music. The piano, well established, respected and promising of a potential career, was Henry's chosen instrument for Julian and he paid for his son to receive professional piano lessons. Julian's fascination with his father's plectrum guitar was not initially encouraged; he was allowed only to play it for fun, the piano being, in his father's mind at least, the serious instrument for the boy with the cello a close second. As it became clear to Henry, however, that his son had a natural aptitude for the guitar, he recognised that this was worth nurturing alongside the piano studies which he continued to fund and sustain. Julian was, after all, a very talented pianist and cellist and continued to play and study both instruments in parallel with the guitar.

The young Bream's innate ability with the guitar inspired his father to teach his son everything he knew about playing it, and ultimately to invest in the purchase of the classical instrument, knowing that the jazz guitar was definitely not the way forward. Julian began the transition from plectrum-style to finger-style and in the following year, 1945, was accepted as a pupil by the émigré Russian, Dr Boris Perrott, who was then chairman of the grandly named Philharmonic Society of Guitarists (PSG). By the autumn of that year, Julian had given modest recitals and was clearly making great strides with the guitar.

The Williamses knew of Julian and had some ideas of where he fitted into the guitar world. Even before they met him they had some sense of just how good he was. Terry Usher sent Len a recording of Bream playing the last two movements of the Rodrigo Concerto on the BBC and he and John were knocked sideways by it. That performance set such a high standard that when they subsequently heard the work played by Narciso Yepes they were very disappointed by his rendering. They got to see Julian perform the Concerto later when he played at the Tottenham Municipal Baths.

Julian and John first came across each other at the PSG meeting in 1952. Bream had proved himself to be an extremely accomplished and promising guitarist and was the great white hope of the society which was so keen to demonstrate to the world that an Englishman could compare with the best. John was then performing for the first time in England and his playing drew generous compliments from Julian. Both men went on to great things and their achievements were to make them, along with Segovia, the most important and influential guitarists of their time and it is a matter of taste, debate and very little meaning as to which of them one prefers.

Richard Wright, who has been the guitar teacher at the Yehudi Menuhin School at Stoke D'Abernon since the instrument was added to the curriculum there, identifies what he sees as the single most defining distinction between the three men he considers to be the giants of modern classical guitar. He points out that two of the three, Segovia and Bream, were largely self-taught, while John Williams received tuition from an early age from someone now universally recognised and acclaimed as a great teacher. Further, by virtue of that teacher being his father, John's progress would have been monitored and his practice observed and directed on a daily basis with the particular kind of discipline that comes only from a parent. This distinction is of fundamental significance and may provide clues about the different ways in which the three approached the instrument and the repertoire.

Segovia stands alone; a consequence of his time as well as his talent. Bream and Williams are not quite of the same generation but they overlap significantly and have been comrades in arms and, in the eyes of their public if not in reality, gentle rivals. The trajectory of their careers could hardly be more different but the enormous mutual respect is evident when talking to either man. Each recognises and appreciates what the other has achieved and given to the world of guitar music. They also accept that they are very different. There are as many opinions about the variation in the styles of the two performers as there are commentators and some go so far as to invoke the Apollonian/Dionysian dichotomy to characterise the differences between the two guitarists. Most would characterise Bream as the more emotionally expressive but they may be persuaded of this by his physical animation. His intense involvement with his music is visible as well as audible. Julian's face grimaces and distorts to reflect his passion about whatever he is playing and he stamps his own interpretation on the piece. He works hard at his art, almost having to fight to make his inner voice heard. Williams, by contrast, seems more in control; he rarely moves much more than the occasional eyebrow and may, rarely, be seen to move on his seat. His playing has great colour and, his adherents declare, is truer to the composers' intent, something for which they say he has a god-given talent. The Almighty may have played a role but it was Len who helped develop and instil the technique that removes the barrier and filters between what John is thinking and what he conveys to his audience. Rodney Friend, the virtuoso violinist who was Leader of the London Philharmonic Orchestra at the age of twenty-three, has the highest regard for John's musicianship. He says:

> Musicians have an inner voice and that it is what they wish their audiences to hear. They can be inhibited or constrained by their instrument and their own capabilities but John Williams's skill and technique transcend any limitations imposed by the guitar. He can express his 'voice' far easier than others, almost without thinking about it.

This is not to say that he does not have to work at his art but everyone who works with him will recognise that John learns quicker than others and needs to practise less; this is one consequence of his superb technique. Regardless of their individual approaches, there will always be those who prefer one over the other but, hopefully, many more who are grateful that both Bream and Williams emerged to enrich the world of guitar music in their own distinctive ways. A review by Harry Broad in *Guitar* magazine in 1977 celebrated their individuality:

> ... the contrast in personality and style ... was never more obvious than when they played together – Williams's detachment, Bream's bodily involvement; the differences in technique and sound; the different viewpoint ... It is probably their difference in background and experience which creates so much life, mutual awareness and enjoyment in playing together.

Between 1975 and 1994, early Saturday evening TV viewing of a family programme called *Jim'll Fix It* was a must for millions, a large proportion of which were children aspiring to be on the show. The eponymous 'Jim' was the somewhat eccentric disc jockey Jimmy Savile, later to be knighted for his services to charity. The format was simple and constant: children and, indeed, some adults wrote in to the programme, spelling out their often quite bizarre ambitions in the hope that Jim would fix it for them to realise their dreams. Having achieved them, they were awarded the coveted keepsake of a large and quite kitsch medal on a ribbon, to be placed around their necks by someone involved in their stunt or by Jimmy himself.

Memorable examples of 'fixes' include a young girl who

drove a red London double-decker bus on a skidpan, a boy sitting in on drums with New Romantics pop group Adam and the Ants, and actor Peter Cushing having a variety of rose named after him. All very innocent and highly entertaining fun but essentially trivial in nature and not at all where one would expect to see a classical musician. John Williams, however, had no qualms about appearing and was quite happy to fulfil the dream of some young guitar players from Yorkshire. He showed them a few moves and played with them, completing his role by placing the beribboned medals around their necks.

By sheer coincidence and in extremely telling contrast, a week or two later Julian Bream was also on BBC television giving a master class of great gravity to a few young students. It would be neither fair nor accurate to suggest that Julian does not have a lighter side to his personality or is devoid of a sense of fun but in some ways these two television appearances were a metaphor for the different approaches of the two great players – Julian appearing serious, almost grave, in a niche programme for the committed, John informal and content entertaining the mass audience of a prime-time Saturday evening show designed mainly for children.

Williams and Bream have always been good friends despite the efforts of many to make them otherwise. Subtle but determinedly poisonous concert and record reviews, divisive comparisons of their chosen repertoires, performance styles and techniques have all been employed by small-minded critics and correspondents to letters pages. Lesser men might have been affected but it is gratifying that Bream and Williams have always stood above such petty spitefulness. The writers' motives are perplexing – it is difficult to know how anyone might benefit from the gulf they sought to create.

Julian, John and James Burnett inspect the Silver Discs for the duo's Together *recording.*

The older man was ever generous in helping John with recommendations and referrals of work; they were to be found at each other's parties and went together to those thrown by mutual friends. The two have performed as a duo in venues ranging from the little church in Semley, the village where Julian lived, to the greatest concert halls and, in the three albums they made together, these extraordinary musicians created some of the most sublime guitar music ever. They have also looked out for each other. During a trip to Sweden in 1978, John broke a couple of ribs by falling off a sled. He returned to England to honour touring commitments with Julian and, although he was able to play, it fell to Julian to carry two guitar cases and other luggage as they travelled by train, something he did with great good humour and just a little teasing of his partner.

In the December of 1962, Julian dropped into the Queen's Elm Pub in Fulham Road for a quick pint and a smoke on the way home from a rehearsal. When he returned to his car he found that his guitar, his second by Robert Bouchet, had been stolen. He had owned the guitar for just two or three years and was very attached to it; it was certainly the best by the French luthier that he had played. The guitar fraternity soon became aware of the theft and sensitised to watch out for its emergence into the small market for such instruments. A short while after the theft, during a time when Sebastian Jörgensen and his partner were lodging in the attic flat at Brunswick Gardens, Williams spotted an advertisement for a Bouchet and, hoping to find and recover Julian's guitar for him, the two Aussies decided to investigate and drove together to the seller's address armed by Julian with a description of its marks and blemishes. Seb suggested that John should stay in the car, knowing that he would almost certainly be recognised and the game would be up. A man answered the door and Jörgensen told him he was interested in the guitar. He was welcomed into the house to play it and he inspected it thoroughly then sadly returned to the car to share his disappointment that it was not Julian's, the crucial identifying marks on the headstock being absent.

John and Julian's work together had begun when Christopher Nupen went to Julian's home in Dorset to direct and record two television programmes featuring the guitarists in 1967. They enjoyed themselves so much that Bream suggested they might do something together as a duo. This was the beginning of a collaboration which would include an ecstatically received US tour, and the inevitable recordings followed. The first, released in 1972, was aptly titled *Together*. It was huge success and followed a year later by *Together Again*. The two discs in the double album, *Julian Bream and John Williams Live*, were recorded in Boston and New York respectively. The two men put a great deal of preparation into those recordings and their effort was reflected in the results. Some of the long rehearsal sessions into the night at Broad Oak might well have seen the end of several bottles of wine from Julian's excellent cellar!

Many believe that the work these extraordinarily gifted guitarists recorded together is unlikely to be surpassed for its musicianship and near perfection. Convention states that duets should be played in a similar style by both contributors; these recordings are the most resounding rebuttal to that view. John says: 'These recordings are more than the two of us. We create dynamics and life because we are as different as chalk and cheese.' He is especially proud of the live albums.

After having lived there for forty-two years, Julian Bream put Broad Oak House up for sale in 2007. Always a planner, he decided it was time to realise its substantial value and, after purchasing a far more modest home for himself, his dog Django and his old MG, still in his beloved Dorset, Julian committed some of the funds to a musical foundation. Characteristically, Bream chose to use the fruits of his success to provide five scholarships for guitar students and, acting on his conviction that new repertoire is needed to sustain the interest and vitality of the instrument, to commission even more new works for the guitar. The first of these was by the British composer, Harrison Birtwhistle.

In yet another act of great generosity, Julian donated his impressive and substantial art collection to the Royal Welsh College of Music and Drama. He spends a lot of his time in a gazebo in his garden with just a desk, a thesaurus and his dog Django for company. This is where he is working on writing his memoirs which he says, with typical Bream humour and practicality, are in stand-alone sections, 'So that there will be something publishable, even if I drop off my perch halfway through.'

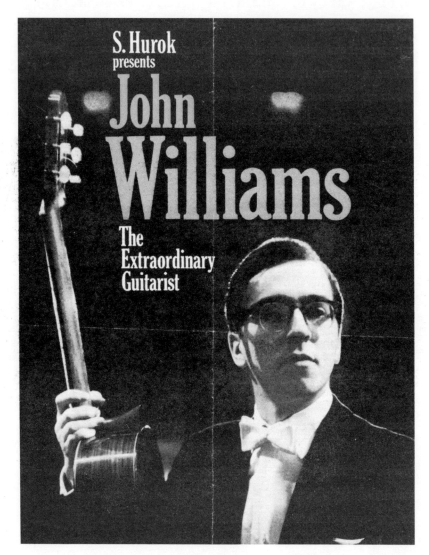

White tie and tails for a New York concert.

SIX

NEW HORIZONS

John's career was starting to take shape. A successful Wigmore Hall recital under his belt, the completion of his musical education was now underway at the RCM and during continuing summertime visits to Siena. There was also the great pleasure of very good friends in London, musicians and others, so the social side of life, too, was definitely on the up. But the relationship between John's parents, separated but living in the same house, was fractious and volatile. The carapace he had developed to protect him from its excesses was invaluable, as was his ability to tread the fine line between appearing to side with one or the other.

Melaan was trying to break free and she continued to emphasise and delineate her independence further by seeking a job. She was bright, articulate and had secretarial experience so she registered with Dutton's, an employment agency in Gower Street. The agency immediately came up with a suitable position and her first paid work in England was as a secretarial assistant. Melaan's efficiency and easy charm were well received by her employer and the agency was soon in touch to ask if she would be interested in being considered for a permanent position. The job concerned might have been custom tailored for her, as, although it was another assistant role, this time it was at the *New Statesman*, the respected and established left-wing political and cultural magazine which had been required reading for the Williamses. Kingsley Martin had been editor for over twenty-five years when Melaan joined the staff in the early sixties and he had been very effective in keeping the two sections of the magazine equally vital and distinct.

John's mother was delighted to be hired on the literary side of the outfit and found herself completely at home. She was admired and appreciated by her colleagues and superiors, and worked her way up to become the assistant to the literary editor, Janet Adam Smith, a distinguished critic and journalist who was eventually succeeded by Karl Miller and later, Claire Tomalin. Melaan could not have been happier with her job; it was intellectually stimulating and she met great writers of the day, such as Nobel Laureate V. S. Naipaul and Eric Hobsbawm (who wrote the jazz column under his pen name, Francis Newton), people who warmed to her and long remembered her affectionately. What made the role so perfect was that it was entirely aligned with her politics and required of her no accommodations, reconciliations or compromises. A family friend declared that he had never seen a better example of 'a round peg in a round hole'.

Some years before Melaan joined the magazine, the Campaign for Nuclear Disarmament (CND) was founded, spawned from an article penned for the *New Statesman* by the Yorkshire-born novelist and playwright, J. B. Priestley, a founding member of the protest organisation when it was established in late 1957. It was Kingsley Martin who chaired the inaugural meeting at which Canon John Collins was chosen as chairman and philosopher Bertrand Russell as president.

Completely independently of what was emerging through his mother's eventual employer, John Williams was already involved with the nuclear arms cause with others whose concern and efforts predated CND. He saw an article in the *News Chronicle*, a now long-defunct national newspaper, relating how Harold Steele, a Quaker, had been arrested after sailing in protest into the nuclear testing zone around Christmas Island and he was inspired by the man's courage. Some years later, John received a letter of appreciation from Steele's widow after she had heard him relate in a radio interview how he had been motivated by her husband's protest. Becoming aware of a campaign against nuclear testing, he approached Peggy Duff, an early activist who was elected as General Secretary of CND at that same meeting, about what he might do to aid the cause. Regardless of his left-wing inclinations, this kind of 'cause politics' would not have exercised Len at all. However, John did consult his father before engaging in activism and received the fairly neutral response, 'there's no harm in it'.

In 1958 John played the first benefit concert to raise funds for the organisation and soon became a great friend of Gwen Crabbe, Peggy Duff's assistant, and her husband John. John Crabbe gave lectures, organised meetings and acted as CND's recordist before becoming editor of *Hi-Fi News*. Duff held the position of General Secretary until 1967 and was a key player in organising the protest marches from the government's nuclear science facility at Aldermaston to London, where huge rallies took place in support of CND.

John has never wavered in his anti-nuclear stance and has held the position of life president of 'Musicians Against Nuclear Arms' (MANA) since its formation. This body superseded the 'Musicians' Organisation for Peace' led in the fifties and sixties by the distinguished conductor Sir Adrian Boult, who made a very eloquent statement as to the distinctive contribution of musicians to this kind of campaigning: 'It is not that musicians with their particular concern for music have a greater interest than their fellows, but that they have special opportunities, through practice of an art which knows no barriers of language, religion or nationality, to foster international understanding and make common cause with their colleagues throughout the world.' John's association with both organisations is detailed in Chapter 14.

While still a student at the Royal College, John made his first recordings in December 1958. These were essentially composed of the works he had performed publicly to date, including pieces by Bach, Albeniz, Ponce, Segovia, Lauro and Scarlatti. There was soon sufficient material from the sessions for two albums, which were recorded and released in quick succession on the Delysé label. Both were launched in 1959 and there was also a single volume released in the USA.

Delysé was an unusual company, founded by concert pianist Isabella Wallich. She was the first woman record producer and the first woman to run her own record company; undoubtedly she received advice from her uncle and mentor, Fred Gaisberg, the man behind both EMI Records and Abbey Road Studios. Isabella started the company in 1954 with the aim of catering to specialist tastes not well-served elsewhere. She began with Welsh folk music and progressed to the more obscure classical works. The lady clearly had an eye for talent as she recognised John Williams's potential when a friend of the Williams family introduced them when he was just sixteen. She went on to record him, producing the sessions herself. She also made the first solo recordings of the opera singers Dame Janet Baker and Sir Geraint Evans, but did not limit herself to classical and folk music. Williams, Baker and Evans had some strange stablemates and the eclectic nature of the label around that time might be illustrated by its 1962 release of the debut recordings of *Thomas the Tank Engine* stories by the children's entertainer Johnny Morris.

To his great credit Andrés Segovia did not bear a grudge – something well illustrated by his recommendation of John Williams to his agency, the legendary London firm Ibbs and Tillett. The company enjoyed an enviably illustrious client list over the years; it had included Clara Butt, Fritz Kreisler, Pablo Casals, Sergei Rachmaninov, Kathleen Ferrier, Myra Hess, Clifford Curzon and now represented the likes of Vladimir Ashkenazy and Jacqueline du Pré. Control of the firm was now in the hands of the redoubtable Emmie Tillett, the widow of one of the founders. Emmie was known as 'The Duchess of Wigmore Street' and very much of the old school. It was at Ibbs and Tillett that John later met Martin Campbell-White who, as joint Chief Executive at Askonas Holt, remains his manager today.

John and Emmie Tillett enjoyed a very good relationship. Anxious to ease him into regular performances, she started him on a circuit that comprised mainly of music clubs and colleges, many of which were supported and sustained through funding from regional arts councils. He played solo concerts and frequently with Musica da Camera, a group consisting of a string quartet led by flautist Harold Clarke. This little ensemble had a repertoire of works by Haydn, Boccherini and the like, and provided John with an introduction to music-lovers around Britain, many of whom became committed fans and followers of the gifted and youthful guitarist. For many of them, the only other classical guitarist they might have seen would have been Julian Bream and this fresh face presented something new. The ensemble played a few dozen performances each season over several years, providing income as well as invaluable visibility for John. It was much better than just studying and practising and he greatly enjoyed this baptism into working regularly with other musicians.

With his first recordings under his belt and well received by both critics and audiences, John's career was starting to take off. In 1959 he made his French debut, appearing in Paris, again to both critical and popular acclaim – his technique was declared to be greater than any ever seen. The performance drew critics not just from within France but beyond: there were reviews in the press of Germany, Spain and the UK. He was still only eighteen years old.

John's studies and career were developing well but the strain of living in the topsy-turvy world of the flat at 40 Gordon Square was upsetting and exhausting. Tensions in the house were always lurking and it took just the tiniest provocation for Len or Melaan to let fly. There were some periods of calm when things seemed to be managed reasonably well, with the distractions of music, political discussion (sometimes quite heated) and an even more open house. One highlight at this time was the musical quizzes featuring their friend Basil Hogarth, who had once played piano accompaniment to silent films. He could play anything and everyone tried to guess what tune was being performed and in whose style.

The peace was superficial, however, and the whole household was affected by the continuing tension between Len and Melaan. John strove desperately not to take sides or to do anything that could create any suspicion that he was doing so. The couple would argue about anything – over moral principles or John's future and relationships with others; Sadie Bishop was making waves in Gordon Square just by being herself as well as at the Guitar Centre, where she was starting to carve out a musical career. Melaan and June had a very strange relationship; even as Melaan and Len were at each other's throats, she was counselling June that more children would be good for her and her new husband. Life in this small part of the select square in Bloomsbury was becoming ever more peculiar for, in addition to the usual pre-occupations of newly-weds, Len and June had acquired a mongoose that lived in their room, an active little creature that would often hide their slippers.

Len then began his love affair with *Lagothrix lagotricha*, the Humboldt woolly monkeys that would become his last great cause. The flat was fairly close to London Zoo in Regent's Park, where Len had been a frequent visitor since returning to the city. He might have met woolly monkeys as friends during his time as a Melbourne zookeeper, but he certainly grew fascinated by one in London. He crouched by the enclosure and mimicked the creature's sounds, seemingly finding some way to communicate with what he describes as 'the most beautiful monkey I had ever seen'. The keepers at the zoo kept a watch on him since he also carried out similar exercises at the wolf pen. They told him to keep away because they thought he was disturbing the animals, so he decided that since he couldn't come to the monkey, then perhaps one could come to him. There was a pet dealer who had premises quite close to the zoo, and there he acquired his first monkey, duly taken home to join the mongoose. From a plaque displayed on the monkey cage, Len learned the name of the lady who had donated it to the zoo when it became too dangerous for her. He found some way to contact her, and Mrs Rex of Weeley Heath entered the story, soon to play her small part in the extraordinary life of Len Williams.

It was tough for John to pay proper attention to his studies at the RCM, practise regularly and maintain his own social life, and a chance to liberate himself from Gordon Square came out of the blue. Christopher Nupen emerged one day from his troglodyte refuge in the coal cellar to give notice to his landlord; he too was finding it increasingly difficult to live in the dysfunctional surroundings of the flat. He declared that he and Luc Markies, his Dutch friend and fellow student, were going to find a flat for themselves. Without hesitation, John said: 'And I'm coming with you!' He was seventeen, solvent, totally fed up with the attitude of his parents and ready to take responsibility for his own life. The chance to get away presented itself and he grabbed it with both hands. The three young men found a suitable apartment at 42 New Cavendish Street: flat 3, just around the corner from BBC Broadcasting House. The rent worked out at £3 each per week and the trio set about furnishing their new home.

Both John's parents were distraught at their son's break for freedom and Len was fearsomely angry, accusing John, against all evidence and reason, of having taken his mother's side against him. In addition to the belief that John was being disloyal there was probably some sense of guilt and Len also felt he wanted a year or two more to influence his son's musical development. It was a highly emotional time for everyone involved and the fragmentation of the Williams family was about to become complete. On the night John left, a distraught Len asked June to sleep elsewhere so he could deal with his emotions. Tearfully, he summoned Nupen to his room and asked him to 'Keep an eye on John, he's not as ready for this as he thinks.' The younger man thought differently. Christopher felt that the prevailing climate in the Williamses' flat was unhealthy for all concerned and he had no worries about John's ability to run his own affairs. One positive thing that had resulted from John's distorted child-hood and adolescence was the self-reliance and particular kind of maturity and resilience that he had been obliged to develop. Nupen remembered well the analytical logic that fourteen-year-old Williams junior had displayed when returning home from school, having clearly taken odds with the French language he was being taught: 'It is not *of* the bananas? That's just nonsense.'

Studies at the RCM finished in 1959 and John was invited to help establish and then run the guitar department at the college, quite something for a teenager. His profile and success had encouraged many prospective students to come forward and the college was keen to satisfy the demand with the most qualified person available and that, patently, was Williams. He held the position of head of guitar studies continuously until 1973 when he was sacked, to be succeeded by Carlos Bonnell, one of his former students. His dismissal was a consequence of him doing things his own way: he encouraged the better students to take on small concerts, something frowned upon by the college. Conflicting dates meant that some of them missed lessons with him and, ingrates that they were, a few complained about the loss of tuition. John maintains that they learned more from the performance experience than they would have done from another lesson. By then, though, his time at the RCM had run its course in any event and life was busy and full of music.

The celebration for John's arrival in Madrid for his debut in 1961 exceeded even that of Paris. He was the first performer ever to be invited to give a recital in the Prado Museum and the gallery chosen for the performance was hung with works by Velásquez. John's reception in Segovia's homeland was little short of ecstatic from an audience who had thought until then that the culture of the guitar was theirs and theirs alone. The organiser of this performance was one of the patrons of the Santiago di Compostela summer school and an important official in a major Spanish bank. She loved the plaudits she received for the coup of promoting the concert and was gushing about John. Only a year later, however, she expressed a very different view.

She was at Santiago when John was there giving lessons. There was a severe outbreak of food poisoning due to salmonella and many of the students became very ill. John was unaffected but, in addition to providing support to the English-speaking musicians who found themselves in hospital, he was at the forefront of a group organising a petition about the lack of hygiene at the residence. The patron took great umbrage and she complained to the harpsichordist Rafael Puyana, 'When John was in Madrid he was a nice young man but now he is an ungrateful pig.'

Things were looking up for John on the work front. Julian Bream had been touring very successfully with the British tenor Peter Pears, collaborator and life partner of the great composer Benjamin Britten. Emmie Tillett saw an opportunity to replicate this successful duo and, indeed, mop up some of the dates that they could not accommodate or chose not to accept. She partnered Williams with Wilfred Brown, an older man and established oratorio tenor, and they went on to become a successful touring attraction. They also recorded an album of folk songs with the stunningly unimaginative title *Folk-Songs*, released in 1961.

John had relied on buses, taxis and the Tube for local transportation and trains for concerts elsewhere in the country but the volume of work was increasing and, in 1963, he finally got round to purchasing his first car, a shiny new Morris Minor, which made life much easier.

Julian was delighted that his young colleague was making serious headway and adding to the credibility and popularity of the instrument he had fought so hard to help establish. He generously passed over to John many of his connections, including the Melos Ensemble, an accomplished outfit famed for a wide range of chamber music, including much contemporary music for the BBC. Julian also ceded to John his role in a trio with the cellist Amaryllis Fleming and violinist Alan Loveday. Some years later the trio, together with viola player Cecil Aronowitz, were to make a recording of works by Paganini and Haydn, something of a rarity since Fleming was a perfectionist and made very few records. The cellist had a background as exotic as her delightful Christian name, daughter of the artist and prolific breeder Augustus John, something she did not discover until she was twenty-three, and a half-sister to James Bond creator Ian Fleming.

In 1961 John Williams entered into something either brave or foolhardy, but it came off well and, arguably, set him on the road to gaining the popular following he has enjoyed since. Colour TV was still six years away when he made his first proper appearance on television as a guest on a Christmas variety programme, the *Billy Cotton Band Show*. This show had transferred to the screen from its long-established slot on radio at Sunday lunchtime. Cotton was a bandleader who announced his shows with a cry of 'Wakey, wakey!' followed by an up-tempo rendering of his theme tune, 'Somebody Stole My Gal'. He was something of a national institution and it seemed a safe bet to move the programme to television as Cotton's big band was a solid and proven outfit which could attract big name guests.

The Christmas show in question progressed through a number of pantomimes, with Eric Sykes appearing first as Robin Hood then as Aladdin, with Kathie Kay popping up as Cinderella. The programme was pure variety with pop singers, a sing-along with pub-style pianist Mrs Mills and a skit on the popular *Come Dancing* ballroom competition. John was slotted in somewhat incongruously to play some Bach. Later in the show, Eric Sykes performed a sketch in which he mimed to a recording of Segovia playing a Bach Gavotte. He was sitting at a desk when the telephone rang. He answered it, having to put down the guitar and, of course, the music continued playing. Soon after the show, knowing that the young man had a great sense of humour, Eric contacted John to ask whether he would be prepared to pay the role of the stooge sometime instead of the Segovia recording. Over the years he developed this idea for the two of them in various TV programmes and he became a very dear friend of John's.

To put this event in the context of John's establishment as a serious concert performer, this appearance was only three years after his first at the Wigmore Hall. By Christmas 1961, Williams had released only five albums, all of uncompromisingly serious music and on small labels: the Delysé recordings, *Folk-Songs* with Wilfred Brown and two for the US company Westminster, later released on Decca. So taking on the *Billy Cotton Band Show* gig at that juncture was a brave step and something of a risk, although John himself simply thought of it as an enjoyable opportunity. He was, however, only twenty, on the threshold of his career, and the classical establishment was very conservative and only just opening the door of acceptance to the guitar.

There was criticism, of course. Self-righteous keepers of the classical guitar flame tutted and huffed, declaring that Billy Cotton was not suitable company for Williams, but this fresh young talent determinedly made the first step towards personal acceptance by mass audiences and showed them the classical guitar as something accessible and to be enjoyed. Len was totally relaxed about John's excursions into popular entertainment circles but Melaan had reservations about the direction in which her son's career was going.

The Swinging Sixties were building up to full swing and London was the place to be. The three young men, Williams, Nupen and Markies, were living in the middle of what, by common consent, was the most exciting place on the planet. They lived independent lives but their flat was the scene of many parties and John partied with the best of them. He was, though, somehow different from the other two – more direct, brutally honest, disinclined to or dismissive of diplomacy.

Flatmate Chris Nupen recounts a couple of illustrative examples, fairly trivial but telling: at breakfast, which the three often shared, Luc was taking some marmalade for his toast. He spilled some and it ran slowly down the outside of the jar. John admonished him harshly, 'Clumsy!' Luc's relaxed reply was that it could happen to anyone. Williams shot back quite curtly, 'It doesn't happen to me.' Luc went into a furious rage but John was unmoved. He knew what he said was accurate and probably had difficulty in understanding why the large Dutchman looming over him was so angry. It is also telling that this little domestic vignette has since been forgotten by Williams. For him it has little meaning or significance, whereas Nupen and Markies remember it vividly, fifty years on.

On another occasion, John was working on an arrangement

for the guitar of an arpeggio Prelude by J. S. Bach but found one bar that could not be made to work. Nupen, who believed the piece in question to be that most compelling among all of Bach's to be played on the guitar, encouraged him that it would be easy to fudge it – 'Go on, fake it for one bar.' John simply would not countenance such a thing and abandoned his efforts in an example of what Christopher cites as the pure honesty that he counts as one of his friend's defining and enduring qualities.

The UK was beginning to take serious notice of its new young star of the guitar and he was soon to be found back on the nation's TV screens. Granada Television, the Manchester-based company, invited him to make thirteen programmes, each of fifteen minutes, with the producer Douglas Terry. Another groundbreaking achievement for the young artist came the following year. In 1962, Williams toured the Soviet Union at the time when the Cold War was at its most heated and the Cuban Missile Crisis in full swing. Demonstrating that art can rise above politics, he played to audiences who embraced the Australian prodigy and demanded encore after encore.

The tour came about through one of the few more positive aspects of the prevailing regime. The invitation came through Ibbs and Tillett, together with photographs of an engineer named Gyorgi Khodakov playing copies of John's Delysé records to an audience in a library hall in Moscow. Khodakov had first heard a recording of Williams on the BBC World Service and had been moved to suggest to the state entertainment agency GOS that the young star should be invited to perform for the Soviet public. John toured for a month, starting in the Baltic satellite states of Latvia, Lithuania and Estonia and then playing four dates in Moscow, followed by four more in Leningrad. Some performances were broadcast on radio and television.

John was paid for his work, but in local currency that he was not permitted to take out of the country. His solution was to use up his roubles by paying for flights and accommodation for his mother, who had always wanted to visit the USSR. When she arrived, mother and son attended a performance of *Spartacus* by the Soviet composer Khachaturian at the Bolshoi Ballet, at which President Nikita Sergeyevich Khrushchev was also present. When Melaan telephoned her new husband John Bunting to share her excitement at having been to the Bolshoi, he was very concerned for their welfare, having heard about the growing tension between Khrushchev and Kennedy over the situation in Cuba.

In Leningrad John and Melaan visited the Hermitage and other museums and discovered that Sir Malcolm Sargent was staying at their hotel; he was conducting a concert of the Leningrad Symphony Orchestra in the city. One evening they made their way down the grand but slightly faded staircase under massive chandeliers to take their place for dinner. Sir Malcolm joined them and together they watched a visiting American group, The Robert Shaw Chorale (halfway through its seven-week tour), and a Cuban variety band, all having a high old time with the hotel's resident band and seemingly unconcerned by the critical political situation unfolding on the other side of the world.

Leaving the Soviet winter behind, it was back to London, where at the Wigmore Hall, John received the ovation of an enthusiastic public; even the grudging critic of the London *Times* expressed recognition of the maturing in his performance since his debut at the Wigmore.

Invitations to tour flooded in from around the globe and following the recording of two more albums, John set out for tours in Japan and North America, where he played to packed auditoria in the USA and Canada. He was under the watchful eye of one of the most successful impresarios in the States, the legendary Sol Hurok, and during this hectic round of concerts CBS Records offered him a contract that made headlines in the national press. The amount of publicity generated was unknown for a classical player and far more like that of a pop star. The following year saw the release of his first album for the label, with which he shared bland and equal billing: *CBS Presents John Williams.*

John's interests beyond what might be termed 'the Segovia repertoire' were exercised when he played at the premiere of Michael Tippett's Iliad-based opera, *King Priam*, in May 1963 as part of the celebrations of the consecration of the new Coventry Cathedral designed by Sir Basil Spence. His involvement with 'new music' surfaced again when he contributed in 1969 to *Anton Webern: The Complete Recordings* conducted by Pierre Boulez, on which he played 'Three Songs for Voice, Clarinet and Guitar' with Halina Lukomska and Colin Bradley.

These excursions were not universally well received, predictably offending some of the guardians of the 'traditional' repertoire. The classical guitar world remained very small and introspective even through the sixties and seventies. It appeared factional; bitchy and snide comments were still to be found in exchanges in the magazines and journals. The 'camps' were established around choices of repertoire, of technique and of instrument. There was elitism and patronage. Self-appointed critics with dubious credentials made vitriolic and unfounded remarks based upon their prejudices and envy rather than stepping back and marvelling at what was happening with the classical guitar.

‡

Melaan now had her own life in good order; her job was fulfilling and through her work she had met and married John Bunting, an executive with the publishing company Barrie and Rockcliff. Bunting, too, had been married before and he provided John with a stepbrother named Michael, who now lives in Hong Kong. The couple were convivial company and they were very welcome at some of the parties that the three young flatmates held at New Cavendish Street. They were well suited in many ways, sharing a love of books and having literary friends in common, although there were two issues: Melaan was frustrated by her husband's complete indifference to the charms of music of any kind – and he drank too much. Like most irritations, this grew more significant over time and as John Bunting's drink problem worsened, the couple eventually split up.

For their part, June and Len were still involved with the Spanish Guitar Centre but were becoming increasingly pre-occupied by their other interests. In 1959 they moved from central London to live in Chislehurst, a small town in Kent most famous for its labyrinthine caves. By now the mongoose was no longer around but the number of woolly monkeys had increased, one of them an unusual bequest from Mrs Rex, with whom the couple had developed and maintained a friendship. After passing her first monkey to the zoo, she had acquired another that she called Sambo, later to be renamed Samba after she left it to Len and June and they correctly determined its sex. The monkeys were provided with outdoor spaces but also had access to the house. Len, who had recognised from the outset that the monkeys were not happy alone or in pairs but needed to live in groups, was seriously studying the way in which they conducted themselves and became engaged in correspondence with other researchers, some quite notable academics.

Len published his findings and experiences in 1965. *Samba and the Monkey Mind* was to be the first of several books, and his acknowledgement of suggestions and help from Dr Konrad Lorenz, Sir Kenneth Clark and Sir Julian Huxley indicate that this was not the lightweight dabbling of a well-intentioned novice but a substantial study worthy of serious consideration.

After several years in Chislehurst, the visionary who had founded the Spanish Guitar Centre decided to move on completely and it was duly sold, something that should have been quite straightforward. There was, however, the issue of Lock Aitken's financial and material contribution towards its establishment and Len spectacularly failed to ensure an equitable and fair outcome for his old friend and sponsor. Alan Gubbay, the buyer, was someone who could be totally relied upon to continue the ethos of the centre. Once an admiring student of Len's, he was still studying musical theory with Jack Duarte at the time of the sale, but many of Len's supporters and associates felt abandoned and rejected when he sold the centre. This extraordinary man had been the hub of their universe. His energy, vision and talent had underpinned their lives and their feelings were akin to bereavement. He had beguiled and enslaved them with his personal charisma and the mission he shared with them; there was devotion and dependency and it is small wonder the term 'disciples' was so commonly used to describe them.

John visited his father and June at Chislehurst a few times but he and Len had a major falling-out over a guitar student. John had been asked by someone at the RCM to recommend a guitar teacher for his brother, a complete beginner. Knowing that Lock Aitken had been the beginners' tutor and also having some sympathy with him over the way the old family friend had just been cheated on the sale of the centre by his father, John recommended and provided an introduction to Lock. Len heard of this and exploded at his son, calling him an ungrateful pig. Len's creed on loyalty was 'If you're not for me, you're agin me' and this event compounded John's act of moving out of Gordon Square; the rift between father and son was to last for years.

Len and June Williams left their home in Chislehurst in 1964 to found a sanctuary for woolly monkeys, where they could study them while educating visitors in the way in which the creatures lived and socialised. Their search for a suitable site took them first to Paddock Wood in Kent, but eventually they lit upon a site at Murrayton, between Looe and Seaton on the south coast of Devon and Cornwall. They purchased the property and, with the help of a few people who wanted to join their venture, began building the housing and other infrastructure for their monkeys. It was not just a community of monkeys they established, however; the way in which the place was run had echoes of Montsalvat. Len established a place where his will prevailed and where the inhabitants would become a 'group family'.

John met Lindy Kendall, the woman whom he was to marry, at the RCM, where she was studying cello and piano. When she graduated she supported herself teaching piano to students of all levels and abilities, although there were rather more young beginners than she would have liked. Lindy was a gifted teacher and a striking young lady and John a fellow student with an established career and a very promising future; it seemed they were made for each other. They married and bought a home in Brunswick Gardens, a street that runs parallel with Kensington Church Street and a short walk from Kensington Palace. Williams had no problem securing a mortgage – his earnings at the time were good and the bank manager who approved the loan accepted the income projection that was the surety. The couple still needed to find a contribution of their own. Lindy's family helped out and, once more, the generosity of Lock Aitken came into play and he gave John a small loan.

Christopher Nupen had also tied the knot by then and he and his wife, Diana, rented the basement of the house, becoming very much part of the family. Lindy and John had always had many musician friends in common and her onetime flatmate later married Patrick Gowers, an organist and composer. John admired Patrick's music and the men got on well together but for many years Gowers resisted the guitarist's suggestions that he should compose for the guitar. He finally agreed that he should and, importantly, could, quite a few years later.

In 1964, John made two more albums for CBS Records, both released the following year. *Virtuoso Music for Guitar* was recorded in New York in May at the same time as his first CBS release, *CBS Presents John Williams*, which was the beginning of a long relationship with producer Paul Myers. It included works by Paganini, Granados, Falla, Villa-Lobos, Castelnuovo-Tedesco and his friend and mentor Stephen Dodgson. The other was simply called *Two Guitar Concertos*, namely the Rodrigo *Concierto de Aranjuez* and Castelnuovo-Tedesco's *Concerto for Guitar No. 1, Op. 99*. The location was Philadelphia, this time the producer was Thomas Frost and two weeks before Christmas 1964, the youthful Williams, together with the Philadelphia Orchestra, found himself under the baton of Eugene Ormandy.

John flew back to London excited and elated but soon a mood of depression descended. He felt he had reached a monumental milestone and was gripped by a hollow sense of 'What next?' – a feeling that he had somehow reached a zenith that could not be surpassed. This wonderment at attaining such a level of achievement is a reminder of John's modesty: what he had done was unprecedented and he was very conscious that this was uncharted territory for a classical musician of his age. By the time the records were released in 1965, however, he was ready for the new challenges and opportunities opening up for him. His life changed completely in May of that year when Lindy gave birth to their daughter, Kate, at the old Elizabeth Garrett Anderson Maternity Hospital in Belsize Park, somewhere now long-demolished. Having a child caused John to take a long, hard look at himself and he made a number of adjustments to his life, not least to his working schedule.

Kate remembers her mother giving piano lessons at the house and she was allowed to sit in and listen if she remained quiet. Lindy taught her to read music and helped train 'her ear' with melodies, intervals and so on but did not teach her to play the piano. There was obviously something musical in Kate's genes as, even before tuition of any kind, she was able to tell the black notes from the white and whenever her mother played in a key such as F#, the young girl would comment, 'It sounds all watery.'

Kate does not remember much of John in that house; her memories of him were nearly all formed after her parents decided to part in 1969. She was to be their only child. It was all very amicable and has remained so ever since; Lindy and her second husband have always been friends with John and his wife, Kathy.

John moved out of the house and it was sold in early 1970. Lindy and Kate relocated to a flat in Lansdowne Road in Ladbroke Grove and John to St Marks Road in North Kensington, a location he chose so as to remain close to his daughter. Even though she was not yet five years old, Kate clearly remembers her mother nervously watching her precious grand piano being hoisted outside the building, dangling and swinging on ropes as it was brought over the balcony of the third-floor flat. Kate had a room at her father's home at that time and everywhere he lived subsequently, and she was a regular visitor. She tired of hearing her mother's piano students struggling through much the same pieces and enjoyed the company at John's place, which was livelier than her home.

The estrangement between John and his father continued. As John's career went from strength to strength and his own family life seemed to be taking shape, Len continued to build and run his community at Murrayton. He was earnest and thorough about his studies of the Humboldt woolly monkey and was becoming something of an authority on the species. The academic world was cautiously accepting of many of his findings on the subject and the sanctuary was visited by a number of experts in the field. Williams published two more books in 1967. The first of these, entitled *The Dancing Chimpanzee*, brought together the two main interests of his life, music and monkeys, and was a fairly superficial treatise on how humans and apes understand and exploit music and sound for various purposes. *Man and Monkey*, the second book published during that year, built on his earlier work, *Samba and the Monkey Mind*, expanding some topics and adding new strands of observation, knowledge and argument. As part of the preliminary matter, Williams listed the characters in the book, starting with the two dogs, the two donkeys and then the seven humans, followed, in more detail, by the twelve monkeys. Getting his thoughts into print with highly respectable publishers was an extraordinary achievement for a man of Len's limited education and was an excellent example of his self-belief and resourcefulness. As with his approach to music, he was not cowed by or in awe of the relevant establishment.

Len was still Len and the odd visitor to the sanctuary felt the rough edge of his tongue when he thought it appropriate. Monkeys and visitors mixed and, at some point during their visit, people were invited to sit while the monkeys explored them and the residents gave talks and answered questions. As the tourists sat, a monkey jumped onto the lap of a woman who reacted furiously, shouting, 'Get that dirty thing off me!' Len calmly picked up the monkey by its tail and, bringing its rear end close to her face for inspection, replied, 'Madam, when your arse is as clean as that, you can call my monkeys dirty.'

By the time the books were published, John had two half-brothers, Sam and Dan. June seems to have taken Melaan's suggestion that more children would be good for Len seriously and, as they grew, the two boys absorbed music from their parents and acquired a wide range of experience from watching the adult group go about its business of running an extended family household, caring for their animal charges and operating the business that sustained it all.

In 1971, Len wrote what was to be his last book, *Challenge to Survival*, subtitled *A Philosophy of Evolution*. The subject matter was far wider than he had previously considered and quite polemic. He rejects institutionalised religion, as does John, and condemns 'a monogamous morality that has reduced woman to a sex-object and a biological machine' and offers his own community at the sanctuary, along with other group families, as 'the answer to the dilemma of the nuclear consumer-family'. The book ranges far and wide, including much research into animal behaviour and other group families around the world, a number of which he had links with. He wrote frankly about the detail of the 'family fraternal sex' within his group, saying that for them it had become 'as natural as dancing and music'.

For all this, the sanctuary was not a democracy; Len was very much its master and it is impossible not to see the spirit of Justus Jörgensen in the way he chose to live. All income was dedicated to sustaining the community so none of its members were ever able to develop the economic independence that would allow them to leave easily. And as with those who might wish to leave, so too with those who might wish to enter: Len would not take into the group anyone who he thought might upset his personal applecart. He guided and controlled every aspect of life at Murrayton.

‡

It had long been apparent that John Williams was not going to be a typical classical concert performer. He had already broken new ground and a few taboos along the way, but in 1968, he took a high-profile part in a move that would change the way that concert platforms would look from then on. He had always been unhappy about the formality of wearing white tie and tails for concerts. John thought that although tails looked very elegant for gentlemen who were standing, they were most unsuitable garments for professional musicians, who worked sitting down and whose first action on taking the platform was to tuck them away behind their seats.

The London Sinfonietta was thinking along the same lines around the same time as John. He was on tour in the USA and decided it was time for a change, so he went on stage wearing black trousers topped with a white turtleneck shirt. The audience did not seem too upset – this was the Swinging Sixties after all, and the influence of Carnaby Street was evident worldwide. It was, however, too much for the critic at the *New York Times*, who dedicated much of his review to sartorial matters, concluding that Williams had appeared like a cross between a refugee from the Don Cossack Chorus and Dr Kildare. Others followed suit – not quite the right word – with varying responses. Vladimir Ashkenazy agreed about changing things but he felt it was easier for John as a guitarist to get away with it. Some time later, Ashkenazy appeared at a Swansea Festival in a lounge suit and turtleneck shirt and the organisers wrote to his London manager complaining bitterly about his lack of professionalism.

It is ironic that John helped lead the way to less formal dress. His dress sense as a teenager had been extremely conservative and he tended to look older than his years; it was only as he became older that his style became more relaxed and consequently looked more youthful. A friend remarks that he compares to Benjamin Button, saying when he was sixteen, he looked like he was forty and when he was forty, he looked sixteen. John continued to push the sartorial boundaries, moving from the conciliatory white turtlenecks to looser shirts with bold floral patterns. And his hair was probably at its longest during this period.

It wasn't all work for Williams. In the middle and late sixties he was part of a 'rat pack' of precocious classical musicians who made London their home. He had met Jacqueline du Pré when she lived with her parents in Portland Place and she visited him at New Cavendish Street occasionally at teatime. He recorded with her in 1963 when he accompanied Jota from the 'Suite Español' by Falla on her EMI album *A Jacqueline du Pré Recital*. John had been in contact with her future husband Daniel Barenboim since his Siena days and they were close friends, a relationship that still continues. Others in the group included Fou Ts'ong, Itzhak Perlman and Vladimir Ashkenazy, who might be joined by friends who happened to be passing through London on tour or in transit. Christopher Nupen, who was beginning to make a name for himself as a documentary film producer, was also one of this glittering gang. They went to concerts and then on for a sometimes rowdy meal at a favourite Italian restaurant in Dean Street. John preferred a slightly quieter life and, although the friendships endured, his participation in this kind of socialising became less frequent.

The house that John had at St Marks Road was huge and he had no hesitation in offering a home there to the McKay family, whom he met through their shared concern over the political situation in Greece. Brian McKay was an Australian artist who, with his wife Jo and their children, had travelled to Europe to allow him to absorb some old world influences and develop his art. They chose Greece as their initial destination and lived there for a year, during which time Jo became fluent in the language. Afterwards, they moved on to London, where Brian became part of the vibrant artistic scene, although it was a much more expensive place to live and he had to compromise on his ambitions there. He continued to produce paintings when- ever he could make time while barely supporting the family through his work designing and producing graphics for the mass-market furniture company MFI.

The couple shared a strong social conscience and when Brian spotted a small announcement in the *New Statesman* inviting anyone interested or concerned about the prevailing situation in Greece to a public meeting at the Bird in Hand pub in Hampstead, he decided to go along. A group of right-wing army officers had seized power in the country in April 1967, just weeks before scheduled elections. He walked to the meeting from the family's lodgings in Muswell Hill and was surprised to find himself one of around 400 people there. They included those whose main focus was on similar situations elsewhere, such as Argentina and Chile; democracy seemed to be under threat in many places around the world at the time.

The meeting was noisy and confused but it eventually took some shape and agreement was reached about the need for action. Attendees were invited to declare what skills and contacts they had that could be of use to the cause. Brian immediately volunteered his services as a designer and copywriters, finance people, musicians and others joined him, with one man who offered the use of three vans complete with drivers being roundly cheered for his generosity. Publicity was obviously something that was key to success and there was a discussion about inviting celebrities to become involved, both to raise the profile of the group and help give it credibility. 'John Williams' was among the names mentioned who they thought might prove sympathetic and it was agreed that he was just the kind of person they needed. Nobody actually knew him or even how he might be contacted but someone put themselves forward to try and enlist his help. The effort was successful and, two or three meetings later, John went along to see what was happening, a little wary of the fledgling group. He became convinced that the cause was worth pursuing and threw in his lot to help. It was through this connection that he and Brian became friends as they worked together; John helping with fundraising and the artist designing posters and other graphics.

Brian and Jo are warm and open people and Williams soon became close to the McKay family, recognising very quickly the financial difficulties they were trying to deal with. There was also pressure from Brian's agent in Australia, who told him in very direct terms that if he could not provide enough new work for a forthcoming show, he was in danger of being brushed aside by a new generation of artists. John found this offensive and resolved to help. He offered to act as patron for Brian so that he could give up his job and concentrate on his art. The family moved into St Marks Road, taking over the top three floors of John's house while Williams retained the ground floor and the basement. Brian's pride dictated that he would contribute something tangible and it was agreed that he would pay the rates or local taxes for the house in lieu of rent. Jo helped by getting a job in a school nearby and the household was set.

The arrangements were not exactly communal but came pretty close to that. John would pop upstairs for meals from time to time and when Brian became a househusband, the two men spent time on their respective occupations of painting and music, and would get a Jamaica pasty from Portobello

Road for lunch together. Jo made a unique contribution to John's stage wardrobe in designing and creating his first 'Mao jacket' in black velvet, which he wore for many years. He later had another one made in purple velvet to exactly the same design. He wore the new outfit when he played for the Greek Democracy movement with the exiled composer Mikis Theodorakis and the famous Greek singer Maria Farandouri. They finally got around to making a recording of their work together for CBS in 1971. It was called *Songs of Freedom* and re-released on CD by Sony in 1995.

‡

John was in great demand. He made eight albums for CBS between 1964 and 1969, and his concert schedule was burgeoning with dates at prestigious venues and with top-flight orchestras and conductors. His willingness to embrace music of any kind, as long as it was good, was widely applauded and very welcome to all but the usual curmudgeonly guitar traditionalists. In 1968 he met composer John Mayer, who had been working with the Jamaican alto-sax player Joe Harriott, and began taking an interest in Indo-jazz fusions. Mayer wrote a particularly notable piece called 'Ragamalika', which he and John played together a number of times, including one performance at the Chichester Festival. It was at this time that John first met Kesh Sathe, the great tabla player, who remained a dear friend until his death in 2012.

Another genre-breaking event occurred when Williams made history of a modest sort by becoming the first classical musician to be invited to play at Ronnie Scott's jazz club. Scott was a big fan of the guitar and he floated the idea of John appearing at the club when they met at a 1968 benefit concert for the African National Congress (ANC), where he was performing with John Dankworth and Cleo Laine. John was really keen to play at the club and a date was found in both diaries for the following year. He has been back several times since. It was around this time that he was also introduced to the London Contemporary Dance Theatre. Robert Cohan, who had been Martha Graham's dancing partner, was the Artistic Director at the time. He was soon to retire and he asked John to work with him on what was to be one of his last dance compositions, 'The Constellation of the Rising Moon'. John was not required to actually compose anything for it but Cohan asked him to use his knowledge and experience to put together various pieces, including Indian and Spanish music, to suit the dance.

John met Paco Peña in 1969 – through the guitar, naturally. Paco, a native of Córdoba, had come to London a few years earlier and was beginning to make a name for himself in England as the major force in flamenco guitar, effectively creating the concept of solo performance in the style. He began by playing in restaurants and small venues. His English was poor and he was somewhat reserved as a consequence, something that seemed out of character given the fiery nature of much of the music he played. Paco knew about John, of course, but he was in awe of being intro-duced to him, not least because he had somehow gained the impression that the Australian was rather serious. John admired Peña's playing, loving his strong and natural sense of rhythm, and told him so after seeing him perform.

Unsurprisingly their friendship sprang from a shared love of music and of the guitar but Peña had strong humanitarian sensibilities and the two found they had this in common as well as their music. John had largely acquired his leftie social conscience from his parents' intellectual convictions, whereas Paco's attitude was more instinctive and less political – not surprising given his circumstances. The Spaniard was one of ten children born to a peasant family. Under the shadow of the Franco regime they lived in two rooms in a house shared with nine other families and this experience could not fail to help form his strong sense of community and justice. The way in which many Spaniards reacted was just to keep their opinions to themselves; to do otherwise risked retribution so Paco was less well versed and practised than John in active protest.

These two men would have become friends regardless of profession or politics – they are both warm and thoughtful people. One topic of discussion in the early days was their differing views on the English way of life. Paco seemed impressed with what he had found in the country – it was freer and more open than Spanish society at that time – but John still had issues with the double standards and class obsession he saw around him. Williams certainly influenced Paco's politics and there were many things in which they became involved that might not have called Peña, had he not met John. With music, friendship and politics binding them, it was inevitable that they would end up working together and so it would prove. These two superb musicians would help make London the guitar capital of the world.

János Starker, Peter Calvo, John Williams and
Peter Sculthorpe appreciate the joke from Joe Pass.

SEVEN

SKY'S THE LIMIT

By the start of the seventies John Williams was professionally very well established with recognition and money
aplenty for a 29-year-old. He had a beautiful and lively
daughter on whom he doted and although his marriage to
Lindy was over, it had ended amicably with no recrimination
from either side. His house in Ladbroke Grove was full of
life and company, courtesy of the McKay family and all the
visitors and temporary guests it never failed to attract.

It was a decade of solid progress and great change for
John. He was happy with life and busy, not just in his
prolific recording and touring schedule but also with various political activities. Rarely for him, one of these was very
local, almost literally on his doorstep. London was in the
process of change and there were plans for a major new
road route, the so-called inner ring road. John's attempt to
become elected to the Greater London Council on a platform of resistance to the plan features in Chapter 13. As well
as resisting the planned road, the campaign was also about
utilising some available space for the benefit of children.

In 1971 Williams contributed to two movie soundtracks.
The first, *The Raging Moon*, was scored by Stanley Myers,

a seasoned composer with several films to his credit. The soundtrack album was released on EMI Records and featured John playing on six tracks in total; others were performed by pop band Blue Mink, whose bass player Herbie Flowers would later join Williams in SKY. The other film was something very different, a low-budget creation by American guitarist Frank Zappa and the British director Tony Palmer. It was called *200 Motels* and starred Theodor Bikel, Ringo Starr and the latest incarnation of Zappa's band, The Mothers of Invention. John's part in proceedings was playing with two other guitarists, classical player Tim Walker and Big Jim Sullivan, session player and member of Tom Jones's band. This was also the year when he reached one million record sales with CBS, who marked the accomplishment by the presentation of a specially commissioned glass sculpture of his left hand arched in a playing position.

He had enjoyed working with Stanley Myers and when the composer suggested they might make another album together he jumped at the idea. Myers had quite a commercial streak and the choice of material for the disc reflected it. *Changes* was a significant new departure for Williams, outraging the classical establishment who had just about been able to live with what the guitarist had done to date. The record included arrangements by Myers of Bach and 'The House of the Rising Sun', plus four of his own compositions, including 'Cavatina', then 'Nuages' by Django Reinhardt, 'Because' by Lennon and McCartney, Joni Mitchell's 'Woodstock', 'Theme from Z' by Theodorakis and 'Good Morning Freedom', more usually associated with Blue Mink, Herbie's day job. John was aided and abetted by fifty or so of the top session musicians in the UK, very different company to the great orchestras of the world with whom he usually shared the studios. It was ironic that the image of the CBS 'glass hand' award was used as the sleeve illustration for *Changes* since it was released on the Cube label.

The premiere of the guitar concerto Williams commissioned from André Previn, then principal conductor of the London Symphony Orchestra, was well received and released on record the following year, together with the *Concierto Del Sur* by the Mexican composer Manuel Ponce, Previn again conducting the LSO. One critic, Peter Moffatt, expressed some reservations but, promisingly, wrote that he was 'glad to get away from the run-of-the-mill potboilers, and this was no potboiler!' Williams and Previn worked together again, including the odd appearance on television.

John made many guest appearances on TV through the early seventies and they were varied, to say the least. They included guest spots with his friend Val Doonican, folk singer Julie Felix, Vera Lynn, Roger Whittaker and Nana Mouskouri on their regular shows. His showing up on the comedy show *Not Only, But Also* with Peter Cook and Dudley Moore was something of an oddball but there was one programme that gave him more than the usual guest slot. *André Previn's Music Night* featured the multi-talented conductor, composer and jazz pianist in the role of host, with the London Symphony Orchestra as the 'house band', and Previn took the opportunity to have a number of distinguished guests. Williams was able to stretch out on the programme and played the Rodrigo *Concierto de Aranjuez*. It was typical of the way he was forging his musical identity that in the same year that he appeared to be kicking over the traces with *Changes,* he also released an album that was as strait-laced as could be. Rafael Puyana, the great Colombian harpsichordist, partnered John for *Music for Harpsichord and Guitar* (Jordi Savall also featured on viola de gamba), and became an enormous influence on the guitarist, teaching him about baroque style and giving special insights into the work of Scarlatti. Included on the recording was *Duo Concertante,* a new composition by Stephen Dodgson, whose *Concerto Number One for Guitar and Chamber Orchestra* John had recorded in 1968 with the English Chamber Orchestra under Sir Charles Groves.

Like Puyana, Groves was generous in sharing musical knowledge and friendship with Williams and over many years, John became close to Sir Charles, whose wife, Hilary, was something of a confidante for the young guitarist. Sally and Jonathan, the Groves's children, always felt that although their parents generally kept their musical life separate from their personal life, they embraced John, treating him like a son and always speaking of him with real affection in a way they did of no one else.

Len, June and their sons arrived on a trip to London to stay with John. He took them, along with his daughter Kate, on a sightseeing trip around the city, showing their children, Dan and Sam, where they had lived and the area where Len had grown up. Six-year-old Kate enjoyed the outing but had great difficulty getting her head round the idea that these young boys were her uncles! Later during that visit Len and John had an argument about one of John's girlfriends at the time, something that got completely out of control.

This might have been expected; Len was more irascible than ever and John now entirely his own man, mature, established and confident. Things escalated and neither would back down. John reflects, 'We both behaved pretty badly – we should both have known better.'

The silence between father and son resumed as, once more, each retreated to his own world. John had commitments galore while Len and June took the boys back to the rest of the extended family in Cornwall and continued to throw themselves into making a go of things there. They were thriving as a community and, to a lesser extent, as the operators of a self-sustaining business. Tourism in the southwest of England enjoyed a boom when the M4 motorway opened in 1972 and the monkey sanctuary benefited. In addition to welcoming paying visitors, Len was deeply engrossed in observing and recording the behaviour of the woolly monkeys, sharing and publishing his findings. He was also applying his mind to weightier matters and encouraged by the respect he had gained through his work with primates, in 1971 he published his polemic *Challenge to Survival*, generating some welcome income and a great deal of interest.

By this time Melaan was back in Australia. Her marriage to John Bunting was over and her health had deteriorated badly. Having finally given up smoking, her doctor suggested that the climate back in Australia would be better for her emphysema than that of London, still very polluted despite the improvement since the 1956 Clean Air Act and creation of 'smokeless zones'. Encouraged by her sister, Toylaan, she moved back to her homeland, not to Melbourne this time but to Sydney, which proved to be even more polluted.

John's circle of friends, always so important to him, was growing, not least with musicians he encountered as he travelled around. He first met Gerald Garcia when he accepted an invitation from the Oxford Guitar Society, which Gerald had helped establish. Before Williams went on stage to perform at University College, Garcia, with the encouragement of his pals, took the opportunity to play for him and received compliments on the way he performed a Villa-Lobos Prelude. John gave the student his address and when Gerald and his fiancée moved to London the young guitarist called on John. He was warmly welcomed and the two sat and talked for a while about life in general. From then on, Garcia dropped by once a week or so and they chatted about music and the politics they shared. By chance, he happened to be visiting when Rafael Puyana called in to discuss his recording with John and, on another occasion, he arrived to find Julian Bream already there for lunch. 'This was a dream for me,' says Garcia, 'Although I was no one really, John accepted me with open arms and there I was, having coffee and lunch with my heroes.'

Williams and Garcia began playing together occasionally; they did the odd concert supporting CND, mainly solos but a few duets, too. One of these events was at the Wigmore Hall, something that was an absolute thrill for Garcia, as was the chance to engage John in discussion on the long train journey from London to Barrow-in-Furness when they were headed there to support a nuclear protest. John was also close to Paco Peña and his Dutch wife Karin; they were an important part of the circle of friends and Paco, too, played at many of the protest gigs, sometimes solo and occasionally in duets with John. Also in the circle were Rigas and Sally Doganis, who Williams first met through his involvement with the Greek movement. John has always had the happy knack of bringing people together; he has been the catalyst of many friendships and his house was always a great place to meet new and often surprising people, none of whom could ever be described as dull.

Sadly, one particular friend was going through great difficulties. John had known Jacqueline du Pré for many years, since she was sixteen, long before she married Daniel Barenboim in 1967 in what *Time* magazine called, 'One of the most remarkable relationships, personal as well as professional, that music has known since the days of Clara and Robert Schumann.' Now she was suffering from multiple sclerosis, a disease particularly cruel to a musician. There was a small group of close friends who arranged a schedule between them to keep company with her, to try and sustain her spirits and talk to her about music, the thing she loved most. Daniel, of course, Rodney and Cynthia Friend, Maggie Cowan, Anita Lasker, Christopher Nupen and John were among that number. Jackie died in 1987, aged just forty-two and twelve years later, John was in the front rank of friends of the cellist who expressed their outrage at the interpretation of du Pré's life in the film *Hilary and Jackie*, which they condemned as a gross distortion of reality.

‡

Humphrey Burton was the up-and-coming producer of *Aquarius*, an arts programme for London Weekend Television and he decided that he would like to make a piece featuring

John Williams. Burton contacted Christopher Nupen, now well established as a filmmaker, knowing that he was a good friend of the guitarist and could help recruit him to the project. Nupen was deterred by the small budget and pressed Burton for more funds, but without success. However, a TV contract of any kind was not to be sneezed at and he could ill afford to waste this opportunity, especially as it gave him a chance to work with his old friend. He approached John and they agreed that they would shoot the feature at Ronnie Scott's Jazz Club. Ronnie would be keen, it could be contained within the budget and it would show off John's talents as both a superbly accomplished classical guitarist and someone who was prepared to venture off the concert platform. However, when Burton saw the film he was not at all satisfied with what had been delivered. Nupen vigorously defended his work, complaining that he had been obliged to work within extremely tight financial constraints and, given that limitation, it was a fine piece of filming. Burton disagreed and refused to take the film.

The filmmaker now had a completed project with no prospect of it being shown. Somewhat cheekily he took it to Burton's rivals at the BBC. They were delighted to have the option but shared some of Burton's concerns. Fortunately, they were prepared to remedy them by giving Nupen extra funds to extend the scope of the film from a simple, if very elegant performance piece to something more extensive, to be shown as part of the Corporation's respected *Omnibus* arts programme. New segments were filmed of John working in the studio with Patrick Gowers and the CBS record producer Paul Myers. They also showed a working discussion between John and Stephen Dodgson, then in the process of writing his second guitar concerto for Williams. The film starts with a short biography and the action then moves to the club, where Ronnie Scott's introduction of his guest is typical of his style:

I first met John Williams about two and a half years ago when we were both appearing on an anti-apartheid concert at the Albert Hall and we were backstage. For a long time I'd entertained the idea of having John work here at the club. And someone told me that John was a very charming, very approachable young man so I thought I'd ask him. I did find him very charming, very approachable. I said good evening, he said get out and we took it from there. And eventually I did manage to get John to appear at the club and he did, over the last couple of years, two two-week seasons and we're very happy to have him here again tonight. We'd like you to welcome to the stand one of the world's greatest classical guitarists, Mr John Williams.

The film also included the first public release of the message that John had recorded, aged six, to be sent from Australia to his grandparents in England. The programme was a great surprise; many critics had doubted that Williams could cut it in a smoky, noisy jazz club but the audience was stunned into respectful silence. Scott himself had been concerned that John might struggle to make himself heard over the clattering of cutlery and took some pride that it all worked out as planned. Television viewers were impressed by the boldness and lack of compromise of John's set and he added a few more jazz fans to his roster of admirers. The imprimatur of Ronnie's unstinting approval was a coup but he, like Williams, was never constrained by prescriptive musical boundaries. The BBC, Nupen and Williams all received praise; a compliment even came from sculptor Dame Barbara Hepworth, who felt that it reflected John perfectly. She knew him well as a friend who had played at her seventieth birthday celebrations in Cornwall.

John and Julian Bream had made their first record, *Together*, for RCA in 1972. It was a huge success, critically and commercially, and had a simultaneous release in the USA and Japan with the alternative title *Julian and John*. The UK album had a gatefold sleeve with what became an iconic picture of the hands of the two musicians, shown larger than life-size; the liner notes explained helpfully that the upper pair were Julian's and the lower ones John's, although the denim shirt sleeves might have been a giveaway! Listeners were informed in the notes that, in the stereo mix, Bream was to be heard on the right, Williams on the left. All this information, and more, was printed over a large sepia photo of the two guitarists playing table tennis in a field of cows and it is easy to believe that this was exactly how they might be found down in Dorset when the guitars were set aside for a break.

With works by Carulli, Falla, Sor, Lawes, Ravel and Albéniz, the record company took no risk; it was an interesting but safe selection. Bream and Williams 'toured' their album and critic John Devereux was inspired to write in *Guitar* of their having surpassed all expectations. He contrasted the 'ice-cool precision' of Williams with the 'emotional intensity' of Bream; he wrote of 'perfection' from the former and 'zest' from his colleague, concluding that the pair demonstrated 'how much Togetherness [*sic*], a guitar duo can achieve.' Rather less conventional than the material on that record was the *Gowers Chamber Concerto* which John recorded with, among others, Tristan Fry and Herbie Flowers. The album was completed with a number of Scarlatti pieces and 'Double' for guitar and electric organ by Patrick Gowers (after Scarlatti).

Although still recording regularly, John effectively gave up solo tours abroad in 1972, with the unsurprising exception of his visits to Australia. He had complained regularly in interviews that he hated travelling and although he never said as much at the time, it was travelling on his own that he found so dull. Williams is a man who loves company and conversation, and solo tours meant that he spent a lot of time alone. The main reason that John did not tour, however, was so that he could be around for Kate. For the same reason, he also turned down work that would fall during school holidays and refused engagements at weekends. His disinclination to tour disappointed and frustrated many promoters around the world because John Williams had become a very popular musician who could guarantee sell-out houses.

A 'greatest hits' album is regarded in the record industry as a milestone of acceptance and longevity for pop stars. How much more remarkable then was the release in the USA of *Greatest Hits – The Guitar*, the first compilation of his work and another compilation album in the UK, *John Williams Plays More Spanish Music and Other Favourites*. On the performance front, Williams continued to push the musical boundaries. Within a period of four days in August 1972, for example, he first shared the stage at the Queen Elizabeth Hall on the South Bank with Joe Pass and André Previn when he gave a lecture recital on sixteenth-, seventeenth- and eighteenth-century works. Next he performed with Imrat Khan, a virtuoso of the surbahar, which is a lower-tuned version of a sitar. These were followed by two dates with another great jazz guitarist, Barney Kessel, the second of which was at Ronnie Scott's. It seemed John Williams was everywhere. Correspondents to the letters page of the new *Guitarist* magazine bickered over the provenance of obscure compositions he played and helped each other find the recordings of pieces that John performed on *The Val Doonican Show*. Even his students were beginning to make a serious name for themselves. For example, Jiro Matsuda, who also studied briefly with Segovia and Díaz, made his Wigmore Hall debut in January 1972.

Brian McKay suffered problems with his sight, something he, as a visual artist, found truly terrifying and it was concerns over this matter that finally drove the family reluctantly to leave London and return to their home just outside Perth in Western Australia. Their departure left quite a gap in John's life; they had filled the larger part of his home with life and energy for the past four years and the whole family had become very important to him. Their presence had helped give the house its vitality and that had made it an even more attractive place for his daughter Kate to visit, something she did frequently.

John loved having her around. The musician in her was already showing signs of emerging. When she was six she had, on her own account, decided to take up the cello. Kate says, 'I messed around with the cello until I was about twelve but it wasn't really for me. I never took grades or anything like that.' She had other talents though and she used her skill with a pencil to fill the time when John was away and Lindy was at rehearsals with the orchestra she was now involved in managing. As the musicians were put through their paces, Kate sat quietly and drew very good sketches of them at work. 'Perhaps that's where I got a lot of my music. I suppose I was soaking it all up. It's funny that both my parents were musicians but they weren't the pushy type and I probably had less music tuition as such than many other kids of my age.'

Although tinged with the sadness of the McKays' leaving and concern over Brian's wellbeing, 1973 was a very important year in Williams's life. He and Bream were awarded a Grammy for *Julian and John* (Best Chamber Music Performance) and they continued to work together on the concert stage. John, thinking about new projects, had enjoyed making *Changes* so much that he decided he would do something similar. Wheels were put in motion and Brian Gascoigne assembled another amazing array of session musicians at Air Studios in Oxford Circus, where 'Fifth Beatle' George Martin produced *The Height Below*, a title worthy of M. C. Escher and dreamt up by Williams himself. The album is dominated by compositions from Brian Gascoigne who, with Tim Walker contributing one movement, wrote the suite *Emperor Nero*, which fills side one. Side two begins with Gascoigne's title track, then one piece each from George Martin, John Dankworth, John Williams and Dudley Moore, who played organ on the album. Sir George Martin was in awe of John Williams's ability. He says:

> I think he is the best classical guitar player in the world. All instruments have some things that can't be played or don't work well. I am not a guitarist so I didn't know what to avoid and so I asked John how I should write for him. He said that I should just write what I wanted to hear and he would tell me if there was anything in it that could not be played. When I showed him what I had written he simply rattled through it – amazing! I was thinking about learning the guitar at the time but after seeing him play, I soon gave up that idea.

Ivor Mairants, one of the great British jazz guitarists, revealed in a review of the record that he had been involved in helping John find the right electric guitar for the album, guiding him to settle on a Gibson Les Paul De Luxe. *The Height Below* sessions proved to be something of a nursery for bands that John would form later: Tristan Fry and Herbie Flowers would join him in SKY and Gascoigne and Williams co-founded John Williams and Friends. Brian was much more of a backroom boy than his brother, Bamber Gascoigne, who was a household name through his role as the original presenter of the cerebral TV quiz programme, *University Challenge,* a job he held for twenty-five years. By contrast, Brian did most of his work in the anonymity of recording studios; he was an established session player who also had great talent as a composer and producer. At that time he was to be seen on stage touring with the phenomenal Japanese artist Stomu Yamashta, playing keyboards in his band. John got on really well with Brian; they had many things in common and during 1973, with another friend, they bought a house together. The McKays were about to leave for Australia and John heard that there were two adjacent houses for sale at South Hill Park, near Hampstead Heath. He and Brian bought one and his friends, the Doganises, the other.

Soon after *The Height Below* was released in May, Williams took the material on the road. He styled the touring band John Williams and Friends. The first to enjoy the privileged epithet 'friends' were Brian Gascoigne, Carlos Bonnell (John's successor at the guitar department of the RCM), bassist Chris Laurence and Maurice Pert on percussion. One of the fundamental ideas behind the group was to play baroque music with two guitars but with the innovation of using marimbas instead of harpsichord for the 'continuo' parts. John truly believes in this approach to the repertoire that the Friends played and would love to see it used more widely. The tour was a great success and since his colleagues shared or were easily persuaded by John's sympathies with Greenpeace, they did a benefit concert for the organisation along the way. This was the first 'band' with which John had spent time on tour and the camaraderie and shared excitement of gigs gave him a real buzz. Although he had worked with many orchestras and ensembles of various types, he was somehow always apart from them; this was a new and exhilarating experience after such a long time of relatively solitary work.

Brian Gascoigne wrote the arrangements around John: 'I wanted him to sound and look wonderful so I wrote for that. The arrangements were concerto style – centred on him, with Richard Harvey and Carlos as soloists.' Gascoigne was surprised how well John fitted into a group set-up: 'Most prodigies don't have an adolescence – they lose the ability to react in the superficial way that teenagers do but John re-found that. To have the strength to give solo concerts at the age of thirteen you have to lose your teenage inhibitions and angst pretty quickly. I take my hat off to him, extraordinary man!'

John still continued to find time for TV guest appearances, holidays in the south of France, time with his friends in London and the occasional trip to see Len and the family in Cornwall, but 'the friends' was something new and very enjoyable. Ivor Mairants was in the audience in May 1975 to watch John Williams and Friends at a sell-out concert in the Royal Festival Hall. He was very impressed with what he saw and, in his review, took issue with the critic from *The Times*, who said he would have preferred to see a solo recital, going so far as to suggest that rather than playing with them, John should simply have given free tickets to his friends to watch him perform. Mairants's comments are an important indicator of how the Friends would be received because he had his finger on the pulse of the guitar world at large and although known best for his jazz playing, he was also a competent classical player who knew what he was listening to. He remarked on John's 'benign leadership', saying that it contributed to a 'relaxed, informal atmosphere', exactly what Williams had been aiming to achieve, and after expressing some concern about amplification, applauded John's solo rendering of the J. S.

Bach 'Chaconne' as the best live performance of the piece he had ever heard.

The excellent and by now well-established Paul Myers/ Mike Ross-Trevor partnership was responsible for two of John's 1974 albums, which were very different in nature. The first, *Rhapsody*, which Roy Emerson co-engineered with Ross-Trevor, included Patrick Gowers's *Rhapsody for Guitar, Electric Guitars and Organ*, on which Gowers also played, combined with the Villa-Lobos *Five Preludes for Guitar*. Williams had premiered the work in January that year with his friend Peter Hurford, the organist, choirmaster and Bach scholar who established the St Albans International Organ Festival, an event that always draws musicians and spectators from around the world. They made a delightful recording of works by Bach together some years later with Peter playing the organ at St Catherine's College Chapel in Cambridge.

The other record also featured Villa-Lobos, this time his *Concerto for Guitar and Small Orchestra*, and the extremely popular *Concierto de Aranjuez* by Joaquín Rodrigo. Daniel Barenboim conducted the English Chamber Orchestra for this landmark recording of the piece which was to be used in numerous later compilations. Rodrigo, or to give him his full name and title, Joaquín Rodrigo Vidre, Marqués de los Jardines de Aranjuez, composed this piece in 1939 and it has become one of the best-known and most popular orchestral guitar works ever. Many of those who bought this work have no other orchestral music in their record collections and this modest contribution to popular culture owes a lot to John Williams's interpretations. He was quite surprised when, at a presentation line-up to meet members of the royal family after the Last Night of the Proms, Prince Philip said to him, 'We've got your record of Rodrigo.'

Rodrigo was a remarkable man. Blind from the age of three, he first studied music in Valencia, moving to Paris when he was twenty-seven, where he was a pupil of the French composer Paul Dukas. His achievements undoubtedly merited the honours and awards he received, not least from the King of Spain and the French government. He died in Madrid in 1999 at the grand age of ninety-seven. John Williams says of the concerto: 'the solo part, particularly in the second movement, has surely not been surpassed as an example of expressive and inventive instrumental guitar writing.' Something that intrigues many guitar fans is that Segovia never played *Concierto de Aranjuez*. Composition of the work began in 1938, two years after Segovia left his homeland for Uruguay at the outbreak of the Spanish Civil War. He did not even know of the piece until 1947 when he heard it played in South America by his compatriot, Regino Sainz de la Maza, the guitarist who had been involved with the work since its inception and to whom it was dedicated by Rodrigo. Segovia's reaction and subsequently professed view of the concerto was that he 'liked it, but not for playing' and he may have felt slighted by it not being linked with him by Rodrigo.

Sainz de la Maza premiered *Concierto de Aranjuez* in November 1939 at Palau de la Musica, Barcelona, reprising it a month later in Madrid and is credited with its first recording. Segovia remained in Montevideo and later in the USA until some time after the Second World War when he returned to Europe. He subsequently commissioned Joaquin

Rodrigo to compose 'Fantasia para un Gentilhombre' for him in 1954, Segovia himself being the 'gentilhombre' or gentleman, but *Concierto de Aranjuez* can be said to have passed him by perhaps as a consequence of politics or, perhaps, of pique. Having first been associated with Spanish guitarists Sainz de la Maza and then Narciso Yepes (who played it at his own Madrid debut in 1947), this evocative piece passed to the next generation of guitar players, including John Williams, and was adopted by musicians in other interpretations, perhaps the most famous and influential of which was the Gil Evans arrangement of the second movement as played by Miles Davis on the 1960 album *Sketches of Spain*. In another of the great coincidences that occur in the world of the guitar, Regino Sainz de la Maza was also the teacher with whom Alirio Díaz studied when the scholarship from the Venezuelan government enabled him to travel to Spain to develop his playing.

Williams was back in the studio with Julian Bream for *Together Again*, a follow-up to their highly successful first recording as a duo. Again, the material chosen was solidly from the classical stable and, again, the magic that the two guitarists each brought combined to make this another milestone in the history of recorded guitar music. A year later they were presented with Silver Discs for sales of the first album. There was some uncertainty around as to exactly what level of sales or income this award represented but industry insiders put the number at 50,000. When he got home from the presentation ceremony, John put his disc on the record player to see if it actually played; it did but the blues refrain that came out of the speakers was certainly not by John or Julian!

Williams thought this was hilarious and called his partner to tell him about it. Intrigued, Julian played his own disc to see if he had suffered the same fate. No blues for him, but 'his' Silver Disc turned out to be by Paul McCartney's Wings.

Williams participated in another programme in the *Omnibus* series for BBC television with the colourful couple who performed as Dorita y Pepe but in real life were the rather less exotically named Dorothy and Peter Sensier. John's role was to perform work by Agustín Barrios Mangoré but it seemed, in the eyes of one critic at least, that the Sensiers, particularly the exotically garbed Pepe, were determined to steal the show. John was able to put things right by Barrios over the next two evenings when he presented a programme at the Wigmore Hall that, unusually, was made up of works by just two composers, the Paraguayan being one. The first half comprised the three suites by the Frenchman, Robert de Visée; the second, which was far better received, was made up of works by Barrios.

Williams continued the season by sharing the platform with cellist Rohan de Saram at the Queen Elizabeth Hall the following month. They each played Bach, the *Third Lute Suite* and *Third Cello Suite* respectively, but the remainder of the programme was rather less predictable. Williams performed 'Nunc' by Goffredo Petrassi, a piece that imposes demands on both player and listener alike. The unaccompanied cello was played by de Saram with alternative tuning to the lower strings for 'Finale' from the Sonata by the Hungarian Zóltan Kodaly. Their duet piece was Stephen Dodgson's 'Duo for Cello and Guitar'.

Soon after, John and Paco Peña played one of their

informally structured concerts at the Fairfield Hall in Croydon. Together they played solos and for the encores, duets, in which they showed enormous generosity and sensitivity to each other's playing, something the knowledgeable audience recognised and appreciated. For the encores Williams played one of the Spaniard's flamenco guitars for a *farruca*, followed by a crowd-pleasing *bulerias*. It was a bitterly cold evening just two weeks before Christmas but the audience left the hall having been warmed by the musical sunshine of Spain.

Just six days later, John and Daniel Barenboim were to be re-united at the Royal Festival Hall together with the London Philharmonic Orchestra. It was an extraordinary time for the guitar: the diary pages of guitar magazines were full of notices that performers such as Carlos Bonnell, Gerald Garcia and Alison Roseveare, Alice Artzt, Narciso Yepes, John Mills and flamenco player Juan Martin could be found playing not just in London but all around the country. In May 1976, the John Williams and Daniel Barenboim recording of the Rodrigo concerto reached number twenty in the pop album chart, the highest placing achieved to date by a classical album. John received another Silver Disc for this recording – which this time he did not even attempt to play – awarded to him by Maurice Oberstein, chairman of CBS Records. In the middle of that month, Julian Bream played three concerts at the Wigmore Hall, the first with tenor Robert Tear, then with his consort and actress Dame Peggy Ashcroft and finally with the Gabrieli String Quartet. The second of these was in competition with John Williams and Friends at the Royal Festival Hall. Ivor Mairants had a hit single as the soloist in Manuel and his Music of the

Mountains when their rendering of the Rodrigo Concerto went soaring up the Top Twenty. Extraordinary times indeed!

Williams finally got around to making his first recording with Cleo Laine, appropriately called *Best Friends*, for RCA in 1976. John had long been friends with Cleo and her husband John Dankworth and it was inevitable that their friendship and music would find its way onto vinyl. The three had often worked together since the early seventies and the two men loved the sound of Laine's voice with the guitar. Cleo was the most popular female jazz singer in the UK and had successfully extended her audience by venturing into the pop world and through her forays into acting and musicals. Brian Gascoigne was involved in the album and John Dankworth and Paul Hart produced it, all three contributing songs to go along with Lennon and McCartney's 'Eleanor Rigby', 'If' by David Gates, 'Killing Me Softly' and 'Wave' from the Brazilian bossa nova master, Antonio Carlos Jobim. Given Cleo always called it 'He Was Beautiful', the final track is curiously and quaintly listed as 'He's so Beautiful (a lyric version of the musical composition entitled "Cavatina")'.

The story of 'Cavatina' in its various instrumental forms and its subsequent incarnation as the song 'He was Beautiful' is long, complicated and highly fortuitous. It is also quite romantic. During 1969 and 1970 John Williams worked with composer Stanley Myers on his soundtrack for the film *The Raging Moon*, a touching and provocative tale of the relationship between a paraplegic and a polio victim featuring Nanette Newman and Malcolm MacDowell, who became famous for his role in the notorious *A Clockwork*

Orange. The film, directed by Newman's husband Bryan Forbes, was considered quite shocking at the time as it dealt directly with the sexual relationship between the two disabled characters.

Stanley Myers, who was particularly noted for his collaborations with director Stephen Frears, was a prolific composer who scored the music for over sixty movies before his untimely death from cancer at the age of sixty-three. Among his most familiar work is the theme for the popular BBC TV discussion programme *Question Time*, which has been heard since the programme started in 1979. It is still broadcast today.

Williams's work on *The Raging Moon* was the first of a number of collaborations between the guitarist and the composer. The theme that was to become known as 'Cavatina' was composed for and first widely heard in *The Walking Stick*, a movie in which he was not involved. It starred David Hemmings and Samantha Eggar, both extremely popular, headlining actors, and was a gritty drama set in London's run-down and edgy Docklands area, based upon Winston Graham's novel of the same name. The alluring Eggar falls for Hemmings and then, of course, it all goes wrong.

John Williams and Stanley Myers were very different characters, Stanley perhaps slightly harder-edged and commercially-minded, but they greatly enjoyed each other's company, and regularly spent time together after sessions; there was a genuine friendship between the two men that was built upon more than mutual musical respect. They decided to work together again on the album, *Changes*, released in 1971. This happy collaboration was John's first involvement with a tune that would subsequently become so closely identified with him, particularly as a favourite with his popular audience.

John recalls that a couple of nights before the last session for this album they were discussing what to do in the next session. He and Stanley met for a meal at a restaurant in London, long since disappeared, which he describes as 'a very elaborate Italianate place on the corner of Fulham Road in South Kensington', where Alan Clare, the jazz pianist known as the 'musician's musician' and some-time Spike Milligan collaborator, was playing in the downstairs room. The subject of 'Cavatina' came up over dinner and Stanley took over Alan's piano stool to play the theme from *The Walking Stick* to John and, from that moment, the tune was set to take on a new life. The guitarist immediately warmed to the seductive melody and it was decided that it should be included on *Changes*. This recording featured an incredible line-up of top-class classical, jazz and rock musicians including Rick Wakeman of prog-rock band 'YES', Canadian flugelhorn player Kenny Wheeler, trombonist Don Lusher, Tony Coe, bassist Danny Thompson and the future SKY members Tristan Fry and Herbie Flowers.

A few years later, in one of those strange events of fate, a production assistant to the Hollywood director Michael Cimino gave him a copy of *Changes* for his birthday. 'Cavatina' might have lodged itself in Cimino's subconscious. Some time later, when the director was in London consulting with Stanley Myers on the end music for his current movie project, he complained to Myers that he was very unhappy with what the composer had offered him so far. Richard Harvey, the multi-instrumentalist who was to work with Williams for many years to come, was a long-time associate of Stanley's and he recalls being at a party at Myers house in Barnes on the River Thames in Cimino's honour. The house and the party were both special: the house because it was the former home of composer Gustav Holst and the party because it was a celebration of the annual Oxford and Cambridge University Boat Race. Despite Stanley's best efforts, Cimino was not enjoying the party, distracted by his worry over the music he needed and he took Myers aside from his guests. He told him, in very direct terms, that a solution had to be found. What had been delivered was simply not suitable since he wanted a very memorable and hence commercial theme. He wanted something else and he wanted it now!

The two men went into Stanley's home studio in an extension at the back of the house and the movie director told Myers to play him anything he had already written that might fit the bill. After playing three or four recordings, 'Cavatina' was offered up and worked its magic once again. Cimino decided there and then that this was what he wanted for the film, the compelling and complex anti-war Oscar-winning movie *The Deer Hunter* starring Robert De Niro and Christopher Walken. Before long, John Williams was on his way to Hollywood with Stanley to record the piece in the studios of MGM.

There was something special about the space where John sat to record. He could see no particular reason why his chair and footstool had been placed on an area of the studio floor that was of a different wood from the rest of the space. When he took his seat, he was quite disgusted to see this little patch was disfigured with lots of dents and cigarette burn marks. After the recording he asked the studio manager about the wooden panel. 'That was put there for Fred Astaire to tap dance so we could synch' the sound to the movie track and he smoked all the time he was dancing!' Hallowed ground indeed!

The tune has since become known as 'The Theme from the Deer Hunter' as well as 'Cavatina'. As with many iconic moments in musical history, there are numerous and varying accounts about exactly how 'Cavatina' took on its new life as a movie theme. The one related here has the blessing of both John Williams and Richard Harvey, and that was good enough for the author.

The film was awarded Oscars in five categories and had nominations in a further four. Surprisingly, given its popularity and durability, the score received no recognition although the soundtrack album, released some time after the movie, sold very well and together with the single version instilled 'Cavatina' in the public consciousness.

In 1976 Cleo Laine wrote the moving and beautiful words for the vocal version of 'Cavatina' and describes them as 'the first "important" lyric of my career'. In her autobiography, *Cleo*, she relates how she heard John play the piece at his home as they discussed what tracks to record together for the *Best Friends* album. She and her husband John Dankworth were due to leave for their holiday home in Malta and when she learned that there was no lyric for the piece, she asked the publisher to commission a songwriter to write one. Fate intervened and nothing arrived before the Dankworth family set out for the Mediterranean so, haunted by the melody, she decided to write her own words.

Maybe she was inspired by the stunning surroundings of the family's Maltese refuge and from somewhere came that first, gripping line, 'He was beautiful' and she built upon that to complete the song. Back in England she took her work to the studio to find that the publisher's chosen lyricist had now finally come up with a lyric. She tried it but didn't like it. Reluctant to criticise the work of a professional, she left it to others to decide which of the two was better. The publisher hadn't seen the commissioned version so someone suggested that copies of both were submitted with the originators' names blacked out. Although Cleo liked her own better, she thought it fairer if the publisher made an objective decision about which lyric would make the cut. The publisher got in touch and he must have been wondering how to break the bad news to her, thinking as he did that 'He was Beautiful' was so good that it had to be the work of the experienced songwriter. Cleo took great pleasure in the look on his face when she told him that the winner had come from her hand. She has been asked many times, not least by her great friend and fellow jazz singer, the late Marion Montgomery, just who was that beautiful guy? Her answer never changes: 'He's a compilation.'

Two other versions of 'Cavatina' featured in the bestseller charts. The Shadows, who had originally been the backing band for Cliff Richard, had made a parallel career for themselves as the most notable guitar-based instrumental group in the UK. Probably due to the band's established fan base, its version of the tune sold very well but failed to match the lofty position of number three in the pop charts that John Williams achieved. It remains one of the very few occasions in the history of the charts when two instrumental versions of the same tune were fighting it out for sales.

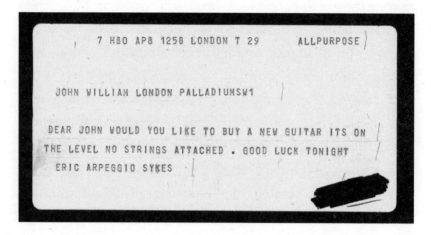

7 H8O AP8 1258 LONDON T 29   ALLPURPOSE

JOHN WILLIAM LONDON PALLADIUMSW1

DEAR JOHN WOULD YOU LIKE TO BUY A NEW GUITAR ITS ON
THE LEVEL NO STRINGS ATTACHED . GOOD LUCK TONIGHT
ERIC ARPEGGIO SYKES

Good luck telegram to John Williams from Eric Sykes.

Perhaps surprisingly, 'Cavatina' also found favour, albeit very briefly, with Andrés Segovia. In 1977, John was about to play a week-long season at the London Palladium with John Dankworth and Cleo Laine, an event for which his great friend Eric Sykes sent his best wishes by telegram. Segovia was in London that week and Williams paid a courtesy call, making his way through a city darkened by a power cut to the Westbury hotel in Conduit Street, where the Spaniard was staying. Segovia was quite disparaging when Williams revealed that he was currently working with Britain's top jazz singer and her husband, at the Palladium of all places! Swiftly steering away from that subject, Segovia asked what repertoire John was playing and was treated to a rendition of 'Cavatina'. He commented that it was a very pretty tune and asked about its origins, declining to add further praise or comment when they were revealed. This is a perfect

LEFT Len with baby John aged four months.
RIGHT AND BELOW Early lessons for the young John. The guitar is believed to be the Martin, before and after modification to the neck.

Melaan, John and Len in the garden at Alston Grove.

Melaan, John and Len with Lock Aitken, Bob Wilson and Brice Wilson (unrelated) before boarding RMS *Orontes* for England.

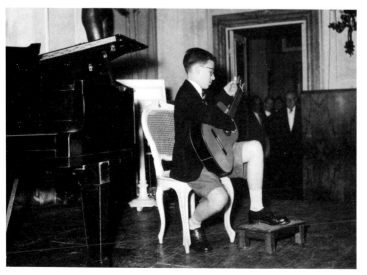

Tuning for a performance at Accademia Musicale Chigiana.

John stands shyly behind Segovia as the Maestro plays for Count Guido Chigi Saracini, founder of Accademia Musicale Chigiana. Fourth from left is jazz guitarist Charlie Byrd. Alirio Díaz is second from left, Rodrigo third from left.

John and Daniel Barenboim debate who should pay for the drinks.

Young Kate explains her cello to Brian McKay. John is on the phone in the background.

John helps Charlie get to know a woolly monkey.

John and Julian Bream practising together.

John with John Dankworth, Cleo Laine, Richard Rodney Bennett and a young Alec Dankworth at the Dankworth home in Wavendon.

SKY on tour – the band and their road crew.

Eric Sykes sent this photograph, suitably annotated, as a 'thank you' for John's appearance on his TV show.

Greg Smallman explains the intricacies of an early version of 'lattice bracing' to John.

John and Paco
Peña on stage
with Inti Illimani.

'John Williams
and Friends'
rehearsing.

Len Williams
promotes his first
book with a little
help from his
friends.

Harpo Speaks! – and so, happily, did father and son.

An unlikely duet – John Williams and Pete Townshend at The Secret Policeman's Ball, July 1979.

Giants of the guitar: (l–r) Paco Peña, John Williams, Joe Pass and Leo Kottke.

John Williams and Sir George Martin discuss Martin's composition 'Westward Look' at Air Studios. Giles Martin awaits the outcome.

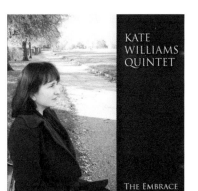

LEFT Kate's album, *The Embrace*.

BELOW John in Air Studios with the 'Stavrou' microphone set-up.

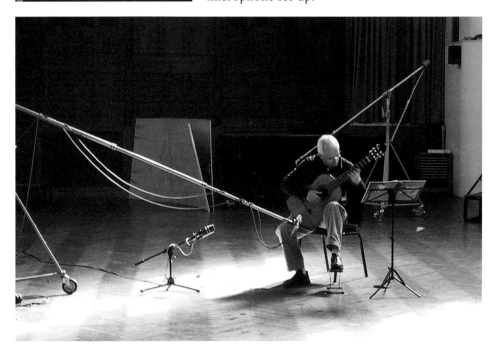

Tim Kain, John Williams, Raffaele Agostino and Richard Charlton at the Darwin International Guitar Festival.

Old friends: John and Alirio Díaz.

illustration of what Williams characterises as the musical conservatism and snobbishness of Segovia; he liked the piece but was reluctant to give it credit because it did not have the right provenance.

In 1989, John played the tune during The Secret Policeman's Ball, a benefit concert for Amnesty International. He had received the same invitation to perform from John Cleese as every other target artist and it had that distinctive Cleese touch about it. Addressed: 'Dear Esteemed Jewel of the Firmament (or Occupier)', it ended with advice for anyone who indicated they might be willing to participate to 'Not be too shocked when we call you in mid-August to see if you're the generous public-spirited person you're reputed to be and not the selfish contemptible little shit the Archbishop of Canterbury says you are.' John's presence on the night confirmed that His Grace was mistaken and there was a nice set-up to his entry onto the stage, with Dawn French and Jennifer Saunders acting as stagehands in the black clothes typically worn by those unsung technicians. The stage set for the previous act had been cleared and the two comediennes made their way across the stage with their backs to the audience, hilariously displaying buttock cleavage that would embarrass the most shameless and scantily trousered builder. They set John's chair and microphone in position then departed stage right.

Williams, tanned and in jeans and a colourfully striped shirt, came on stage with his guitar to great applause. He settled himself on the chair and began playing 'Cavatina'. After a couple of choruses, Saunders wandered back on stage with a flashlight. She went over to John, who was still playing, and touching his shoulder said, 'Stop it, stop it! I think they're bored'. She then addressed herself to John Cleese, who was approaching from the other side of the stage, 'He's your friend, you tell him, go on, tell him', and, picking up the microphone, she exited the scene. Cleese shrugged, looked apologetically at the apparently perplexed and disconsolate guitarist, then put a comforting arm around his shoulders and steered him off-stage, pausing to pick up a half-eaten apple left by a previous act, which he offered to John by way of consolation.

There is a clip of this performance on YouTube and many of the touching but completely misguided comments on it are expressions of sympathy for John Williams from people who clearly failed to appreciate that the self-effacing Aussie was obviously aware of what was going to happen and delighted to be the butt of the joke. The whole point!

Regardless of how many other interpretations there might be, 'Cavatina' will always be most closely associated with John Williams. Over thirty years since he first recorded it, the tune retains a special place in the hearts of a particular section of his fans and he still occasionally plays it in concerts, often as part of a group of movie themes, including those from *Cinema Paradiso* and *Schindler's List*. On one notable occasion, not long after the movie had been re-released in the UK, John deliberately presented it as 'The Deer Hunter'. He was performing along with many others at a Red Nose Day benefit concert for the charity Comic Relief at the New Theatre in Oxford. As if his name alone was not enough to help ensure a full house, he allowed his programme to be billed as including 'The Deer Hunter'. Came the evening of the concert. The enthusiastic and slightly rowdy applause with which he was greeted fell to a respectful hush as John settled on his chair at front of stage, adjusting his footstool and his seating position. He was picked out by a single spotlight, the lustre of his guitar sending dancing reflections randomly into the darkness of the auditorium as the first notes of 'Cavatina' floated across the muted footlights. Behind him the stage set was bathed in a sombre blue wash to reflect the mood of the movie which the haunting melody had come to embody. John infused his rendition with great emotion and the audience listened reverently, many with bowed heads and half-closed eyes, perhaps reflecting on some of the more sombre scenes that the music evoked. The audience sustained the tension through its consciousness of the background to the theme as John continued to play, hunched over his guitar. He was about three-quarters of the way through the piece when, from the wings upstage, there slowly emerged an enormous pair of antlers followed by an equally immense pantomime deer. The creature moved onto the stage, doing some theatrical 'business' behind the guitarist, wandering around and foraging. Apparently deaf to the sniggering of the audience, John played on until he could no longer ignore the distraction. As he turned around to see what was going on, the deer hit him full in the face with a custard pie. Cue uproarious laughter, the audience erupted! Inside the deer costume was John's brother Sam who had hired the outfit from a local costumier. A delightful example of one of the world's greatest musicians being prepared, literally, to take one on the nose for charity in an occasion made all the happier through it having been a family event.

When Stanley Myers died in 1993 John Williams played

'Cavatina' as a tribute at both his cremation and the memorial service that followed.

The album, *John Williams and Friends*, was in record shops in 1976. It was made three years after the concept of the group became reality when the band was tour-hardened and the material very familiar. It was light-hearted and accessible, and the public liked it enough to buy it in large numbers. Many other recording sessions, including one with virtuoso violinist and old friend Itzhak Perlman, were fitted in between touring and recital obligations and the time that John had to spare was largely devoted to various good causes. He became known as someone with a strong social conscience and was in demand from many quarters. One particular cause was close to his heart but this one was different: it was a matter of music and it led to one of his most important recordings. John had loved the work of Agustín Barrios Mangoré since his first exposure to it back in the days of his summer visits to Siena. He now had the opportunity to pay tribute to the peerless Paraguayan guitarist and composer.

John's worldwide recognition was not only as a virtuoso musician but also, crucially, through the work he had done as someone who was open to new ideas, new repertoire, and new ways of doing things. This reputation for receptiveness was a major factor in the way that a large quantity of music by Barrios came into his hands with an implicit plea to share it with the world. The full story is related in Chapter 12. Suffice to say here that the trust placed in him was well founded and *John Williams Plays Barrios* was the vindication of the choice of John to use his talent to bring the music of the great Barrios to a global audience. He had answered the prayers of many Paraguayans and provided inspiration for some of that nation's great guitarists, Berta Rojas being a superb example.

There were other South American-centred activities for John in 1976 when Alirio Díaz invited Williams to go to Venezuela and perform in Caracas, and the two old friends made the most of their time together. Alirio took John to the small town of Valencia, some way from the city where they visited a family who made and played their own instruments: guitars, a bass and cuatros. The plan was that they would arrive for lunch and then spend some time with the family so John could experience this 'home-made' music, but when they reached their hosts, the two professionals were sat down under a sprawling mango tree to watch the family perform. John and Alirio were plied with whisky, a drink that Williams usually avoids but that was what was on offer, probably as a special treat for the visitors, and it helped the music flow. Everyone was soon playing and dancing together, Alirio and John whirling with the best of them.

Back in Caracas, John played a successful concert in which he combined the European tradition of J. S. Bach with the work of the local composer, Agustín Barrios Mangoré. The concert was later hailed by the musicologist and historian Alejandro Bruzual as 'the single most important performance by a visiting guitarist in the second half of the twentieth century'. Alirio had also requested that his friend serve on the jury of a guitar competition in which he was involved. This presented John with a problem because he has always had a very jaded view of this kind of contest.

This may have some echo of Len's attitude but it is a position to which he has always held firm. In this instance, however, John agreed to do so out of respect for his great friend. It was to be the first and last time he was ever involved in judging such an event. He was in good company on the panel, though; fellow jurors included Leo Brouwer, Robert Vidal and Rodrigo Riera and the chairman of the jury was Antonio Lauro – this was guitar music royalty. It was all a bit irregular: for example, Riera was disqualified from voting on the rounds in which his teenage son Ruben was competing. Other factors in this episode helped confirm John's prejudice against competitions.

He and Alirio spent most of their time together during the visit and John remembers that he learned a great deal about the roots and culture of Venezuelan music first-hand through the various excursions from the city that he went on with his old friend. Incredibly, given how long they had known each other and how great their mutual regard, it was still another year before Alirio Díaz and John Williams actually performed together. It was during the ninth International Guitar Festival in Paris, an event arranged as always by the formidable Robert Vidal. Both men played solo recitals but the last night of the festival was reserved for them as a duo. Reviews of their performance were mixed but there seems to have been a general feeling that, geniuses though they both may be, a strong bond of friendship was no guarantee of complementary interpretations of their chosen programme.

‡

Melaan died in February 1978 at the John Radcliffe Infirmary in Oxford. The arrangements in Sydney had not worked out for her as planned and she had returned to England a few years earlier. Her health continued to deteriorate and she had little option but to resort to entering a care home for people with literary associations in Summertown, a suburb of Oxford whose name contrasts starkly with the unremitting nature of her illness. Emphysema or 'chronic obstructive pulmonary disease' is even more closely linked to tobacco smoking than lung cancer and would also claim the life of John's other parent.

Happily, though, their granddaughter was doing well. She and her mother moved to Highgate when she was eleven and Kate was sent to King Alfred's School in Golders Green. It was what was termed a 'progressive' school, similar to, if not modelled on, A. S. Neill's Summerhill School, founded as a place where 'kids have the freedom to be themselves'; where 'success is not defined by academic achievement but by the child's own definition of success' and where 'you can play all day if you want to'. The very particular regime meant that she needed to develop her innate instinct for self-discipline. She had given up the cello by now; her father saw that her heart was not in it and said, 'Don't force yourself. If you are not interested you don't have to do it.' The school offered no musical education whatsoever but like most girls her age she was into pop bands, especially Ian Dury and the Blockheads. She started picking out their tunes on the piano and was encouraged when John told her she was doing it well. That was hardly a surprise since she had been steeped in music all her life, her mother's piano students and rehearsals, her father's performances, but she was also much influenced by what she heard on John's record player: Django Reinhardt, Stravinsky, Haydn, Bach and lots of Beatles records.

On her own initiative Kate told the school that she wanted to take music as one of her O level subjects. There was a performance component to the exam so her mother's friend Clare Sutherland was conscripted to give piano lessons. She was the only pupil taking the music O level so an examiner was brought into the school for the performance test. After Kate had played, the examiner was full of praise and asked if her parents were musical. Not wanting any favours through her blood link to musical royalty, she mumbled that her mother was a piano teacher, thinking she had successfully navigated around the question. 'What about your dad?' insisted the adult. 'He plays guitar a bit.' The examiner knew nothing further about John until after Kate was marked 'pass with distinction'. Lindy and John were both delighted, regardless of their separation, she was very, very close to them both. Kate was also very fond of her maternal grandmother but her relationship with grandfather Len was limited for some time by the animosity between him and John.

John was a good father in the less than ideal circumstances. Kate was a frequent visitor wherever he lived and she had her own room in every one of his homes. She was a real chatterbox, always asking questions, and during an election year, aged six years, she asked John to explain the difference between the Conservatives and Labour. He said, 'The Conservatives make the rich richer and the poor poorer. Labour make the rich a bit poorer and the poor a bit richer.' She was not hugely aware of her father's fame until he appeared on television with Eric Sykes or being interviewed by Michael Parkinson and SKY became a big thing.

Williams regularly took his daughter on holiday and, perhaps through some sense of his own childhood, always invited her to bring a friend or two along. Kate understood that her father had some special qualities and she recognised and appreciated John's way of dealing with things. She remembers him arriving at her school to pick her up. She and her friend were due to spend the evening at John's home and while they waited for him they bought ice creams for themselves. Her father had a beautiful Bristol coupé at the time and as the girls got into the car, her friend accidentally smeared ice cream across the headlining. The girl feared the worst but John remained calm throughout as Kate knew that he probably would. She contrasts this with how Len might have reacted: 'He had a real temper, he was really snappy. He could be quite scary.' She says:

I'm sure John's [she always calls him John] character is a reaction to Len. He is a peacemaker who will speak his mind but with great balance. He will definitely have his say but is never out to seek conflict whereas Len had lots of anger, he had a hell of a temper. Len was very dominating. John must have been influenced by that but somehow he has managed to become particular without the need to be dominating. Len was aggressive, John isn't.

Kate formed these views, she says, when she was quite young and she is grateful but not surprised that John never tried to impose his own views of his father on her. 'He let me find my own Len and I felt that showed he trusted my judgement. John was always the sort of parent who gives wise but quiet guidance and then lets you get on with it.'

Although Kate, like most other people who know him, will testify that John is enviably mild of temper, she does recall one occasion when he was so frustrated that 'He really lost it.' It happened at the house in South Hill Park, where an electric toaster raised his temperature, if not that of the bread he had inserted. John remembers, 'I was so pissed off that the toaster wouldn't work that I threw it out the window. When I looked down, hoping to see it smashed to smithereens, the bloody thing was still intact so I went outside and collected it. Then I took it up to the top floor and chucked it out again and it still didn't break so I jumped up and down on it until it did!'

Williams was never out of touch with Australia and he made sure that Kate had the chance to become familiar with his birthplace. He toured there regularly, solo and with 'the Friends', and often stayed in Sydney at the invitation of Peter and Athalie Calvo, sometimes taking Kate along with him. His performance schedule was always punctuated with master classes and it was at one of these, in 1978, that he first met George Black, a student of Calvo's, who remains one of his closest and most trusted friends. George had been mainly a folk and blues fingerstyle guitarist and was now studying jazz and classical guitar, soon dropping the former to concentrate on his chosen style. Like thousands of others across the world, his inspiration was seeing John Williams, in his case at a concert in Sydney Town Hall, and his life changed as a consequence. Two years later John was in town with Joe Pass, the top American jazz guitarist described in *Jazz: The Rough Guide* as a musician who 'summarised all of the bop-based players of the last forty-five years' and 'someone few guitarists could surpass'. Joe and John were there for the Sydney Music Symposium when they performed the world premiere of Peter Sculthorpe's 'Cantares for Guitars and String Quartet' with the Sydney Spanish Guitar Centre Players (which included Calvo and Black), the Petra String quartet and four electric guitarists.

Peter Calvo was a visionary who promoted not just guitar in all its forms but also strings and another of his guests was the Hungarian cello virtuoso, János Starker. Paco Peña was a frequent companion on trips to Australia and, with John, he was to take part in a memorable class and concert some years later with Joe Pass and Leo Kottke, the great steel string fingerstylist. One person John always spent time with while he was Down Under was his cousin, Paul Ket. Paul is a man of many parts: an engineer and model maker who designed and constructed the 'ball-juggling' machines for the Australian National Lottery, a carriage driver who has competed against Prince Philip and was Australian champion for pairs and fours; farmer and all-round good bloke! He and John were 'as thick as thieves' according to a friend.

Paul spent some time in the UK during which he joined John, Kate and a number of friends for a memorable holiday at Plan de la Tour in Provence, where his mischievous sense of fun was exercised to the full. When John was considering spending three months of each year teaching at the Victorian College of the Arts, an idea inspired by his great friend John Hopkins, dean of the college, he decided to buy a home in the land of his birth. He and Paul went house-hunting together then found and jointly purchased a beautiful farmstead on the Mornington Peninsula, south of Melbourne. Paul took on the responsibility of running the farm and John and many famous friends, including the Dankworths and the Hurfords, stayed there while touring or simply visiting until plans were changed and Paul bought out his cousin's share.

After Melaan died Len picked up the phone to call his son and ask him why he had chosen not to pass on the news of his mother's death. He asked the question in sadness, without recrimination or probably any real expectation of an answer, but the call broke the seven-year silence and brought the two stubborn men back together. John was very apologetic. They would become quite close again and, from then on, he visited his father two or three times a year, right up until Len's death some ten years later from the same relentless disease that had killed his second wife. Even by the time of Melaan's death, Len was already quite physically limited by his health and its constraints were a source of anger and enormous frustration for a man whose mind was still buzzing and whose curiosity was unquenched.

When he was sixty-eight, Len was interviewed at the monkey sanctuary by George Clinton, the founder and editor of *Guitar* magazine, a unique publication that was highly influential in its day but which was sadly to die with him in the early 1990s. Clinton was clearly highly respectful of Len's profound influence on the development of the guitar, respect that was ultimately reflected in the title of his piece: 'The Man Who Started it All'. The journalist travelled down from London not quite sure what to expect from his interviewee. Clinton had gone to enquire about lessons at the Spanish Guitar Centre in the late fifties and was auditioned there by Williams. He was as impressed by the teacher's playing as Len was dismayed by his own and came away without lessons but with a lasting recollection of the older man having a cigarette at the corner of his mouth throughout their encounter. (George took lessons privately with a teacher from the centre). Now, twenty years later, he was about to meet Len Williams for the second time. His interest in Len was all predicated on the image he had formed of him as a visionary man who had successfully established possibly the most important institution in the world devoted to the classical guitar. This great benefactor of the instrument and its players had then disappeared completely from the guitar scene to set up a commune that would share its home in the backwoods of Cornwall with a load of monkeys. This was to be a voyage of discovery!

George Clinton was received by a man looking much older than his years, a victim of the smoking habit he had successfully warned his son against. Len was evidently keen to do the interview and had even prepared a written script ahead of time, which he invited Clinton to use and modify as he thought fit, although the journalist still recorded another three hours of discussion. Not much emerged that was new to interested parties but when the two reached the subject of teachers, Williams was very direct, scathing even, when talking about old colleagues who had been with him at Cranbourn Street, Jack Duarte in particular. Beyond that, he repeated tales told many a time before, the essential folklore of the Williams clan, and shared his thoughts on swearing, string squeaks and the music of Barrios. The overwhelming mood of the interview is of his nostalgia but, like much nostalgia, it is selective and sanitised by hindsight and experience. Len did not even attempt to answer the direct and fundamental question 'Why the move from the guitar to monkeys?' settling instead for expressing a view that music and nature are never far away from each other before deftly changing the subject. His enduring love of the guitar shines through the article and it is a shame that more of his notes for Clinton and what was recorded over three hours were never published.

The community now rather ran itself but Len's work with the monkeys and his correspondence with scientists and others continued to be the main inspiration for all the 'family'. The sanctuary went from strength to strength. Visitor numbers grew and there was a great breakthrough in both publicity and recognition when, in 1981, the BBC included a half-hour episode in its popular *Nature Watch* series documenting the institution and its achievements. A book based on the series was published, co-written by the programme's presenter, Julian Pettifer, in which he confirmed that Leonard, as he was referred to throughout, remained a 'vigorous polemicist' despite his failing health, who had 'a formidable reputation among musicians, behavioural scientists, moral philosophers and many unsuspecting persons who have felt the sharp side of his tongue'.

The author was content to acknowledge that it is beyond question that the sanctuary, under Len's total control and direction, had enormous success in its care and treatment of Humboldt's woolly monkeys. At London Zoo, their typical lifespan was two years and nine months whereas in the radically different environment of the sanctuary, the eldest monkey was twenty-four at the time of recording. No woolly monkey had ever been born in a zoo but the breeding record at Looe was consistent and staggering. Pettifer looked somewhat askance at the 'extended family' lifestyle and noted that many would regard Williams as 'an eccentric and even a disagreeable customer'; someone who had 'upset a good many establishment figures' in fields ranging from science to politics, economics, sociology and religion – quite an achievement! But to Len's credit, he and his extended family not only achieved great things through their husbandry of monkeys but observed and recorded their findings, adding substantially to the sum of knowledge on the subject.

‡

Back in London John was still extremely busy. Dodgson's *Second Guitar Concerto* was written for Williams and he recorded it with Sir Charles Groves and the English Chamber Orchestra on a disc that included 'Serenade for Guitar and String Orchestra' by another English composer, Malcolm Arnold, and Castelnuovo-Tedesco's *Concerto No.1 in D (Opus 99)*. The Emerson/Ross-Trevor production team who made the Barrios and Malcolm Arnold/Leo Brouwer albums were joined on this one by Michael Gore. Having missed out on being part of the Amnesty International benefit show *Pleasure at Her Majesty's* the previous year due to other commitments, John was delighted to be able to join John Cleese and his wife Connie Booth, Python Terry Jones, Peter Cook, Jonathan Miller and Sir Peter Ustinov at the Mermaid Theatre on the embankment of the river Thames to contribute 'Sevilla' to the proceedings. Six months later he was at 'Her Majesty's', but this time it was *Her Majesty's Silver Jubilee Royal Variety Gala* at the London Palladium. Queen Elizabeth II had been on the throne for twenty-five years and she and HRH the Duke of Edinburgh were sharing this particular celebration of the anniversary with Bob Hope, Julie Andrews, Tommy Cooper, Harry Belafonte and The Muppets. John Williams was also on the bill, performing with John Dankworth and Cleo Laine and not looking at all out of place.

Four recordings made in relatively quick succession over 1978 and 1979 stand as markers of the broad musical spectrum that John Williams was exploring and occupying. The first was the soundtrack for the movie *Stevie*. Directed by Robert Enders and starring Glenda Jackson in the title role, this was a biopic of the troubled British poet, Stevie Smith, who had died at the start of the decade. Patrick Gowers composed the score on which John played solo and with string and accompanied spoken poetry. The soundtrack now has a cult following and Gowers revisited it as the basis for his 1987 *Stevie Concerto*. Another was *Julian Bream and John Williams Live*, a double album recorded during concerts at Symphony Hall, Boston and the Avery Fisher Hall at the Lincoln Center for the Performing Arts in New York during the pair's highly successful North American tour. They also played to packed houses in Washington, Ann

Arbor and Toronto. At the Lincoln Center, Rodney Friend watched from a box with Julian while John performed his solo part of the programme. Friend recalls that Bream turned to him at one point and said, 'What he is doing is astonishing, nobody else could do that!' In a review of the New York concert by Gregory D'Alessio of the Society of the Classical Guitar he wrote of the 'ravishing music' and asked rhetorically when were two other comparable virtuosi such as Hofmann and Rubinstein on pianos, Milstein and Heifetz on violins or Rostropovich and Piatigorsky on cellos ever seen on stage as duos? The tracks selected for the album were an inspired choice and it's no wonder both guitarists have such affection for this peerless record of their finest work together. It was arguably the classical guitar at its peak. The third recording, in enormous contrast, was *Travelling*, another Stanley Myers production that included 'jazzed up' Bach with a strong bass line from, predictably, Herbie Flowers. Francis Monkman was on keyboards, playing lines that would not have seemed out of place with his old band, Curved Air; Adrian Brett contributed pan pipes, 'Friend' Richard Harvey recorders. John played Spanish and electric guitars alongside three other guitarists and worked, for the first time, with American sound engineer Michael Stavrou, the auspicious beginning to what would develop into a lasting relationship. If *Travelling* struck observers as a radical departure for Williams, they were in for an even greater adventure. The fourth album of the year was called *SKY* and it would be like nothing they had ever heard.

*Programme for the South Bank Summer Music Festival 1984.
Artistic Director: John Williams.*

EIGHT

THE WIDE BLUE YONDER

When John Williams gave an interview to Lance Bosman for *Guitar* magazine in August 1978 the concept of SKY was definitely on the horizon: 'I'm putting together a group ... It will comprise six of us and we're going to do a week at Ronnie's at the end of the year and some concerts. There'll be three guitars, Kevin Peek and Tim Walker, and we'll all play electric and acoustic; Francis is going to play harpsichord and electric piano, Herbie will be on bass guitar and, almost certainly, Maurice Pert will be on percussion.' It did not happen quite as John outlined but it was pretty close. SKY was one of the most unexpected musical phenomena of its time, extreme even for the unpredictable Williams. For the curious and confident John Williams, however, it was somehow a natural next move, building on his earlier flirtations with re-interpreting and presenting classical music while making the most of the technology of the day to do so. The story of SKY is covered extensively in Chapter 9.

SKY might have remained earthbound without John's popular success with 'Cavatina'. He had played and recorded the tune years before but it was only when it was employed as 'The Theme from the Deer Hunter' that it acquired a new life, released as a single to be propelled into the bestseller charts. Had this not happened, giving Williams a new, even higher level of exposure and popularity, the record industry, so reluctant in any event to take a chance on SKY, might have stalled the project entirely. Even if the enthusiasm and commitment of its members had been enough for them to go ahead without a record deal it is unlikely that the band would have made much of an impact or lasted very long.

Confusingly, in the same year that the band's first album (*SKY*) was released, Cube Records put out *Morning Sky*, a compilation of tracks from *The Height Below* and *Changes*. The only track on the Cube disc that has the remotest link with the sky in any way is 'Horizon', so it is understandable why some saw it as an attempt to cash in on the new band.

John invested a huge amount of time and energy into his venture with SKY but did not let up on his continuing sched-ule of performance and recording. Even so, he was accused by critics of failing his classical audience, of not taking seri-ously his responsibilities as an artist. One commentator on a radio arts programme became quite emotional when voic-ing his opinion. He said, 'I expected more of John Williams than getting involved with this rock and roll nonsense. When God gives you a talent like that, he gives you a duty, too', before confessing in response to the inevitable question that he had not personally ever heard anything played by SKY – 'And I don't want to!' There were mutterings that Williams had sold out and was doing it for the money. This matter is covered more extensively in Chapter 10. Throughout his time with SKY John actually played more concerts than before, confounding the critics who said he had abandoned 'the true path' and was squandering his talents on pop trivia. The first example of his fidelity on the record front was the solidly classical *Guitar Quintets*, a collection of works by Boccherini and Guastavino performed with the London String Quartet. Around the same time, K-Tel, the unashamedly 'pile 'em high, sell 'em slightly cheaper' record company released a compilation album fittingly called *Bridges* on its Lotus label. The sleeve notes expand the theme of the title: 'John Williams is something special, a rarity, an example of that occasional talent, the ability to span more than one musical arena. John bridges all areas of popular taste…' It included 'Cavatina' with *The Deer Hunter* billing so was likely to be popular but even K-Tel was surprised by its sales success; it spent several weeks in the pop album chart.

John was soon to acquire new house-mates. He was on a plane bound for London when he stumbled across an article in the culture section of a newspaper revealing that Rodney Friend was returning to England from America, where he had been concertmaster for the New York Philharmonic Orchestra. As soon as he landed, Williams called Rodney in New York to talk to him about the news and to offer that the Friend family could stay with him while they got themselves re-established. They enjoyed his hospitality for three months and greatly valued the breathing space in which to find themselves just the right home. The family joined a circle of friends which, as always, included the Peñas and Doganises at its heart and now embraced the SKY members who came to the house to rehearse in the basement.

John was due to leave for his regular solo tour of Australia

and went upstairs to see Rodney and Cynthia to say his fare-
wells. They went down to the front of the house, chatting
while John waited for his taxi to the airport. Rodney looked
around and saw there was just a guitar case and a weekend
bag by the door. He offered to get John's suitcase, assuming
there was one. 'That's all there is,' said John, nodding at the
small grip. Rodney, used to carrying up to eighteen dress
shirts for a US tour, was flabbergasted to learn that John
was setting out across the world with just two velvet 'Mao'
jackets, a couple of pairs of trousers, some underwear and a
shaving kit.

Williams was awarded the Order of the British Empire
(OBE) in 1980. He had just returned from his annual trip to
Australia and was on tour with SKY at the time he was due
to receive it from the Queen at Buckingham Palace. Although
he was aware of the importance of the honour, John was
uncomfortable with its imperial overtones and minded to
decline it. Like some others with similar concerns, he felt,
however, that by doing so he would simply draw attention
to himself, the last thing he wanted to do.

Williams has good reason to remember the circumstances
surrounding the event. He invited Paco and Karin Peña as
his guests for the presentation ceremony and he and Paco
had gone together to Moss Bros a few days before the event
to hire their morning suits and top hats. Both men had
playing commitments the evening before the investiture:
John with SKY in the north of England and Paco a little
closer to home. It was arranged that Karin would pick up
the hired outfits and that she and Paco would meet John's
train at St Pancras station. The three would then drive

directly to the palace. Both the train and the Peñas were late arriving, leaving them desperately short of time. John and Paco had no choice but to change clothes in the car park, crouching behind the open boot lid of their car to avoid outraging public decency.

John was soon back in Australia again for the first tour Down Under by SKY. Peter Lyster-Todd, the band's manager, was understandably a little nervous about how the band might be received as they had sold only a few thousand records before they arrived. With sales having reached eighty thousand by the time they left, combined with sell-out concerts, the tour and the band were an undoubted success. It was during that time that Greg Smallman, the innovative Australian luthier who John had met through Peter Calvo three years earlier, brought two guitars to show him. John bought one of them and has not wavered since in his belief that Smallman guitars are right for him: 'He understood from when we first met what I wanted and his guitars have continued to give the responsiveness and variety of colour which I think make the instrument more musical; the traditional design has some limitations in this regard, even if their basic sound is also beautiful but more typically "Spanish".' The Smallman design changed the history of the classical guitar, and its story is in Appendices B and C.

SKY kept John busy but he maintained his classical output. *Echoes of Spain*, an album devoted to the works of Isaac Albéniz, was followed by the duet recording with organist Peter Hurford, *John Williams and Peter Hurford Play Bach*.

The touring and recording continued and, on 24 February

1981, the band played the first concert ever at Westminster Abbey to mark the thirtieth anniversary of Amnesty International. The event was recorded for BBC television and broadcast two weeks later. Such a high-profile performance had the predictable effect of prompting critics to renew their questioning of the band's right to exist, with Richard Williams (no relation!) of *The Times* in the lead with the charge that the music of SKY was less than meaningful.

In 1982, during a very brief second marriage to the broadcaster Sue Cook, John became a father for the second time when his son Charlie was born.

Julian Bream's fiftieth birthday came around and a celebration of the milestone was held at the Wigmore Hall, where a procession of composers (including Dodgson and Tippett), actors, writers, poets and the BBC's guitar champion Gareth Walters all paid tribute to the great man. Bream played, of course, and he was joined by Robert Tear, William Bennett, John Underwood, Stephen Orton and John Williams. As part of an interesting and varied programme the two guitarists duetted on 'Partie Polonaise', a lute piece by Telemann. The evening was a delightful marking of what Bream the cricketer called his 'half century'.

Another friend with whom Williams worked that year was Cleo Laine. Their second album, six years after the first, was co-produced by Cleo's husband John Dankworth and Rod Argent, a keyboard player who will be remembered by many for his bands of the sixties and seventies, The Zombies and Argent. The album was a beautiful collection of tunes that seemed made specifically for Cleo's unique voice – in fact, at least three of them were! John was very much at ease working with the Dankworth couple; he had known them for many years and had been one of their collaborators in setting up the Wavendon Allmusic Project, a bold initiative to provide the highest quality of tuition and encouragement to young musicians, one of whom was Richard Wright. This took place at the Stables, converted from its original purpose: friends including Williams, John Ogdon and Richard Rodney Bennett were all roped in by 'JD' and Cleo, ostensibly as 'artistic directors'. Dankworth said: 'We wanted them to help with matters of policy but they all also offered their services for tuition and performances.' The three also threw themselves into the physical side of things as the project took shape. Cleo was terrified by some of the work she saw them take on: 'I remember seeing those precious hands of John Williams clutching a club hammer as he was knocking nails into a fence. I was so scared he would hurt them. We should have put a blue plaque on that section of fence!' The original Stables has been replaced by an excellent concert hall that provides a great programme through the year; the summer garden party and the famous Stables Christmas Show are highlights.

Sir John Dankworth, one of the jazz world's true giants, died in February 2010 on the eve of the fortieth anniversary of the opening of the Stables. The show to celebrate the anniversary has entered showbiz legend: Cleo decided to go ahead with it and not to reveal to the audience that John had died until the end of the programme. She, together with her son Alec, daughter Jacqui and other family and friends made the event a truly fitting tribute to a delightful man and one of Britain's greatest musicians.

John Dankworth loved any kind of challenge – he was an avid crossword fanatic – and he recalled the particular difficulties of writing for Williams, having done so on many occasions. Of course he wanted to take full advantage of John's supreme musicianship but Dankworth was hampered by not being able to play the guitar and he had to work out for himself what was possible on the instrument. Working on some arrangements for John while at the family holiday home in Malta, he experimented with diagrams of the fretboard but finally decided that the only way to truly get a grasp of the issue was to have a guitar to hand to see what was physically beyond the pale. He ventured into town and bought from a modest and unprepossessing music shop something he recognised and subsequently described as 'looking like a guitar'. When he got back to the villa, he reviewed the work he had done so far and checked the demands of what he had already written against the physical limitations of the fingerboard. After a number of tweaks and adjustments, he felt satisfied that he had created something that would be eminently playable on a classical guitar by his friend. The score was faxed to John Williams back in London. He declared himself to be pretty pleased with the arrangements but identified a few sections where certain chords were, to his mind, unplayable. Rehearsing the piece, he worked around the parts in contention, settling to talk to John Dankworth about them on his return from the Mediterranean.

When the two Johns met to discuss and resolve the fingering problems, there was some banter about the lowly workhorse that had been used; Williams suggested that Dankworth may have been misled into working with something that wasn't really a guitar at all but perhaps some local variation on the instrument. In fact, John and Cleo had brought the Maltese guitar home with them and it was produced for Williams's examination. He gingerly picked it up, pored over it and finally declared that it was, indeed, a reasonable approximation to a guitar. In which case, he concluded, the fault must lie with the composer so he challenged his knighted namesake to demonstrate how one particular chord could possibly be played as written. Dankworth showed, somewhat awkwardly, that by curling the thumb over the top of the fingerboard the offending note on the bottom 'E' string could be 'thumbed' rather than fingered. This device would be anathema to any modern classical player of a six-string guitar but Dankworth had observed jazz guitarists often hanging the thumbs of their left hands over the fingerboard, sometimes barring not just the low 'E' but both the bottom two strings. Williams was not buying this technique at all but a compromise was reached and the arrangement concluded to the satisfaction of both Johns. The guitar in question still sits in the hall of the beautiful old rectory that has been the Dankworths' home since 1967. Cleo Laine has fond memories of a party at which Paco Peña 'really made that cheap little guitar sing'.

John played Paul McCartney's theme for the film based on Graham Greene's novel *The Honorary Consul*. Paul liked it but he had quite a problem with another piece he needed for the movie. He knew of Richard Harvey's work for the screen and wanted him to write it. The commission intended for Harvey was sent out but, by mistake, somehow went to another composer who had a similar name. McCartney was disappointed when he received the piece, believing it to have been composed by Harvey. Running short of time and not knowing anyone else he might ask to do the job, he called Stanley Myers and said, 'Can you find someone to write this? I need it fast.' Knowing that Myers and Harvey were old friends, Paul kept the earlier attempt to himself. Myers looked at the brief and knew exactly the right man for the job – the next day he passed it on to Richard Harvey!

In that same year, notwithstanding SKY and all his other commitments including the premiere of Patrick Gowers's *Stevie Concerto* at the Royal Festival Hall, Williams found time to bring John Williams and Friends together again with a slightly modified line-up. Carlos Bonnell's replacement on guitar was Gerald Garcia and Richard Harvey brought his multi-instrumental talent to bear. There is more to read on all the Friends' line-ups in Chapter 10. An album called *The Guitar is the Song: A Folksong Collection* by a previous incarnation of the group had been in progress over two years. It was finally completed in 1982 and released in '83. The new Friends were ready to take over and they appeared to do so with a vengeance because although the two things were totally unrelated, John's participation in SKY was soon to be over. He finally quit in February; another remarkable and unpredictable episode in the life of John Williams was over.

The high point of the following year was, without question, the invitation for John to take the role of artistic director of the South Bank Summer Music Festival, an appointment with a three-year tenure. One guiding principle was that it should always be run by a musician and not an arts body, although the sponsoring organisation, the GLC Arts and Recreation Council, were on hand to take care of the bureaucracy. The festival had always been a great success, to the extent that it had now spawned a distinct but linked folk festival the previous year. John had a free hand and he used it to present an incredibly varied and eclectic programme.

As was expected of him, he was involved in many performances: with the Australia Youth Chamber Orchestra; Peter Hurford, his organist friend; Cleo Laine and the John Dankworth Quintet; The Medici Quartet with cellist Moray Welsh; Paco Peña and Benjamin Verdery and, in a fantastic final weekend, he played first with The National Youth Jazz Orchestra (NYJO) and then with an extended version of John Williams and Friends. There was both an artistic coup and some innovation that year. The Consort of Musicke, directed by Anthony Rooley, gave three performances of a production of the seventeenth-century masque *Cupid and Death*. Rooley had been unable to secure the funding necessary to present the masque anywhere in Britain but between them, Williams and Anthony Phillips, programme director for the festival, made it happen. The new departure, now quite commonplace, was to have performers from the masque and also musicians from the NYJO performing in the foyer so that concert-goers had entertainment as they filed in and also during intervals.

The way the programme was put together showed great imagination – for example, in how it integrated the folk and main festivals through the guitar. In two sessions called *Contemporary Guitar – State of the Art*, the first featured

John Renbourn, David Bromberg and DADGAD specialist Pierre Bensusan, and the second, Williams, Peña and Verdery. Among the hurdy-gurdy players and folk fiddlers, one indisputable highlight of the folk festival was the 'Boys of the Lough', whose usual energetic line-up of Ali Bain, Cathal McConnell and Tich and Dave Richardson was supplemented by sword dancers, Irish dancers and clog dancers. NYJO's founder and conductor Bill Ashton stepped aside for Paul Hart to conduct John in his *Concerto for Guitar and Jazz Orchestra*, which they recorded together a few years later. The Friends included, for just two pieces, two members of the Chilean group Quimantu, who had taken part in the 1983 tour by the Friends.

Classical fans remained well served with regular recitals and a splendid recording of concertos by Bach, Handel and Marcello with the Academy of St Martin in the Fields, an orchestra with which Tristan Fry has a long association. Tristan was a special contributor to John's second South Bank event, when he gave lectures and workshops on percussion to young musicians. What should have been John's valedictory festival in 1986 was denied him by the abolition of the GLC by Margaret Thatcher, as if he needed any further reason to dislike 'The Iron Lady'. He had served his first two years as artistic director in 1984 and 1985, and already had plans in place for his third and final year but the festivals, like so many uniquely London events, were brought to a crashing halt. The GLC had previously been the operator of the South Bank complex, and the transfer of control of the venue to the Arts Council sounded the death knell for the summer festivals. The last 'GLC concert' at the

Festival Hall was by the London Philharmonic Orchestra, with a programme that included Haydn's 'Farewell Symphony' and ended with a symbolic candle being extinguished by the Council Leader, Ken Livingstone, who, when the new Greater London Authority was established under Tony Blair in 2000, was elected to the newly created post of London mayor. Livingstone then began his acceptance speech with the words, 'As I was saying before I was so rudely interrupted fourteen years ago...'

Paul Hart's *Concerto for Guitar and Jazz Orchestra*, which John recorded with the National Youth Jazz Orchestra, was an extraordinary demonstration of his ability to play superbly in that setting. His parts, some of which sound like improvisations to which most jazz guitarists would happily aspire, are played as written, just as he would play the most classical of works. What he brings to them, however, in addition to his usual technical precision, is a fluidity and feel for the jazz idiom that is entirely convincing. Paul conducted his own work and the NYJO showed why they are so highly regarded. The nature of this band is that young musicians join, develop and move on so Bill Ashton's achievement in maintaining such consistently high standards is all the more remarkable. A number of musicians in the orchestra at the time of recording, such as Mark Nightingale and Dave Arch, have gone on to become among the most highly rated in the business.

John used some of the time he was granted by the unfortunate circumstance of the festival cancellation to write the score for a film to be made in Australia. *Emma's War* starred Miranda Otto in the title role, Lee Remick as her mother and also, in an early role, a young Sam Neill. It had echoes of John's own time in Australia, as it dealt with the time that the Japanese began to attack Sydney, although nobody in the movie filled their garage with canned food.

This was Williams's first film score and his inspiration for its theme sprang from an unlikely source. He was staying at the farm in Australia with Peter and Pat Hurford – Peter was playing some concerts with him there. As he did quite frequently, John chose to sleep on the veranda and was awoken one morning by the sound of birdsong. The tune he heard amazed him with its almost formal rhythm and shape. He called Peter from his bed to listen to the bird and the organist began to improvise on the tune at the piano. In the post that morning was the script for *Emma's War* with a request that John should write the music for the film. His immediate reaction was that it had been sent to him by mistake and the invitation was really meant for the other John Williams. He phoned to check and was reassured that it was for him. The producer outlined what was required: he wanted to reflect the countryside outside Sydney for which he imagined a quite intimate guitar piece to contrast with the period big band sound that characterised the city at that time. John immediately pictured the Blue Mountains and coupled it with the sound of the bird he had just heard. This was the origin of the main theme for the movie.

As he paid homage to Australia, so he did to his adopted home, London. The 1986 album *Echoes of London* is a curious mix of material, all of which is related to the city in some way. The first side is just guitar, all arranged by Williams, sometimes with him playing an extra overdubbed duet part. It began with 'Streets of London' by folk singer Ralph McTell, a good friend with whom John had played some benefit concerts including one for the Samaritans which was recorded as *Just Guitars*. Another contemporary piece was Alan Clare's 'Holland Park', but the rest were by Handel, Elgar and Byrd and would not have been out of place in the Wigmore or Cadogan Halls. The second side, with orchestral arrangements by SKY colleague Steve Gray, comfortable on his home territory, is a combination of easy listening standards and cabaret pieces with 'A Foggy Day in London Town' given a swinging jazzy treatment. Len did not get a vote on this but would probably have approved. The contrast of styles and techniques is an effective demonstration of the flexibility of the guitar and a re-affirmation of John's total disregard for artificial musical boundaries and ability to play whatever he wishes. Around this time he also played on one track of the *Hounds of Love* album by Kate Bush, one of the most original pop singers and composers around. Another unlikely act by Williams was to permit the creation and 'release' of *Le Grand Classique*, a concoction of tracks by John Williams and Friends, and solos by John. This curiosity was made by CBS for the French fashion house Guy Laroche, as a promotional tool for its perfume. John has always had a creed of never endorsing any products but this one somehow escaped.

John's experience with SKY stood him in good stead when he played one of the biggest arenas in Britain, a place more accustomed to trade shows and rock concerts. The National Exhibition Centre in Birmingham was celebrating its tenth anniversary and his contribution to the celebration was to join Simon Rattle and the City of Birmingham Symphony Orchestra for a live broadcast of the Rodrigo *Concierto de Aranjuez* from this vast venue – all very incongruous!

Daughter Kate had long since left her pop phase, brief as it was, behind and was now becoming quite an accomplished pianist. After leaving school, complete with an A level in music, she thought she would study history at university, but her exam grades would not get her into the institution of her choice. She opted instead to apply to the University of East Anglia (UEA), where her boyfriend was headed; she would study piano with composition as her second subject. When she got to UEA, Kate met Pete Whittaker, another keyboard player whose area was composition and electronic music, and boyfriend number one was no more. Kate and Pete got together and have remained so ever since.

John used to visit and the first time he heard his daughter play what she calls a 'serious performance' was when he came for the third year end-of-term concert to hear her play the Shostakovich second piano concerto with the University Orchestra. She was not a relaxed classical performer and found the performance aspect too restricting. Again, her father was the role model; she thought, 'He is so relaxed so why do I put myself through this?' Kate studied baroque and contemporary classical music but her heart was in jazz and she started playing in local pubs. Up until Len died in 1987, she had been a regular visitor to the monkey sanctuary and enjoyed being around the place. She never really registered the lack of convention there but always felt 'it was different somehow'. What Kate did not fail to notice was something she sees as a paradox and also quite an irony: 'Given the sanctuary was such an unconventional set-up, it's amazing that I never saw a man anywhere else being waited on by a woman like Len was.' Her grandfather, not especially tolerant of anybody, particularly disliked teenagers – 'Although he sat in a winged chair most of the time, he was the antithesis of an old guy giving out Werther's Originals.' She remembers when she first played for the old man: 'There was a large, open-plan kitchen with a big dark dresser like a divider across the centre. He sat one side of it, away from the cooking area – he had a TV and a fireplace and there were a couple of sofas so that people could come and talk to him.' Len was very ill by now and spent most of his time sitting there coughing and chain smoking. 'He would talk engrossingly about politics or human behaviour but if someone came into the kitchen to make some tea he'd get really angry and say "Bloody hell! What's that fucking racket?" He was very intolerant. He asked me what I was going to do with my life and, when I said I was going to play piano, he said, "Everyone here plays piano, that's no good".' She continues, 'I sat down and played a piece of Beethoven and he got really narked – "Why didn't you say you could play like that?"' He softened a little and told her she should play jazz, giving her a list of players he recommended and even got someone to copy some lead sheets for her. He also told her, 'Jazz people are far more interesting!'

When Pete stayed on to do his Masters degree, Kate stayed too, finding work teaching piano in a local school. There was a music scene of sorts in Norwich and she combined her part-time teaching with more and more jazz gigs, on the rare occasion with her on piano and Pete on Hammond organ. Another Williams was entering the music profession. Although Len was grouchy, his sense of humour was not far below the surface. John tells a story about that armchair: 'When you came into the room, Len's chair had its back to you and the first thing to catch your eye was a large poster of a human skeleton hung over the fireplace. Len used to say that he had put it there to make him look healthy by comparison; it somehow prepared you for the shock when you saw him, gaunt and drawn.'

June telephoned John in London in June 1987 to tell him that she thought Len's time was near. Father and son had become much closer over the past few years so he dropped everything and headed for Cornwall, where he found his father very weak and extremely thin but in quite good spirits. All the family were around. John was grateful to be with his father for that last weekend, even though the painkilling drugs he had been given meant that he was not completely coherent. The evening before he died, Len perked up and became quite chatty; he combed his hair to tidy himself up. As he and John talked, he put his hand on his son's and said, 'God bless you.' This was very moving for John, who recalled what his father had said on the subject when he was a child: 'Most people have a belief in God but who knows what that is? But whatever it is, it is good overall and in the end and if you take one "o" out of "good", you get God.' He told John that last evening, 'If I get to come back again, next time I shall have a different philosophy.' Only he knew if that remark was conciliatory or simply contrary.

With his family around him, Leonard Arthur Williams died on a Monday morning in July 1987, aged seventy-six;

he turned in his bed, gave one last sigh and was gone. His funeral was conducted at the sanctuary, a unique ceremony at which Sam's musician friend James played piano and sang 'Georgia on My Mind', Len's favourite song. John played 'La Ultima Cancion' by Barrios as the last tribute to his father. He was buried in the churchyard at Morval, just a couple of miles north of that special place where he had done work of great scientific importance and lived life entirely by his own lights. The family had never had much truck with religion so it was perhaps surprising that it was a priest who conducted the interment service. Len, too observant ever to miss such a detail, would have had a wry smile at the gaffe of the berobed clergyman, who, perhaps a little distracted by the presence of celebrity, solemnly intoned, 'We are here today to say farewell to our good friend Ted!'

John reflects on his father:

I really appreciated his dislike of intellectual dishonesty. His arguments were always very straightforward but he liked to win them. He was driven, ambitious, single-minded and had a bit of a chip on his shoulder about 'out there' – that is how he referred to the rest of the world. Stan Kupercyn, an old friend of the family, once told me that Len had confided in him that he had paranoid thoughts. But he had a great sense of humour, a natural manner and a very pleasant voice. He used all that and his charismatic personality to dominate people. He liked to be in control of small groups, friends and disciples, and he was entertaining and hospitable to eminent visitors to the sanctuary but he wasn't good when he was not on his own turf. He did not like to travel, he was even slightly frightened of travel.

John and Kate agree that Len's sister Marjorie embodies all the easiest bits of Len, in particular the humour, without the downside.

The sanctuary would never be the same. As Montsalvat had mutated with the passing of its master, so Murrayton; each was the creation of a single human spirit without which they were destined to bend to conformity and obliged to shed their unique but contrived character. Although Len had been quite frail and incapable of doing much physically in the last few years, his will was still the mainspring that sustained and defined the place. Negotiations to secure its future took place over the next eight years, during which time most of the focus was on achieving charitable status, an effort successfully led by the head keeper, Rachel Hevesi. She is now director of 'Wild Futures', the charity of which the sanctuary is the flagship project.

The original long-term 'extended family' fragmented without its patriarch and the participants in the project moved away when arrangements were finally agreed with them about the disposal of assets of the sanctuary. June Williams pursued other qualifications so she could begin a new life. Dan had already left to study and develop his skills as a craftsman, making musical instruments and bespoke furniture, and to travel. Sam has become an extremely successful record producer, songwriter and artist, perhaps most famous for his work with Supergrass, The Noisettes, Plan B and Kula Shaker. Both have good reason to thank their parents for the way they were raised but neither has felt compelled to carry on their father's mission.

The sanctuary thrives today in a form that Len would not

recognise but would probably applaud as it has gone full circle to become a refuge again rather as it was at the beginning. The breeding programme is no more, due to the small gene pool within the woolly monkey population at the sanctuary. Few woollys remain there, the majority of animals now being Capuchin monkeys that have been abused, neglected or simply become too much for their owners. Len would appreciate the work that is being done to help end the trade in primates, something he abhorred, and be delighted that the sanctuary is advising the government Department for Environment, Food and Rural Affairs on the matter. Some other important activities are funding overseas conservation projects and sharing best practice with other sanctuaries; Murrayton hosted fifteen for a conference in 2012. The sanctuary, which will celebrate its fiftieth anniversary in 2014, remains a great attraction, drawing around 30,000 visitors a year, and it has the active support of celebrities including Stephen Fry and Katie Melua. John Williams and John Etheridge played a benefit concert in London for Wild Futures in January 2012.

‡

John had a busy 1987, with events scattered across the globe. The first half of the year was taken up with a tour of the UK by John Williams and Friends and then, in a huge boost for Bill Ashton and the band, he set off around the country again with The National Youth Jazz Orchestra. Barely had his feet touched the ground when he was off to Canada to present the world premiere of the *Fourth* or *Toronto Concerto*, by the great Cuban composer and

guitarist Leo Brouwer, composed for Williams and commissioned by the Toronto Guitar Festival. His schedule did not
stop there. John and Paco were still much involved with
their Chilean friends, Inti Illimani, a band in political exile
from their homeland. The name translates as 'Sun God' in
Aymara, a language of the highlands of Chile (there is more
about the band in Chapter 14). They joined the Intis on stage
whenever possible; they played in London first, then around
the rest of the UK and finally at the Edinburgh Festival,
where they gave three performances. Up until this time they
had been contributing solos and the odd ensemble piece but
they now had a completely integrated programme. There
was a wonderful spirit within the extended band and it was
evident in every performance. Peña and Williams joined the
band on recordings in 1987's *Fragments of a Dream* and
Leyenda three years later.

It is difficult to believe that someone of John's standing had managed to evade the Henry Wood Promenade
Concerts until this point in his career, but although
he had been invited many times he delayed his appearance
until he had a work that would truly grace the event.
The Rodrigo Concierto was an obvious candidate but he
had been associated with it for so long that he thought it
would be 'naff' to play that after all the time that had passed.
After an enjoyable jaunt around the UK with the Friends,
the tireless Williams toured throughout the summer and
right into the Royal Albert Hall in August '88 with the
NYJO to play Paul Hart's *Concerto for Guitar and Jazz
Orchestra*. He was not, however, to escape the *Concierto de
Aranjuez* entirely that year as he joined one of his favourite

partners, the English Chamber Orchestra at London's Barbican Centre in December before setting off yet again for a summer season in Australia.

Kate was by now a gigging jazz pianist making quite a name for herself. And like his sister Kate, Charlie found that his genes would not let him go too far through life without being drawn to playing music and, by the time he was about seventeen, he started teaching himself to play guitar. He showed the same kind of natural talent for this as he had for the many sports in which he excelled. John started to teach his son odd pieces and was impressed at the way he observed and picked things up very quickly. Charlie plays well but does not take it too seriously.

Somehow John still found time for a social life and he met the delightful Dr Kathy Panama through mutual friends around 1990. Over twenty years later his friends are still rejoicing that he has finally found his soulmate. There is common consent among them that she has made the man complete. Kathy is a physician who had a general practice in south London at the time they met although her home was north of the river in Pimlico. The couple share a worldview, political inclinations, social sensibilities and the same kind of curious, inquiring intellect; crucially for both, they each have a sense of humour that was written on the same page.

They set up home together in a house in north-west London and Kathy gave up her practice to take a Masters degree in the History of Medicine. When that was completed, she flirted with a PhD in an esoteric aspect of medical illustration that combined her professional knowledge and artistic bent. She has since used her extensive and formidable skills to work as a craftsman ever since. The couple moved on after a few years, staying longer at the next house before moving on in 2001 to their current stylish but homely property, still in north-west London where Kathy has a studio, and they are well-placed to make the most of what London has to offer. Like John, Kathy was born abroad, the USA in her case, and like him, she came to England at a young age, when she was twelve. No longer an American national, she is content to be, in her own words, 'a happy cultural mongrel'. It is difficult to think of a more apt and succinct phrase to also describe John.

The rich musical partnership that was Inti Illimani, Paco Peña and John Williams made a tour of Europe at the beginning of the new decade, one venue being the stunning Philharmonie concert hall situated just across the square from the enormous gothic Cologne Cathedral. The concert was recorded and released as *Leyenda*. By March, John was Down Under and Australia featured even larger than usual for him in 1990. The Adelaide Festival of Arts, directed by Cliff Hocking, was an absolute treat for guitar lovers, featuring Joe Pass, Paco, Leo Kottke and Williams, each representing a very different facet of the instrument, each a master in his own field. Time pressures meant that rehearsals for ensemble playing could simply not be fitted in so the audience enjoyed what were really four short individual concerts at the Thebarton Town Hall. Something that made John's contribution special was that he performed *Stele* by Philip Houghton, the Melbourne-based composer and guitarist for whom he has enormous admiration and respect. John brought the enigmatic Houghton up from the audience to take his share of the credit for the performance. Clifford Hocking and David Vigo could always be relied on to set up suitable venues and they were behind a ten-date tour that Williams made with Paco and the Intis in September, taking in Sydney, Brisbane, Melbourne, Adelaide, Canberra, Newcastle, The Gold Coast and Perth; there was not a spare seat to be had at any of the venues. While John was in town, he took time to pay respects to the work being done by Australian guitar teachers, singling out Tim Kain and Jochen Schubert for particular praise.

The geographic tension between London and Australia that seems both to stretch and to inspire Williams was at the heart of his totally impractical ensemble with musicians hailing from and, crucially, still living in the two places. Although it was impossible to keep the band together for long, Attacca (see Chapter 10) was a project that he felt he simply had to do. It was a seven-piece chamber group that, sadly, is not preserved in any recording other than a single track on Nigel Westlake's album, *Onomatopoeia*. One member of the group, Tim Kain, went on to work with John as a duo, performing and recording *The Mantis and the Moon*, an interesting mix of music that shows off the skill of both men and their instinctive and sympathetic duet playing. Kain is one of the leading and most popular guitar teachers in Australia. He was the creator of Guitar Trek, a four-piece group based in Australia which, in addition to conventional guitars, also features treble, baritone and bass guitars.

Another mighty Aussie, Adrian Walter, has sometimes been described as the powerhouse of Australian guitar.

He certainly qualified for that epithet in the effort he put into securing sponsorship and support for one of his career triumphs, the Darwin International Guitar Festival. The first festival ran through June and July 1993 and, although barely justifying its 'international' billing through the contributions of the Hungarian composer and guitarist Stepan Rak and Britain's Julian Byzantine, the event was largely a celebration of the guitar in Australia. It featured compositions by Peter Sculthorpe and Philip Houghton, guitars and lectures by Greg Smallman and recitals by a host of home-grown guitarists including Walter himself, Timothy Kain, Peter Constant, Carolyn Kidd, Jason Waldron and long-time Londoner John Williams. The festival included a guitar competition with a strong focus on the interpretations of Australian compositions and a Smallman instrument as the top prize. Its value was declared at a mere $A8,000 and whoever won it surely gained a greatly appreciating asset. Walter was head of guitar in the Music Department of the Northern Territory University in Darwin at the time and his idea for the festival was inspired. Darwin is on the shores of the Timor Sea on the extreme north coast of Australia and although the festival was staged in the middle of winter, daytime temperatures there were around 30°C. Festival-goers recall how relaxed the event was, even by Australian standards! John, as always, was happy to be among his compatriot friends, Philip Houghton, Raffaele Agostino, Richard Charlton and Tim Kain and, as they will tell you, he is always just one of the crowd and only uncomfortable if he is being paraded or feted as 'a star'.

John later celebrated the music of his homeland by

releasing *From Australia*, with music by Peter Sculthorpe and Nigel Westlake. The two come from opposite sides of that vast country; the former from Tasmania, the latter, Perth, places further apart than London and Moscow. The evocative music on the album reflects some varying geography, too; 'Nourlangie' and 'From Kakadu' named for and inspired by the Northern Territory set against Westlake's *Antarctica Suite*. John had played the European premiere of 'Antarctica' at the Barbican with the American conductor Kent Nagano and the London Symphony Orchestra in 1992. His busy touring schedule meant that only two albums were made in 1992 but it was not just their rarity that made them special. With the Finnish conductor Esa-Pekka Salonen and the London Sinfonietta, Williams dedicated a whole CD to the music of the great Japanese composer Toru Takemitsu; John had given the first performance of one of these works, 'Vers l'arc-en-ciel' with the City of Birmingham Symphony Orchestra, conducted by Simon Rattle in 1984. Also featured on this recording are Sebastian Bell on alto flute and Gareth Hulse playing the beautifully-named oboe d'amore. The other recording that year was *Iberia*, a collection of pieces by Rodrigo, Llobet, Granados and Albéniz. This time the orchestra was the London Symphony under the baton of Paul Daniel.

The film *The Seville Concert* and the album of the same title were made in 1993. The concert was recorded in the stunning surroundings of the Royal Alcázar Palace and was a visual and audio tour de force. Neil Mundy was its producer and John's Aussie friend Nathan Waks, distinguished cellist and wine-maker, the sound producer. The film was issued on DVD and included the biographical film profile of John Williams that had been made for the prestigious ITV arts series, *The South Bank Show*, which the company strangely abandoned in 2010. Fortunately it was promptly picked up, along with its regular presenter, Melvyn Bragg, by Sky Arts Television. John was accompanied by the Orquestra Sinfónica de Sevilla conducted by José Buenagu. The programme includes both favourites and the odd surprise, such as Koshkin's 'Usher Waltz' and 'Sakura Variations' by Yuquijiro Yocoh and the album is widely considered to be one of John's greatest.

Apropos the film profile, which is very entertaining and informative, John said at the time it would be the only biographical document he would allow; there would be no more. Peter Sculthorpe gives a picture of the man he knows: 'He likes staying up late and getting up late in the mornings. He's relaxed, enjoys relaxing; he cherishes a small group of friends. He likes wearing old clothes, he has a rather insane, sort of democratic view of things.' John is driven around the farm that he still owned at the time by his cousin Paul and is seen playing in the beautiful practice room he built at the end of the house. He makes reference to Montsalvat, coyly referring to it only as an alternative community based around arts and music. Sculthorpe articulates the same thought as Rodney Friend, that the instrument becomes part of the man. There is footage of John visiting Greg Smallman in his old workshop and two men discussing guitar construction. It was the time of Attacca and John and Tim Kain are seen in rehearsal with Sculthorpe, who talks of the powerful influence of the Australian landscape on his music and John's sensitivity to this relationship. Cutting to London, John and

Sebastian Bell talk about Takamitsu and Williams focuses the listener on the importance of the decay of notes on a guitar. Barrios is mentioned, played and lauded. Segovia is shown in black and white, conversing with a youthful John who, back in real time, expresses his reservations about the Maestro's teaching style. The relationship between John and Paco Peña is introduced via Scarlatti and his use of Spanish guitar harmonies. The two play and relax just as they have so many, many times, the Spaniard helping with interpretations demanding the constant rhythm that is essential to dance in flamenco. The profile ends with John and Kathy entertaining friends at a dinner party at their home, Paco and Gerry Garcia among them. The film certainly catches something fundamental of John.

The fiftieth anniversary of the death of Agustín Barrios Mangoré called John and Kathy to Paraguay. John was presented with an award, Orden Andrés Bello en la Clase Banda de Honor, a distinguished decoration named for Andrés de Jesús María y José Bello López, a highly esteemed legislator and philosopher whose political and literary works form an important element of Spanish American culture. This was a fitting recognition as the music of Barrios appears, to many, to be a part of John's soul. His 1977 album was one which he held to be very important and he decided that after a seventeen-year interval he would make another recording devoted to the guitarist and composer whose work he had loved and enjoyed for so long. His appreciation of Mangoré had continued to grow over that time, recording techniques had improved and this release would be on CD. Always someone to plan and manage detail, he was determined to make this recording very special. The pieces he chose for the album overlapped substantially with *Barrios*, but others were added.

He decided to use Air Studios, now relocated to north-west London, and determined that Mike Stavrou would again be the engineer and co-producer for the record. Williams worked with great technical people over the years; his record company knew he expected the best and they delivered. Mike Ross-Trevor was, and remains one of the best in the business and he and John have an incredible back catalogue together. There was something about Stavrou and his almost obsessive approach, however, that had struck and impressed Williams in the same way as it had Sir George Martin. During the recording of *Travelling* in 1978, John had been impressed with Stavrou's 'genius' at getting right into the essence of the guitar sound he makes. Stavrou was not a classical specialist by any means but he had also engineered the highly classical 1988 *The Baroque Album*, recorded in Australia, his new place of residence, and had done an extraordinary job. Williams says: 'Stavrou brought the best from "pop" sound; pop producers often have a very real appreciation of sound that most classical producers do not possess and Stavrou had it in spades.'

Mike Stavrou is an American who began messing around with recording while he was still in short trousers. With his defining analytical approach, he went to studios in his native country to see whether the reality of being a sound engineer matched his expectations. Not totally convinced, he went to London, then the recording capital of the world, and after diligently learning his trade, landed a choice job with Air

Studios. A little history is appropriate: when George Martin decided to set up his own studios, he spared no expense in the facilities and equipment. As a result, his outfit became the one to work for and Stavrou counts himself very lucky to have been hired. In 1979, Sir George opened a studio on the Caribbean island of Montserrat and Stavrou fought hard to get a position there, impressing Martin with the meticulous way he went about his work in helping set up the new facility. When Stavrou wrote and published *Mixing With Your Mind*, an extraordinary and very personal treatise on recording, Sir George Martin wrote in the foreword of his appreciation of Mike's cerebral and experimental approach and added that he wishes the book had been available to him in the 'days of wax and shellac'. When John began rehearsing at home for the album, Stavrou asked if he could be in the room and just listen to the guitar. He walked slowly around the guitarist as he played, listening at different heights and angles to try to discern the best place to hear different frequencies, harmonics and other characteristics of the sound. The two men placed absolute trust in each other's abilities and it paid off – the album was a triumph.

A year before he was knighted, George Martin, with his son Giles as assistant producer, made what can best be described as a musical pot pourri with the Medici Quartet and guests John Williams, John Dankworth, Jack Brymer, Francis Monkman and Barbara Thompson. The tracks ranged from 'The Snowman Suite' through 'Eleanor Rigby' and 'Delilah' to a medley of traditional tunes and 'Les Barricades Mysterieuses'. The three tracks contributed by Williams are the only compositions on the album by

Martin himself and are entitled *Three American Sketches*. Unsurprisingly, given Martin's credentials, the record has excellent arrangements throughout and the Medici Quartet provided a solid base for the guests to excel.

In 1998 John was invited to perform on another album by Martin and son, another intriguing mix, this time not in the material but undeniably in the artists contributing. The album *In My Life* was a nostalgic collection of Beatles tunes played by 'friends and heroes' of the great man; Williams played 'Here Comes the Sun', the only George Harrison tune on the disc. He was in truly eclectic company: Billy Connolly, Jeff Beck, Sean Connery, Vanessa Mae and Bobby McFerrin among them. Martin's tribute to Williams in the sleeve notes reads:

> John Williams is not only a good friend but certainly one of my heroes. Without doubt he is the finest classical guitar player in the world and he is avidly interested in all forms of music, continually exploring new territories and techniques. Whether it is a great guitar concerto or a collaboration with a jazz master, delving into the avant-garde or playing a rock song, he is always at ease. And he seems capable of playing absolutely everything brilliantly.

Williams and Martin have the same grace and humility about them: someone who observed their behaviour at a party commented that they were the epitome of English gentlemen, each insisting that the other be first to go through a doorway in something akin to a parody of deferential manners.

John's colleagues Richard Harvey and Steve Gray both

wrote concertos for him and, fittingly, he recorded them for release together although they are dissimilar works. The two composers have very different influences and inclinations; Harvey began his musical career by forming Gryphon, a folk group with a predisposition to using crumhorns and the like. By contrast Steve Gray was from the jazz world and his scores have graced the music stands of Count Basie, Thad Jones and master of the valve trombone, Bob Brookmeyer. Harvey's *Concerto Antico for Guitar and Small Orchestra* was the core of the programme for a UK tour with the Bournemouth Sinfonietta before the release in 1996 of the combined works recorded with Paul Daniels and the LSO.

Williams toured Japan again in 1995, travelling on to Australia for the Darwin Festival specifically to play the premiere of Ross Edwards's *First Guitar Concerto*. John's aversion to travel was eased considerably by having his wife Kathy along for most of his long-haul trips and he was content to do a major round of Europe before setting off for recitals in Chicago and New York.

Although not in exactly the way that was planned, in 1997, John and Kathy went to China with Gerald Garcia and his partner and fellow guitarist, Alison Bendy. The original invitation from Chen Zhi, the most famous guitar teacher in the country, was to John Williams and Friends but this was deemed unrealistic for a number of reasons: the band was expensive to tour and there were misgivings as to whether the now-routine onstage tomfoolery would be appropriate for what was, to some extent, a kind of cultural mission. Having his invitation declined, Chen Zhi persisted, inviting John to come alone, but after careful consideration of all the implications of the trip, Williams decided to ask Gerald Garcia to join him. Gerald hailed from Hong Kong and had toured in China before, and John felt he would be the perfect travelling companion and could, of course, share playing duties.

The four went to Hong Kong first, immediately splitting up! Kathy and John stayed at the Peninsula Hotel in Kowloon, Alison with a friend and Gerald took the opportunity to catch up with his family. Garcia had arranged some concerts in Hong Kong that were to be performed after the visit to the mainland; there would be little if any payment in China and these would help cover the costs of the trip. Crossing to the mainland, they started in the south and toured the country. The travellers arrived in Beijing after a fourteen-hour train journey to be warmly received by a delighted Chen Zhi. There was a surprise in store for them. As they set out to take in the spectacular sights of the Great Wall of China, Richard Harvey popped up! He was at a bit of a loose end and just decided to come along.

In Beijing, the guitarists had a full programme of concerts and master classes; John even gave a talk on the amplification of guitars to an audience that soaked up everything on offer. It was then that the second of the great John Williams myths began its life. During this visit they were all impressed by the playing of Xuefei Yang, among others. Contrary to the myth, Williams did not give her his Smallman.

Gerald described the tour of China as, 'Sensational, some of the students were outstanding. Chen Zhi gets the best because there are so many to choose from.' During the trip the five met thousands of guitarists and Harvey avoided dozens of dishes that were served. He is a vegetarian and it seemed that almost everything on offer was cooked or served in a chicken broth. Whether it was because of that or not, he returned to England when the others headed back to Hong Kong for the concert obligations. While they were sitting around in the hotel bar one evening, John said how impressed he was with what Chen Zhi had started and was achieving. He mused for a while and eventually revealed his thoughts; he knew that despite all the good work in Beijing, there really was not even one top-quality guitar there, so he decided that he would leave his Smallman behind and send another one from London to Chen Zhi for the use of his best students at the Beijing Institute. Xuefei was one of a number of students to use the Smallman and now, as a gifted player with an established international career and reputation, she has one of her own.

On leaving China, John did not return to the UK but went south to Australia for the Melbourne Festival and to receive an Honorary Doctorate in the Faculty of Music from the university in his old hometown, something he regarded as a great and particularly personal honour. John always felt so at home in Australia but even there his comfort zone could be breached. On one occasion when he was in Darwin, he was invited to a reception hosted by a French dignitary in honour of his friend and regular promoter, Robert Vidal. Most of the guests were diplomats or business types but a few token musicians were invited along too. John does not enjoy this kind of event – he hates to be treated as a celebrity – and, after having been button-holed by a particularly obsequious guest, he resorted to pleading with Raffaele Agostino to rescue him: 'Come and talk to me, I can't stand this shit.'

There is a unique and delightful open-air performance venue just outside the city of Berlin and it was there at the Waldbühne that John joined Daniel Barenboim and the Berlin Philharmonic on 'Latin American Night'. The Waldbühne accommodates an audience of 22,000 and it was close to full that evening. In a programme of full-blooded music, Williams performed the *Concierto de Aranjuez* and 'La Ultima Cancion' by Barrios to a German crowd that showed its appreciation very enthusiastically. The concert was filmed and issued on DVD. For someone who had declared he was going to stop touring, John's globe-trotting was still quite extensive. Although it is a market he has never really sought to make his own, the USA has always welcomed Williams and, in October 1998, he began what has since been a fairly consistent touring schedule. He tends to play tours on the west and east coasts in alternating years, generally around the same time each year.

John's recording career went through a period of great activity and diversity, and it gives some indication of how broad the market for his work was at that time. He paid his respects to the Cuban composer by recording *The Black Decameron*, which was released before he launched himself into more extensive touring. The next album to hit the shops on which he featured was the soundtrack from *Great Expectations* and although he had made *John Williams Plays the Movies*, a collection which includes his sensitive and emotional arrangement of his namesake's theme from *Schindler's List*, this was his first contribution to a movie for nearly ten years, since the John Cleese comedy *A Fish Called Wanda*. John's own composition, 'The Aeolian Suite', was featured on *The Guitarist*, an album the title of which, with its definite article, reflected his standing. He chose to include works by Theodorakis and Erik Satie with Domeniconi's 'Koyunbaba' and all four sections of Houghton's *Stele*.

After completing the sessions for this CD, the end of an exhausting period spent in the confines of recording studios, John was off to Italy, where he famously played the Guiliani *Concerto in A Major Op. 30* on the early nineteenth-century guitar owned by Carlo Barone, the conductor and musicologist historian. Barone had invited Williams to play the piece, which he conducted, and the two had agreed that it merited the use of the small-bodied Guadagnini guitar. In December 1998 he played the piece with the Australian Chamber Orchestra (ACO), with his own transcription of Schubert's 'Arpeggione Sonata' in collaboration with the multi award-winning British composer and arranger Christopher Gunning. The arpeggione is a long-forgotten instrument that had six strings, frets and the same tuning as a modern guitar so it is not surprising that the transcription is so elegant. Both Barone and Adrian Walter encouraged Williams to record the Guiliani and they took the opportunity to do so at the ABC studio at Ultimo in Sydney, adding the Schubert to a disc that was released the following April, as usual on the Sony label. John was particularly happy to have done this work with the ACO and the orchestra came to Europe for his tour of Germany, Spain and England in May 1999. To the delight of many frustrated fans, at long last a recording of Richard Harvey's *Plague and the Moonflower* was released, ten years after its debut in Exeter. John is very proud of his involvement in the work, even though he was

but one of a number of soloists to feature on it (see Chapter
10). After some domestic festival appearances, he was
off to the Darwin Festival, stopping off in Sydney on the
way through.

Something happened during that break which is a superb
illustration of John's incredible memory. He was at dinner
in Chinatown with a number of friends including Greg
Smallman, Adrian Walter, Richard and Fiona Charlton and
Raff and Janet Agostino and, as was inevitable at such gatherings, the jokes started to flow. Richard Charlton delivered
what he thought was a gem but John said, 'Do you know,
Richard, you told us that same joke ten years ago at this very
restaurant?' Memories were searched and it was agreed that
they had indeed been at the restaurant at that time although
nobody else recalled the joke – except Richard, who admit-
ted he had been recycling it for years!

John played only solo recitals at Darwin and caught up
with many more of his Aussie friends there. Kevin Peek joined
him for some workshops and as usual, whenever there was
free time, all the guitarists hung out together – Tim Kain, Phil
Houghton, Richard Charlton, Raff and Janet Agostino. The
Agostinos have good reason to remember that festival as they
almost never made it home from the event. When they left
for Sydney, the plane they were on had a technical problem
and needed to return to Darwin but the landing gear was
stuck, possibly due to a tyre having burst on take-off. The
aircraft circled for two hours, using up and dumping fuel,
and finally came in for an emergency landing on its undercar-
riage. Raffaele says, 'There were fire trucks and ambulances
all around. We thought our number was up.'

The plane landed safely and the passengers went back to the terminal, where Raff and Janet bumped into John, whose own flight had just been called. As they waved him off he kept setting off the alarm at the security check; he had forgotten to return his hotel key. He gave it to Raff to put in a post-box and left for his flight. The passengers on the Sydney flight were all going to be stuck in Darwin for at least another day so they were given assigned hotel accommodation. Janet and Raffaele were driven to their nominated hotel but when they went to check in, the receptionist turned to select the key for their room, only to find it was missing. Raffaele reached into his pocket, where he still had John's key, and said, 'I think I might already have it!'

The two Johns, Williams and Etheridge,
getting their act together.

NINE

BEYOND THE MILLENNIUM

The first performance of the new millennium for John was a benefit concert with the English Chamber Orchestra at the Barbican. It was for victims of the earthquakes that had caused so much devastation in Turkey a few months earlier. Williams is a great favourite with the musicians of that orchestra and they welcome any opportunity to work with him but it was with a very different kind of ensemble that he set off around Europe. It was time for another tour with Paco and the Intis and they took in a total of seven cities during March. Soon after his return, he and Kathy were on their way to Cuba. He had visited before but never performed on the island and he was there at the invitation of Leo Brouwer to appear at the country's Tenth Guitar Festival, where he gave a recital including Brouwer's 'El Decameron Negro'.

The Williamses spent some time in Cuba and were moved by the friendliness of the people and impressed by the safety of the place, travelling around in a hire car to places like Trinidad and happily giving lifts to hitchhikers on the way. They had both followed events in the country's history over many years and they enjoyed long and interesting discussions with Leo about them. After the festival performance in Havana, John took the opportunity to play in two smaller towns – free concerts for the benefit of the locals. The first of these performances was in Matanzas, east along the coast from the capital, and the other in a hospital at Cienfuegos, where he played in a lecture room sometimes used to provided performances and entertainment for the staff during their working day.

Like Brouwer, Francis Bebey, who came from Cameroon, was also a great musical influence. He had lived for a long time in Paris, where John had visited him frequently over the past few years as the musicologist and musician encouraged Williams in his passion for the music of Africa. John decided it was time to do something with the music that he enjoyed so much so he rounded up old Friends Richard Harvey and Chris Laurence, then enlisted percussionist Paul Clarvis and star jazz guitarist John Etheridge to record *The Magic Box* in a number of sesssions split between Paris and London. Between this recording and its release, to the great delight of their friends and families, John and Kathy Panama were married on New Year's Eve, 2000. Due to her father being wheelchair-bound, the ceremony was held in his apartment in Los Angeles.

The Magic Box album was heavily promoted and well received, its rhythms and spirit infectious to audiences and listeners and the group, who adopted the name of the record, were soon on tour around the UK, then to Europe, Australia and New Zealand over the second half of the year. Such was the reception that the band was almost obliged to make further tours in Europe and the UK before playing the second of the 'John Williams' contributions to that year's

Proms, the first being John with the Australian Chamber Orchestra. Over two nights at the Royal Albert Hall, audiences were treated first to the evocative music of Australia and then to the loose, informal sounds of Africa. World music remained the theme when, after his now-routine October visit to America, John joined forces with Paco Peña and Inti Illimani for emotional concerts in Chile, the land from which the Intis had been exiled for so long. This was to be their last tour all together, as the Intis split into two; John Williams's loyalties remained with Horacio Salinas, the composer, arranger and musical director of the original group, now called Inti Illimani Historico.

The following year, John turned his focus to the musical heritage of Venezuela, having spent three years of research and preparation for what was about to unfold. The full story of how Caroni Editions made possible John's landmark recording *El Diablo Suelto* is in Chapter 12. Williams chose again to work with Michael Stavrou as his co-producer and engineer, feeling it essential to fly him in from Australia for the task, and again this partnership came up trumps. These two near-obsessives pushed every boundary to get the best solo guitar sound they could. Their relationship is reminiscent of John's with Greg Smallman, equally demonstrating a characteristic willingness to consider and embrace experiment and innovation.

El Diablo Suelto was being made at Air Studios, London and when John came in for the first session, the mikes were already set up, based on the engineer's assessment of the optimal positioning gained from his extensive critical appraisals during practice and rehearsal. One of them was placed at the end of a long boom in close proximity to the soundhole of the guitar and Williams assumed, quite reasonably, that this was the business part of the equation rather than the other that sat on a floor-based stand, some six or seven feet to his right at about the level of his knee. Stav had both mikes in position for the first day of recording and the session went well – John likes working at Air. He, John, George Black and assistant engineer Jake Jackson listened to the day's takes and were delighted with them. When John arrived at the studio the following morning, however, he was dismayed to find the boom mike gone, and only the floor-based one in position. As Stavrou arrived, an unhappy John said, 'The bloody cleaners must have moved the boom, Mike. We'll have to go through the whole set-up again.' His partner came clean: 'That boom mike was only there for show. It was me who moved it. We didn't use it at all yesterday but I wanted to be sure that I was right about the other one doing the job to everyone's satisfaction, not just mine!' John was amazed but not surprised, his faith in Stavrou's approach vindicated.

What Mike did was quite revolutionary but John also made an incredible mark on these sessions with what Stavrou refers to in his book as 'the missing skin'. When Mike and John were listening to some recordings of the day's work over coffee during the evening, the guitarist was quite sure that what they were listening to had been taken from a digital version rather than an analogue one, even though they had requested and thought they were hearing an analogue copy. When Stav asked how he could possibly know, John said, 'The sound of the skin is missing.' To explain: when he plucks a string, the flesh of his fingertip touches the string before the nail and for an extremely short time it imparts a virtually inaudible sound of its own. John was able to detect its absence. They went back to the studio and compared the digital and analogue masters. Sure enough, this time to Stav's amazement, Williams was proved right. It seems that limitations of digital technology meant that the skin sound got lost on that medium whereas it was retained on analogue tape. No wonder these two worked so well together.

To listen to Stav talk about 'the piece of air' that he is trying to secure and capture is a fascinating experience. Like John, Greg and, indeed, many of the greats in their fields, Stavrou is perfectly content to share his knowledge, philosophy and approach – in his case to sound engineering. Not content with being an exceptional sound engineer, he is also a 'close-up magician' who is good enough to be a member of the London Magic Circle and beyond that, has won awards for the design of a revolutionary mixing desk and water-saving devices for domestic use. The guitar sound on *El Diablo Suelto* has to be heard to be appreciated and is widely recognised as the quality benchmark for recorded classical guitar. John's other personal 'guitar sound' favourites are *The Baroque Album* and *The Great Paraguayan*, both engineered by Mike Stavrou.

At the time when Eric Sykes was about to celebrate his eightieth birthday, he was appearing in a production of *The Three Sisters* by Anton Chekhov. The cast presented him with a birthday cake during the interval and he was delighted that they had chosen to celebrate with him when all he had done in return was 'get older'. Little did he know that at the end of the performance, when the cast were taking their bows, they would invite the audience to sing 'Happy Birthday' to him, with John Williams appearing on stage to accompany them in honour of his great friend.

Val Doonican received his own tribute when celebrating sixty years in show business. It was not a surprise but it was something he prized greatly. A number of his friends appeared with him at a special show at the London Palladium for a showbiz charity. Val had always loved an arrangement of 'Beautiful Dreamer' that John had once played on his TV show as a duet with Doonican's regular guitarist, Max Brittain, and that is what they played that evening. Val says, 'It was just like a music box, a delicate little arrangement. Only John can play like that!'

‡

Williams had a Magic Box tour of the USA lined up for the autumn slot of 2003 but he cancelled as an expression of protest at the invasion of Iraq by the alliance headed by the American and UK governments. He felt that President George Bush and Prime Minister Tony Blair seemed determined to ignore the will of the people. It was one of the most unpopular and, arguably, undemocratic actions ever taken by a British government, provoking unprecedented demonstrations in London by well over a million people, Williams among them. John had also resigned his membership of the Labour Party that year for the same reason.

John's children continued to make their mark in their chosen fields: Kate as an award-winning jazz pianist whose first CD, *Scenes and Dreams*, was rated in the top ten jazz albums of 2005 by *Mojo* magazine, as was her 2011 *Made Up* recording with her new septet of Gareth Lockrane, Steve Fishwick, Ben Somers, Julian Siegel (a friend from UEA days), Jeremy Brown, Oli Hayhurst and Tristan Mailliot; the septet was nominated for a Parliamentary Jazz Award in 2012. Kate has made several more recordings which display her distinctive talent for composition, the latest of which is *Smoke and Mirrors*, on which she is partnered by the great British saxophonist Bobby Wellins, a long-time colleague of Stan Tracey, and the disc includes a number of co-compositions by the two musicians. Kate maintains her interest as an educator, and she teaches on the jazz degree course at Middlesex University.

By 2006, Charlie Williams was already beginning to demonstrate his abilities as a talented filmmaker. Having studied at the University of Edinburgh and La Universidad de Las Americas in Puebla, Mexico, he had an MA in Anthropology under his belt and he created a thoughtful and provocative film documentary, *The Guitar is Their Song*. Telling the story of the Mexican town of Paracho, where the economy is overwhelmingly based on guitar making, the work illustrates the way of life of the townspeople and reveals how it is threatened by savage competition from guitar factories in China and other countries in the Far East. Charlie cleverly sets this harsh reality against the gaiety of the town's 2006 Guitar Festival to emphasise how the traditions and identity of the community face an uncertain future. Many viewers must surely be hoping that he will revisit and review the situation of Paracho after a few years to satisfy the concern and curiosity he raised so effectively with his touching film. The work was released on DVD in 2008, since when Charlie has gone on to study at the New York Film Academy and continues to advance his career in the film industry as a director, cinematographer and editor.

The year 2004 was spent in Europe. John Williams joined Costas Cotsiolis in Athens to perform the premiere of his Leo Brouwer's *Double Concerto* with the Kamerata Athena, which the composer himself conducted in what proved to be the highlight of the Volos Guitar Festival. He also performed the Guiliani Concerto while in Greece and the whole of the programme was repeated in mid-July in Córdoba, Paco Peña's hometown. Staying for a while in the UK, he had the chance to join Greg Smallman speaking at the Dundee Guitar Festival about guitar design, a session that had its moments! Whenever Greg steps up to share his thoughts there are always luthiers who are prepared to travel many miles to argue and this event was no different. Even after the formal discussion he was pursued to the bar by guitar makers trying to convince him how misguided he was.

The other feature of John's attendance at the Scottish festival was to perform some of the African music of The Magic Box in a new, smaller set-up called WEB, an acronym of the surnames of the three musicians it comprised: Williams, Etheridge and Bebey (Francis's son, Patrick). Another festival appearance soon afterwards was at Bath, where he was a guest of the Venezuelan harpist Carlos Orozco, and the Venezuelan motif was also evident in John's solo tour of the UK that summer as he included much of the material from *El Diablo Suelto* in his set. More touring with

WEB ensued over the next few months and in November 2004, he had the great joy of working again with charango player Horacio Durán of Inti Illimani when they, together with Richard Harvey on flutes and pipes, played *Danzas Peregrinas* by Horacio Salinas. At the request of Williams, Salinas had built this work on some of his original pieces for Inti Illimani. The premiere of the piece was given with the London Symphony Orchestra at London's Barbican concert hall.

John Williams and John Etheridge have enjoyed a professional partnership for many years and it is one that perfectly illustrates Williams's oft-expressed view that there is a kind of brotherhood of the guitar that transcends different styles of playing. In 1999 he said, 'There's a kind of togetherness about guitar players; they always have a good time together ... They tend to feel a kind of bond across the music.' But if Bream and Williams were 'like chalk and cheese', it is difficult to find a simile with a span of difference that is ample enough for Williams and Etheridge. They have been equally eclectic within their own worlds but have different approaches to their instruments and to their music. When they play together they are most assuredly greater than the sum of their parts and produce some extraordinary music.

They continued the work begun with The Magic Box by going on to WEB and in 2006 came together again as 'John Williams and John Etheridge'. When they premiered their new programme ahead of recording it as *Places Between* live in Dublin, quite apart from the superb music they were making, they were responsible for a rather special phenomenon in the guitar world. Williams was playing his customary

Smallman with its revolutionary construction, and along-side him, sitting among his armoury of other guitars, Etheridge was playing a steel string acoustic that was also dramatically advancing the state of the art in design. His instrument was an Ergo Noir, hand-built by the American luthier, Charles Fox, a master craftsman with forty years' experience of making guitars and of teaching others how to make them. There were many special features in the design of the guitar but perhaps the most radical was the virtual absence of strutting to the soundboard, which was constructed as a sandwich of tonewood and the space-age material Nomex. It is pulled into playing position by the tension exerted by the strings. Etheridge's Ergo was the only one in Europe at the time and it was quite fitting that this incredibly innovative steel string should have its first outing on the same stage as a Smallman.

When the two Johns appeared on the BBC radio programme *In Tune*, its long-time host Sean Rafferty sparked a discussion about the Ergo by remarking on its luxurious appearance. John Williams commented that not only did it look good but 'it even sounds expensive'. In this he was paraphrasing Mike Stavrou, who, when assessing two slightly different sounds in the studio, would ask 'which sounds the most expensive?' During the tour of the USA, there was a lengthy interview by Bill Piburn, published in the American magazine *Fingerstyle Guitar*, with Williams and Etheridge that perfectly caught the kind of banter that characterises most of their conversation. The first comment from Piburn was, 'In watching you guys do your sound check today, I noticed you have a good time together.' This remark could have been made of any of the 'band' combinations in which John Williams has worked over the years.

The two Johns have played their double act in an enormous variety of places, from dyed-in-the-wool jazz venues such at London's Pizza Express Jazz Club to Carnegie Hall, to the Sydney Opera House. Williams's comment about guitarists being less bound by their playing genre than other instrumentalists seems to apply equally to their audiences, who can be captivated and moved by his solo 'La Ultima Cancion' and then wildly applaud a jazz standard such as 'Goodbye Pork Pie Hat' by his partner in crime before laughing out loud when Etheridge goes into a routine with his looper. This is a device that he has on stage that allows him to instantly record what he plays and then overdub that recording several times, building up quite complex layers of sound. What amuses his audience is that sometimes he will stop playing altogether and just conduct the sound coming from the little box at his feet!

Williams has another regular duo partner, Richard Harvey, and like the Williams/Etheridge pairing, they tour quite extensively and have great fun while doing it. They have made a DVD, *John Williams and Richard Harvey's World Tour*, recorded at World Expo 2005 in Aichi, Japan, and it captures faithfully the extraordinary range of musical delights they present at their concerts. A similar mutual respect characterises their performances and they generally leave the stage with one resting an arm affectionately on the shoulder of the other.

When John Williams travelled to the historic Ridderzaal in the Hague, Holland to receive the 2007 Edison Lifetime Achievement (Klassiek) Award, Etheridge was there with him. The event was broadcast by Dutch television and contained a huge surprise for the guitarist. Bringing him back to the stage, the presenter led him on by asking whether he had any musical children. John spoke warmly about his jazz pianist daughter Kate, who, he said, was back home in London. She was, in fact, just about to walk on stage to play a salute to her father's achievement. The look of surprise on John's face was truly a delight to behold.

In 2008 John recorded *From a Bird*, a CD for his own label that, apart from five short traditional Irish tunes, was made up entirely of his own compositions. Williams is unduly modest about his skill as a composer but this album includes not only some virtuoso pieces that show off his playing but also 'Hello Francis', his warm tribute to Francis Bebey, fittingly played in the characteristic rhythm of a 'makossa'. His technique remains, to use Brian Gascoigne's term, 'blistering'. He was influenced in some of his works by the birdsong in Australia that had inspired the theme for *Emma's War* and Kathy Panama used the image of a fantastic bird with a long, multi-coloured tail as the centrepiece of her design for the CD cover. As has been the case for so much of John's publicity and promotional material over the past decade, it is her photographs that adorn the cover. Jake Jackson, who has previously worked with Mike Stavrou on Williams's albums, recorded, mixed and edited the album.

The 2008 solo tour of the UK had an interesting programme that speaks of a journey through music: Vivaldi, Scarlatti, Granados, Albéniz, Williams (J. C.), Barrios, Morricone, Myers, Williams (J. T.), Sculthorpe and the Irish harpist O'Carolan. There can be few world-class musicians, regardless of their instrument, who would offer such a mix of material with confidence that few in their audience would fail to enjoy it all.

The Wigmore Hall Guitar Series 2010 was kicked off by John Williams on 13 October when his programme included Villa-Lobos, Brouwer, Bebey, Barrios and four of his own compositions. Reflecting the theme and patronage of the event, he chose to play exclusively Australian music for his performance at the 2011 City of London Festival. After the English Chamber Orchestra under Paul Watkins had played some very English Elgar, Peter Sculthorpe's 'Nourlangie' sounded extremely exotic and decidedly Antipodean. The superb concerto for guitar and string orchestra *Arafura Dances* by Ross Edwards was also unambiguously Australian and contrasted strongly with the Dvořák 'Serenade in E Major' that followed it. The High Commissioner for Australia was an honorary patron of the festival, which shed a distinctly Australasian mood across the city during its run.

Sadly, in July 2012, John and Kathy had to bid farewell to a friend of very long standing when the writer and comedian Eric Sykes died at the age of eighty-nine. John and Eric were always very close. It was a year when John had taken sabbatical leave from playing solo guitar but seemed to remain as busy as ever. He and Kathy were spending more time in their home in Cornwall, a place they both love but that will never entirely replace the capital in their affections – 'We will always keep a foothold in London, I can't imagine life without it,' says John.

In the spring, John did the odd gig with Richard Harvey

and he and John Etheridge continued to play around the UK. During a break between dates, when Williams was back in London, he had the chance to meet up with Sadie Bishop's son, George Washingmachine, who was in the UK for a successful tour of his own. John's schedule took in more performances with John Etheridge in Turkey and Poland, and he marked the fiftieth anniversary of the City of London Festival with a new and specially assembled John Williams and Friends to give the UK premiere of *Light on the Edge* by Philip Houghton. The City of London Festival, which featured John Williams in its inaugural year, 1962, and again fifty years later, could stand as a metaphor for Williams: immensely varied, it is mindful of tradition but always open to new ideas, international, durable and ever capable of the unexpected.

THREE

STRINGS
ATTACHED

The Magic Box: John Williams, Richard Harvey,
Paul Clarvis, Chris Laurence and John Etheridge.

TEN

THE BANDS

It is surprising how many people, fans and others, think of John Williams simply as a solo artist, carrying a mental picture of him either front and centre of a stage with just his guitar and footstool to keep him company or as the featured virtuoso performing with orchestras great and small. This is an appealing and romantic image and it is true that it accurately reflects a large part of John's career, certainly the part that his father might have hoped for and predicted. Any review of Williams's musical life must, however, take full account of the numerous collaborations with other musicians ranging from the determinedly classical end of the spectrum populated by the likes of Wilfred Brown, Peter Hurford, Rafael Puyana and Julian Bream to the other, less formal end that would include Cleo Laine, John Dankworth, Paco Peña, Joe Pass, Leo Kottke, Richard Harvey and John Etheridge. The orchestras and ensembles with which he has played also span the musical spectrum ranging from The Royal Philharmonic Orchestra to The National Youth Jazz Orchestra.

Then to be considered are the groups and the bands that Williams created and chose to play in as opposed to with: SKY, the varying and multiple incarnations of John Williams and Friends, WEB, Attacca. None of these was ever part of some early career roadmap that charted goals and ambitions. It would seem that the opposite is true: the cover of the very first issue of *Guitar* magazine in August 1972 features a grainy picture of the 31-year-old Williams beneath a banner headline of his quote, 'I'd be bloody awful with a group'. To be fair, the statement was taken from an unlikely conversation staged by the magazine between Williams and Andy Powell, one of the guitarists with rock band Wishbone Ash, and was in response to the fairly unfocused question 'Would you be interested in playing with a rock band?' posed by the magazine's facilitator. John goes on to cite his 'background and experience' as inhibiting factors and suggests that it would be pointless for him to do what others can do better and that he is far happier doing what he does well than being 'tenth rate at something else'.

SKY

John Williams (guitars), Herbie Flowers (bass and tuba), Kevin Peek (guitars), Francis Monkman (keyboards), Tristan Fry (drums, percussion, trumpet).

John's most controversial and solitary rock'n'roll venture followed less than seven years after his declaration to the *Guitar* staff writer. SKY was based upon and emerged from the comfortable nature of the relationships and mutual musical respect that existed between its founding members. From the time that Williams made his first non-classical album, *Changes*, with Stanley Myers in 1970, he began to work more and more frequently with some of the cream of Britain's session musicians. The studio roster for *Changes* is truly star-studded and included two players who would grace the recordings and performances of the first SKY lineup, namely percussionist Tristan Fry and Herbie Flowers, the noted bass player who features on the Myers album. Rick Wakeman, he of the long blond hair and the golden cloak in his role with YES, was also involved in the *Changes* sessions as keyboard player and would make an appearance in that role for SKY during a tour of Australia (although this was in 1985, long after Williams had quit the group). Francis Monkman was the original man at the keys and an important composer for the band, he too having worked on *Travelling* with Williams.

It is no surprise that John Williams should have formed his first band on the basis of friendships as much as part of some great musical plan. Some might suggest it flows from his being an only child, but whether or not that is a factor, John has always placed an enormous importance on friendship. He values and enjoys his friends and is a loyal and generous friend himself. In the event, after recording *Travelling* in 1978, he and Monkman thought that they might enjoy seeing what they could do as a band combining acoustic and electronic instruments, and they tried out the idea on Flowers and later Fry, both of whom embraced it. John decided that they needed a second guitarist so he contacted Kevin Peek, a fellow London-based Aussie working as a session guitarist and composer, who was also a very good classical guitarist. He and John had met at a benefit concert following the devastations of Darwin in 1974 by cyclone Tracy. Peek joined and the band was complete. They eventually came up with the name SKY after some inevitable false starts, including the far less rock'n'roll 'London Pride'. Another suggestion offered by Len Williams from his home in the monkey sanctuary in Cornwall was 'Andromeda'. Perhaps surprisingly, Len seemed to have no issue with his son's planned venture into a rock-style ensemble. The band was to be purely instrumental, run on its own terms and much fun was to be had in coming up with a repertoire.

The founder members of the groundbreaking SKY deserve some introduction. Tristan Fry is a classically trained timpanist and percussionist who worked with the Academy of St Martin in the Fields and the London Symphony Orchestra among other august institutions. He has banged and shaken an enormous variety of instruments on countless sessions and for innumerable bands. Tris played drums, percussion and, extremely occasionally, trumpet for SKY.

In the annals of pop music, the name Herbie Flowers must be inscribed in the section headed 'Legends'. After stumbling into a musical career during his national service in the army, where he learned to play the tuba, Herbie swiftly added double bass and bass guitar to his armoury. He is one of the most witty and personable people on the planet and there is no doubt that these attributes, combined with his musical invention and flexibility, helped make him the in-demand player he became. He had made his name in another band made up of session players, Blue Mink, which featured singers Madeleine Bell and Roger Cook. The band had a string of hits including 'Good Morning Freedom' and 'Melting Pot'. Herbie went on to the Diamond Dogs tour with David Bowie and then joined Marc Bolan in T-Rex. For some, Flowers achieved immortality by conceiving and playing the iconic bass line on Lou Reed's hit 'Walk on the Wild Side'; for others it was by composing 'Grandad', a schmaltzy novelty song that was a hit for comedy character actor, Clive Dunn.

Francis Monkman studied organ and harpsichord at school before going on to the Royal Academy of Music, where he concentrated on the latter and won a prestigious prize. While at the Academy, he also took up the electric guitar; he found he had an affinity for the instrument and became quite an expert player. But it was in his role as keyboard man that he formed the group Curved Air. This was a prog-rock band at the pop end of the scale, fronted by the striking and ethereal vocalist Sonja Kristina and featured Darryl Way on violin. Way and Monkman had previously been in a band with John Etheridge, one of John Williams's later sparring partners. With the help of the talented and experienced SKY sound team, he was the first to effect a mechanical coupling of a harpsichord to a synthesiser. He left SKY in 1980 after having a notable success with the film score for *The Long Good Friday*.

Guitarist Kevin Peek is a native of Adelaide, South Australia. He moved to England in 1965 and lived there until deciding to return to the Antipodes in 1982. Like Williams, Peek studied music from early childhood and became first a percussionist and later a guitarist with an impressive range of styles at his command. He has recorded with an incredible variety of popular and jazz artists, and a number of important orchestras. At the time when SKY was being put together, Kevin was a busy freelance session musician and relied on his wife to keep his diary and manage his bookings. She also dealt with enquiries relating to private guitar lessons and, when John Williams called, she didn't catch his name properly and thought it was someone interested in taking lessons. She made a note of his number, but when Kevin phoned back, he soon realised that the caller concerned certainly had no need of lessons from him. John invited Kevin to think about joining the new venture and told him who else would be involved in the band. Peek had worked with them all on various sessions and, after they all got together at John's house a few days later, signed up for a project that he remembers with enormous affection: 'Being on stage in the middle of a concert somewhere and looking around at the smiling faces of all the other guys in the band … we genuinely all had a great time up there. It was a wonderful feeling – brilliant musicians, mutual friendship and enjoyment, irreplaceable memories. I shall cherish them always.'

Another claim to fame for Kevin is that he was with John Williams in Sydney when Greg Smallman arrived at the hotel with two guitars that he had developed and refined in response to input from John. Greg had a good day – Williams bought one, Peek another. He rates it as the best classical guitar he has ever owned, 'An incredible instrument.' Sadly, Kevin Peek has made the headlines throughout the past two decades for reasons other than music, having been involved in a number of financial scandals back in Australia.

John Williams wanted the SKY venture to be parallel and separate to the other work he intended to continue in the classical world so he chose not to invite his agent, Harold Holt Ltd, to manage the band. He knew that the type of management required was totally alien to the classical world. At first this infuriated his personal manager, Martin Campbell-White, but after he had calmed down he came to recognise that John had probably done him a favour. He was not used to the world of rock bands and had never felt any inclination to enter it. It's an experience he continues to deny himself. It fell to Herbie Flowers to help out on the management front and he got in touch with Peter Lyster-Todd, whose wife Isabel was a 'fixer' who had booked the bass-player many times. Lyster-Todd was mainly involved in managing the affairs of a number of high-profile photographers, a business in which he had been in partnership with David (now Lord) Puttnam, who had by then steered his own career into the world of movies. Peter admits that he may have been less inclined to sign up to the venture had it not been for John Williams, who he knew was a major factor in making the band marketable. Inevitably Lyster-Todd and Campbell-White had dealings over the years and they went on to become friends.

All of the members of the soon-to-be band had other commitments to fulfil and they each continued with work alongside SKY throughout its existence. When the idea of the band was gelling they started writing and getting other material together but had to wait for John to return from the US, where he had been touring with Julian Bream, before they could get recordings together for Lyster-Todd to pitch to the all-powerful A & R (artists and repertoire) men of various record companies. They recorded a demo of the tune 'Westway' by Flowers and Monkman at the London CBS studio and began what turned out to be the surprisingly difficult task of getting a recording deal. It could be that the record companies were unsure as to what category they could position and market the band. On the basis of the limited demo recordings available to them, the best fit was probably 'progressive rock' and, regardless of the incredibly high standing in the music world of all the band members, there seemed to be a feeling in the business that the market for what was considered to be prog-rock was saturated and perhaps waning. Emerson, Lake and Palmer, YES, Genesis, Soft Machine, Gentle Giant, Mike Oldfield and many other acts in the genre were still alive and kicking and it was quite a shock to the band that they were turned down by company after company before Ariola, a relatively unknown German label, took them on almost exclusively because of its faith in the magic of John's name. The band was resolutely democratic, however, and with Williams's full support, Lyster-Todd was able to insist that his name could not be used in isolation. The band's first album illustrates this well, having the names of all five members emblazoned across the top of the cover.

Kevin Peek is certain that a band like SKY would never have got off the ground without a big name fronting it. He says: 'We were an already-ageing group of guys doing strange things with classical and quasi-classical musical arrangements and compositions, and not a vocal in sight.' But it happened and the next step was to put a disc together.

The friends laid down a number of their own compositions and transcriptions of classical pieces at Abbey Road Studios at the tail end of 1978.

The eponymous album *SKY* was released in May 1979, along with a single that had Monkman's 'Cannonball' as the 'A' side, backed by the percussion-fest that was 'Tristan's Magic Garden', a track that was not even on the album although it was to be included on *SKY 2*. The single bombed but the album sales soared, no doubt propelled by the record company's unremitting exploitation of John Williams's name and fan base. The company also tapped into the substantial existing audiences for Herbie in the pop world and Francis in progressive rock circles. Another extremely valuable catalyst for sales was John's unrelated solo success with 'Cavatina', which topped the charts just a month after the *SKY* album was launched. The record quickly sold in great numbers, probably to a very catholic audience, and went on to reach platinum status.

Ariola's gamble had paid off beyond the company's wildest dreams and SKY was now firmly on the map, as was Ariola itself. The recordings quickly established a musical identity for the group outside of any existing genre and any fears about the viability of a purely instrumental outfit playing classics soon evaporated. Star impresario Mel Bush, who remained the band's UK promoter throughout its existence, set up the band's first English tour to coincide with the release of the record and, after a series of provincial dates, this climaxed with a sell-out concert at London's Royal Albert Hall.

The record sales and clamorous audiences were not matched by critical acclaim, however. This may have been partly because of the expectations raised by the reputations and musical history of the band's stellar members, most notably, of course, its most bankable member, John Williams. But it was primarily because no one on the receiving end of the SKY output really knew what to expect. Advertising and promotion had been largely aimed at existing fans of John Williams, a broad church indeed. It was a conglomerate of devoted admirers of his sublime classical works, watchers of prime-time television who has seen the gifted guitarist often playing straight man to Eric Sykes and later on Les Dawson and duetting with the ever-popular family favourite Val Doonican, plus a new group of followers who had recently been introduced to John through the soundtrack of *The Deer Hunter*, a multi Oscar-winning movie. Little wonder that the reviewers did not know whose voice they were representing. The critics, who were used to pronouncing on prog-rock bands, probably didn't take the band seriously to begin with, while the more po-faced Williams's watchers in the classical community declared themselves appalled by this travesty of both the music and the talent of the players concerned. It was a reprise of the furore that Bob Dylan had faced in 1965 when he first went on stage with an electric guitar, outraging his established and avowedly acoustically minded followers.

Convinced that John had sold out and was in it just for the money, Len Williams's old colleague Jack Duarte puffed himself up to ask in his review in *The Gramophone*, an unlikely place for the album to have been reviewed in any event: 'What does an artist, whose performances of the guitar classics set a standard others strive for, find in music as inconsequential as this? Perhaps the album's achievement of a high position in the LP charts makes the question irrelevant.' Coming, as it did, from a bastion of the conservative and introspective classical guitar establishment, it is this pompous example of criticism of John in the context of SKY that is most frequently cited to illustrate the critical reaction but there were many more in similar vein and the letters pages of guitar magazines and journals were hysterical with concern about John's wayward direction and 'the loss to the guitar' that was being felt. This was patent nonsense, of course, because John actually performed and recorded the classical repertoire more during the SKY years than at any other time.

Len Williams was in quite poor health and never saw SKY perform live. He probably heard very few recordings, even, because he was not one to listen to records at that time of his life. The band performed alongside fellow guests Patti Boulaye and Alan Price on *The Val Doonican Show* and, in a perfect example of the spirit of the show, Herbie and Val played a tuba duet. Len certainly saw that programme and no grumblings of disapproval came out of Cornwall. Overall he seemed to quite like the band but was pretty selective about the offerings that he was prepared to applaud. And he particularly liked the Bach 'Toccata'.

The SKY didn't fall as a consequence of misguided and self-righteous criticism and the band went back on a tour of England and Scotland in September, playing twenty-six dates, the last five of which were to packed houses at the London Dominion Theatre. The band took stock at the end of the 1979 and put out a new double album with the imaginative name of *SKY 2*; for a rock or fusion album it contained a lot of classical material, including Monkman playing Rameau on harpsichord and Williams and Peek playing Praetorius duets. John is immensely proud of that album.

Far from being bloody awful in a group, Williams appeared comfortable and at home. He did not want to be 'the leader of the group' and took great pains to dispel any such notion. The programme for the *SKY 3* tour included this banner statement: 'There are no stars in the group. There is no leader. Our music represents all the things we do individually' – and this really was the SKY manifesto. The ethos of equality extended to earnings, particularly income from publishing and 'mechanical' rights; the composer(s) received the lion's share of royalties but everyone in the band got something in recognition for their contribution. Lyster-Todd must take some credit for that as for another innovation of paying the core technical crew a monthly retainer; this ensured continuity for the band and some security for the techs.

John loved the company and camaraderie of being with engaging, seasoned and gifted musicians, who were great fun but on whom he could rely absolutely when performance time came around. He sometimes got to play electric guitar and it was evident that he enjoyed sharing his platform. This was the closest Williams had been to a full-blown rock tour and he relished and rose to all the challenges and demands it imposed on him. At the infrastructure end, he soon got used to venues that were new to him, to huge PA systems, massive lighting rigs, dry ice and explosions, and at the more personal end, he accepted that he simply had to use guitars like the nylon-string Ovation because it had a pickup system. Although perfectly adequate to do the job in the maelstrom of noise of a SKY stage performance, it was a guitar that he would certainly never have used for a classical recital as a substitute for a Fleta or a Smallman.

A DVD of the band's performance in 1980 on the German television programme *Musikladen* shows Williams appearing to make other concessions or gestures towards looking more like a rock star, albeit a seated one. Seated beneath a revolving glitterball, his footstool is beneath his right foot and the Ovation perched on his right thigh rather than the 'classical' posture, something that must have made a lot of conservative guitarists very twitchy. John makes clear that this was a purely practical adjustment; he needed to be able to communicate with his colleagues by looking around and nodding or making some other sign. This would have been impossible with the classical stance applied to holding his guitar with the left leg and foot tied to a footstool.

Despite the band having been around long enough by the time of the concert for members of the audience to know what to expect of the evening's entertainment, the DVD reveals a significant proportion of them determinedly avoiding expressing any form of appreciation. Defiantly crossed arms and stern expressions convey distaste, disapproval and probably disillusionment. It would be nice to think there were at least some among their number who were worried about the welfare of John's fingernails when he took up his solid body Gibson RD Artist with its abrasive steel strings. The appearance of the individual musicians varied, with John's stage look probably the median in terms of style – longish hair showing the first signs of greying, blue jeans. At the rockier end were Monkman and Peek, Francis prowling his array of keyboards looking every bit as if he had just stepped off-stage at a Curved Air gig, with the Aussie guitarist centre-stage with John, cool in a waistcoat and fashionably moustachioed. Tristan Fry sits above them all on a drum-riser with the air of a slightly out-of-place but highly enthusiastic ex-public school boy who would easily have won a Roy Orbison look-alike contest, if only had there been one. And then there is Herbie in his blue jumper with the red banding; he embodied the persona of the game and youthful sixth-form music teacher, sitting in and bringing his effortless experience to help out.

SKY 2 was a double album that continued the sales success of SKY and became the tenth best-selling album of 1980 in Britain. It is probably best remembered for the highly customised electric version of Bach's 'Toccata and Fugue in D Minor' that, in its subsequent release as a single simply called 'Toccata', peaked at No. 5 in the *Melody Maker* chart. This dizzying achievement brought the band the distinction of an appearance on BBC TV's *Top of the Pops*, an event that must have had the more conservative John Williams fans around the country reaching for their smelling salts. Had they been brave enough to buy the album, they would have heard some completely unsullied and probably familiar pieces of chamber music. True, they would also have had to endure Herbie Flowers's 'Tuba Smarties' and Francis Monkman's three-movement rock suite 'FIFO'.

More tours followed on the back of the album including one in Australia, promoted by Paul Dainty and helped along by Clifford Hocking, one of Len's old crowd in Melbourne days and a long-time friend and supporter of his son. Peter Lyster-Todd had reason to be grateful to Hocking as it was his reassurances that made the tour happen. The band had sold only a small number of records in Australia ahead of their visit and the costs and logistics were quite a risk, but with the help of Hocking and Dainty, it was a great success and record sales rose to a very respectable level.

Francis Monkman chose to leave the band soon after the Australian tour. His place was taken by Steve Gray, a pianist, composer and arranger who had a strong grounding in jazz, having worked with luminaries in that field including Quincy Jones and Lalo Schifrin. Gray was on board in time for the first European tour and in February 1981 he took his place alongside his bandmates at Westminster Abbey for the first rock concert ever to grace that magnificent venue. The concert was to benefit the humanitarian charity Amnesty International and came about as a result of John's performance at The Secret Policeman's Ball two years earlier, when he played an unlikely and memorable duet with Pete Townshend of The Who's 'Won't Get Fooled Again'. Williams had been involved in numerous other shows in aid of Amnesty that preceded the Ball and producer Martin Lewis had come up with the idea of SKY doing something special in their own right to mark the charity's twentieth anniversary in 1981. Quite apart from the enormous benefits for the coffers of Amnesty, the sole motive behind the event, the band received much positive media coverage.

The Westminster Abbey Concert was recorded by the BBC, to be subsequently released on video and it was also shown later on television. The concert provided a great launch pad for *SKY 3*, the only classical content of which was 'Sarabande' by Handel, and the band set off around Europe, the UK and Australia to promote it. *SKY 4 Forthcoming* followed, with far more representation from the likes of Bach, Ravel, Berlioz and Katchaturian as well as more modern works from Theodorakis and Villa-Lobos. After the completion of more tours to Europe and Australia, and for the first time, Japan, came *SKY 5 Live* with a release date in January 1983. *SKY 4* might have been the beginning of the end of SKY as far as John Williams's continued participation was concerned. He thought that the arrangement of Wagner's 'Ride of the Valkyries' was embarrassingly awful. He now admits that he agreed to its inclusion as it massacres Wagner, a composer he does not like. He says: 'That piece is so overblown it was OK to send it up, even if it was done badly.'

Herbie was and will always be, first and foremost, an entertainer who John has always liked and admired. He used to open the second set with his solo piece 'Tuba Smarties', something that the more serious Francis tended to look down upon but that most audiences loved. Flowers would be dressed as Noddy and sit by a giant teapot with a dry-ice haze across the stage. At one gig, the crew decided it would be a wheeze to hide Herbie's trousers so that when he finished his solo and came off-stage to make the necessary quick change, he would have nothing to wear. Being Herbie, he quickly gathered what had happened and returned to the stage to join his bandmates. As the dry-ice cloud dispersed he was revealed in his underpants, wandering round the stage, looking for his stage kit. In December 1983 the band released *Cadmium*, having finally thought of an original name for an album. John finally left, disillusioned with the material it contained, and he later mused on the unfortunate use of the name of a poisonous metal for its title.

He had never planned that SKY should be a permanent part of his life and, by February 1984, Williams reached the conclusion that the band was becoming something he had not anticipated or, indeed, planned. The quality of the album *Cadmium* had fallen short of his wishes, sounding 'like a cross between MOR and jingles'. Back in 1979 he had told journalist Chris Dunkley in an interview for the *Sunday Telegraph* magazine that he was sure that for 'at least four or five years' SKY would be the most important part of his musical life. That time-span proved to be prophetic. He had become disenchanted with the band and he implied that SKY had entered the realms of self-parody. It was time for him to move on and that is what he did. His departure did not result in an immediate end for SKY, but the band would never be the same without him, either as a draw for audiences or as a fully paid-up member of what had been a brave musical co-operative and adventure.

In 1984 the band set off for an Australian tour as a quartet, to be joined by various guests along the way. The first of these was Rick Wakeman. In the middle of that year, another UK tour unfolded with other guests and this coincided with the release of a compilation album by Telstar Records. It was back to Australia in September, to Kevin Peek's studio, to record album number seven, entitled *The Great Balloon Race*, on the Epic label, Ariola having decided that SKY sans Williams was not worth retaining. The disc received favourable critical acclaim but fans proved fickle and sales were poor.

There was a landmark event for the band and especially for Tristan Fry when, on 1 November 1987, SKY and The Academy of St Martin in the Fields collaborated in a performance at the Royal Albert Hall with a programme appropriately heavy in content, given that it was the bicentenary of his death, with the work of a certain Wolfgang Amadeus Mozart in arrangements by Steve Gray. An album called *Mozart* was forthcoming, falling between the two stools of the classical and popular worlds in the UK although it became the band's biggest seller in the USA. Things went quiet for some time until the release of another compilation album, *Classic SKY*, the first to be exclusively available on CD, and brought the band together for a few performances to promote it. At this point Kevin Peek decided that commuting from Australia was becoming too onerous and he too left.

SKY had stood alone, it was unique. Most forms of entertainment that become popular or successful generally inspire imitators hoping to cash in but there was never to be anything remotely like SKY.

JOHN WILLIAMS AND FRIENDS

There have been numerous iterations of John Williams and Friends from 1973 right through to the present day. In forming them, John always started from a solid baseline of friendship and musicianship. The concept has proved very flexible but the standard of musicianship has never been compromised, although it has sometimes been threatened by the eccentric and unpredictable behaviour of some 'friends'. The Friends that most people will recognise by the name was very much a touring band and, as happens with many such outfits, familiarity with the programme grows steadily, imposing fewer demands of concentration and application as the tour proceeds. This is a dangerous development as it leaves capacity for mischief. Gerald Garcia's revolving bow tie would qualify – but rank among the tamer examples. The extreme stuff came from Brian Gulland, an old bandmate of Harvey's in Gryphon. He began by coming on stage with no shoes and a rainbow-coloured Afro wig. He progressed to wearing a toque or chef's hat until this became too common-place to cause even a raised eyebrow among his bandmates. Upping his game, he decided to pursue the theme and, as John and Gerald began a guitar duet, Gulland wandered on in a full chef's outfit bearing a camping stove, which he set up directly between the two guitarists and their audience. The duo played on gamely as the chef lit the stove and placed a frying pan on it. He reached into his pocket, took out two eggs and made an omelette, which he offered to the two players.

John Williams always insisted that all the Friends, including himself, received an equal share of what the band was paid, even to the extent that although Mauricio Venegas and Claudia Figueroa played on only two pieces at the South Bank Festival, they too benefited from this generous arrangement.

JOHN WILLIAMS AND FRIENDS
(AS AT THE RECORDING IN 1976)

John Williams (guitar), Carlos Bonnell (guitar), Brian Gascoigne (marimbas and vibraphone), Morris Pert (marimbas and vibraphone), Keith Marjoram (bass)

The CBS recording *John Williams and Friends* was produced by Paul Myers and engineered by Mike Ross-Trevor, both long-term contributors to John's career. The content would have been unremarkable but for Brian Gascoigne's arrangements and the unusual instrumentation that made this something new and special.

JOHN WILLIAMS AND FRIENDS (MOST DURABLE LINE-UP, INCLUDING THE SOUTH BANK FESTIVAL, 1984)

John Williams (guitar), Gerald Garcia (guitar), Brian Gascoigne (musical director and tuned percussion), Chris Laurence (bass), Gary Kettel (percussion), Richard Harvey (flute, recorder, crumhorn, tin whistle), Brian Gulland (bassoon, crumhorn, tin whistle), Claudia Figueroa (guitar), Mauricio Venegas (charango, quena, pan pipes), Richard Studt (violin), Hisako Tokue (violin), Stephen Tees (viola), John Heley (cello)

This is the extended 'Friends' line-up of the 1980s, most of whom were involved in the many tours of the UK and Ireland and, memorably, Italy.

JOHN WILLIAMS AND FRIENDS
(ONE-OFF LINE-UP, 2012)

John Williams (guitar), Craig Ogden (guitar), Tristan Fry

(percussion), Peter Didg (didgeridoo), Max Baillie (violin),
Lucy Wakeford (harp), Tim Gibbs (bass), Kelly Lovelady
(conductor)

It is something of a stretch for this line-up to justify the name since it is simply a convenient label for a combination that has never played together before and is unlikely to do so again. The occasion for which it was assembled was the fiftieth City of London Festival. This unique annual event is a musical extravaganza that takes place in numerous venues around the capital, many of which are not generally accessible to the public. John and his friends played at the ornate and historic Fishmongers' Hall, one of the greatest of the remaining Guildhalls in the city. Aussie Williams is happy to declare that he is first and foremost a Londoner and this appearance in his adopted city was special because he also performed at the very first City of London Festival in 1962. He was reunited with his SKY colleague Tristan Fry and had two fellow Australians along, Kelly Lovelady and Craig Ogden, both now based in England and on didgeridoo, Peter Didg, who contributed to the UK premiere of *Light on the Edge* by Sydney's Philip Houghton, a gifted composer and guitarist and old friend of JW.

In addition to more established pieces by J. S. Bach and Guiliani, the programme also featured the world premiere of a piece commissioned by John Williams for this event. Taking its title, *The Flower of Cities*, from William Dunbar's poetic tribute to England's capital, 'London, thou art the flower of cities all', the piece was written by the English composer and guitarist, Steve Goss. There was something especially romantic about new musical works being performed in the

Grade 1 listed home of a mediaeval Guild with a 700-year history. The juxtaposition of great tradition and a brand new commission reflected perfectly the approach that John Williams has taken throughout his career – respect for the established canon combined with a determination to avoid stagnation by continuing to push every boundary and add to the guitar repertoire.

ATTACCA

John Williams (guitar), Tim Kain (guitar), Michael Askill (percussion), Rita Manning (violin), Chris Laurence (bass), Nigel Westlake (clarinets and saxes), Paul Hart (piano, synthesisers, violin, viola)

If the method of creating the group is the criterion, Attacca was just another iteration of John Williams and Friends, but this time with the distinction of an original name although it had been used before. 'Attacca' is a musical term meaning 'to follow on immediately' and Gerald Garcia had once had an ensemble of that name that was now defunct. John liked the term and Gerald had no objection to it being used again, so Attacca it was. What distinguished this group from other versions of John Williams and Friends was that the friends in this case were drawn from either side of the world. Three British players, three from Australia and, uniting their origins and masterminding the group, Williams himself.

John started with a sense of what instrumentation would best suit the music he had in mind; he liked the idea of two guitars, knew that percussion worked well with them and that a bass adds enormous depth. He steered away from cello or viola because he felt that they competed in terms of texture and colour with the guitars over which they had more sustain, and opted for violin. Clarinet was an ideal complement and Paul Hart's jazz sensibilities were just what was required so keyboards were added.

The idea to form the band seems to have surprised nearly all concerned. By way of example, Tim Kain, a superb guitarist and professor of guitar at Canberra conservatory, first heard about it when he received a late-night phone call at home in Australia from John Williams in London. Tim was already settled in bed when the call came through at 11 p.m. He was in two minds whether to let it ring and go to answering machine but something called him from the warmth of his bed. John always introduces himself in the same way on the phone. In a very upbeat tone of voice he would have said, 'Hi Tim, it's John Williams', with an uplift on the 'Williams' and it is easy to imagine that Tim was immediately pleased to receive the call since the two were old friends. Even though he was in his pyjamas, he could not have dreamt what was coming next: 'How do you fancy joining a group I'm putting together? Think about it.' Tim picked himself up from the floor and mumbled that he certainly would think about it and that was really that. He went back to bed, where his wife, Chris, was already asleep. Shaking his head, he thought he must have been dreaming. The other musicians concerned would each have received similar calls, though perhaps at more sociable hours.

The band toured for the first time in May and June of 1992, playing eleven dates around the UK, with the last on 13 June at London's Barbican. Attacca toured Australia, playing the Sydney Opera House and Melbourne Concert

Hall. The group's programme included Sculthorpe's 'Tropic', pieces by Nigel Westlake, Paul Hart, Michael Askill and Brouwer's 'Micropiezas' for the two guitarists. That the group was made up of musicians drawn from opposite ends of the globe, all heavily engaged in other projects, suggests that Attacca was never intended or likely to last and so it was. Apart from the tours mentioned above, there were invitations for the band to give odd performances but they never amounted to the prospect of viable tours. This factor combined with other obligations on the sought-after musicians and the cost and time involved in getting together to rehearse before concerts imposed barriers that were simply too difficult to overcome. The same issues prevented the group ever getting together in a studio; even had they done so they could not have supported the tour necessary to promote an album, something that Williams greatly regrets. There were sadly no recordings released so the sound of this intriguing and inspired assembly of fine musicians lives on only in the memories of the few audiences privileged to have seen them play. Few people would have had John's vision or determination to bring together the players and friends that he thought would make Attacca work so successfully but their bases on Antipodean extremes were always going to impose limits. John Williams and Tim Kain, who had a great relationship musically and personally, got together again as a duo, touring and then making an album in 1995. *The Mantis and the Moon* was an eclectic and international mix of music that showed off both guitarists to great effect and celebrated a special partnership. The last track on the album – 'Guitars' by Dmitri Shostakovich – is a real surprise.

THE MAGIC BOX

John Williams (guitar), John Etheridge (guitars) Paul Clarvis (percussion), Richard Harvey (sanza, flutes, pipes, clarinets, percussion), Chris Laurence (bass) – guest Francis Bebey (sanza and vocals)

A great favourite among audiences at concerts over recent years has been John Williams's composition to honour the memory of Francis Bebey, his great friend and inspiration, who died on 28 May 2001. 'Hello Francis' beautifully evokes the musicality and joie de vivre of the Cameroonian ethnomusicologist through a combination of the affection that shines through every performance and the use of the makossa rhythm, something in which Bebey excelled. On his website, John reveals that it quotes from Bebey's own piece 'The Magic Box' and includes 'a hidden bit from J. S. Bach'.

Had it not been for John's friendship with Bebey, it may have been some time before he began to record and perform the music of Africa. The idea had been suggested to him in 1997 by a producer at Sony who saw a ready market for a crossover record and realised it could easily be produced by calling in some increasingly well-known African musicians to work with the guitarist. John dismissed the suggestion because he had no inclination to do such a crossover for its own sake. Just because he had already played music from most parts of the world he felt no particular need to 'complete the set' even though he was knowledgeable and enthusiastic about African music. Williams had met Francis Bebey (birth name, Francisco Birago Diop) in Paris around 1980 when he had seen him perform as guitarist and singer-songwriter, but not seeming to be any great champion of *la musique Africaine*.

By the time they met again, some fifteen years later, John had read and absorbed a book by Francis called *African Music: A People's Art*. It was a veritable treatise on African instruments and music with great emphasis on the importance of music in the daily lives of the people of the continent. The curiosity that helps define Williams led him to learn more about the extent of Bebey's activities, which included rigorous research on his subject and great accomplishment as a musician, songwriter, poet and novelist. The two musicians met and began to talk more about where the guitar fitted into the history and music of Africa. Encouraged by what he had learned, Williams started to warm to the idea of an album but it would be approached in a very different way than had been mooted by the record executive. John and Francis collaborated in putting together a list of material for potential inclusion and the album would ultimately feature five tracks composed by the man from Cameroon. Among these was his most famous, 'O Bia', and another piece that was to provide the name for the album, 'The Magic Box'. Bebey had used it as a song and a guitar piece. The 'magic box' concerned was an old-fashioned gramophone but could equally refer to the guitar. John, who was to play the tune as a solo, decided the title could also serve to represent Africa itself.

Before John could begin thinking about arrangements he decided that he was going to build them around the guitar rather than use a whole range of original African instruments. The guitar had been introduced to the African continent and islands by travellers from Portugal in the fifteenth century but had never really displaced the wide range of indigenous instruments. It was really only in the twentieth century that it began to take its place alongside more established cousins. Much as he loved their sound, Williams did not want to imitate instruments such as the kora but sought to capture some of its distinctive harmonies by using alternative tunings on his guitar.

Francis Bebey would certainly be involved and when John started to think about the musicians he wanted to work with, he concluded that this project would really benefit from having some of the usual suspects around. He contacted Chris Laurence and Richard Harvey, who were both keen so Paul Clarvis was brought in on percussion of all sorts and John Etheridge provided a different kind of guitar contribution to Williams's own. Part of the recording took place in Paris but most of the work was done at London's Air Studios during September and November 2000. The album comprised fifteen tracks and the core team of musicians were augmented by Bebey himself, listed as a 'special guest', singing and playing the sanza or thumb piano and a tuned percussion instrument. For one track there were more special guests, The African Children's Choir, singing a special arrangement by John Williams of the African National Congress anthem, 'Nkosi Sikelel'I Afrika'. 'Maki', track three on the record, featured cellists Anthony Pleeth, Martin Loveday and Paul Kegg. Track seven, 'Musha Musiki', which John composed, was inspired in part by a dance that his brother Dan had filmed in Zimbabwe. The evocative painting featured on the album sleeve was by Nigerian artist Osi Audu and the original hangs in the Williams home to this day.

This joyous music was too good to leave as just digital encoding on the surface of a CD so the 'five white blokes from north London' (to use John's own description) set off around the UK in May and June 2001 to play their version of African music. Sadly Francis Bebey, then seventy-one, was too old to participate and his life was soon to end. The devastating news of Bebey's death at his home in Paris came through in the middle of the tour and the remaining dates and subsequent tours of Europe, Australia and New Zealand were treated as celebrations of the great artist's life, posthumously raising his profile but perhaps more importantly, spreading his music to a grateful public. Williams has since played other African pieces but those that made up this particular album had a magic all of their own.

The music lived on for a while with WEB (Williams, Etheridge, Bebey). This time the Bebey in question was Patrick, Francis's son and a seasoned musician himself.

JOHN WILLIAMS AND JOHN ETHERIDGE

While a duo might not actually qualify as a band, the Williams/ Etheridge pairing can sound like a much larger ensemble and justifies their inclusion on that basis if no other. The two live in the same part of north London and bumped into each other regularly over the years in the course of everyday life and by meeting occasionally through mutual friends in the music world. They knew of each other's careers and had great respect for each other as musicians, each having watched the other perform many times. Although each has different recollections of exactly how and when they met, Williams made contact with a suggestion that they might work together on the *Magic Box* project. They had such a great time bouncing ideas off each other in that venture that it was likely that they would wind up playing together again some day. John had the idea of them again combining the steel and nylon string guitar sounds, something that had been so successful in *The Magic Box* and in John's former life with SKY.

It is no surprise that Williams chose Etheridge: an extraordinary guitarist, he is equally at home on acoustic guitar as on electric, both of which he uses in this duo. Having started out as an electric player in a variety of groups playing blues and rock, he was asked to play acoustic guitar with Stéphane Grappelli, the legendary violinist and long-time partner of Django Reinhardt, and spent a number of years touring with him. Anecdotes about his time with Stéphane, delivered in a cod French accent, are an important part of his on-stage patter.

John was simultaneously playing cutting-edge jazz-fusion with Soft Machine, a band that commanded similar respect to Grappelli but in different circles. He has played with too many jazz greats to list and had inspiring collaborations with violinist Christian Garrick and Andy Summers, the guitarist with The Police. Etheridge is one of the most in-demand guitarists on the jazz scene, working in an enormous variety of settings as a player, composer and bandleader.

The two Johns put together a set made up of reworks of African pieces from the *Magic Box* repertoire, some superb original compositions by each of them and a lengthy and intricate piece written for them by the American guitarist and composer Benjamin Verdery. This work, 'Peace, Love and Guitars', is multi-faceted and written to give a solid and consistent part from the guitar of John Williams while providing written lines and sometimes providing 'suggestions' as to what Etheridge should be getting up to on his parts and in his solo sections. The jazzer was initially unsure as to what liberties he could take with the composer's suggestions because he wanted to respect Verdery's intentions. He was possibly constrained to some extent by the comment sometimes made about jazz players who wander far from the intended theme: 'Why are they even paying a royalty on that?' He settled into the piece, however, and it made up the larger part of the second half of the duo's set. They recorded an album called *Places Between – Live in Dublin* before setting out to tour in the UK, Europe and the USA and are constantly refreshing their set, with one major addition being 'Ludwig's Horse', composed for them by Paul Hart. This was one of the highlights of their performance at The Queen's Hall during the 2012 Edinburgh Festival, which was also broadcast live by BBC Radio Three. The concert was one of the first of the festival to sell out and the hall was packed. Despite beginning at the unearthly hour of 11 a.m., the two Johns were wide awake and played their varied set to an extremely appreciative crowd. They were back on the radio that same evening, chatting and talking on the *Late Junction* programme. At the time of writing the duo is still going strong, with performance dates scheduled out into the future.

JOHN WILLIAMS AND RICHARD HARVEY

The association between Richard Harvey and John Williams has stood the test of a considerable length of time. They first worked together with Richard in a supporting session role on some of John's recordings. He was an associate of Stanley Myers who had ambitions, to be successfully realised, to compose and perform film music. Myers brought Harvey in to play recorders on the 1978 album *Travelling*, and he has been a recording and performing partner for the guitarist ever since in numerous guises and on innumerable instruments.

The two friends have toured most recently as a duo and the title of their 2009 DVD, *John Williams and Richard Harvey's World Tour*, neatly and accurately reflects the ambit of their music. Some audiences, drawn to the concert hall by the name of one of the most celebrated guitarists in the world, are bemused to settle into their seats in front of a stage bereft of guitars but positively littered with an array of instruments to be blown, plucked or beaten. There are pipes and flutes and psalteries and mandolins and thumb pianos and things to which it is difficult to give a name; the list seems endless but a quick recap at the end of the show confirms that they have all been put to use by Richard, sometimes two or three at a time. These are Harvey's toys exclusively. Williams might employ an alternative tuning or two but sticks stubbornly to guitar. The programme may demand that he makes it sound like something else, perhaps of Chinese or African origin, but it is always a guitar, and always a Smallman guitar at that.

Richard Harvey's career is as diverse as his instruments.

A founder member of the group Gryphon, he has worked with Sir Paul McCartney, composed and played on numerous film scores, was awarded a BAFTA for 'Best Original TV Music' for the score for the hard-hitting *G.B.H.* that he co-composed with Elvis Costello and has also written a superb concerto for John Williams (*Concerto Antico*). His magnum opus is probably the work he created for the 1989 Exeter Arts Festival with artist Ralph Steadman. Williams was booked for the event, Steadman was artist-in-residence and Harvey was commissioned to write something that would combine and exploit their talents. *Plague and the Moonflower* was the result. Its creators describe the oratorio, to which Steadman contributed the libretto and immensely powerful projected images some twenty feet high, as an eco-opera. It is the tale of a world destroyed by a Plague Demon, who falls in love with the Moonflower whose tropical paradise he is destroying.

Steadman says, 'The images emit waves of anger at what man is doing to his only home' and sadly concludes that they resonate even more strongly today than when they were first created. *Plague and the Moonflower* explores the dark side of humanity through the character of Plague. It relates the struggle for the survival of our planet in the face of apathy, pollution and greed. It is, however, redemptive, as Plague is transformed through encountering the Moonflower, and pledges to provide a better future. The Moonflower is a rare cactus that, symbolically, grows in the Amazon rainforest. It only flowers under a full moon, emitting a beautiful perfume while it flowers, but within a few hours it is gone.

This work was subsequently recorded with Ben Kingsley as narrator, Sir Ian Holm as the Plague Demon, John Williams on guitar, soprano Kym Amps and three choirs. Harvey conducted the ensemble and 'Friend' Richard Studt played violin.

John Williams with the author at Pizza Express, Soho.

ELEVEN

FANS, FOLLOWERS AND DETRACTORS

FANS

John Williams has fans in places that many could not point to on a globe. His career has taken him to countless countries and his willingness to explore and perform the music of so many regions has endeared him to the natives of some unlikely places. The gratitude of some governments for what he has done for their culture resulted in a number of medals and other awards but John's popular acclaim far outstrips that of the global establishment. In addition, he has always been prepared to look for new audiences as well as new music and this, too, has been successful and rewarding. Inevitably there are fans who wish he had never stepped off the concert platform or outside of a certain repertoire but John's total absence of musical snobbery endears him to many more people than it deters and his accessibility has been major contributor to his sustained success and popularity.

There can be little doubt that John's appearances on radio and television variety shows helped introduce a significant section of the public to the classical guitar

and perhaps to other classical music too. Audiences for
the prime-time Saturday evening shows hosted by Val
Doonican, Eric Sykes, Nana Mouskouri, Roger Whittaker
and Les Dawson spanned a diverse demographic; there
might be three generations of a family all enjoying the
show together. John's willingness to fit in with the character of the host and the format of the show meant that
his appearance onscreen in 'the classical slot' was not a
signal to leave the room to put the kettle on, go to the
loo or put some more coal on the fire. This cohort of fans
also included 'serious' followers, who would welcome
an opportunity to see John play live, regardless of the
context and even if they were not regular viewers of variety programmes.

Martin Campbell-White, the joint chief executive of
John's management company, Askonas Holt, strongly holds
the view that his client being prepared to play on such
shows was a major factor in his popular acceptance and
continuing success. Campbell-White is uniquely qualified to
comment as his association with Williams goes back to the
sixties. He elaborates on how and why John was so sought
after by the producers of the shows:

> Most of them wanted someone of status for their classical
> slot and John was ideal. He was a good-looking young man
> with an instrument that was growing in popularity, portable
> and self-contained. It is far easier to accommodate an artist
> who would walk in carrying his own instrument then sit
> down and play than to have, say, a violinist who needed an
> accompanist with a piano. The guitar could be used for a

range of music and, when necessary, John could accompany a singer or, in the case of someone like Val Doonican, play a guitar duet with him.

Add to this John's willingness to play straight man to comedians Eric Sykes and Les Dawson and it is easy to conclude that he was an ideal and welcome guest for this kind of programme.

John's appeal to the producers of such shows is clear but it is perhaps less obvious what convinced the musician himself that it was a good idea to play on them. He recently contributed to a programme celebrating the work and career of Val Doonican, erstwhile host and a great friend. He said, 'People used to say to me, "Are you going on that?", implying that it was demeaning for a classical musician to do so. On the contrary, I was absolutely thrilled and honoured. If I could go on a show and play "Recuerdos de la Alhambra" or "Cavatina" or a Bach Gavotte, whatever Val wanted me to play, it was not just luck or good fortune for me but also for the classical or Spanish guitar. You have to do a lot of concerts at the Wigmore Hall or the Festival Hall to play to 18 million people. It cannot be over-estimated the part over the past thirty or forty years those shows played in the popularity of the Spanish guitar today.'

Wherever he plays and in whatever context, John is invariably available to sign autographs after the show. He bridles occasionally when asked to pose for a photograph with a stranger's arm flung around his shoulder, his standard protest being, 'I am a musician, not a model' but he makes time to answer questions, preferably when there is time to do so properly. A few years ago, at the Bridgewater Hall in Manchester, he experienced both the demands and devotion of fans. As he sat at a table signing CDs and concert programmes, one man had the effrontery to tell him, in a most unpleasant manner, that he had incorrectly described one piece he had played. John chose not to enter into debate but others who were waiting let the man know their feelings in no uncertain terms. Having satisfied the long queue, John went back to his dressing room to get changed and prepare to set off on the drive back to London. He got to the stage door lobby to find a young couple who had been waiting there for over an hour. The young man, who was on crutches, was a guitar student desperate to see his idol but the nature of his injury meant that he could not have stood in the queue. He apologised for bothering Williams and humbly asked for the autograph, proffering his ticket. John spotted the distinctive fingernails of a guitarist and talked to him for twenty minutes or more, giving advice on technique, repertoire and practice, despite it now being close to midnight and knowing that he had a long drive in front of him.

The public are not held at a distance; John is a modest, approachable man who never projects an image of remoteness or grandeur. When he speaks from the stage, it is with humility and respect for his audience and he takes great pains to explain the background of what he is about to play, translating the titles when necessary. Because he can appear so 'ordinary', some devotees, in addition to sending fan mail of the predictable kind, are emboldened to contact John by his obvious openness to new things. Many years ago he received a beautifully written letter to which was attached a design for a nine-string guitar, hand-drawn in exquisite detail. The writer had spent a great deal of time developing the ideas around the instrument and he addressed matters of construction, playing technique and application – there were suggestions for the repertoire to which it would bring new possibilities. The effort involved was considerable and Williams corresponded with him. Although the design was never pursued and is now outmoded, John met up with the writer, an inmate of HMP Parkhurst, one of the few UK prisons ever given a 'top-security' rating, when he was released at the end of his sentence. Williams still keeps the letter, in the same file box as treasured pictures drawn by his children and correspondence from the great and good.

Peter Lyster-Todd identified something of a trend in the fan mail that SKY received. It never arrived in the multiple postbags that teen idols get every day but was regular and substantial. The SKY manager recognised that a significant proportion of the letters came from people who, suffering some kind of setback in life, found solace, uplift and warmth in the work of SKY. John says he has never known anyone, not just among managers, who was so sympathetic and helpful to fans as Peter Lyster-Todd.

Lyster-Todd put this type of correspondence down to two factors: the projection of the camaraderie and good-natured relationships within the band and the type of music that was played. The members of the band were not strutting young bloods, they were mature and extraordinary musicians whose mutual respect and sheer enjoyment at playing together was infectious. And SKY provided a bridge-head for people to access classical music, just as John has always done through much of his solo playing. The classical music establishment can appear very exclusive and forbidding but SKY and John helped democratise and provide a welcome to great works for eager listeners who would never consider buying a ticket for the Wigmore Hall.

There is one fan of John's who, in the opinion of the author, stands above all others for his extraordinary achievement in developing and maintaining an archive of the guitarist's career, a resource which he generously shares with anyone who cares to look at the website. Richard Sliwa, who declares himself, at least as far as music is concerned, to be possessed of 'anti-talent', first put his site up in 1998. His unique tribute contains extensive biographical material on John Williams and SKY, a near-exhaustive discography (reformatted and employed in this book with grateful thanks) and a now-lapsed discussion section.

FOLLOWERS

This term is used here to refer mainly to guitarists who hold John as a model and an inspiration. They also qualify as fans but their appreciation is technical as well as musical; they study and learn from his playing and emulate or modify what they see to improve their own performance. John 'teaches' mainly by example and even more so by encouragement, his experiences with the 'cloning' approach of Segovia no doubt conditioning his approach. Through his work with academic institutes in the UK, Australia and Spain, John has guided many students and influenced lots more through master classes and workshops. He does not have a dogmatic approach to teaching although he confesses to being disillusioned with the weekly one-on-one concept of tuition. Like Len, he believes students can learn from observing each other and many of his students have followed this example as they move on to teaching. Again like Len, he encourages ensemble playing, believing it is essential that guitarists learn to work effectively with other musicians. John is not a fan of the run-of-the-mill solo repertoire.

Over the years, he has received a great deal of generally positive mail from followers, asking advice, making suggestions and submitting compositions or transcriptions for his consideration. The advice sought spans general matters such as nail care, choice of instrument, string type and tension through to very technical enquiries about fingering, interpretation and even the nuancing of individual notes in nominated pieces. This represents an impressive expression of confidence and trust. Apart from his students and the beneficiaries of master classes it is the most intimate level of communication but John also stands as a role model for thousands of players across the world. In his blog of the trip he made to China with John in 1997, Gerald Garcia writes: 'We met many of the estimated 10 million amateur and professional guitarists in China and taught and played in four cities: Shanghai, Hangzhou, Nanjing and Beijing. The visit was an important one for Chinese guitarists, all of whom seem to base their technique and repertoire on the playing of John Williams, whom they had only heard previously on recordings.' That country serves as an example;

Japan, Europe, North America and South America all have significant populations of guitarists at all levels of capability, who consider John Williams to embody the epitome of guitar-playing technique. In Christopher Nupen's film of John's performance at Ronnie Scott's Jazz Club, Peter Clayton, the leading jazz broadcaster and writer, teased Scott about substituting guitarists for tenor sax players in his bookings. Scott replied:

> By the time John came here, we'd used most of the tenor players in the world ... but I think one reason John's thing worked so well here is that the guitar is such a popular instrument ... I was amazed at the number of guitarists we get in from all fields – classical, jazz, pop guitarists, a lot of young kids who came down and listened entranced while John was playing. It was really very encouraging.

DETRACTORS

Not everyone worships or even likes John Williams as a player or as a person. A large proportion of those agin him are driven by their subscription to the ludicrous Bream/Williams divide. Christopher Nupen, the producer who first put the two guitarists on television together, says that 'Stalwarts of either camp whose horizons are so limited that they cannot find anything good to say about the other are to be pitied.' He rails at such partisanship, calling it 'rank idiocy', but he reflects sadly that it was ever thus: 'Menuhin v. Stern, Perlman v. Zuckerman ... Why can't intelligent people who consider themselves music lovers simply enjoy all the greats of whatever hue for their own special gifts and contributions?' Incredibly, there are even professional critics who wear this particular set of blinkers. It is to be expected that many music fans will have preferences but it is sad when they soar out of all proportion into this kind of polarisation.

There are others who are unhappy that John has failed to comply with convention. Williams has challenged orthodoxy on many fronts during his career, never for the sake of controversy but quite often provoking it. He is disposed, perhaps programmed even, to speak frankly – a trait inherited from Len – and his clear, unvarnished opinions on a variety of subjects have offended listeners or readers. A good example is an English guitarist who put together a bundle of brickbats and published them on a website a few years ago in the form of an open letter to Williams (the letter is a reaction to comments made by John Williams in the 1993 DVD film profile that accompanied the Seville Concert). The list of criticisms is prefaced by a conciliatory expression of pleasure gained over the years from John's work. There are issues expressed on Williams's views about guitar design and his expression of appreciation of the work of Greg Smallman, on his opinion on the limited repertoire of the guitar and on the Australian's views on teaching in which our scornful writer makes what might be read as a revealing confession: 'I really don't understand this approach'.

Williams restated his reservations about Segovia's teaching methods in the profile, views he has expressed many times before but he is accused of being 'cruel and disrespectful in the extreme' about the maestro, this treachery being considered the more shameful 'after all he did for you'. The letter concludes with an expression of disappointment on the part of its writer in what he interprets as John's apparent hatred of the guitar, suggesting that Williams appears to be a man who wished he had done something other than play the guitar!

Anyone in the public eye is liable to this kind of condemnation but it is difficult to see what purpose is being served by something so unremittingly negative. It is doubtful that the writer ever expected Williams to respond and most people reading the letter are likely to consider it unreasonable, even if they have sympathy with some of the points being made. The letter enlightens no one and is a futile exercise.

YouTube carries an enormous number of clips of Williams in performance and in conversation. Each clip attracts many comments, most of which are appreciative, many positively laudatory, but of course there are a number that express a critical view of John's playing. The most common theme is that he plays without emotion or expression, a view encapsulated in this context by references to him as 'MIDI Williams'. MIDI is the acronym for Musical Instrument Digital Interface and, in simple terms, it is a protocol for allowing communication between electronic instruments. In the YouTube context, it is meant to suggest that John's playing is like an automaton and, ironically, given the technology of the metaphor employed, mechanical. However, to paraphrase Oscar Wilde, there is only one thing worse than receiving YouTube comments and that is not receiving YouTube comments.

Even today, after so much advancement and with so many barriers demolished, the world of the classical guitar in Britain remains inclined to the parochial and partisan. It has improved, certainly, but there has always been something about some guitar folk that is bitchy and spiteful. The correspondence columns in guitar magazines and journals used to be filled with lengthy missives that were surely written in green ink, scoring points, 'correcting' facts, challenging assertions and slating performers, transcribers, composers and concert audiences and promoters. When the much-lamented George Clinton launched his new magazine, called simply *Guitar* in 1972, John Williams, as well as being pictured on the cover and featured in a joint interview with Andy Powell of Wishbone Ash, contributed the following message:

One reprehensible drawback to the development of the guitar as an instrument with a classical background and technique has been the narrow-minded, reactionary and, in many cases, unmusical attitude of its most 'pure' advocates. I say 'has been' because this attitude is nearly dead and buried; however, any extra pushing towards this end can only be welcomed, and for this reason I wish you all the best on the occasion of your first issue of GUITAR.

Sadly, he was too positive in his assessment and too optimistic of the influence of the magazine. Time after time, critics, reviewers and correspondents lined up to take John to task for his latest deviation from the straight and all too narrow path of the classical devotee or to accuse him of squandering his talent on undeserving projects.

Someone who may not exactly qualify as a detractor but who expressed concern both about and for John is the priest who wrote to him in 1968 after the musician's appearance on the BBC radio programme *Desert Island Discs*. The show invites its guest to talk about his life and select the eight records he would like to have with him in the unfortunate case of his being cast away on a desert island. Williams was questioned about his religious views during the discussion and, to avoid going into a lengthy discourse on the subject, settled for describing himself somewhat inaccurately as an atheist rather than simply agnostic. The epistle from the clergyman expressed deep regret that John was 'without the fold'. At the end of the programme, the guest has to pick the single disc that he would want most and John's 'must have' was the 'St Matthew Passion'. Seizing on this choice, the priest argued that to create such a work, Bach had been inspired by God and that since John was so fond of the piece that he would have it as his only musical companion on the island, he must have been moved by its spiritual origins and was therefore one step along the path to redemption.

There is an anonymous Australian lady in whose estimation John Williams clearly falls short because she phoned in to a radio show to complain about them playing his music. She was a big fan of the Aussie country singer John Williamson, famous for hits such as 'Old Man Emu', 'True Blue', 'Cootamundra Wattle' and 'Rip, Rip, Woodchip' and would have preferred any one of these to the Bach Gavotte she had just endured, having had her expectations raised by mishearing the introduction to the disc. When the presenter gently chided her, suggesting she might take pride that her countryman John Williams is one of the world's greatest guitarists, she replied, 'Maybe so, but he can only play the guitar – John Williamson can play guitar *and* sing!'

Charlie, John and Kathy Williams with Count
Peter Hamilton MacDomhnaill and Alirio Díaz.

TWELVE

SOUTH AMERICAN MASTERS

John Williams has studied and played music from all over the world. In his long career, he has all but exhausted the European 'classical' repertoire, championed the emerging guitar compositions of Australia, and interpreted and added to the musical tradition of a swathe of African countries. Arguably, however, his most lasting and greatest legacy is his understanding and promotion of the rich music of Latin America. It has always had its own great exponents but sadly and unjustly they were more 'world-class' than 'world-famous' and Williams should be applauded first for researching and absorbing the music so thoroughly and then for using his fame to bring it to the attention of a global audience. Decades earlier, Andrés Segovia had been presented with the opportunity to do just that but for a variety of reasons he felt that music of a traditional or popular inspiration should be kept separate from the purely classical or European form, and he therefore chose to ignore the chance. Although John would protest that he has been but one among a number of people instrumental in achieving the breakthroughs of the last few decades, his role is such that he has been honoured with awards from the governments of Venezuela and Paraguay.

BARRIOS

In terms of repertoire, one of the most important contributions that John Williams has made to modern guitar music has been his part in bringing the work of Agustín Barrios Mangoré to a global audience. He has a fervent and profound respect for the composer and has said that he believes that Barrios may be the greatest of guitar composers. John also talks admiringly of the extremely refined playing technique and deep romanticism possessed by Barrios.

Williams first became aware of the existence and compositions of 'the great Paraguayan' in the 1950s while studying at Siena in Italy. Alirio Díaz, the Venezuelan guitar virtuoso some eighteen years his senior, was in attendance and shared with John two pieces by Barrios, perhaps the only two that had been published at that time. They were enthusiastically adopted by the young Australian and have been part of his life ever since. It is interesting to note that Díaz may not have come to the guitar himself had it not been for an extraordinary six months that Barrios spent playing in Caracas in the 1930s. During the first month he played some twenty-five concerts in a variety of halls and settings and so popular were his performances that they spawned and inspired the interest of a whole new generation of Venezuelan guitarists, in particular Antonio Lauro and Raul Borges. Alirio Díaz was to follow in their footsteps.

In 1969, Carlos Payes, a young medical student and amateur guitarist from El Salvador, arrived in Spain to begin a post-graduate degree in psychology. His home was in San Salvador, where Barrios had taught at the National Conservatory for the last years of his life until his death there in 1944. The Mangoré people of El Salvador had adopted and revered Barrios and they held a strong conviction that the only way that his work would gain the recognition they were sure it deserved would be through its being performed by a great and recognised player. Payes played his ultimately world-changing role in promoting this ambition by carrying some Barrios material along to a John Williams concert in Spain and taking it backstage after the performance to show him. Williams looked at the work and was so impressed that he invited Payes to London, asking him to bring the fifty or sixty pieces he had in total along with him. Williams was already an enormous admirer of what he had seen of Barrios and was delighted to be presented with this heaven-sent opportunity. The compositions revealed to him provided the foundation for a seminal recording. The disc was extremely well received all around the world and, following this exposé of superb compositions performed with immaculate technique by a man who played them with great appreciation, sensitivity and understanding, Barrios finally found the audience his work warranted. There are now around 100 Barrios compositions published.

The release of the 1977 CBS album *John Williams Plays Barrios* is acknowledged in the history of modern guitar music as the event that put the compositions of the Paraguayan maestro on the world's musical map. But Williams did not stop at that. As well as championing Barrios as composer and performer, he has also expressed firm views on the way in which the poetic Paraguayan was ignored and sidelined by Segovia. He makes clear that he has some understanding of the Spaniard's reasons but cannot sympathise with them.

For his own reasons, Segovia was reluctant to extend his repertoire beyond the European tradition. Many of his pieces were transcriptions of non-guitar works and he abhorred the notion of the guitar as a folk instrument; he dedicated his life to cementing its place on the concert platform and may have felt that any concession he might make would undermine his efforts.

When, soon after its release, a copy of Williams's album reached one of today's most gifted and renowned Barrios interpreters, Berta Rojas, at home in Paraguay she felt a sensation that would stay with her forever:

> I will never forget how amazed I was to hear Barrios' music (our *own* Barrios) played so beautifully. John brought the music of Barrios to the attention of the whole world. As a Paraguayan myself, I will always be grateful that a legend like John would take the chance to explore this music with his perfect technique and unique musicianship and make these pieces sound as the masterpieces they truly are.

While applauding the particular support for her countryman, Rojas also pays tribute to Williams's promotion of other South American works including those included on the album *El Diablo Suelto*, a collection of compositions from Venezuela. She has a similarly jaded view of Andrés Segovia's disdain for what she calls 'the popular inheritance of the guitar' in Latin America and contrasts it with the inspiration that John Williams took from that popular tradition with which, she says, 'He broadened the reach of the instrument to a point today where there is no one who has not heard, enjoyed and loved the guitar.'

Rojas, who is currently Professor of Guitar at George Washington University, Washington DC, believes that,

> John dignifies, with his wonderful technique and musicality, these jewels of popular music and makes us feel proud to play them. There are no boundaries when he reaches to these pieces. While Segovia may have penalised us, and I say this with respect to his immeasurable musical status, John allows us to recreate them, live and feel them. He makes them great and worthy in his hands.

Speaking in an interview in 1978, Len Williams also expressed his appreciation of the Paraguayan master with both a surprising comparison and a typically Len-esque sting in the tail that might just have been a swipe at Segovia: 'People who don't like and/or criticise the music of Barrios usually do so because they cannot play it. It is too difficult for them. I've been playing ... for fifty-two years and I can no more play Barrios than I can Reinhardt.' He continues, 'Both Barrios and Reinhardt made and played their own music. Both were great in their own way but they had one important thing in common. Disregarding their creative imagery and their fantastic techniques, they were incurable romantics who never lost touch with beauty. Perhaps that is why some people have no time for either of them.'

Although the Paraguayan held him in the highest regard and wanted to be his friend, Segovia's unfortunate and condescending attitude to Agustín Barrios Mangoré may have derived from some sense of threat of competition from the Latin American. It was almost certainly part of his preoccupation with European classical repertoire and, in John Williams's opinion, a function of the tendency for ex-colonial powers to look down on their former colonies, especially in popular culture. Segovia's prejudice was expressed in many ways, from the trivial to the fundamental, and some certainly reflected the patronising view of a native of the colonial power. Good quality gut strings, the best of which were made at the time in Italy, were almost impossible to come by in Paraguay in the early years of the twentieth century so Barrios was obliged to make do with the more readily available steel strings. Some other prominent performers acknowledged that Barrios had little option than to use metal strings and declared that his artistry transcended their limitations but Segovia loftily stated, 'I wouldn't know what to do with that wire fence', damning the strings and the player. It is known that Barrios, still deprived of a regular supply of gut strings, later tried to minimise the strident tone of their steel equivalents by putting small sections of rubber on the unwound treble strings right at the bridge of his guitar.

When the two men first met in 1921, Segovia, his idol, had expressed his admiration for the playing of Barrios and the Paraguayan was seeking some kinship. Segovia continued to speak well of Barrios but never did anything to help or promote him, either locally or on his return to Europe. Barrios took this badly, never speaking again of the Spaniard. It is worth noting that Segovia was presented with the score for 'La Catedral' but chose never to perform it. By the late twenties the difference in their fortunes was stark. Segovia, with his established international reputation and old-world stature, was widely preferred to Barrios in many parts of South America. The two guitarists both played concerts in Buenos Aires in the summer of 1928 – Segovia to full houses, Barrios being forced to cancel his second concert due to lack of interest. This painful contrast took place seven years after the two had met and their activities during that time illustrated vastly differing priorities. Barrios had been composing while Segovia had been cultivating his international standing and acquiring a repertoire of new compositions written for him and, specifically, in a European classical style that was alien to the more traditionally inspired work of the Paraguayan.

John Williams recalls that Segovia forbade his students from playing Barrios in any of his classes. Other well-known Segovia students have confirmed this as accurate and even a suggestion that a piece by the Paraguayan might be discussed would be met with an angry refusal. In his excellent biography of Barrios, *Six Silver Moonbeams*, Richard D. Stover states that in 1982, he heard Segovia publicly declare, 'Barrios was not a good composer for the guitar.' Williams has also said that he thinks the music of Barrios would be difficult for Segovia to play because he would have difficulty in summoning up the appropriate techniques and expressing the romantic spirit.

Barrios went through sustained periods of depression and disillusionment with his own life and professional standing, although he remained a sociable and social person who never lost his sense of poetry of the guitar. There was inevitably some self-doubt and deprivation at the national level, too. Berta Rojas suggests that the country was slightly behind the rest of the world. Paraguay had suffered a five-year war against Brazil, Argentina and Uruguay (the War of the Triple-Alliance, 1865–70), which took the lives of three quarters of the country's male population of the generation to which Barrios was born. His father was a Vice-Consul of Argentina and his mother was a schoolteacher so he began life in privileged circumstances. As with John Williams and Julian Bream, Agustín received his introduction to the guitar and first lessons from his father, who played folk-style music for dances such as the polca, zamba and vals.

Williams recorded and released another album in 1995 entitled *The Great Paraguayan*, which included new versions of much of the same material as the 1977 recording. His main reason for re-recording was to take advantage of developments in recording techniques and technology, and he chose to use Air Studios and to work again with Mike Stavrou. In many ways, Williams's imprimatur upon the works of Barrios has had the effect of raising the self-esteem of Latin American musicians, who now know that there is worldwide recognition and appreciation for them. And, as Berta Rojas gratefully acknowledges of John: 'His technique has influenced all of us. I sincerely don't think that there is anyone in the field that hasn't been inspired by John's natural connection to the guitar and the ease with which he can run off the greatest and most complex musical pieces from the "wooden mystery box", as Barrios called the guitar.' She does not buy in to the thought that there is a distinctive South American playing technique but suggests that what might distinguish players from that continent is '...the laid-back and fun feeling there is when we play our traditional pieces; think of Brazilian Carnival, but the technique, no, we inherited the European tradition.' This subtle distinction is recognised by many, including Brian Gascoigne, who remarked on the way that Latin American listeners as well as players respond instinctively to traditional music. He recalls John playing some Barrios at a party and the effect it had on a young Colombian woman who came into the room bearing a tray of food. 'That music just seemed to transform her. There was a change in the way she moved – not dancing but some kind of sensuous shimmy, an infusion of rhythm straight to the core of her being.'

Agustín Barrios Mangoré had profound musicality, prodigious skill and, through no fault of his own, possibly the worst timing in the history of the guitar. He was nearly always in the wrong place and at the wrong time. He would not have created what he did without drawing on the wellspring of his native Paraguay but his living there at a time before travel and communications allowed rapid worldwide recognition severely restricted his opportunities. What made him also damned him. His excursions to Europe were cursed by first the Spanish Civil War and then the Second World War. He never set foot in the USA because of trivial reasons to do with paperwork and bureaucracy. The lifeline that Segovia represented was pulled from his reach, the most promising champion failing him badly. It would not be overstating the case to aver that, when set against his potential, Barrios' life was little short of a tragedy – but redemption has come through the eventual and just discovery of his work all over the world.

The introduction and consolidation of the music of Agustín Barrios Mangoré into the repertoire for guitar is an enormous gift to guitarists by John Williams. It added to its compass and diversity and serves as encouragement for others to look favourably beyond the European classical tradition for resources and inspiration.

EL DIABLO SUELTO AND CARONI MUSIC

Count Peter Hamilton MacDomhnaill is the cousin of Count Guido Chigi Saracini, who in 1932 founded the celebrated Accademia Musicale Chigiana with the support of his friend and fellow music lover, Queen Elisabeth of Belgium. The Accademia, in the family palace in Siena, has been the finishing school for some of the world's most accomplished musicians, who studied with the greats of the preceding generation. The teachers include Pablo Casals, Antonio Guarnieri, Sergiu Celibidache, Andrés Segovia, Nathan Milstein and Yehudi Menuhin and among past students who have become great masters in their turn are Daniel Barenboim, Zubin Mehta, Claudio Abbado, Salvatore Accardo, Alirio Díaz and, of course, John Williams.

Peter had the privilege to witness musical history when he visited the palace as a boy and could wander around just soaking up the sounds of great musicians rehearsing and performing; small wonder that his musical appreciation was nurtured by this unique experience. It was an enviable springboard for a lifetime's passionate interest in music that propelled him, together with his lifelong friend, Michel

d'Arcangues, Marquis d'Iranda to make a unique contribution of enormous importance by identifying and confronting
a problem that was denying the world access to a rich source
of music and fair reward for its composers. The music in
question is that of Venezuela, a genre richly endowed with
influences of the traditional and folk roots from which it
springs. Michel d'Arcangues has a cultural heritage that
stands well alongside that of Peter MacDomhnaill. His
family's friends included Jean Cocteau, Igor Stravinsky,
Maurice Ravel and Kees van Dongen.

MacDomhnaill was close to many great musicians of the
twentieth century including the Venezuelan Alirio Díaz,
arguably the most accomplished guitarist to emerge from
South America. Díaz was a generous supporter of the young
John Williams when he first attended the Accademia and
the two have remained close ever since. Although he went
there to study with Andrés Segovia, Williams believes that
he learned much more from Díaz. Peter and the Venezuelan
met after some time in Italy and MacDomhnaill was
dismayed to learn that most of the work that the guitarist
had recorded was not available in the current format of CD,
which was of course significantly displacing sales of vinyl
records. The doughty Scot determined to try and rectify
this situation and he approached the recording companies
concerned, buying up the distribution rights and the master
tapes. He then set up a company with Michel d'Arcangues
and Díaz to remaster the recordings and manufacture the
CDs. Caroni Music was born in a spirit of cultural patronage rather than as a commercial enterprise.

Andrew Walter led the efforts at the EMI studios in

Abbey Road to produce excellent new masters. Along the way, however, the secondary issue arose of the copyright of the works that were the subject of the recordings. The state of publication rights' ownership and registration was dire; many of the works on the recordings were not published and those that were available were bedevilled with errors. Peter and Michel resolved to rectify this too, so MacDomhnaill flew to Venezuela to agree terms for new and accurate editions of the works to be prepared and published. The arrival of a man of such striking physical presence and unshakable determination was an unlikely but very welcome event and the Caroni project was seen by all concerned as a combination of saviour and liberator.

John Williams was aware of what was underway and as a friend and admirer of Alirio Díaz had heard him play many pieces of Venezuelan music over the years. He could not play them himself because no one but Díaz had the arrangements, most of which were his own. For many years, John had longed to record an album of Venezuelan compositions to give due acknowledgement and express similar appreciation to the music of that country as he had previously done with the compositions of Barrios. He had been a lover and champion of the music since being introduced to it by Díaz on his first visit to Siena but had been reluctant simply to include two or three token pieces from the country on an album of other works. Peter MacDomhnaill visited John at his home in London and together they began to discuss the project for a future album. The bold Caroni initiative held out the prospect of Williams being able to do justice to a wider collection of works by a range of Venezuelan composers and the Caroni principals were delighted to work with him on what they later referred to as 'a labour of love'.

John, Michel and Peter worked through the treasure trove of material that had been collected to decide what should be included in the recording while Alirio painstakingly prepared the manuscripts of his arrangements. When he went into the studio, John worked from a combination of finished works and proof copies of what would become Caroni Editions. Another factor contributing to the delay of the project was that John wanted to be sure that he had the right idiomatic way of playing for the varied and complex rhythms. He is committed to paying due respect to the traditional way of playing and is extremely sensitive to the variations in rhythm that are evident in and help define different cultures. There were lots of discoveries and lessons for John to learn during the process of study and analysis in the preparation for this recording:

I had already understood a lot about Venezuelan music from many years' friendship with Alirio Díaz but when preparing the recording I was interested in finding out the background to what I already knew from listening; to take just two examples – first, the huge energy and vitality which comes from the simultaneous duple and triple rhythms which are very difficult to play on one instrument – in traditional groups, the bass which might be the bass line on a harp, usually plays three in a bar while the accompaniment and melody play two to the bar quite apart from continuous syncopations on the cuatro. Second, the grey areas of some rhythms such as the aguinaldo, which is basically in five but usually a bit more when played on the cuatro due to the way it is strummed! Historically, my wife found some very interesting books in the London University library from which she translated fascinating passages about the first instruments taken from Spain to Venezuela in 1529 and many other details about the transformation and integration of mediaeval European dances, secular and religious, with African and indigenous rituals etc., etc.

In May 2003, in north London's Air Studios, John Williams recorded the twenty-six tracks that make up the landmark album *El Diablo Suelto*, for which, as he had with *The Great Paraguayan*, he recalled his co-producer and engineer, Mike Stavrou, from Australia. The pieces recorded represent the finest of Venezuelan music and the range of rhythms covers a large number of the dance forms that ornament this rich culture. Eleven composers are represented on this album, which includes the original compositions by the great Venezuelans Antonio Lauro, Raúl Borges and Vicente Emilio Sojo that have been associated with Alirio Díaz during his long career, as well as his fine arrangements of the works of Ignacio 'Indio' Figueredo, Heraclio Fernández, Pedro López and many others.

John had the idea of using a cuatro accompaniment on certain tracks as he wanted to add the colour and flavour of traditional Venezuelan music. Peter MacDomhnaill suggested that the Venezuelan composer, guitarist and cuatro player Alfonso Montes might be a suitable contributor and he invited Alfonso and his wife Irina to Arcangues Castle to meet John Williams and his wife Kathy. As a result, the recording ends with an original piece, 'Preludio de Adiós', written by Montes, who plays the cuatro on four of the pieces, including the title track. All of the works on the album are included in Caroni Music Editions.

Peter and Michel were involved extensively in the recording, joining John and Kathy in London and hosting them in Arcangues Castle in the south-west of France during the three-year period that was invested in preparation. The album, superbly recorded by John's co-producer, Michael Stavrou, is dedicated to Alirio Díaz and is a homage to Venezuela, her culture and composers. It is also a celebration of the achievements of two extraordinary men whose love of music and respect for its originators drove their philanthropic intervention. It's impossible to overstate the importance of the contribution that Count Peter Hamilton MacDomhnaill and Michel d'Arcangues, Marquis d'Iranda, aided by and in appreciation of Alirio Díaz, have made in bringing the guitar music of Venezuela to the rest of the world.

John Williams helps out with the launch of a new peace initiative, releasing a symbolic dove.

THIRTEEN

POLITICS AND CAUSES

This book touches on a number of aspects of John Williams's life that may or may not be attributable to the influence of his father, Leonard Williams, but there is one legacy beyond dispute. John grew up in a household that was decidedly and unremittingly left wing in its politics and was infused with that tradition but, like Len before him, he is not political in the sense of party politics. True, he would always support the Labour Party over the Conservatives but there is an instinctive dislike of party machinery and the naked ambition of some who loiter and plot within it.

He did join the Labour Party for a while and played his part by knocking on doors to canvass votes for the local candidate but it was not the way he felt he could make the best contribution to serving the community. Although he voted for Tony Blair and the Labour Party in 1979, he resigned from the party over the Iraq invasion in 2003. He cancelled a US tour for same reason. His instinct has guided him towards humanitarian causes and he has made a significant contribution to many of them over a number of years.

FRIENDS OF THE EARTH AND GREENPEACE

It would be foolhardy and possibly ultimately self-defeating for someone whose fingers are his livelihood to put them at risk by getting, literally, hands-on and, tempted though he has been by some of the derring-do exploits of activities by these and similar organisations, John's common sense has prevailed and he supports them in other ways. High on his personal agenda are deforestation and nuclear waste dumping; he is a particular champion of Greenpeace's *Rainbow Warrior* and immensely admiring of those activists who risk life and limb for their beliefs – 'I think what they do is extraordinary. They are very brave people.'

A similar body enjoying Williams's support is the Environmental Investigation Agency. Eco systems and biodiversity, environmental crime and governance and concern over global climate are at the core of its efforts and it conducts scientific investigations to provide data as well as campaigning. The EIA involves itself with the natural world through a focus on animals and wildlife and campaigns on matters ranging from the poaching of ivory and the killing of rare animals for their skins and organs. To give some idea of the challenges with which this organisation and others like it are trying to contend, CITES, the Convention on International Trade in Endangered Species, applies to around 5,000 protected species of animal and 29,000 species of plant threatened by over-exploitation.

AMNESTY INTERNATIONAL

Williams has had a long association with Amnesty International, a body that can be described as an umbrella organisation dedicated to upholding human rights that is active and recognised around the world. In 1994 he made his only visit to Paraguay. It was the fiftieth anniversary of the death of Agustín Barrios Mangoré and John was delighted to learn that he was to be awarded the Presidential Medal in appreciation of his efforts to increase recognition of the composer's work. He received an invitation from the office of the President to visit Paraguay to receive the medal.

Two years earlier, this troubled country had overcome its military rule and realised a democratic form of government that helped establish far more robust rights for its people. In 1993 Juan Carlos Wasmosy was elected as the nation's first civilian president for nearly forty years; things improved for the country but there was still some way to go. Williams and his wife Kathy, being honoured guests of the government, were met at the airport by officials and dignitaries. What they had not anticipated, however, was that enthusiastic crowds holding banners bearing his name aloft would be waiting to greet them, something he found moving and humbling. He made a visit, almost a pilgrimage, to Mangoré's home, where he was received like royalty before going on to play in the local church packed with people anxious to hear him. The church doors were left open and hundreds more thronged outside, listening to him over loudspeakers. At the presentation audience with the President, the First Lady asked John to play a fundraising concert for her favourite charity. Williams agreed only on condition that he could perform another in the name of and for the benefit of Amnesty International, a brave thing to do in the circumstances. It was agreed and both concerts took place in Asunción. The reason for which he was awarded the Presidential Medal makes it one of his most prized possessions.

He made other performances to benefit the charity, including far more light-hearted fundraising concerts in London. The first was in 1977, when he played 'Sevilla' as part of *The Mermaid Frolics*. Two years later, he performed 'Cavatina' and an unlikely and memorable duet of 'Won't Get Fooled Again' with Pete Townshend of The Who at The Secret Policeman's Ball. In 1989, John Cleese sent Williams an invitation to contribute to The Secret Policeman's Biggest Ball, the tenth anniversary show in the series, which he was to co-direct with Jennifer Saunders at the Cambridge Theatre, just down the road from the Spanish Guitar Centre. He agreed, playing 'Cavatina' again, but as the fall guy of the joke was interrupted mid-tune and ushered off-stage by comedienne Jennifer Saunders.

NUCLEAR MATTERS

The first major cause in which John Williams was involved was action against nuclear testing. In May 1957, Britain exploded its own H-bomb on Christmas Island and a brave protestor defied the exclusion zone imposed to sail alone into the testing area. His name was Harold Steele and his personal protest was the inspiration for John to become involved. He performed a benefit concert to raise public awareness of what he considered to be an appalling development and to generate funds to support protest activities. This was before the establishment of the main organisation to take on this cause – the Campaign for Nuclear Disarmament (CND) – which he also supported.

Williams is the President of Musicians Against Nuclear Arms (MANA), an organisation whose list of patrons and past patrons reads like a roll call of the great and good of pop, classical music and jazz. MANA is a fundraising entity rather than being actively involved in pursuing its cause. Its 'Concerts for Peace', often performed in prestigious London venues, feature star names who support its aims. The MANA Chamber Orchestra has, at various times, been conducted by Sir Colin Davis, Paul Daniel, Sir Neville Marriner, Sir Charles Mackerras and Sir Charles Groves. The charity also organises speeches and presentations by leading journalists and politicians. Funds raised from events and subscriptions are disbursed to a number of other organisations including CND, the International Peace Bureau and Chernobyl Children's Project.

John has also been involved in protests against nuclear power developments including the Sizewell 'B' power station in Suffolk and a proposal to build a nuclear waste dump on Bodmin Moor. He and Paco Peña played a benefit concert in Truro Cathedral to help provide funds for the campaign against the plan in the eighties.

COUNCILLOR WILLIAMS?

John has stood for public office just once in his life and it was not on any traditional party ticket. Instead, as most who know him would expect, it was in promotion of a single focused cause for the good of real people. The GLC or Greater London Council is where Councillor Williams would have been found after the 1970 election, had the 437 votes he garnered in Hackney for the 'Homes Before Roads' party been sufficient to put him in office. Luckily for his guitar playing and his audiences they were not. The nub of the issue was the plan to build an inner ring road (Ringway One) within London and the destruction of many homes. Another bone of contention was that the space below what is now the 'Westway' was just neglected wasteland and the campaign wanted it to be developed and used as a playspace for children. The slogan was 'Playspace for North Kensington' and John played two concerts to raise funds for the appeal. For one of these, at the Queen Elizabeth Hall in December 1968, he was joined by Julian Bream and the proceeds from the event were shared between the Playspace Appeal and the Sunshine Fund for Blind Babies and Young People. That particular Playspace campaign was successful: Ringway One was never fully built and the area under the Westway is now being used very effectively for shops, community and sports facilities largely due to the efforts of the Westway Development Trust, a charity which was established in 1971 and grew out of the efforts of the earlier group.

THE MUSICIANS' UNION

This may appear a fairly prosaic cause compared to some of the others mentioned here but John Williams has always been a supporter of the union and, indeed, of his fellow musicians. He enjoys an enviable reputation as one of the most considerate, generous and thoughtful soloists with many of the orchestras with which he has performed. John is never 'grand' in the way he conducts himself and he is concerned for the welfare of everyone in the ensemble; the same is true of his relationship with technicians at concert venues and in recording studios. Many soloists do not feel a need to belong to a musicians' union as they are not involved in any kind of collective bargaining or the setting of basic rates for performance and generally their management controls their representation and handles any negotiations. Although he has the benefits that come with being a soloist, Williams has never subscribed to standing aside from his professional colleagues at any level and this has been recognised and commands respect from other members. In 1989 he was asked to stand for election as a representative on the National Executive of the union for the London region and won. He served a three-year term and, along with any local activities, had to commit three days every quarter to national union meetings, which was something of a challenge when planning tours and concerts. The MU has a regional structure and although its headquarters are in Clapham in south London, at least one meeting each year is held at a regional location.

John found the experience fascinating and fulfilling: 'I learned a lot. Being so closely involved helped dispel many myths about the MU and unions in general. I was left with huge respect for the way it was run.' He also identifies one limitation with which the MU has to cope: 'Strikes have very limited potential in the arts!'

DEMOCRACY MOVEMENTS

Many musicians, writers and artists limit their political involvement either to the big themes or to small, very specific causes. Of the big ones, few compare with the cause of democracy. John has been deeply involved in several, the first of which was the military dictatorship in Greece in 1967. When Williams became aware of the situation, made all the more immediate by his friends and housemates the McKays having so recently lived in the country, he threw in his lot wholeheartedly. He worked from the outset in London with Brian McKay, raising funds and using his public profile to increase awareness.

Famously, he supported and worked with the exiled composer Mikis Theodorakis, and the Greek singer Maria Farandouri, performing and recording with them. In a later adventure more at street level, he and McKay once filled his car with 400 English language copies of a book called *The Method* by Pericles Korovessis, a document of his incarceration and torture, which was, of course, banned in Greece. The books were wanted by the opposition in Athens but for some reason it was illegal to ship them from the UK to Greece so the plan was to take them to France, from where there was no similar restriction on shipment. The Greek exile organisation in Paris was waiting to receive the two men and the books. They sailed across the English Channel to Calais, where the Customs officers took a very dim view of their cargo. In their poor French, the travellers tried to explain what they were doing, protesting that the book was not banned, it was just not available in the English language in France, and that these copies were to be exported in any event. The officials either did not understand or were not buying what they were told so they impounded the books and put the two Australians on the next ferry back to Dover. The Paris chapter were notified and they set off to Calais to investigate, finding that the issue throughout had been to do with paying import duty rather than any concern about the books' subject matter.

Alongside Paco Peña, Williams was involved in a campaign over Chile, where, in 1973, a military coup had usurped the Popular Unity government of Salvador Allende. The group Inti Illimani had been an important cultural force in the country and were considered ambassadors of the nation. After the coup they were exiled from their homeland, a punishment they endured for fifteen years. Williams and Peña had long admired them, becoming friends and touring with the group. To begin with, the two Europeans played as guest soloists but this soon progressed into far more integrated roles with them included more and more in the ensemble. The leader of the group, Horacio Salinas, wrote many new pieces for the extended 'family'. They made two fine recordings together: *Fragments of a Dream* in 1987 and *Leyenda* in 1990. John continues to appear with the band whenever possible, most recently in Sweden in 2010.

One example of this ad hoc activity was after Turkey suffered devastating earthquakes towards the end of 1999. In January 2000, together with the English Chamber Orchestra, Williams played a concert at the Barbican to help victims of the tragedy. They paid special tribute to the victims through the inclusion of Carlo Domenicani's evocative 1985 work 'Koyunbaba', which has great spiritual and cultural resonance in the area where the earthquakes struck.

Whenever the music or entertainment industry comes together to help, John is likely to be found in the vanguard. In 1982, John, in the company of Juan Martin, Bert Jansch and his good friend Ralph McTell and others, played a benefit concert for the Samaritans, a great organisation that provides telephone contact day and night for troubled souls. A recording of the performance added to the funds raised by the event. Williams was also one of the first stars to be contacted by CBS Masterworks when they were looking for big names to participate in the recording of *Classic Aid* in 1986. The event followed a year after the hugely successful Live Aid concerts and it was intended to be a contribution from the classical world with profits going to the United Nations High Commission for Refugees. The cast of high-profile contributors was as spectacular as that assembled for the pop concerts: Anne-Sophie Mutter, Gidon Kremer, Zubin Mehta, Seiji Ozawa and fellow guitarist Narciso Yepes were supported at the Grand Casino in Geneva by conductors Esa-Pekka Salonen and Lorin Maazel. Special guests at the event included Sir Peter Ustinov, Catherine Deneuve and Gina Lollobrigida. Unlikely surroundings for John, perhaps, but there was an important cause to support.

Williams stays in touch; he is very aware of what is happening around the world at any given time and thinks deeply about political and humanitarian developments and their effects. He is not a bleeding heart looking for a cause or a battle to fight but he is always ready to respond to situations as they arise, using his music to raise funds, demonstrate support and increase public awareness.

John deep in thought.

FOURTEEN

A QUESTION OF IDENTITY

'John Williams' – the name is familiar around the globe, courtesy of not one but two highly successful musicians of the same generation. John Christopher Williams, the subject of this book, is sometimes confused or conflated with the American John Towner Williams, the celebrated composer, most notably of film scores. The work of the two John Williamses has overlapped rarely but anyone who has heard the guitarist's interpretation of his namesake's theme from *Schindler's List* might wish it had. J. C. Williams is sometimes approached by members of the public telling him how much they admire him and that they really love his work on *Superman* (or *Star Wars* or *ET*, etc.). Incredibly, this has even happened at CD signings after concerts. John stoically accepts it with good grace but it must rankle sometimes. He was in Darwin in Northern Australia for the Guitar Festival when a young lady bearing a copy of the *Star Wars* soundtrack CD approached him in a café and asked him to sign it. He replied that he could not do so because it was not his work. 'But you are John Williams, aren't you?' 'Yes, but not *that* John Williams.' 'Will you sign it anyway? Nobody will know.' 'No!' John never signs anything by other artists.

343

John has Len and Melaan to blame, of course. Ranking third in the list of the most common surnames in Australia, 'Williams' is somewhat undistinguished in itself. Impediment enough it might be thought but they decided to make their son even more anonymous by choosing to dub him 'John'. But Williams is grateful for the benefits of a commonplace name. His friends' names would leap off the page of a hotel register or a restaurant diary. Someone spotting a reference to 'Paco Peña', 'Cleo Laine' (even without the Dame) or 'Julian Bream' would certainly expect to find a celebrity in the proximity. Their likely reaction to 'John Williams', however, even if it registered at all, would be to dismiss it as statistically unlikely to refer to *the* John Williams (or even the other one). This suits a man who values his privacy immensely; someone who largely relies on his agency, Askonas Holt, to act as his gatekeeper – Melanie Moult and Katie Crisp, his personal management team, are past masters in this role. John has, quite deliberately, not yet caught up with the concept of email.

Given his place of residence, there is one thing that clearly sets him apart. John Williams is Australian, proudly and almost obstinately so, given that he has chosen to live in London for his entire adult life. He has few family members back in Australia and, although he has many dear friends there, they have nearly all become so since he has lived in England. That he was born in Melbourne, the country's second city and capital of the proud state of Victoria, is a matter of historical fact but he was the first son of an Englishman who moved there for a new life yet never gave up his British passport. John left Oz when he was just ten years old, never to return to take up permanent or long-term residence. His secondary and tertiary education was gained in England; he is married to an American, has two English children, two English brothers and is more or less cured of his accent. So why is he Australian?

His choice is not really to be either English or Australian; if London were to become independent, a not totally implausible notion given its current mayor, John Williams might well be first in line for one of its new passports. He points out, quite correctly, that London is not England (and vice versa) and that it is the capital to which he has declared his affection. John has long and often described himself as a Londoner but he is most definitely one with the instincts and sensibilities of a true Aussie. Even if he took Boris's shilling he would remain a champion of Australian culture, especially her music, which he continues to encourage and promote and he would retain the mindset and attitudes of his birthplace. In an interview for the *BBC Music Magazine* in 1999 he said, 'Although I've lived in England for most of my life, at heart I feel more Australian than English, and more a Londoner than either. I have a more benign feeling about Australia than any other country.' In a later interview he added that Australians have the energy and openness of a new world country like America, with their own directness and laconic style. He went on, 'The British are better at satirising themselves – the best sense of humour in the world: but the Aussies are right on the button at seeing through English bullshit and the British class system.'

George Black, resident of London, long-time friend and fellow Aussie, suggests that John's retention of his

Australian passport is a 'get-out-of-jail-free card' in that it allows him to live in England but stand apart from things done in her name and from attitudes prevailing there that he finds unpalatable. Those who know him best accept that he has had a chance to evaluate British and Australian identities and simply stuck with the one closest to his own nature and inclinations. Their explanation for his residence in London is equally uncomplicated; it is one of the great music centres of the world and where he belongs. They add, quite rightly, that we should be grateful for his decision rather than questioning it; he has made a unique contribution to making London such a musical treasure house. His links with Australian music are central to his identity and he is an active patron and ambassador for composers and musicians who reside on the other side of the world. He has played and showcased works by Peter Sculthorpe, Ross Edwards, Nigel Westlake and Philip Houghton that might never have been heard outside the land of their creation.

Australia reciprocates; in 1987 John was awarded the distinction of being appointed an Officer of the Order of Australia (AO) and he was feted at the High Commission in London as the Australian of the Year in 2009. Whenever he tours his homeland, concerts always sell out as soon as tickets go on sale and he can fill the Sydney Opera House at the drop of a kangaroo skin hat with corks dangling from it. Williams's integrity and musical objectivity confound any suggestion that his choice of Smallman guitars, now made in Esperance on the south coast of Western Australia, could even remotely be the consequence of chauvinistic bias but it is a happy coincidence that his association with the country gave him the chance to get to know them. Someone who was aware of Greg Smallman's work before John was Peter Calvo, who represents a strong bond between the Williams family and Australia. A graduate of Len's academy in Cranbourn Street, Calvo took his teacher's methods and, some would say, attitudes, to the Antipodes and played an enormous part in the cause of the classical guitar there through his teaching and performance. Sadie Bishop was another pupil of Len Williams who, on returning to her native Australia in 1959, first set up a guitar school in Melbourne, then taught at the University Conservatorium in that city before going on to become Head of Guitar at the Australian National University in Canberra. John's friend and musical partner Tim Kain studied with Bishop in Australia and another of Len's alumni, Gordon Crosskey, at the Royal Northern College of Music in Manchester.

At one time John Williams had his own plans to teach in Australia, largely due to the infectious enthusiasm of John Hopkins OBE, a Yorkshireman and celebrated conductor who, after making his mark in Britain, emigrated to New Zealand in 1957, moving on to Australia six years later. He had distinguished careers in both countries and while Dean of the Victorian College of the Arts, he impressed and inspired Williams enough that the guitarist considered spending three months of each year teaching at the institute. He went so far as to purchase and develop a beautiful property on the Mornington Peninsula, south of Melbourne. Circumstances intervened to disrupt the tentative plan, however, and any thoughts of spending regular and substantial periods of time in Australia were postponed indefinitely.

Leaving aside considerations and narrow debate about London and Australia, there is no doubt that John qualifies with distinction as a true citizen of the world. As someone who refuses to acknowledge barriers within music, whether of genre or geographic origin, he absorbs influences, melodies, rhythms and harmonies from wherever he finds them and weaves them into his own work and interpretations to share with the world. John was an enthusiastic exponent and champion of world music long before that term came into being; he was born in one continent and has the bloodlines of two others in his veins. Does his passport really matter?

FOUR

CONCLUSION

His own man.

FIFTEEN

REFLECTIONS

I was aware that John Williams owed a great deal to his father long before I started writing this book. As I learned more of their relationship, I became intrigued by its nature and effects.

It takes a great deal of character to survive being a prodigy and John clearly possesses the mental strength he needed to navigate his way through life so successfully and so boldly. Whether this is because of Len or in spite of him is another matter entirely. Or maybe Len is not the key at all.

Someone who has known John far longer than I said that, even without a Segovia or a Len Williams, there would have been a John Williams. And, although John has said many times that it would have been nice to have made the decision for himself whether to be a guitarist, he has always qualified that statement by adding, 'But I might have made the wrong decision.' So it was Len who set him on the path and the world should be grateful for that, but how many fathers in other spheres have tried and failed to bring out the yearned-for prodigy in their offspring? Without the student's latent abilities, even the most gifted teacher cannot create greatness.

Len helped make John a guitarist through a combination of factors, the most basic being his skill as a teacher and John's ability to learn and apply what he was taught. Richard Harvey said that 'John Williams was the ideal person to be John Williams; born at the right time to the right father, who chose the right time to emigrate; he has the right level of intelligence, right physical constitution, the positive attitude. So many planets lined up.' So Len, John and fate all came together splendidly but what price has John had to pay? The great French guitarist Ida Presti regretted, 'I never had a childhood.' Williams has never echoed that sentiment but it is self-evident that his childhood was far from typical and would have been considered unusual even were he not studying guitar. His parents, especially his father, lived an unusual lifestyle that helped deny John peer company and obliged him to grow up in a particularly adult world, effectively bypassing normal childhood. This experience helped make him self-sufficient – it was he who made the monumental decision regarding the Geneva competition – but it could have backfired badly. The worlds of music, sport and showbiz are littered with hot-housed children whose flame burned brilliantly but briefly before it all became too much for them and they fell by the wayside. I believe that Len Williams risked this outcome.

To Len's great credit, John was never set to be a family meal ticket, something far from unusual in similar circumstances. Williams senior positively protected his son from the world of competitive music, even at the risk of alienating Andrés Segovia. By contrast, others sought to exploit John's talent by exaggerating their roles in his development and success:

Jack Duarte's sleeve notes on the Delysé recordings would have readers believe that he did everything but give birth to the guitarist, Andrés Segovia sought to over-ride Len's wishes in many ways and, after the success of 'Cavatina', Stanley Myers tried hard to cling on to John's coat tails. Len Williams's motives were clearly loftier: the service of music and of the guitar, with his son as the vehicle, a Rolls Royce as it turned out. Williams's gratitude to his father is unreserved and unstinting; he never fails to acknowledge him as a great teacher but it remains that John had to have the personality as well as the musical facility to succeed and it is he alone who has realised the potential of all the promise.

John Williams became an artist who would not settle for the expected, who in his exploration and expression was prepared to frustrate and infuriate some admirers by, in their terms, squandering his talents on undeserving projects and music. His achievements as a great musician flow from his own efforts and on his own terms. Rodney Friend told me a story about Itzhak Perlman. The virtuoso was in Zabar's Deli in New York when an elderly woman approached him and said, 'You are Itzhak Perlman?' The violinist acknowledged this was so. She spoke again, quite sternly, 'You take good care of yourself, not everyone gets to be Itzhak Perlman.'

And not everyone gets to be John Williams.

APPENDIX

APPENDICES

APPENDIX A: THOUGHTS
FROM JOHN WILLIAMS

The following are extracts from conversations between the author and John Williams.

GETTING INSIDE THE MIND OF THE COMPOSER
Trying to get inside the mind of the composer is obviously important in playing his or her music – but it is not the only important thing. There are many different ways of interpreting, sometimes you may see something the composer didn't, and composers themselves vary in their 'directions' – some are very detailed about what they want in the way of 'dynamics' (loud and soft, tone colours, slower or faster, etc.), while others give very little guidance. In some senses, performing is a partnership with the composer. Furthermore, composers who also play themselves reflect the musical and instrumental styles of their own times; recordings of the Spanish composer/pianist Enrique Granados from the early 1900s show a kind of almost wayward romanticism, but also a charm that we can miss in the conventions of today's interpretation. With students, I prefer to point out these general factors and not be too specific about all the finer and personal details of interpretation, which in the end is for them to develop in their own way. However, I feel very strongly that the style of the music and the culture which it comes from must be not only respected but obeyed! For example, when the great J. S. Bach and others are composing dance suites in the French baroque style, we must understand that style, because even though the dances were formalised as instrumental pieces, the rhythms and phrases

of those pieces correspond to the actual movement and gestures in the traditional dances. Another example would be traditional Venezuelan music: the characteristic feature of the instrumental rhythms is the simultaneous combination of two and three in a bar, with the bass always in three and often the tune or song above in two – this is what gives Venezuelan music such energy and fluidity, and, in common with the rest of the Caribbean, is the result of the African influence since the 1600s. To ignore all this shows no respect – a bit imperialist, I would say! European and Spanish music in particular have many examples of alternating two or three in a bar, but not simultaneously! Actually, when you think of it, the rhythms in European music are quite 'foot-based' –for example, flamenco is very positive and rhythmically tight. In contrast, African rhythms, especially from West Africa, are looser, more body movement; an example would be the polyrhythms of the 'talking drums', where each drum speaks for a different Spirit with its own rhythm, and all simultaneously.

COUGHING

I have never understood why people don't do more to prevent or control their coughing. How difficult is it to hold a handkerchief over your mouth to muffle a cough? A loud cough in a quiet moment can destroy the essence of the whole piece for an entire audience, not to mention the performers. To me it's simple: audiences have a responsibility to each other and to the performers they have come to see. I really appreciate what some venues do, providing cough sweets in the foyer so that people who haven't bothered to think about it themselves are reminded about coughing and given something to help.

SKY – PUTTING THE RECORD STRAIGHT (MYTH NUMBER THREE)

Accusations of populism and commercialism and snide remarks about me and SKY have come from various places over the years – and still do! Apart from the obvious insults, they often betray a musical snobbishness towards popular music and usually total ignorance of the practical and financial organisation of groups like SKY. A typical UK SKY tour would last three weeks with twenty to thirty crew, management and tour promoters on the road, hotels for all, lighting and sound equipment – and then after management and promotion costs were deducted, the group's share was divided by five! In order for all of us to continue our other musical and social lives we agreed to do only two tours a year, with no one being pressured to do more. This meant we could do tours of Australia and Europe in alternate years, always with a maximum of three weeks. In all, being on my own was a far easier option! In addition, we had five or six crew on yearly retainers and paid all our recording costs, which for a CD would be for a month in the studio. One result of tabloid and celebrity journalism is the false hype surrounding Top Ten single and album charts. Apart from some being one-week wonders, the fact is that the gap between the top few and the rest is enormous. The top bands and singers sell massively more than everyone else – we were with the 'everyone else'!

CONTEMPORARY MUSIC

When I play music by contemporary composers it's because I like their music, not because I think it is a duty. However, back in the sixties and seventies many of us were engaged, usually by the BBC in their Thursday invitation concerts (often called irritation concerts), to rehearse and perform music which fell into the category of the fashionably described 'avant-garde': although much of it was unintelligible, even to the musicians, there was a certain sense of achievement in getting it more or less right – a bit like solving a crossword puzzle! But 'like it'? It raises the question of what music really is, which of course means different things to different people – for example, Webern's Opus 18 songs would be meaningless to most people, but to many musicians, including myself, [they] are exquisitely refined and beautifully balanced miniatures, for the perfectly combined colours of female voice, E flat clarinet and guitar. The trouble with the so-called avant-garde was that you had to spend ages learning a piece before you realised it was either a gem or a load of rubbish! An example of a gem is the guitar solo 'Nunc' by the Italian composer Goffredo Petrassi, which I was asked to play at the Edinburgh Festival in 1973 and grew to love and play often throughout the seventies. In truth, the term avant-garde covers a multitude of sins, and it came with the assumption that it announced the arrival of a new and progressive mainstream – this really was, and is, rubbish! While serialism and atonality are interesting systems for some composers, the inevitable deconstruction of melody, harmony and rhythm which followed ends up in the organisation of sound for its own sake. But musical cultures are about more than this – it would be great to have a book on European music that is not musicological but about its social and cultural meaning.

Mention of the word 'culture' does bring us back to the one development in so-called western or European classical music that began in the late 1940s and has remained a huge influence on all music. 'Minimalism', which can be described as the gradual trans-formation of rhythmic and harmonic patterns through repetition, was inspired by the music of Africa, in particular West Africa. This suggests to me that the influence of other cultures is more 'evolutionary' in music than the restructuring of the elements in our own musical language, however intellectually interesting that might be. There really is such a thing as not seeing the wood for the trees! One might ask if all this has any particular relevance to the guitar: the answer is yes, because it belongs to the world-wide family of plucked stringed instruments with their many cultures – the Japanese koto, the Chinese pipa, the West African kora and ngoni, the American banjo, the Andean charango, the Venezuelan cuatro etc., etc.!

APPENDIX B: IN THE DEN OF THE ALCHEMIST – A VISIT TO GREG SMALLMAN'S WORKSHOP

The following was written in December 2010 as a magazine article.

During the planning phase of a research trip to Australia, there was one meeting to be set up Down Under that demanded the highest priority, the one around which everything else would be shuffled, if necessary. Once arranged, the date that would shine like a jewel in my calendar was the day when I would meet Greg Smallman, the man who makes guitars for John Williams. Greg is not the easiest person to get to see. It is not that he is reticent about discussing his work and methods; in fact, he is lauded and admired for sharing his knowledge and discoveries and, particularly, for not trying to protect them through patents. Rather, it's a simple matter of geography. Greg's workshop, which he shares with his sons Damon and Kym, is located just south of the middle of nowhere in the Australian bush. To use his words, 'If I want to get to a city, it's one day's drive west or three days' east.' I had chosen not to drive, but to fly into the one-building, three-flights-a-day airport that serves the town closest to his home.

I consider myself a pretty experienced traveller, but this was the first flight on which I have heard an announcement from the flight deck asking if any passenger would like a taxi to be booked to meet them at the airport. I concluded that there must be a good reason for this so I took up the offer – I knew I would need a taxi in any event. After I'd picked up my luggage there appeared to be even more passengers buzzing around the single cab parked outside the 'terminal' than there were flies around my head. I pushed my way through, asserted my claim to the car and was soon speeding off to my motel, leaving my travelling companions to wait for my driver's return. For one-horse town, read one-taxi town!

Greg and his delightful wife Robbie picked me up next morning and drove me to their home. We shared the car with their dog Jai, a friendly and boisterous border collie, and, after negotiating roads that would delight a rally driver, we reached our destination. The house and workshop are set on a prominent hill with splendid, 360-degree views across the bush. Kym and Damon each have houses within a kilometre of the shop and right to hand is the bushfire shelter that the boys have built, an underground refuge that would protect the family, the dogs (and the guitars) should fire break out.

Greg's sons joined us in the house and we repaired to the workshop, where they displayed, discussed and shared their tools and techniques for building the guitars that have changed the design paradigm for the classical guitar. There was less wood in stock than I might have expected, but I was reminded that, between them, the family would probably complete perhaps fifteen guitars in a year. I was also surprised by the lack of indulgence in expensive kit and equipment, but soon realised that, when they need something, these guys will simply set about making it. A comparatively unsophisticated example I shall probably try to replicate was a frame made of copper tube, into which a dial gauge is mounted, to be used for measuring soundboard thickness. Simple, cheap and custom made for the job in hand. Not that Greg is averse to the prospect of using modern technology; he just hasn't got around to much of it yet. However, the 'dry room' has a sophisticated control system, and the health and safety people would surely be delighted with the lighting and ventilation standards.

Greg can best be described as a no-nonsense kind of guy. He says what he thinks in very plain terms and did not attempt to duck or avoid any of the questions I put to him. His sons offered the occasional spin on his words but this was generally for the purpose of clarification or expansion, and sometimes took the form of one of them producing a section of a guitar work-in-progress to illustrate the point under discussion. As we talked, I concluded that his guitar design philosophy (not that he would dream of calling it anything so pretentious) for delivering *what he is aiming for* seems to rest on a very few articles of faith. This is how I would summarise them:

The first is his re-appraisal of the influence of the back and sides on the tone of the guitar. The choice of wood for these, bearing in mind the influence on sound of particular woods, remains one of the most powerful decision factors for most players (and luthiers). Greg settles for a laminate based mostly on Australian hoop pine, which is widely used as a substitute for spruce in boat and aircraft construction. While acknowledging that some instrument makers and some players like to feel bass notes reverberating through their guitars into their bodies, Greg would prefer that the back and sides were made of concrete or some similarly inflexible material, since 'You don't want the back and sides pumping, that just mucks up what the top is trying to do.' This overstates the point, but Greg is clear that even small changes to the soundboard make big differences to sound, while changes to the back and sides make little differences to the sound: 'Torres made a papier-mâché back and sides, I think to draw attention to the soundboard.' Certainly Smallman found by experiment that a heavy back, side and neck gave him the best result. 'They have an influence on sound by not moving as much as lighter ones. This makes the soundboard pump into the back and sides instead of moving the whole guitar. The heavy back and sides I use are not inert (as concrete might be); there is still resonance and movement.'

Concrete is not completely dismissed: 'I think concrete would work with some changes to the soundboard, but it would be impossible to play or to transport!' Regardless of that flight of fancy, Greg limits the weight of his guitar bodies to 3kg '...as players crack up at any more than that. Players take weight seriously: they think heavy is bad and makes them hear bad things in the guitar, but they are actually playing a very light, responsive soundboard.' This leads to the second article of faith, which concerns the soundboard material. Simply stated, it is: 'No particular piece of wood has great sound locked up in it just waiting to be released.' Smallman uses western red cedar for his soundboards, simply because it is lighter than spruce. These are then married to the famous lattice bracing to produce an assembly with considerable flexibility.

Article number three is that there is 'no formula or "set of numbers" that are the key to enabling the building of consistently great guitars'. The timeworn analogy involving typewriters, monkeys and the works of the Bard was used to conclude that any set of relevant numbers may produce the odd, excellent guitar, but that life was too short to rely on such a random approach. Although he does not see himself in any way as a guitar design evangelist with a passion to change the world, Greg is happy to share his experience and approach to guitar building and has addressed audiences of luthiers around the world. I sensed his frustration as he recalled the kind of questions many of them ask. Some wanted him to deliver unto them a stone tablet inscribed with a strict, formulaic template that would be beset – ironically – with inflexibility. Others clearly had no intention of abandoning traditional methods and phrased their questions in such a way as to reinforce orthodoxy in design. I asked Greg how much this bothers him and his response was that, ultimately, it is their choice what they do and, as long as he is allowed to carry on doing what he is doing, he is content.

Article number four is that an essential input to the design is the informed and detailed critique of a player who understands exactly what he wants from his instrument. This was a veiled acknowledgement of the synergistic relationship Smallman enjoys with John Williams, from whom he receives honest and critical feedback. I have had the privilege of observing Williams very closely for the past couple of years, and I know from experience that he evaluates and manages every aspect of his musical life to ensure the best possible performance. He is observant, keenly analytical and frank in his comments, and will not be swayed or diverted from his objectives. He is ever the gentleman, but a gentleman who is firm and detailed in all his requirements, whether these concern his sound technicians, the temperature of his performance and dressing rooms or, most crucially of all, his instruments.

John was in Sydney in 1978, delivering a master class to students of Peter Calvo, when Greg Smallman, who was still working with Pete Biffin at that time, arranged to show him three guitars during a lunch break. Williams was very impressed that

Smallman was totally undefensive when he pointed out the various faults and limitations that he had identified in the guitars. Rather than argue or try to justify his work, Smallman merely said, 'What do I need to change to make it better?' He praised Williams's Fleta guitar and asked if there was anything that could be improved about it. For John Williams, he could not have responded in any better fashion. This was a seminal meeting: the perfect combination of one man, genuinely prepared to listen, and another who has something immensely valuable to be heard. Greg is quick to acknowledge his debt for this and for subsequent guidance from his most important client:

'If it wasn't for John Williams, I'd probably be making furniture. He talks to me, he lets me know what he likes, what he doesn't and why. John would play a guitar and, when he reached a "bad" note, or short note, he'd look at me to let me know he had found it and that it was no good. Lesser players thought these were good notes because they were louder!'

Greg absorbed Williams's comments on his Fleta, particularly that he found Fletas generally a little too percussive, especially on the top string. Taking this invaluable information into account, Greg headed back to his shop and set to work. Some time after that Williams was back in town, on tour with SKY, and Greg took three more guitars for him to see. History records that John took one and Kevin Peek, the other SKY guitarist, snapped up another. Williams has played guitars by Greg Smallman and Sons ever since.

John Williams has a profound respect for Greg's approach to his guitars. Smallman has studied the work of the noted luthiers of the past and measured their instruments, seeking clues to the characteristics he would like to achieve, and he has a healthy respect for tradition, particularly acknowledging his appreciation of Fleta. He recognises that, since the tradition is still so young, it is unlikely that every desirable variation in design has been imagined and explored. He seeks to build upon tradition, not to rubbish it. And he is no fool; leaving aside any personal philosophy, he knows that the guitar-buying market will tolerate only so much novelty. By way of illustration, he mentioned his experiment of making a guitar without a traditional heel. There was so little interest in this slap in the face to conventional construction that he only ever made one to that design.

The most obvious consequence of the articles of faith philosophy is that all Smallman guitars (by father and sons) are physically very heavy. They would apportion this as 'back and sides at least twice as heavy as the average guitar, top half as heavy'. This characteristic has been apparent in every Smallman I have ever picked up, and it seems that there are some very seasoned guitarists who reckon that the sheer weight of an instrument may just be a promising indicator of its quality. Greg recalls Ry Cooder picking up one of his guitars with the comment, 'Hmm, heavy, gonna be a good one'. Cooder was just one of a number of famous names that Greg had approached over the years, with varying degrees of success. He would find out which hotel they were staying at and sit in the lobby until an opportunity presented itself for him to introduce himself and his guitars. Others he canvassed include Bob Dylan, Alirio Díaz and British jazzer John Etheridge, who purchased an early steel-string guitar that Smallman had co-produced with Peter Biffin. For steel-string guitars of that vintage, Smallman made the tops and necks and Biffin made the rest to Smallman's design and moulds. Etheridge was using the guitar routinely for his 'Hot Club' style playing until just a few years ago. I suspect it is now tucked away in a bank vault as part of his pension fund.

Mention of Peter Biffin provides an opportunity to put the record straight on who actually conceived 'lattice bracing'. There are a number of websites (particularly that of Aussie Jim Redgate) that aver that it was a joint Smallman/Biffin concept, but I am happy to help correct this – it was Greg's alone! The invention of lattice bracing is possibly the most important development in the modern history of the instrument and, as such, deserves to be recorded accurately. In 2009, Biffin, concerned about the incorrect attribution, wrote to Redgate regarding a 1997 interview by the latter, which remains on Redgate's website:

> In the section on soundboards, you mention that the lattice bracing you use was developed by Greg Smallman and myself. Just for the record, I would like to point out that this is actually not the case. Greg and I did much experimental work together but the lattice bracing was not part of that collaboration. The lattice form of bracing and the slightly later development of using balsa and carbon fibre to make the lattice, in my opinion, were flashes of genius and belong to Greg alone. I was in India at the time he developed those ideas and he showed me what he had been

doing when I returned (by which stage we were no longer working as partners). With Greg's blessing, I then pursued the same ideas applied to the lute family of instruments I was making at the time.

Smallman was well aware of the impact of his developments and, as already noted, has no problem in sharing them. This did not, however, stop him setting out to have a joke at the expense of other luthiers, whom he knew would be keen to inspect his early instruments. The great Spanish maker Paulino Bernabe was one of the first to get forensically inquisitive with the Smallman guitar owned by Luis Grimaldi. When Bernabe inserted a mirror to inspect the interior structure, he was puzzled to find a label with three words beautifully presented in copperplate 'mirror writing'. Not being able to understand English, he was obliged to ask Grimaldi for a translation of Greg's pithy inscription, only to be told that it read, 'Piss off, nosey!'

But back to the workshop! The first part of the guitar that I saw in the making was a fretboard. A development in the past few years, this is moulded, complete with fret slots, in a carbon fibre compound that is agitated while being cured to ensure that any air bubbles are eliminated. Greg chooses a synthetic fretboard over any of the usual rosewoods and ebonies to provide stability and straightness. He said that he wonders we guitarists don't go crazy when the fretboard is moving from too short to too long with every change in humidity, causing upward and downward changes in the action and also affecting intonation. The neck is made of a single piece of mahogany, and my question about options in its profile prompted smiles all round, just as my early enquiry about alternative scale lengths had. The necks are completely hand-shaped and there is no template to tell any of the three men when to stop carving. I am 'neck-sensitive' so I questioned this, and a discussion ensued centring upon the correct positioning of the fretting hand and how indifferent a player well disciplined in this respect would be to the profile of the neck. I was assured that no complaints or questions had ever arisen about this aspect of Smallman guitars from any good players. When I demonstrated my right hand position, I was immediately recognised as 'one of those sloppy steel-string players'.

Next I got to see the mind-bending internal structure of a Smallman guitar before final assembly. It does not remotely resemble anything I have seen before in classical guitar execution, and clearly illustrates the thoughts of a man who, although respecting tradition, refuses to be fettered by it. There is a small amount of carbon fibre used on the struts, and much more of this material is used in the frame that supports the soundboard. Greg uses it to provide long-term stability as it does not 'creep' like wood and thus increases immunity to changes in humidity. The back is markedly arched – the wooden former for this is constructed of a laminate of sections of varying thickness, the lines between each layer emphasising the contours and making the arching look even more dramatic. There is another, three-dimensional template for the soundboard that includes some compensatory shaping to anticipate the pulling up of the board under string tension. The back and sides had beautiful and suitably expensive-looking face woods but were very substantial hoop pine-based laminates (or plywood, as Greg irreverently calls them). There is a frame that goes around the edge of the soundboard contributing to the focus on the relatively small area that Greg, Damon and Kym want to excite when the instrument is played, and another, quite substantial frame angled obliquely across the length of the body. The bridge is mounted without a conventional bridge plate on carbon fibre 'pins'. The body has no taper over its length, the top and back being parallel.

Then there is the lattice bracing array, the defining characteristic of a Smallman guitar. It is a balsa wood confection of great beauty and even greater precision. Damon joked about the frustration he feels about the increase in thickness of each element that occurs when the assembly is moved from the dry room to the shop. The lattice bracing with its small amount of integrated carbon fibre imparts considerable strength without causing local rigidity. It flexes in every direction on the plane that will be the underside of the soundboard. A tap tuning technique is employed, but not in a wholly conventional fashion. There is no mystic tapping of virgin soundboard panels to divine those boards with hidden greatness (see Article of Faith number 2), but there is considerable tapping of the assembled soundboard. Checking for the required response, both in functional area and amplitude of movement, is carried out by 'watching the sawdust dance', a reference to the use of the dust as an indicator of excitation.

Quality control for tone is by assessment against two 'reference' guitars. I imagined these existing in two arcs: one physical, the other metaphorical. On the day I visited, there were several guitars arrayed in a physical arc around one end of the shop, with the reference instruments one at each end. Just away from these, on the most elaborate and substantial guitar stand I have ever seen (constructed by Damon and Kym), rested Greg's first guitar. When I asked the three guitar makers how they know when they have got a guitar 'right', the reply was that: 'Its tone fits between that one (reference guitar at one end of the arc both physical *and* metaphorical) and that one (reference guitar at the other end of the arc).' Greg chimed in that, 'Sometimes there is one (metaphorically) out there', gesturing to the other side of the shop, 'and we then have to work on it to bring it into the (metaphorical) arc'. In reality, the guitars that were in the shop were all works in progress. Greg told me that, when a guitar is 'finished', it is tuned and put aside (in the physical arc) to settle and stabilise. The guys will not touch it for at least a month but will then, over anything up to six months, tweak and adjust so as to bring it into the tonal quality control (metaphorical) arc.

The kind of subtle rework that brings a guitar into the arc may be no more than the slightest shaving of a critical part of the bridge, or an increase in the scalloping of the saddle between the string seats – something I had never seen on the scale that was evident on a number of the Smallman instruments. This, of course, contributes to the degree of flexing that can be achieved. Greg demonstrated the reference guitars and one or two others, and the famous Smallman sustain was abundantly evident. He knows that this is a somewhat controversial characteristic of his work, and commented that it is better to damp out sustaining notes when you don't want them than to live without them when you do, as would be the case with a less lively instrument.

We left the workshop and went back to the house, where Robbie had laid on a delicious lunch with homemade bread and a memorable banana cake. Over the meal I asked Greg whether Damon and Kym had had to be press-ganged into guitar making but, before he could answer, the boys emphasised very positively that it had been their choice. They are both into building and riding off-road motorcycles and had concluded that it was great to have a job where they could manage their work schedule around time to hit the dirt on the bikes or to indulge their other passion: surfing. As a steel-string player, I simply had to ask whether there was ever likely to be a Smallman for the likes of me. Greg indicated that he had little interest in that idea, but pulled out a guitar that was resting in the corner of the room. Looking for all the world like a regular Smallman, it was strung with a combination of nylon bass strings and steel strings for the G, B and top E with the fourth string missing. Greg picked up a router bit and proceeded to play some slide on the top three strings, using the lower ones as drones. It sounded sublime and, do you know what? As unlikely as that little performance was, it was no more surprising or unexpected than anything else I'd seen since I entered the den of the alchemist.

APPENDIX C: TOOLS OF THE TRADE

A mong the many contributions and controversies for which John Williams has been responsible during his career, one of the most influential is his role in the development of his chosen instrument, the acoustic, six-string classical or Spanish guitar. His endorsement and adoption of a radical new design for the structure of the instrument helped ensure that the work of his countryman Greg Smallman received worldwide recognition, changing the way guitars were made by many other luthiers. Smallman had been making guitars for some time and was well known within the Australian guitar community when Williams became inspired by what he was trying to achieve and began encouraging and advising him, ultimately choosing to play exclusively guitars from Smallman and Sons. Greg is now by far the most influential guitar maker of his time.

Guitarists of all types, not just classical players, are always searching for the perfect instrument: one that has the playability, action, look and, most importantly, the sound that they have heard in their heads; a perfect combination of tone, balance, the right level of sustain and decay and of volume and projection. For many, the quest for perfection lasts their lifetime and is never realised. For what is essentially a simple device, a box with some strings attached, the number of variables makes for enormous complexity. Confining these to the factors that affect just the quality of sound still presents a huge number of considerations to be managed and translated into a physical instrument. The wood for the soundboard (the resonating plate on top of the guitar, the movement of which creates the sound) is critical, of course, but so too is the internal bracing underpinning it that is required to achieve the fine balance between flexibility and strength. The pattern and structure of the braces has always been one of the most defining elements, and guitars that may vary in other respects are often considered predictable and desirable to a particular player because of the bracing pattern employed. The pattern which is probably in most common usage today is based upon that developed by Antonio de Torres, who built guitars in the nineteenth century. The history of Spanish guitar design and the vexed question of exactly who developed what is a minefield into which we need not to put a foot, because what Smallman conceived and created is so radically different from anything that went before. He developed a lattice of braces that gained and imparted its strength through its geometrical form and integrity. Having proved and utilised lattices made from wood, he enhanced the concept by using a space-age material – carbon fibre – to contribute its extraordinary strength and weight properties to the mix. What he has done is revolutionary, and guitarists tend to either love or hate the sound of Smallman guitars. More details on Smallman's design philosophy and the history of his association with John Williams are detailed in Appendix B.

His father first sat John behind a guitar when he was four years old and could probably barely see around it. When he was given the first professional lessons that would set him on his way, the only guitars that his father could find for him still dwarfed the boy. Even with his extensive connections in the music trade, Len could not find a small-scale Spanish guitar of any quality. He did, however, find a small oddball steel-string Martin and, deciding this was the best available, began to modify it. There is a substantial difference between steel-string acoustic guitars and classical nylon-string guitars. Apart from the size and the construction of the body or sound chamber, the variation in the neck is the most notable feature. The neck is wider on a classical guitar, and hence the fingerboard also, and it feels 'chunkier' in the hand than its steel-string equivalent. In order to make the Martin neck feel more like a conventional classical neck and provide the same practice experience as a conventional classical guitar, Len built up the neck with layers of wood filler and fitted a wider fingerboard. The Martin did its job through those very early years. John's progress soon merited a far better guitar and, although the choice of top-class instruments was very limited in

Australia at the time, a Panormo, made by a French luthier in London, was found and selected over a Parisian Lacote, and John graduated gratefully from the Martin. These two were the guitars on which John did all his practising until the move to London, but by then his hands were significantly larger, as was the selection of instruments from which to choose. The first 'London guitar' was one made in Germany by a maker called Edgar Mönch. It served purpose for a while but was fairly soon replaced with another, constructed in Spain by Juan Estruch. This guitar is remembered most by the Williams family for its bid for freedom from its case. The bridge had come unglued and the string tension had drawn it violently into contact with the case. It was repaired, but by this time Len Williams had engaged the Dane Harald Petersen to make high-quality instruments for the Guitar Centre, and a hand-picked example from his workbench became John's next guitar.

All of these instruments were soon to be outgrown by John's playing, and by the mid-1950s it was time to move on again. After lots of research and recommendations from Segovia, Len found a luthier whose guitars would be his choice for many years. The guitars of Ignacio Fleta met all his needs and aspirations, and he used the first of these for three or four years. The first Fleta guitar had to be collected from the workshop in Spain, and Christopher Nupen was dispatched on the errand. John stuck with Fletas and they saw him right through the sixties. In 1971 he tried and briefly played a guitar by Archangel Fernandez, a gifted young maker who had been apprenticed to Marcel Barbera, but he opted to stick with the Fleta. Later he added a Hernandez y Aguado and then a guitar from the great British maker Martin Fleeson, using it in parallel with the Fleta – for example, on his album with organist Peter Hurford, where a particular articulation was required. He felt it had 'an English sound' and, fittingly, used it for one track on his recording *Echoes of London*.

Although he toyed with other guitars, this is really the sum of John's guitar history until he embraced the Smallman. There was, however, one situation that demanded a special instrument, and that was when performing and recording the Guiliani *Concerto Opus 30* with the Australian Chamber Orchestra in 1998. Williams had recently learned a great deal from the Italian musicologist Carlo Barone about the performance practice of the early 1800s and, in particular, the music of Mauro Guiliani. His work combines virtuosity and simple melody in the Italian 'Bel Canto' style and is best expressed on the smaller guitars of the time, which have a lighter and clearer sound than modern instruments. For that project he borrowed an 1814 Guadagnini after 'auditioning' eight guitars in total.

There have also been times when he has had to step beyond the classical guitar because of the nature of the work involved. For his parts in the Patrick Gowers *Rhapsody for Classical Guitar and Two Electric Guitars*, he used a fairly conventional Gretsch electric guitar, selected mainly because it had a wide fingerboard. He used Gibson Les Paul de Luxe with John Williams and Friends in 1975 but he had to have a real rethink about his guitars when SKY was formed. Although much of what they played still required John to use a classical guitar, it was within a rock environment, so the guitar had to be heard and not feed back through the usual microphone. The only classical-style guitar available at that time with a pickup built in was the Ovation. An aeronautical engineer named Charles Kaman, more used to working on helicopters, was responsible for the design of the Ovation guitars, with their strange-looking round-back bodies. They had a parabolic shape and were made from a material called Lyrachord, supposedly developed for the purpose, which was essentially a glass-fibre and resin compound. They are interesting guitars and did a great job for John and his fellow Sky guitarist Kevin Peek in that context, but they were really only chosen because they gave the two a chance to compete with drums, bass and keyboards through a huge PA system. John's other guitars with SKY were also far from his usual choice of instrument. Later he had a Japanese Takamine classical guitar, also with a pickup. If John Williams's adoption of an electric guitar per se was radical, he went even further in his choice of instrument. The Gibson RD Artist was a top-of-the-range solid-bodied instrument with an entirely new body shape supposedly designed to provide ergonomic advantages for the player. The guitar's, and John's, secret weapon, however, was the 'active' electronic circuitry designed by Dr Robert Moog, the engineer who became most famous as the creator of the Moog Synthesiser, one of the first widely used electronic musical instruments. This feature allowed for a much wider range of sounds to be produced from the pickups. Conventional electric guitar pickups have specific dynamics that constrain the amount of expression and colour that can be attained. This is a major limitation compared to what an expert player can get from a classical guitar, the characteristics of which could be more closely replicated with the Moog electronics.

Unsurprisingly, over the years many guitar makers have tried to get John to appraise and – they hope – adopt their instruments; an endorsement from Williams would make their reputations and guarantee fame and fortune. Most have been grateful merely that he has taken them seriously, and many have benefited from comments he has made on their work. It is difficult to think of anyone more qualified to offer an opinion, and Williams is always generous with his advice. There have been one or two unfortunate occasions when a luthier has left a guitar with John for him to try and has then used that very tenuous association as the basis for promoting their work. Williams hates this and has a very characteristic way of dealing with the acquisition of his guitars. Because he knows how personal the relationship between a musician and his instrument is, he will not endorse guitars and nor does he ever accept them as gifts, always insisting on paying for them – including the Smallmans. He wants to be in the moral debt of no one.

Aside from his being able to choose any guitar he wishes, John possesses one of the most important tools for any classical guitarist: a set of strong fingernails. He has been blessed with them and they are the envy of many other players. Fingernails are of fundamental importance to a modern-day classical guitarist, and it was Segovia who really changed the way the guitar was played when he began using his nails to increase the range of sounds he could generate. Until he successfully championed this major shift in technique, guitar players relied on the flesh of their fingertips to pluck the strings, giving a more muted and limited tone and considerably less volume and projection of the sound. Every guitarist has his own way of caring for his or her nails. Some anoint them with various home-brewed or commercial concoctions to nourish and strengthen, while others advocate diet as the most important influence on their condition. The length to which nails are cut and the shape to which they are filed is also a matter of personal preference and the result of experimentation. Nails may be reinforced with varnish or, in extreme cases, layers of tissue paper bonded with superglue. Some players resort to visiting nail bars to have false plastic nails attached to their natural nail. The attack angle of the nail on the string has a very significant effect on sound quality, as does the position on the string where it is applied. A guitarist's fingernails are kept well tended and smooth-edged, and the necessary files and very fine sandpaper are essential components of any player's kit. When John Williams was asked to contribute to a regular magazine column entitled 'I couldn't live without...', he chose his nail kit as his most indispensable article. He went so far as to say that a broken nail immediately before a concert would mean its cancellation, and he revealed that only on a very few occasions has he been obliged even to repair a crack in a nail with glue and polish. It is only the nails on the plucking hand that demand all this attention and concern. The nails on the hand that fingers the fretboard are simply kept clipped short. A good way to identify a guitarist in the audience at a concert is to look at their nails. If they are long-ish and beautifully manicured on just one hand while those on the other hand are cut back, you have probably spotted a player.

Another key part of the guitar/guitarist assembly is the strings. For a classical guitar these are called nylon strings, although generally only the three that are pitched highest are all-nylon. The lower three are bundles of nylon or other filaments wrapped tightly around with metal wire. Again, Segovia is behind their introduction and he must be credited for the enormous advance that nylon strings represent over the gut strings that they super-seded. His association with Alberto and Rose Augustine resulted in DuPont, the creators of nylon, co-operating with them in the manufacture of nylon strings for the guitar. Segovia's long-term partner, Olga Coelho, is reputed to be the first player to have used them when she played a concert in New York in 1944. The quality of guitar strings is absolutely critical: they must be of constant thickness and section to play in tune and they must retain their tone for as long as possible. The wire-bound strings give a problem to most guitarists. As they move their fingers along the string from note to note, there is often an annoying squeaking or whistling sound. This is partly a consequence of technique: if the fingertip is lifted right off the string before being moved then no sound will result, but there are very few guitarists who have such a 'clean' technique and even they find that there are some pieces where it is physically impossible to avoid the problem. John Williams has an extremely clean technique, but he also gave himself a further edge in reducing string squeak by lightly sanding the affected strings to make them smoother. He told John D'Addario, the head of the D'Addario string company, about this some years ago, and the string maker decided that this was a good idea that his company could adopt and put into production. John is adamant that squeaks are not musical and he always uses D'Addario semi-polished bass strings.

As audiences for classical guitar music have grown, so too has the size of the concert halls where it is performed. This has prompted the use of amplification, which has proved to be a thorny and contentious subject. John's first few performances of the Rodrigo *Concierto de Aranjuez* in the sixties were played without amplification, and he felt obliged to use a microphone and the hall PA system to avoid feeling that 'the guitar was just a little music box in the middle of an orchestra'. He gradually moved on to using amplification for solo recitals in larger halls, particularly because the people at the back in the cheapest seats really do not get the richness and colour of the guitar when it is so distant and soft. Some aficionados will not countenance going to a concert at which guitars will be amplified, and the poor quality of equipment and lack of technical expertise at some halls where guitars are amplified can spoil even the best performance. John is very sensitive to this and invests considerable effort into examining how he might ensure that his audiences hear the best sound possible. His actions at the Sydney Opera House in the eighties are a good example of this. Whenever he was due to play there, he called upon his friend George Black for help. The two would go to the venue together for sound checks and, as John played onstage, Black, who knew exactly what Williams was trying to achieve, would move around the auditorium to hear how the guitar's sound was reaching every part of the room. The sound engineer would make adjustments on his instruction and, when George was finally happy with the results, the two would swap roles, Black playing and Williams taking on the evaluation role, confirming for himself that every member of his audience would enjoy the best possible listening experience. He has used pickups in his guitars, installed by the British guitar maker Gary Southwell, together with a small 'pre-amplifier' onstage, the output of which is then plugged into the hall's PA system. This guarantees that he is in control of the quality of the signal from his guitar at least as far as the junction box of the hall system; beyond that he is at the mercy of the hall's equipment and the sound engineer's skill. For small venues he has used a microphone and his own PA system, which is of hi-fi quality. As a general rule, Williams uses a microphone for concertos and solo recitals, and pickups when playing with, for example, John Etheridge or Richard Harvey. Whatever system is being employed, he will ensure the best possible outcome: rare among musicians, he is technically savvy enough to be able to specify quite detailed requirements of the sound engineer.

For John Williams, the whole array of 'tools' that he employs are simply enablers that help him convey his inner voice to his audience. He applies the same study and attention to them as he does to his music, choosing and managing them to make that voice as clear and pure as possible.

APPENDIX D: DISCOGRAPHY (INCLUDING COMMERCIALLY AVAILABLE VIDEO RELEASES)

Courtesy of Richard Sliwa.
Guitar Recital Volume 1, Delysé ECB.3149, 1959
Guitar Recital Volume 2, Delysé ECB.3150, 1959
Folk-Songs, L'Oiseau-Lyre OLS 131, 1961
With Wilfred Brown, Tenor
A Spanish Guitar, Westminster Gold WGS 8109, 1961
Schoenberg: Works, L'Oiseau-Lyre OLS 250, 1962
With Melos Ensemble of London, Bruno Maderna Cond., ft John
   Carol Case (Baritone)
Sor Studies, Westminster WGS 8137, 1962
Fernando Sor: Studies 1–20
Tom Krause: Songs by Sibelius and Strauss, London 5783, 1963
With Tom Krause, Tenor
Jacqueline du Pré: Recital, EMI 5659552, 1963
With Jacqueline du Pré, Cello
CBS Records Presents John Williams, CBS 6608, 1964
Virtuoso Music For Guitar, CBS 6696, 1965
Two Guitar Concertos (Rodrigo & Castelnuovo-Tedesco), CBS
   6834, 1965
With Philadelphia Orchestra, Eugene Ormandy Cond.
More Virtuoso Music for Guitar, CBS 6339, 1967
Haydn & Paganini, CBS 72678, 1968
With Alan Loveday (Violin), Amaryllis Fleming (Cello), Cecil
   Aronowitz (Viola)
Two Guitar Concertos (Rodrigo & Dodgson), CBS 7063, 1968

With English Chamber Orchestra, Sir Charles Groves
Virtuoso Variations For Guitar, CBS 7195, 1969
Anton Webern: Complete Works, CBS 45845, 1969
With Colin Bradley (Clarinet), Halina Lukomska (Soprano)
Vivaldi and Giuliani Guitar Concertos, CBS 72798, 1969
With English Chamber Orchestra, Sir Charles Groves (Cond.),
    Colin Tilney (Harpsichord Continuo)
Songs for Voice and Guitar, CBS 61126, 1969
With Wilfred Brown, Tenor
John Williams Plays Spanish Music, CBS 72860, 1970
The Walking Stick, 1970, Film Soundtrack (unreleased)
Music by Stanley Myers
Songs of Freedom, Mikis Theodorakis CBS 72947, 1970
With Maria Farandouri Singer
The Raging Moon (a.k.a. Long Ago Tomorrow), EMI SCX 6447,
    1971
Film Soundtrack, Music by Stanley Myers
Changes, Cube Records Fly 5, 1971
Ft Rick Wakeman (Keyboards), Tristan Fry (Drums/Percussion),
    Alan Parker (Guitars), Chris Spedding (Guitars), Herbie
    Flowers (Bass)
Pomegranate (B/W Bach Changes), Cube/Fly Records BUG13,
    1971 (7' single)
Frank Zappa's 200 Motels, United Artists UAS9956, 1971
Film Soundtrack Conceived & Written by Frank Zappa
Music for Guitar and Harpsichord, *CBS* 72948, 1971
With Raphael Puyana (Harpsichord), Jordi Savall (Viola da Gamba)
Together (AKA Julian and John), RCA SB 6862, 1972
With Julian Bream (Guitar)
Gowers and Scarlatti, *CBS* 72979, 1972
With Godfrey Salmon (Cond.), Feat John Scott (Sax & Flutes),
    Pat Halling (Violin), Stephen Shingles (Viola), Denis Vigay
    (Cello), Herbie Flowers (Bass), Tristan Fry (Drums)
Previn and Ponce Concertos, CBS 73060, 1973
With London Symphony Orchestra, André Previn (Cond.)
The Height Below, Cube Records HiFly 16, 1973
Ft Brian Gascoigne (Percussion), Tristan Fry (Percussion),
    Charlotte Nassim (Koto), Dudley Moore (Organ)
Arnold Schoenberg: Complete Works, Decca SXLK 6660-64,
    1973

With Members of the London Sinfonietta, David Atherton (Cond.), ft John Shirley-Quirk (Baritone)
Music from England, Japan, Brazil, Venezuela, Argentina and Mexico, CBS 73205, 1973
Rhapsody, CBS 73205, 1974
With Patrick Gowers (Electric Organ)
Rodrigo and Villa-Lobos, CBS 72728, 1974
With English Chamber Orchestra, Daniel Barenboim (Cond.), ft James Brown (cor anglais)
Together Again (AKA Julian and John 2), RCA ARL0456, 1974
With Julian Bream (Guitar)
Bach Complete Lute Suites, CBS 79203, 1975
Best Friends, RCA 60961, 1976
With Cleo Laine, singer, ft John Dankworth (Sax, Clarinet), Paul Hart (keyboards), Tony Kinsey & Kenny Clare (Drums), Dave Markee (Bass), Chris Hartley (Viola), Gerry Richards & Celia Mitchell (Violins)
Duos for Guitar and Violin, CBS 76525, 1976
With Itzhak Perlman, Violin
John Williams and Friends, CBS 73487, 1976
With Carlos Bonnell (Guitar), Brian Gascoigne & Morris Pert (Marimbas), Keith Marjoram (Bass)
Castelnuovo-Tedesco, Arnold and Dodgson, CBS 35172, 1977
With English Chamber Orchestra, Sir Charles Groves (Cond.)
The Sly Cormorant, Argo ZSW 607, 1977
Music by Brian Gascoigne, story by Brian Patten
The Mermaid Frolics, Amnesty International Benefit Concert, Polydor 2384, 1977
Barrios, CBS 76662, 1977
Arnold and Brouwer Concertos, CBS 76715, 1977
With London Sinfonietta, Elgar Howarth (Cond.)
Stevie, CBS 70165, 1978
Film Soundtrack by Patrick Gowers
Travelling, Cube Records HiFly 27, 1978
Ft Vic Flick, Les Thatcher, Lawrence Juber (Guitars), Barrie Morgan, Harold Fisher, Stewart Elliot (Drums), Adrian Brett, Richard Harvey (Woodwind), Francis Monkman (Keyboards), Herbie Flowers (Bass)
Manuel Ponce, CBS 76730, 1978
Sky, Arista 14162, 1979

With Francis Monkman (Keyboards), Herbie Flowers (Bass), Tristan Fry (Drums & Percussion), Kevin Peek (Guitars)
SKY: Dies Irae 12' Single, Ariola, 1979
The Secret Policeman's Ball, Amnesty International Benefit Concert, Island IL 9630, 1979
Live, RCA 03090, 1979
With Julian Bream (Guitar)
Guitar Quintets, CBS 36671, 1980
With Carl Pini, Benedict Cruft (violins), Rusen Gunes (viola), Roger Smith (cello)
Sky 2, Arista ADSKY2, 1980
With Francis Monkman (Keyboards), Herbie Flowers (Bass), Tristan Fry (Drums & Percussion), Kevin Peek (Guitars)
Echoes of Spain, CBS 36679, 1981
Sky3, Arista ASKY3, 1981
With Steve Gray (Keyboards), Herbie Flowers (Bass), Tristan Fry (Drums & Percussion), Kevin Peek (Guitars)
Sky at Westminster Abbey BBC BBCV3017 (VHS/Videodisc), 1981
Live at Westminster Abbey in aid of Amnesty International
Bach for Organ and Guitar, CBS 37250, 1981
With Peter Hurford, Organ
Sky Forthcoming, Arista ASKY4, 1982
With Steve Gray (Keyboards), Herbie Flowers (Bass), Tristan Fry (Drums & Percussion), Kevin Peek (Guitars)
Portrait of John Williams, CBS 37791, 1982
Sky Five Live, Arista 302171, 1983
With Steve Gray (Keyboards), Herbie Flowers (Bass), Tristan Fry (Drums & Percussion), Kevin Peek (Guitars) Recorded live in Australia
Let The Music Take You, CBS 39211, 1983
With Cleo Laine, singer, ft Rod Argent (Keyboards), Kenny Clare (Drums), Alec Dankworth & John Mole (Bass), John Dankworth (Sax & Clarinet), Tristan Fry & Morris Pert (Percussion), Tony Hymas (Piano)
The Guitar is the Song: A Folksong Collection, CBS 37825, 1983
Ft Chris Taylor (Flutes & Recorders), Chris Laurence (Double Bass), Gary Kettel (Percussion), Brian Gascoigne (Marimba & Celesta), Paul Hart (Fiddle), James Brown (Horn), Les Thatcher (Mandolin)

Just Guitars, Concert in Aid of The Samaritans, CBS 25946, 1983
Sky Cadmium, Arista 205855, 1983
With Steve Gray (Keyboards), Herbie Flowers (Bass), Tristan Fry (Drums & Percussion), Kevin Peek (Guitars)
Sky Why Don't We, Ariola AROD306, 1983
Why Don't We/Troika (Edit) (12' single) Rodrigo, CBS 37848, 1984
With Philharmonia Orchestra, Louis Fremaux (Cond.) ft Christine Pendrill (Cor anglais)
The Honorary Consul AKA Beyond the Limit, Island IS 155 (single) 1984
Ft Richard Harvey, woodwind
Concertos by Bach, Handel and Marcello, CBS 39560, 1984
With Academy of St Martin-in-the-Fields, Cond. Kenneth Sillito
Kate Bush: Hounds of Love, EMI 46164, 1985
With Kate Bush, Singer
Echoes of London, CBS 42119, 1986
Classic Aid, Concert in aid of The UNHCR, CBS M42404, 1986
Emma's War, Moment 106, 1986
Film Soundtrack Music by John C. Williams
Fragments of a Dream, CBS 44574, 1987
With Inti Illimani, ft Paco Peña
Concerto for Guitar and Jazz Orchestra, CBS 42332, 1987
National Youth Jazz Orchestra, Paul Hart Cond./Violin, ft. (Three Pieces): Dave Arch, Synthesiser, Paul Hart, Piano
The Baroque Album, CBS 44518, 1987
A Fish Called Wanda, Milan RC 270, 1988
Film Soundtrack Music by John du Prez
Spirit of the Guitar: Music of the Americas, CBS 44898, 1989
Leyenda, CBS 45948, 1990
With Inti Illimani, ft Paco Peña
Vivaldi Concertos, Sony 46556, 1990
With Franz Liszt Chamber Orchestra, János Rolla Conductor/ Violin, ft Benjamin Verdery (Guitar), Norbert Blume (Viola d'amore), Agnes Szakály (Cimbalom), Mária Frank (Cello), Zsuzsa Pertis (Harpsichord)
Takemitsu, Sony 46720, 1991
With London Sinfonietta, Esa-Pekka Salonen (Cond.), ft Sebastian Bell (Alto Flute), Gareth Hulse (Oboe d'amore)

Benjamin Verdery: Some Towns and Cities, Newport Classic
 NDP85519, 1991
With Benjamin Verdery, Guitar
Iberia, Sony 48480, 1992
Ft London Symphony Orchestra, Paul Daniel (Cond.)
The Seville Concert, Sony 53359, 1993
Ft Orquestra Sinfónica de Sevilla, José Buenagu (Cond.)
From Australia, Sony 53361, 1994
With Australian Chamber Orchestra, Richard Hickox (Cond.)
London Symphony Orchestra, Paul Daniel (Cond.)
Nigel Westlake: Onomatopoeia, Tall Poppies TP047, 1994
The Great Paraguayan, Sony 64396, 1995
George Martin Presents The Medici Quartet, Classic FM CFMCD
 5, 1995
Ft Medici Quartet, George Martin (Cond.)
The Mantis & the Moon: Guitar Duets, Sony 62007, 1996
With Timothy Kain, Guitar
Concertos by Harvey and Gray, Sony 68337, 1996
With London Symphony Orchestra, Paul Daniel (Cond.)
John Williams Plays the Movies, Sony 62784, 1996
The Black Decameron, Sony 63173, 1997
With London Sinfonietta, Steven Mercurio (Cond.)
Great Expectations, Atlantic 83063-2, 1997
The Guitarist, Sony 60586, 1998
Ft string orchestra, William Goodchild (Cond.)
George Martin: In My Life, MCA 11841, 1998
Schubert and Giuliani, Sony 63385, 1999
*With Australian Chamber Orchestra, Richard Tognetti (leader/
 Cond.)*
Richard Harvey & Ralph Steadman: Plague and the Moonflower,
 Altus ALU0001, 1999
Various musicians, Richard Harvey Cond.
Jonathan Elias: The Prayer Cycle, Sony 60569, 1999
Angelika Kirchschlager: When Night Falls, Sony 64498, 1999
With Angelika Kirchschlager, Soprano
Classic Williams – Romance of the Guitar, Sony 89141, 2000
With String Orchestra, William Goodchild, Cond.
The Magic Box, Sony 89483, 2001

With Richard Harvey (Woodwind), Paul Clarvis (Drums &
Percussion), John Etheridge (Steel-String Guitar), Chris
Laurence (Double Bass)
Bela Fleck: Perpetual Motion, Sony 89610, 2001
With Bela Fleck, banjo
El Diablo Suelto, Sony 90451, 2003
With Alfonso Montes (Cuatro)
Rosemary and Thyme, Sanctuary Classics PCACD002, 2004
Julian Bream: Testament, BBC SBT 1333, 2005
With Julian Bream, Guitar
Bryn Terfel: Simple Gifts, Deutsche Grammophon 477202, 2005
With Bryn Terfel, Baritone
Sky Live in Bremen Quantum Leap QLDVD6250, 2005 (DVD),
    2005
(Sky's first public performance in May 1979 in a German jazz
club recorded for German TV)
Places Between, Sony 700907, 2006
With John Etheridge, Guitars
(Recorded Live in Dublin)
From a Bird, JCW1, 2008
Pure Acoustic, West One Music WOM142, 2008
Latin American Night (DVD) Arthaus Musik 107168, 2008
Berlin Philharmonic, Daniel Barenboim (Cond.)
Recorded live in Berlin, 1998
Message to the Future (DVD), Altus ALU0008, 2011
With Richard Harvey
Recorded live in Japan, 2005

APPENDIX E: LINKS

More information on the monkey sanctuary:
  http://www.wildfutures.org

On Charlie Williams's *The Guitar is Their Song* DVD and other projects:
  http://charliewilliamsfilms.com

On Kate Williams's recordings and gigs:
  http://www.kate-williams-quartet.com

On Sam Williams's career and achievements in music:
  http://www.samwilliamsmusic.com

On Dan Williams's design and craftsmanship:
  http://www.danwilliams.co.uk

On guitars by Smallman and Sons:
  http://gregsmallmanguitar.com

On Ergo guitars by Charles Fox:
  http://www.charlesfoxguitars.com

On Caroni Music Editions including the Díaz arrangements of Venezuelan and other pieces:
  http://www.caronimusic.com/pagesAnglais/accueil.php?idsession=&pagec=

On Mike Stavrou and his book, *Mixing with your Mind*:
  http://www.mixingwithyourmind.com

On John Williams and Richard Harvey's World Tour DVD:
  http://www.cdsouk.com

PICTURE CREDITS

INDEX